FROM GENERATION TO GENERATION, THE GREAT SAGA CONTINUES . . .

The Bouchard family line was established by Lucien, a proud Frenchman of noble lineage and lofty ideals, who fled the horrors of the French Revolution to settle in what was then—in the 1790's—an isolated corner of America . . . the rich land along the upper reaches of the Alabama River, ancestral homeland of the Creek Indians. Living with the Creeks in gentle harmony, Lucien carried out, in word and deed, his creed of honor, justice, and compassion for his fellow man.

Nearly one hundred years later, his memory lives on, though his Southern homeland has seen the bloodshed of Civil War, the travail of racial hatred, and the horrors of occupation by Northern troops and carpetbaggers. As the steel rails of modern life extend like tentacles down into the heart of old Lucien's dominion, his values endure, as his descendents struggle to preserve their beloved sanctuary, called Windhaven Plantation.

It falls to Laure Bouchard Kenniston, once married to Lucien's grandson, Luke, and now a well-to-do New York City matron, to return to the plantation and to fight off marauders who threaten the very fabric of Windhaven. At the same time, she must meet new and unexpected challenges within the bosom of her family. Her courage and independence of spirit will determine whether the legacy of Windhaven survives to the next generation. . . .

"The Bouchards are a memorable clan, larger than life."
—Donald Clayton Porter, author
of the *White Indian* Series

WINDHAVEN'S HOPE

Marie de Jourlet

Created by the producers of
**Wagons West, Daimyo,
The Australians,** and
The Kent Family Chronicles.

Chairman of the Board: Lyle Kenyon Engel

PINNACLE BOOKS **NEW YORK**

WINDHAVEN'S HOPE

An original Pinnacle Books edition, published for the first time anywhere.

Produced by Book Creations, Inc.; Lyle Kenyon Engel, Chairman of the Board

First printing, December, 1983

ISBN: 0-523-41889-2

Can. ISBN: 0-523-43056-6

Cover illustration by Bruce Minney

Printed in the United States of America

PINNACLE BOOKS, INC.
1430 Broadway
New York, New York 10018

9 8 7 6 5 4 3 2 1

Once again, to my readers.

ACKNOWLEDGMENTS

The author is indebted to Joseph Milton Nance, Professor of History, Texas A & M University, for helpful verification of historical data, and to Dr. Edward Wolpert of Michael Reese Hospital, Chicago, for background information on diseases of the mind. If liberties have been taken in the presentation of some facts, they are for the purpose of enhancing the story.

Also, thanks are due to Fay J. Bergstrom, who for over seven years has faithfully transcribed the author's manuscripts.

Finally, the author acknowledges her debt to the team of Book Creations, Inc., and in particular the following: Editor-in-Chief Philip Rich, whose overall coordination has helped mold the Windhaven Saga; Marjorie Weber, whose judicious copyediting and checking of facts have ensured the consistency of the series through a number of volumes; Pamela Lappies, whose graceful editing and substantive suggestions have enhanced this as well as previous volumes; and, most especially, Project Editor Dale Gelfand, whose unstinting efforts have helped the author through several volumes, and without whose creative guidance and imaginative contributions this book could not have been completed.

Marie de Jourlet

The Windhaven Families

(Old) Lucien Bouchard
1762-1835

Dora Trask = Henry Bouchard = Sybella
1798-1816   1796-1836   1802-1870

Mark Bouchard   Arabella Bouchard   Fleurette Bouchard
1819-1864   1824-   1832-1869 = Leland Kenniston
                                                                            1837-

Lucy Williamson = Luke Bouchard = Laure Prindeville Brunton
1817-1866   1816-1877   1841-

Lucien   Paul   Celestine   Clarissa   John
1866-   1868-   1871-   1873-   1877-

Lucien Edmond Bouchard = Maxine Kendall
1838-   1840-

Geraldine = Lopasuta Bouchard = Lu Choy
Murcur   (adoptive son of Luke)   d. 1878

Carla   1860-
Hugo   1861- = Edwina
Diane   1870-
Gloria   1872-
Ruth   1878-

Dennis   1877-
Marta   1879-

Luke   1878-

Ramón Hernandez = Mara Bouchard
1840-   1837-

Luke   1868-
Jaime   1869-
Dolores   1871- = Cecily = Franklin
Edward   1872-
Mara "Gatita" 1877-

Millie Landry 1834-1865 = Henry Belcher 1821-1879 = Maybelle Williamson 1820-1879 = Mark Bouchard 1819-1864

Conchita Valdegroso 1859- = Timmy Belcher 1853-
- Luisa 1879-
- Thomas 1881-

Connie Belcher 1856- = Walter Catlin
- Henry 1878-

Laurette Bouchard 1837- = Charles Douglas 1835-
- Arthur 1865
- Kenneth 1865-
- Howard 1868-
- Fleur 1872-

Samuel Parmenter 1820- = Arabella Bouchard 1824- = James Hunter 1822-1876

Andrew Hunter 1854- = Della Morley 1856-
- William 1877-

Joy Hunter Parmenter (adopted by Samuel Parmenter) 1869-

Lawrence Davis 1849- = Melinda Hunter 1852-
- Gary 1871-
- James 1873-
- Denise 1875-
- Arabella 1877-

Fleurette Bouchard 1832-1869 = Ben Wilson 1834- = Elone 1850- = Kiowa brave
- Thomas 1865-
- Sybella 1868-
- Bartholomew 1872-
- Jacob 1873-
- Amy 1876-
- Dorothy 1877-

Tisinqua "Little Fawn" 1869-

PROLOGUE

It was the New Year of 1883, ninety-four years after old Lucien Bouchard, founder of the Bouchard dynasty, had fled his native France to seek the New World, there to explore the Alabama River valley and lay claim to the matchless piece of land that one day would become Windhaven Plantation.

It was eighteen years after Appomattox, and though ostensibly the wounds of that internecine conflict between brothers of North and South had superficially healed, in reality they were still festering. The economy of the South, brought to the verge of bankruptcy during those four years of arduous and debilitating warfare, had still not fully rebounded. The economic panic of a decade earlier had hurt the South more than it had the North; in the northern states there were varied industries, while the South still clung to its tradition of cotton and tobacco, even though the land was barren from scores of years during which those crops had drained the soil of its nutrients and fertility. Upon that arid land had come the carpetbaggers and the scalawags, like a plague of hungry locusts, to render the land still more barren and hopeless. True, the blacks had been emancipated, and acts of Congress had given them equality—but it was only theoretical. The now-free blacks of the South were hired at wages that were a mere pittance. The original decree of the postwar years, giving to each black man fifty acres and a mule, had not been followed by other political, economic, or social advantages, and black people were little better off than they had been before the war. The only difference was that they were now joined in their poverty by the newly humbled class of former white overlords, stripped of their property and prestige by the harsh regime of Reconstruction. In this climate of degradation

1

and hopelessness, the seeds of hatred were quick to take root and flourish, to bring yet more bloodshed to the beleaguered land.

As 1883 began, the Northern Pacific Railroad was sending agents to Europe and the British Isles to encourage immigration to the Northwest. In the desperate hope of restoring the economic balance, Southern whites had formed the Southern Immigration Association, ostensibly to encourage European immigration to the region. But the association was also an attempt to supplant freed blacks with whites who would work for low wages—thereby insuring the exclusion of blacks from the work place. Thus racial tensions continued to flourish like rank weeds, and they could no longer be overlooked even by the most optimistic.

Chester A. Arthur was beginning his third year as President of these United States. He found his administration powerless to turn the economic tide, and there were mutterings among his constituents that he had not delivered them from the aftermath of the economic panic and that the rich were richer and the poor, poorer. There was talk now of a man called Grover Cleveland who, the previous November, had been elected governor of New York on the Democratic ticket with a plurality of nearly two thousand votes.

Ferdinand de Lesseps had begun construction of the Panama Canal for the French Canal Company. Joseph Pulitzer had just bought the New York *World* from Jay Gould, an event that marked the rise of contemporary American journalism. This same year, the *Ladies' Home Journal* was founded in Philadelphia with Mrs. Cyrus H. K. Curtis as editor, and the first of eight volumes of J. D. McMaster's ponderously comprehensive *History of the People of the United States from the Revolution to the Civil War* appeared. Marking the beginning of an American sociology, Lester Frank Ward's *Dynamic Sociology* was published, a work that called probing attention to class and racial differences in these United States.

In the annals of American history, the year 1883 does not figure as outstanding or significant, yet one event was to occur this year that would have far-reaching consequences: The Supreme Court would render a momentous verdict that would destroy all that Abraham Lincoln had sought in his Emancipation Proclamation, and would make a terribly agonizing demarcation between blacks and whites in the South. . . .

On a frosty morning early in January, Benjamin Franklin Brown, a tall, good-looking young black man, descended the steps outside the kitchen of the red-brick chateau at Windhaven Plantation. With him was Burt Coleman, a white man in his early middle years, whose genial smile indicated that he was on the friendliest of terms with Ben.

Until recently, Burt had been the assistant foreman at Windhaven, but he was now employed at a neighboring plantation belonging to Andy Haskins, an old friend of the Bouchards. Burt still lived at Windhaven, for his lovely octoroon wife, Amelia, was employed there as cook. Residing at Windhaven required him to ride several miles to work, but he relished the long journey, even on cold mornings such as this. He always took the road that ran downstream along the swift-flowing Alabama River, on whose banks both plantations were built, and whose ever-changing scenes of natural beauty were a source of constant wonder to him.

Benjamin Franklin Brown had been hired three years earlier by Marius Thornton, the black foreman of Windhaven, and last year had been made assistant foreman, succeeding Burt. As he came down the kitchen steps with his friend, he complimented Burt on his wife's cooking, for the two men had just enjoyed a sumptuous winter breakfast of flapjacks, sausage, and good, rich coffee laced with chicory.

In the courtyard, the two men shook hands, and Burt Coleman went to the stable to saddle his horse for the ride down to Andy Haskins's land. It would be his last such trip for a week, as he planned to stay down on the Haskins property to finish up some repairs without returning to the chateau each evening. Ben Brown, for his part, harnessed a horse to one of the buggies in the barn; his task today was to drive into Montgomery to buy supplies that Marius Thornton had requested.

Ben, who had studied at Tuskegee Institute, had learned that the Lowndesboro General Store had run out of the fertilizer that the imaginative young man felt was essential to prepare the rich arable land for the produce it bore, as well as a limited amount of cotton. Additionally, Marius had stipulated that Ben should see if there were any bargains in feed for the pigs and the small herd of cattle the plantation raised. Ben and Marius often commented that old Lucien and his beloved grandson, Luke, would have been overjoyed if they could see to what diversified uses this fertile soil had been put. Both black men toiled assiduously to continue the Bouchard dream of a commune where whites and blacks would live and work together in harmony, with complete disregard of race or background or economic status.

After the ride into Montgomery, as Ben Brown descended from the buggy and tethered the horse's reins to the post just outside the town's largest general store, he did not notice a group of four white men seated in chairs on the porch of the small, shabby hotel directly across the street, fanning themselves in the already oppressively humid heat. At the sight of Ben, one of them—a fat man in his late forties, with porcine features and beady little eyes—sat upright in his chair and glowered at the young black's retreating form as he entered the store.

"You see that, boys?" Magnus Borden, who was owner of undertaking parlors in Montgomery and Lowndesboro, wanted to know. He glanced indignantly at his cronies, first to one side and then the other. "You see how that uppity nigger acts, just like he's as good as we are?"

"Yup, Magnus," the man seated next to him glumly observed. The gaunt-faced man ran his fingers through his short-cropped graying hair and added, "It's come to a purty pass when quality white folks have to 'sociate with niggers."

"I know that," the fat man angrily retorted. "Look at him, struttin' into that store like he owned it. You know who he is, don't you?"

The third man—nearest the door of the hotel and leaning back so that the top of his chair touched the discolored wooden wall behind him—now offered, "Everybody knows that nigger. He's Ben Brown. I hear tell he lives in that big red-brick castle down by the river near Lowndesboro—yah, that's a fact. Where the Bouchards live. I remember back when Luke Bouchard was still alive—he married that purty N'awleens gal 'n brought her up to live there. You remember, Magnus, he's the one took a bullet meant for Governor Houston 'bout six years back. Well, he's the one started

4

lettin' the damn niggers workin' his land live right in the same house with him, would you believe?''

The fat man dolefully shook his head and scowled at the store across the street. "Bouchard sure started somethin' when he did that, Tobias boy. Seems to me like somebody oughta teach them niggers a lesson, or next thing you know they'll be buyin' up houses here in town, an' tryin' to rub elbows with us. Or, worse yet, Gawd forbid, feelin' they got a right to marry our daughters.''

"I'd see them in hell first," the gaunt-faced man, Cyrus Williams, growled. He was taking a week off from his barbershop, turning the trade over to his new young assistant whom he had induced to work for half-wages in order to qualify as an apprentice, with the hypocritical promise that if the youth made good, he would take him on as a full partner.

The fourth man, youngest of the group, was Bodine Evans. Not quite thirty, the towheaded, lanky man was a clerk at the hotel. He now spoke up: "From what I heared tell, that nigger took the place of a white man, and that white man up and married a bitch with black blood in her. She's an octoroon, true enough; she's got one-eighth nigger blood in her veins, and he married her! You ever heared of such craziness? And that white man and his black wife, they're livin' right in that red-brick house you been talkin' about, too.''

Magnus Borden muttered, "Here he comes again." The funeral director stiffened in his chair and pointed across the street as Benjamin Franklin Brown came out, accompanied by a clerk, carrying sacks of feed and fertilizer that both men hefted into the buggy. Finally, his voice tight with anger, the fat man declared, "There's lots of other folks who feel as we do. I think maybe we ought to have a meeting of the minds and see if we can't all settle our differences in a way those nigger-lovin' trash in the red-brick palace will understand.''

"Makes some sense." Williams nodded heavily. He eyed Tobias Hennicott, a pious-featured, short little man in his early forties.

The man blew his bulbous nose and nodded his balding head. "Yes sirree! Why don't we have a meetin' this afternoon— maybe out to my farm where it's good and private!''

"Sure!" the hotel clerk eagerly volunteered. "We can all get drunk on your good homemade whiskey, that way!" He chuckled, then continued, "I'll just bet you all that if we put

5

our heads together, we'll come up with a great way to put these niggers and nigger-lovers in their place once and for all!''

Marius Thornton looked older than his forty-two years because of the great grief he still bore three years after the death of his lovely young wife, Clemmie. He had inspected the supplies that Ben Brown had brought back from Montgomery late that afternoon, and the two men, together with several other workers, had carried them off to the storage shed. ''In the morning, if it isn't raining, Ben,'' Marius said to the personable assistant foreman, ''we'll spread the fertilizer over on the southwestern acreage. Then, in the afternoon, perhaps, you and I can sit down and write a letter to Miz Laure, lettin' her know what kind of yield we're expectin' to have this year. Even though she's livin' in New York City now, she still loves this land and is bound to it just like she was bound to Mr. Luke.''

''I know, Marius. In fact, I had the feeling that when Miz Laure married Mr. Kenniston—I guess it's going on three years now—she found it hard to leave Windhaven Plantation. But a woman's got to follow her husband, and since his primary place of business is New York City, it's only natural that she and the children went there to live.''

Ben rubbed his chin thoughtfully. ''I wonder if she would find the place much changed,'' he finally said. ''Certainly a lot of the workers would be new faces to her, that's for sure. . . . Damn!'' He paused to speak to a huge dog at his heels. ''Goliath, go on home! Quit messing around here, you big ugly hound! That's it, go on home to your mistress.'' He grinned as the dog, whose coloring, shape, and size suggested that one of his parents had been a brindle mastiff, lumbered off toward the cottage of Elmer and Tess Gregory, one of the several tenant families at Windhaven.

For years, while the Bouchard children were growing up on the plantation, there had been many pet dogs to be seen roaming the fields. But in these days of hard economic conditions, the workers gave little thought to such things—all except Tess Gregory. She loved Goliath, who, for all his enormous size, was exceptionally gentle. Indeed, the dog had been like a surrogate baby-sitter to her four children—Boyd, Larry, Norene, and Lucille—while they were growing up, for whenever the children were placed in his care, Goliath never allowed them to wander off or get into danger.

When Tess, Elmer, and their children had first come to Windhaven Plantation, they had immediately become on good terms with another family new to the plantation, the Larsons. Tess and Elmer Gregory and Doug and Elinor Larson were all forty years old—a fact that merely underscored their strong bonds of friendship. They also had another reason for being close: Eighteen-year-old Boyd Gregory was courting seventeen-year-old Maisie Larson, and both families expected the romance would end in marriage before too long.

Sent on his way home by Ben Brown, Goliath reached the Gregory cottage just as the sun was setting. As he approached the door, he saw the entire family emerge from the house, for as was often their custom they were this evening going over to the Larsons' cottage for dinner. And so Goliath cheerfully fell into step behind the family, which now proceeded along the short path to their friends' home. Goliath, for his part, was full of anticipation, for he knew full well that the Larsons were generous with their offerings of food to hungry and well-behaved dogs. Little Edward Larson in particular, who at seven was the youngest child in both families, liked surreptitiously to give the dog bites of his meal.

All during the dinner, Goliath stayed close by Edward's chair, and his patience and persistence were rewarded to such an extent that Edward's father had to order the boy not to give Goliath any more. By this time, the huge mastiff was replete, and he left the table to go outside and lie down. He promptly fell asleep and enjoyed so deep a sleep that at the end of the evening, when the Gregorys tried to rouse him and take him home, they could not stir him. They knew he would find his own way home in any case, when he was ready.

At eleven that night, a quarter moon rose, and it shone brightly until clouds moved swiftly over the sky to obscure it. There was a stillness to the air, save for an occasional gust of wind off the top of the bluff, the soft splash of the flowing Alabama River, and the occasional call of a night bird. Once, just before midnight, there was the faint hoot of a screech owl. Years before—after old Lucien's beloved woman, Dimarte, had died from the bite of a cottonmouth that had invaded their hut—the Frenchman had stood many a night at the top of the steps of the red-brick chateau and gazed yearningly out toward the red bluff, silently praying and communing with his adored wife, who lay buried there. Throughout his life, the call of the owl had presaged some momentous happening, and often, too, it had conveyed the promise that Dimarte, in her eternal sleep, was still with him in truest spirit.

Goliath lay in front of the Larson cottage, stretched out, his head poised on his front paws, one eye slightly open. He was dreaming of bones, of a particularly succulent beef bone he had buried near an azalea bush at the base of the tall red bluff. In his sleep he uttered a wheezing sigh of contentment, and he drifted into even deeper unconsciousness.

From the northeast, a group of riders on horseback came slowly toward the acreage of Windhaven Plantation. Each of the twelve was masked, but not with the white hoods and robes of the dreaded Ku Klux Klan; rather, they had used burlap gunnysacks with openings cut out for their eyes, noses, and mouths. They paused now near a huge live-oak tree at the eastern boundary of old Lucien's land, to confer and plan their course of action.

The leader of the group, Bud Corley, was a man of forty-six, tall and sullen-faced. Magnus Borden had approached Corley to lead this raid, knowing of the sharecropper's hatred for blacks—especially those in a better financial situation than himself. He positively loathed whites who treated blacks as equals. Through the slits in the mask, his arrogant, dark-blue eyes shone with an ugly light as he turned to the other men and murmured, "Mind you, Magnus don't want no killin' of anybody unless we have to. Just burn as much as you can, and if there are any crops around, set the torch to them, too. When you hit a nigger-lovin' white man in his pocketbook, that hurts him the most, I reckon."

"If they put up a fight, what then?" Sam Arlen, a heavy man in his late forties, fearfully whispered back.

"Hell, Sam, you've got a pistol, and some of us have got rifles. Just fight back—or could it be that the thought of hurtin' some nigger hurts your fat belly? Maybe you should of stayed at home and taken a poke at a black wench."

"Now look here, Bud," Arlen whined, "no need for you to act so damn uppity."

"Sam, you're a born complainer. I think maybe that big belly of yours is givin' you trouble because you had exercise that you're not used to," Corley sneered. "Listen, if you're afraid of gunfire, just make yourself a torch and get to work. The rest of us here, we know how to deal with trash and niggers, don't we, boys?''

There was a low chorused mutter of agreement.

Corley chuckled and nodded, satisfied with the reaction. Then he gave whispered directions: ''You, Tobias, take two men and ride off there to the southwest. See those nigger cottages there right alongside of the bluff? Set the torch to them. You, Cyrus, take two more men and handle the sheds and the warehouse they've got there near the big house, get me?''

''I'm right on your trail, Bud.'' Cyrus Williams wickedly grinned. Turning to two of the men in the group, both younger men from the poorer areas of Montgomery, he directed them to follow him, and the three rode off toward the redbrick chateau.

''You, Bodine, and your three men, come with me, and we'll see about the wharf they've got by the river. We can set the torch to that, and it will be a spell before they'll be able to ship their cotton or produce down to market. Now, let's use our torches fast, before anybody wakes up and gives the alarm!''

The small groups moved off in the directions to which they had been ordered, lighting their torches as they rode. Almost instantly the torches leaped into life, casting eerie patterns on the growing crops, on the sheds, and on the cottages. The men saw none of the fanciful shapes created by the flames; their minds were on only one thing: destruction.

Old Goliath raised his head and sniffed the air. The smell of burning pitch and tar had come to his nostrils, interfering with his dream of the buried bone. Slowly he got to his feet, stretched his massive body, and turned to look in the direction from which the odor came. Then he emitted a loud bark, baring his formidable teeth, as one of the riders neared the Larson cottage. It was Sam Arlen who, with an angry oath, drew his pistol from its holster and fired point-blank at the mastiff, killing him at once.

Bud Corley swore viciously. ''That stupid son of a bitch! Now everybody in tarnation'll know we're here! We'll have to work fast. Let's do some damage before everybody in that big house turns out to find out what's going on!''

Arlen had already put the torch to one of the cottages, and

9

the building immediately began to smoulder. It was the home of Ezekiel West, a forty-two-year-old former slave, and his wife, Marva, four years younger, and their two children. John, their nineteen-year-old son, was an apprentice wood-worker with Elmer Gregory, and their daughter, Felice, an extremely beautiful, light-skinned young woman of seventeen, worked in the kitchen of the chateau with Amelia Colemen.

Wakened by the smoke and the crackling flames, Ezekiel West stumbled out of his bed and wakened his wife. "Marva honey, I smell fire! Go out the back door and go over to the well and get me a bucket. I'll wake John and Felice. How the devil could a thing like this start?"

Marva, still drowsy, hesitantly got out of bed and put on her robe. Ezekiel hurried into the next room, where John slept, and shook him by the shoulder, calling, "Wake up, son. There's a fire going! Come on, I need you to help!"

Felice, in the next room, was wakened and quickly got out of bed, putting her robe over her thin cotton shift. The acrid smell of smoke came to her nostrils, and instinctively she hurried to the front door of the cottage and swung it open to let in the purifying air. Meanwhile, John, Marva, and Ezekiel had gone out the back of the cottage from the kitchen door and hurried to a nearby well, buckets in hand.

Sam Arlen had ridden back to see the progress of the fire he had started. He saw Felice and grinned: Here was a tasty black piece for the taking; it had been a while since he'd had a nice black woman. Swiftly dismounting, he hurried to Felice, who, petrified with horror and surprise, was powerless to move. "You come along with me, you sweet black bitch," he muttered as he seized her by the waist and dragged her toward his horse.

"No, let go of me! Help, Papa! John, please help me! No, let go of me! I won't, I won't go with you! Stop it!" she screamed.

In his room in the chateau, Marius Thornton had been wakened by the sound of the pistol shot that had killed the faithful mastiff. He got out of bed and slowly walked over to the window to draw the curtain. But when he saw the torches of the several fires that had already been started in that darkened landscape, he uttered a horrified cry and hurried to drag on his trousers and shirt, and thrust his feet into his work shoes. Once again he peered out the window, and then hurried over to the dresser, opened a lower drawer, and took out a loaded pistol. He had made out the vague figures of several men on horseback, but even that brief glance had been enough to ascertain that they were not garbed in the white hoods and robes of the Klan. But then who could these raiders be? Cursing his ill luck that Burt Coleman was not here to help him, Marius quickly left his room, descended the stairs of the chateau, and went out into the yard.

At almost the same time, Benjamin Franklin Brown, who lived in a cottage somewhat distant from the immediate field of operation of these nocturnal marauders, climbed quickly out of bed and drew on his trousers and shirt. Opening a closet door, he took out a loaded rifle, checked it once, and set off in the direction of the chateau.

Meanwhile, Sam Arlen was still struggling with the beautiful young Felice West; cursing at her struggles and cries for help, he clamped his left palm over her mouth and, doubling his other fist, struck her a brutal blow on the cheekbone, dazing her. She slumped to the ground, and he grinned down at her. "I'll take you along with me as a souvenir, you pretty black bitch. Risking my life's worth something, I'd say—and you'll do as a down payment."

But her mother, father, and brother had hurried back from the nearby well at her first cries. John West saw Arlen stooping down to lift his half-conscious sister up on his horse, and screamed, "Let my sister alone, mister!" Then, running forward, he swung his water bucket like a club and smashed it heavily against Arlen's neck.

"Oww! Goddamn you anyhow, nigger!" the white farmer hoarsely yelled as he turned to confront his attacker. He made a move toward his pistol, which he had thrust back into its holster after having killed the mastiff, but young John West perceived the movement and again swung his heavy bucket in a backhanded blow that smashed the hard round edge against Arlen's wrist. There was another shriek of pain, and the portly raider ran for his horse, which had backed away and was whinnying in terror, seized the reins, vaulted astride it, and rode off into the night.

The Gregory cottage was on fire at one side and at the back, and Elmer, Tess, Boyd, and Larry ran back and forth to the well with their buckets to do their best to extinguish the spreading flames. Thirteen-year-old Norene stood nearby wringing her hands and trying to console her eleven-year-old sister, Lucille. Two of the raiders rode up, one of them Bodine Evans, the hotel clerk. He pointed to Norene and muttered to his companion, "Let's take her along with us; she's young but comely, I'm thinkin'!"

"Yeah, let's. White trash what associates with niggers deserves the same fate. And I'd rather poke me a white gal than a black one any old day—even if she is a mite young," his companion agreed.

Both men dismounted, hurried forward, and seized Norene by the wrists, dragging her away from Lucille, who at once began to call out for help. "Pa! Mama, Pa! There're some men trying to take Norene away—please come help her! I'm so scared!"

Cyrus Williams had held his torch to the wooden wall of the warehouse, near the red-brick chateau, and had seen the flames begin to lick away the paint and take hold and rise upward with quick, darting, rippling movement.

As Williams was torching the warehouse, Bud Corley was still at work. Having set fire to the Windhaven wharf, he turned to his two companions: "There's a dam they built when there was a flood about three years ago. From what I can gather, the 'Bamy River's gonna overflow any day now 'cause of all the rain we've been havin' lately. It's a small dam, and all it needs is one good breach. Here now—"

Opening his saddlebag, he handed his companions sticks of dynamite to which fuses had been attached, some five feet long, coiled around the menacing gray-colored cylinders. "Get over there fast, you two—light the fuses and then skedaddle. Circle off to the east, and we'll all meet on the road back to Montgomery when the job's done. Those nigger-lovers won't forget tonight, not for a long time! And this is just the start of what we can do to them to teach them a lesson!"

"We got you, Bud. We'll set it off right now." His companions eagerly nodded, wheeled their horses, and galloped downriver to the dam that Ben Brown and other workers had built after the flood of 1880 to control the irrigation of the acreage nearest to the towering bluff.

Doug Larson hurried out of his cottage, instructing his wife, Elinor, to stay inside with Maisie and Edward and keep away from the windows. Doug had only a hammer as a weapon, and after he had heard the shot that had killed

12

Goliath, and had seen the fires, then heard the screams of both Felice and Norene, he had seized the hammer and now brandished it in his right hand. Just as he came out, he almost stumbled over the inert body of Goliath.

Infuriated by the sight of the dead mastiff, which everyone had loved so much, he ran forward, heedless of any danger to himself, and before the two startled marauders could turn to confront him, he had brought his hammer down against Bodine Evans's right shoulder near the collarbone. The hotel clerk uttered a shriek of pain and slapped his hand to his shoulder, releasing Norene and then stumbling back.

But his companion, quick-witted, drew a knife from his belt and taunted Doug. "Just try it, mister; I'll cut your tripes out for you and let your wife cook them for supper tomorrow. Now drop that hammer or I'll let you have it!"

"You scum, go back to where your kind skulks! I'm not gonna drop my hammer until I see you get on your horse and ride off. And take your friend with you!"

Ben Brown was running now as fast as he could toward the workers' cottages and saw the confrontation between Doug Larson and the two raiders. He cocked his rifle and yelled, "Get out of here, you men, or I'll shoot to kill! I mean it!" With this, he fired a warning shot into the air.

"Christ Almighty, who'd have thought these niggers'd have a rifle?" Bodine's companion snarled under his breath. Then, with a philosophical shrug, he moved away, lowering the knife. "All right, mister, we're going!"

Marius Thornton had come running, his pistol in hand. Cyrus Williams, busy with his two companions in setting fire to the warehouse, now turned and saw the faithful foreman coming toward them. "Here's another nigger that lives in that big house with the white folks," he jeered. He cocked his pistol and snapped off a shot in Marius's direction. "Ha! I got the black bastard!"

Marius had seen the pistol come up and had tried to move to one side to avoid the bullet, but still drowsy from the deep sleep from which he had been awakened, he couldn't quite avoid it. He felt a searing pain as the bullet bit into his left side, and when he put his left hand to the wound, he felt the hot, wet blood. Pressing his palm against the wound, he forced himself despite the pain to lift the pistol and pull the trigger at one of the fleeing horsemen. There was a yowl of

13

pain in the darkness, for his bullet had taken the night raider in the fleshy part of his right arm, but the man rode on toward the river, taking the trail that led to Montgomery, and vanished in the darkness.

Suddenly there was an explosion, and Ben Brown and the other workers stopped dead in their tracks, startled.

"That's no gun! I'll bet that's dynamite," Elmer Gregory said to his wife, Tess.

But Tess's concern was elsewhere, for she saw Marius trying to make his way back to the chateau. "Oh, look, Elmer! Poor Mr. Thornton's hurt—I can see he's bleeding! There's blood down his shirt, and it's running down his trousers! He needs tending to."

"You do that, honey, while Boyd, Larry, and me'll go see what was blown up by that explosion. Those damned night raiders—wonder who they could be? Well, no matter now, come along, boys!"

Tess Gregory reached Marius just as the foreman became faint and tottered. He dropped his pistol and put his right hand to his forehead, closing his eyes.

"Mr. Thornton! You'd best let me help you back into the house and do something about that wound—you're bleeding something awful," Tess solicitously murmured. Looking around, she saw Ben and called to him, "Please help me, Mr. Brown; I don't like all that blood he's losing!"

Williams had lurked in the shadows by the side of the house and had overheard this conversation. He swore under his breath. "They need one more lesson, that's for sure—a white woman calling that nigger 'mister.' In the old days, they'd have taken a nigger-lover like her out, tied her up to a tree, and laid on the whip until there wasn't an inch of skin left on her white back and hind end. I'd like to do it myself— but I'd best get out of here. We left them a few reminders of what might just happen if they go on treating niggers like equals, though!"

Ben and Tess helped Marius back into the red-brick chateau and made him lie down on the sofa, heedless of the fact that his blood stained the upholstery. Amelia Coleman, who had been awakened by all the noise, had put on her robe and come into the living room to see what was happening. When she saw Marius, she grew pale, then told Tess, "I'll heat

14

some water and get some towels. I thought we were done with all of this—was it the Klan?''

"Sure didn't look like it, Miz Coleman." Tess shook her head. "Just some hateful white scum who just can't stand to see folks get along the way the good Lord meant them to do.''

Ben Brown knelt down and gently ripped away Marius Thornton's shirt. The bullet had gone in at the edge of the foreman's side and come out of his back, missing a rib that might have deflected it or halted its progress.

Amelia came back now with a pan of hot water and an armful of towels, and she and Tess began to do what they could to make Marius more comfortable. "I'll go get Dr. Kennery," Ben volunteered. "Mr. Thornton needs medical attention. Please try to do everything you can until the doctor and I get back from Montgomery.''

A little over four hours later, around dawn, Ben and Dr. Abel Kennery rode up to the red-brick chateau, dismounted, and hurried into the house.

Amelia had given Marius a sleeping potion, helping the kindly black foreman to drift off into unconsciousness. "I hope I didn't do wrong, doctor, giving Marius just a bit of laudanum so he could go back to sleep—he seemed in such pain," Amelia worriedly explained.

"I think it was a good decision. Now let me look at his wound." Swiftly, Dr. Kennery examined the bullet hole. When he rose, his face was grave. "He's in very serious condition. He lost a lot of blood, which is quite obvious, and although it looks as if the bullet went on out and left a clean wound, I'm not sure whether it touched any vital organ or artery. I'll rebandage the wound for now and let him sleep, but I'll stay here through the day to keep an eye on him.''

"I'm grateful to you, Dr. Kennery," the young assistant foreman earnestly declared. "He gave me my chance here— enabled me to get my schooling and then come back to a good job with responsibility. I love this man, and I don't want Mr. Thornton to die—''

"I'll do everything in my power to prevent that, Ben. You know I will," the young doctor avowed.

*　　*　　*

The raiders had ridden off whence they had come, all of them taking various circuitous routes to avoid detection. Bud Corley met them at the bend of the road about three miles north of Windhaven Plantation. "You men did a great job. Even you, fat belly," this to Sam Arlen who shot him a look of undisguised hatred at the insult. Suddenly there was a flash of lightning and a rumble of thunder. "And here comes the rain—wait till the river floods over that dam we blew up! They'll be busy for the next few days, mark my words. They surely won't forget tonight real quick. That's the way we pay nigger-lovers back, boys."

"Just the same," Bodine Evans—grimacing with pain and rubbing his bruised shoulder—petulantly spoke up, "I sure wish I'd brought that cute little girl back with me to rub some liniment where that black bastard clobbered me with his damn hammer!"

"Forget the wenches for a change, Bodine," Corley snapped. "The important thing is, not one of us got left behind, so they won't know who started this. That's exactly the way Magnus wants it. We'll all lie low. And let me tell you one thing, fellows—we're not the only ones in Montgomery who don't cotton to the idea of lettin' these niggers ride roughshod over us whites just because somebody signed a piece of paper and freed them out of slavery where they belong for all their stupid lives! There's gonna be plenty of other good, hard-thinkin' Southern men who're gonna root out these folks who want to pretend that blacks and whites are the same breed of cats, which they never will be. Maybe we'll inspire a couple of others to do elsewhere what we've just done tonight."

There was a spontaneous cheer from the others as they headed back with him. They galloped now, for the rain was falling hard. And the rumble of thunder grew louder and more frequent, as did the flashes of lightning. It was an ominous presentiment of what was still to come in the strife-torn South that eighteen years of peace after Appomattox had failed to quell.

Chapter One

The first Wednesday of the new year, the day after the attack on Windhaven Plantation, was blustery and cold in New York City. About six inches of snow had fallen during the night, and the temperature had markedly dropped, owing to a violent wind that had come in from the North Atlantic. To the west, the city of Buffalo was buried under nearly two feet of snow, and the state capital at Albany, upriver along the Hudson, had not fared much better. Yet at dawn of this day, the sun rose to a nearly cloudless sky, so that the landscape, touched by the whiteness of nature's wintery paintbrush, shone and glistened with a crisp freshness. To be sure, those who had to use their carriages or horses and buggies for transportation in the teeming city sighed apprehensively when they saw the streets: It would take an expert driver at the reins to avoid mishaps. Those who had sturdy boots and sturdier constitutions preferred to trust their own two legs to walk to their jobs.

During the two and a half years that had elapsed since her marriage to Leland Kenniston, Laure had come to love the winter season of this eastern metropolis, so vastly different from New Orleans and Montgomery, where she had lived all of her foregoing forty-one years. Part of this, to be sure, was because her home on East Twenty-first Street, facing Gramercy Park, was so very comfortable and spacious. She loved the imposing formality of the brownstone town house, so appropriate for the busy round of social obligations incumbent upon the well-to-do city matron. Immediately behind the massive oak front door of the house, on the ground floor, was an imposing foyer graced with a crystal chandelier overhead

17

and a mahogany table, the sole purpose of which was to hold an ornate silver tray for mail and calling cards. Those visitors whom Laure and Leland consented to receive were led to the right of the foyer into a small but elegant parlor or—on more formal occasions, such as when musicales were held—into the drawing room. Behind the drawing room was the large dining room, where the Kennistons took nearly all their meals, and whose handsome wood paneling glowed from hours of polishing by the maid.

A hallway led to a set of back stairs that took one down to the all-white-tile kitchen, whose many modern conveniences were appreciated by the hardworking cook, Anna Emmons. Downstairs, too, was the laundry room, where the newest convenience—a washing machine—was proudly housed. Its agitation action saved hours of hand labor, although even with the machine, the household washing and subsequent drying took an entire day out of each week. The following day was generally spent laboriously ironing all of the newly cleaned clothing and linens.

Going back up the stairs into the main foyer, family members and household staff would then climb the stairway up from the high-ceilinged first floor to the second floor. There, the atmosphere of the house was less formal than in the public rooms, for it was here that Laure and Leland each had a comfortable bedroom—with a large connecting dressing room. The spacious landing at the head of the stairs doubled as a sitting room, and Laure would frequently lie on the chaise longue reading a book by the excellent light that streamed in through the bank of windows that overlooked Twenty-first Street and the park.

Laure's five children had their bedrooms on the third floor, with Clarissa and Celestine sharing one as did Paul and John. Lucien, by virtue of his seniority, had his own bedroom, although Laure's oldest son was at present away at an Irish boarding school.

Clarabelle Hendry, Laure's indispensable governess and dear friend, occupied a large room on the fourth floor—a room that served as John's schoolroom, as well. Mrs. Emmons also occupied a bedroom on the top floor, and Laure often worried about the many steps that the two women had to climb each day, going to and from their rooms.

The tall, narrow town house was a dramatic contrast with

18

Windhaven Plantation, for the broad layout of the red-brick chateau had encompassed the entire family as well as servants in two stories.

Across the street from the New York residence, Gramercy Park lay silent and serene under its cover of new snow. The grounds were virtually deserted at this early hour, and so they would remain throughout most of the day, the snow on the pathways and benches undisturbed except by sparrows and squirrels. The park was surrounded by a wrought-iron fence and closed to all but residents of the square, who had keys to gain admission; thus, it could not be used as a path by casual visitors seeking a shortcut to their places of work, or by schoolchildren hastening to the grammar school on Fourteenth Street.

It had been that school that had quieted Laure's last remaining doubts about leaving Alabama with her children to take up her new life with her Irish-born husband. This particular New York school was considered excellent, a reputation that Laure had been able to confirm for herself when she had called upon the principal and been introduced to the instructors.

New York also offered exceptional opportunities for entertainment and recreation—in utter contrast to the bucolic life at Windhaven. Now in winter, the children could skate, use their sleds, make snowmen, and throw snowballs; or, if more cultural pursuits were desired, see vaudeville, enjoy concerts, and attend the best theater to be found in the country. There were museums, libraries, and art galleries, as well, to enrich the spirit and the mind.

The only cloud on Laure's horizon was the knowledge that the miscarriage she had suffered the previous year meant she could never bear Leland a child. Because she had fallen so deeply in love with him when he had first courted her—completely winning her heart three years before—she could not help feeling that somehow she had failed him. To be sure, her feelings sufficiently convinced her that she had not chosen the good-natured, cultured Irish businessman simply out of the loneliness that had shadowed her life after Luke Bouchard's tragic death. No, no woman could seek more in a husband. Leland was not only the perfect lover to her but also a gracious father to her children, showing them as much tenderness and concern as if they had been his own flesh and blood. And since that terrible day when she had learned of the impossibility of conception, Leland had gone out of his way to show her even more tenderness and thoughtfulness, allowing her little chance to brood upon the misfortune for which she still could not entirely pardon herself.

Indeed, he had, during the past several months, made almost every new day an occasion for some delightful surprise that would turn her mind from any such gloomy thoughts. He would, for example, stop at a florist on his way home and present her with two roses, one red, one yellow, saying softly and with an endearing smile, "Red for passion, yellow for fidelity—always, Laure, my beloved." Or after dinner he might take out of his pocket a prettily wrapped pincushion, so fancifully decorated and designed as to seem a gift of greater worth than it really was. Then, last week, he had taken her to one of the many department stores on Broadway's "Ladies' Mile" and told her, "I shan't let you leave this store, dearest, until you've chosen three of the loveliest dresses in stock, and"—he added, in a soft whisper meant for her ears only—"some appropriately dainty garments to be worn beneath, which only I shall have the privilege of viewing!"

No, she frequently thought to herself, there was no woman in the world who could have asked more of a man to stand by her in moments of crisis, to be loyal and loving, gentle and never possessive, witty and always with an ingenious turn of mind, knowing exactly how to bring a smile or laughter when at times the doubts every woman has about her marriage came like a mocking goblin to taunt her away from serenity into a somber mood.

It was as yet an hour before either Laure or Leland would need to rouse themselves to dress and breakfast with the children. After Paul, Clarissa, and Celestine left for school, Laure—like other well-to-do housewives throughout the city— would have to plan the day's shopping with Mrs. Emmons, while Leland would depart for his office uptown, where he presided over his thriving import-export firm. But for the moment, Laure was free to lie in bed, recalling the previous evening. . . .

Disturbed by a vague headache for which there was no apparent cause, Laure had last night excused herself from where she sat with Leland in the parlor and had gone to bed at ten o'clock. Leland had been going over his accounts, particularly some reports from Hong Kong and San Francisco, his brows furrowed with concern. Laure had seen that her husband was troubled, and she had not wanted to interrupt him; nonetheless, looking at him seated at his desk with his back to her, she had impulsively put out a hand toward him, as if hoping that somehow he would, by telepathy, recognize her need for assuagement and comforting. But since he had not moved and went on scribbling notes in the margin of the document he was reading, she uttered a soft little sigh, turned, and went up to her bedroom.

All of a sudden, a brooding melancholy came over her. She knew that Leland, Irish as he was, might whimsically say that she was "fey," meaning that she had the gift of communication with the spirits and could sense things that the ordinary mortal could not. Nevertheless, though she could not explain it, a kind of foreboding tugged at her heart.

She prepared for sleep, taking from the huge wardrobe her usual shift and robe. But at the very last moment, some piquant desire led her, almost out of caprice, to choose a lace-trimmed green silk nightgown, one that Leland had bought for her during his last trip to Hong Kong. It was exquisitely sewn and designed, and when she wore it, it gave her the exciting and stirring beauty of a siren.

She smiled at herself in the mirror, knowing why he had selected green: During their courtship in New Orleans, he had presented roses to her, tied with a green ribbon that was, as he had told her, to symbolize both her beautiful eyes and the country in which he had been born. Looking at the reflected gown, she was now reminded her of his romantic wooing, and it softened her melancholy. At once she felt both contrition and compassion, for if he was perturbed over his business affairs, it was something that she could not entirely share with him, since his enterprises were so widely spread and diversified. Nor did she wish to play the role of nagging shrew to question his every decision or mood.

Drawing back the covers of her bed, she climbed beneath them, then turned off the incandescent lamp. She drowsed for about an hour, and when she wakened, it was as if she had suddenly come alive again, as if she had cast aside that dark shadowy mantle of presentiment and misgiving. It was as if the negligee had become a magic Tarnhelm, that legendary treasure both the gods and the Nibelungen of ancient legend had so fiercely coveted, by which she could transform herself into that which she desired. And what she desired then was to be reunited with Leland, to seek his strength as reassurance to dispel her uneasy mood.

She sat down at her dressing table, before the beautiful oval-shaped, silver-framed mirror that Leland had bought for her shortly after they had moved into the house on Gramercy Park.

The mirror was reassuring. Laure saw that there were few noticeable lines in her forehead, and her skin was still soft and smooth—though, admittedly, the weather of New York had dried it somewhat more than it had been in the humid climes of Alabama and New Orleans. Her luminous green eyes, her sensuous mouth still had the power to evoke a magical allure. Her figure showed only the slightest trace of sag and middle-aged fleshiness—despite the fact that she was now forty-two-years old. Seemingly, the new climate and the new serenity of her life had, far from diminishing her beauty, enhanced it, and she had attained that degree of maturity in which an alluring and happily married woman can truly discover her finest attributes.

Then she smiled at her reflection. She knew very well what her self-appraisal augured: She was judging herself perhaps as Leland would judge her, as a man would judge a woman who was coming to his bed eager and yearning for his embraces. And eager she was, for she wanted to bask in the knowledge that she was still desirable to him, because this would be the last time he could impart that knowledge to her for weeks. Tomorrow at five, he would sail on the newest Cunard steamship liner, *Aurania,* beginning a European business trip during which he planned to stop over in Dublin and visit Lucien, Laure's eldest son, at St. Timothy's Academy. Their act of love this night, Laure told herself, would be by way of farewell to her husband; it would also confirm that she was truly at peace with him over every issue. Gone now was the unhappiness she had felt when he had induced her Lucien to go so far away to school, and gone, too, was her distress over the boy's subsequent involvement—to a dangerous extent—in the cause of Irish freedom. . . .

Yes, they had had their first really serious quarrel the previous year over that issue, but now, from Lucien's letters, it was evident that he had realized the folly of acts of physical

22

violence, however noble or patriotic their motivation. Besides, he was in love with Mary Eileen Brennert, daughter of the games master at his school, and because he wanted to deepen that love and perhaps one day marry her—as he had confided in many a recent letter—he had given up the rebellious outbursts that had so concerned Laure and made her impulsively blame Leland for having influenced her son to endanger himself.

This love she bore for Leland must be communicated in as sweet and fiery a union tonight as had been theirs on their honeymoon. So, drawing a deep breath, Laure left her bedroom and tiptoed through their connecting dressing room, then cautiously paused at his bedroom door. She smiled to herself, amused that she should react as if this were a clandestine tryst, and a warm blush suffused her lovely face. The house was still, so still indeed that she could hear the beating of her own heart. Putting her hand on the knob of the door, she turned it gently and entered.

Leland lay on his side, in his nightshirt, already deep asleep. She could hear his regular breathing as she came close to the bed and stood there looking down at him. He was her true love, constant and devoted, and all her hopes for the years ahead lay with him. When she had agreed to marry him, she had also broken with the past, firmly resolving that in no way would she ever compare Leland to Luke Bouchard. Just as no woman ever cares to hear her lover or husband nostalgically reminisce about earlier loves or spouses, so, she reasoned, must Leland feel; never for a moment would she let him believe that he in any way was playing second fiddle to the ghost of Luke Bouchard. He was his own man, just as Luke had been; each of them was different, albeit they had the common traits of idealism, character, and a gusto for living that, though it might have its conventional aspects, nonetheless left ample room for imaginative and even capricious behavior.

In Leland's fitful sleep, he had cast aside the bedcovers, and very carefully she slipped into bed next to him, turning on her side to stroke his neck, and then to lean over and kiss him on the cheek.

He wakened, his eyes widening with delighted surprise, and then he turned to her and passionately embraced her. "My darling Laure! No man was ever wakened more beautifully," he told her in that low, caressing voice he used with her alone during their conjugal intimacies.

"Muhammad didn't come to the mountain, so the mountain decided to come to him," she playfully teased, nibbling at the lobe of his ear and with her fingertips tracing the firm outline of his jaw and chin. "Tomorrow afternoon, you'll be going off to Europe, and I didn't want you to leave without knowing how very much I need and want and love you."

"Laure," he murmured back to her, as his hands gently and slowly caressed her trembling body through the negligee, "I've told myself a thousand times I'll never make you feel that I take you for granted. Each time we're together, darling, I want to court and woo you, as if for the first time."

"That's the loveliest way of all; it keeps a marriage long-lived and happy," she rejoined with a smile; then their lips met in a long, ardent kiss.

The night was fraught with delicious love, passionate and yet tender, each improvising new ways to please the other, thus carrying out Plato's maxim that man and woman had originally been one pole, then divided, and throughout the rest of eternity would forever seek to reassemble into the oneness that was divinely intended.

They fell asleep in each other's arms, replete with love, and if Laure had had the slightest doubts over her husband's ardent and unflagging love for her, she was more than ever reassured. . . .

At dawn of this Wednesday morning, as the already bright sun promised a crisp, clear day, Laure dozed, then awoke again. Still in her husband's arms, she uttered a soft sigh of contentment. Boldly, almost wantonly, she had taken the initiative last night—and she knew that he held her no less in his esteem for that carnal forwardness. *There can be no shame or pretense between two lovers,* she thought to herself, and smiled and sighed again.

Very gently, she disengaged herself from his arms, careful not to waken him, donned her negligee, and then, since she had brought no robe from her bedroom, rummaged a moment in his armoire to find one of his and put that on, belting it tightly. Then she tiptoed downstairs to the kitchen.

She knew that Leland enjoyed a hearty breakfast, especially on cold winter mornings. It was still too early for Mrs.

24

Emmons to be up, and so, smiling to herself, Laure began to prepare bacon and scrambled eggs. She brewed a pot of strong coffee, intending to join him for a cup and some toast. He liked his bacon crisp and the scrambled eggs cooked hard, almost with the texture of an omelet. Finally, she toasted four slices of bread, darkening his rather more than hers, spreading the butter liberally and then adding some cherry jam that Mrs. Emmons had made the previous summer. From another cupboard, she drew out a large hand-carved wooden tray, which Leland had bought in a little shop in County Cork on one of his earlier visits to his native land.

Quite pleased with herself, Laure quietly carried the tray up to the bedroom. Having left the door slightly ajar, she pushed it open with the front of the tray, which she then placed on a little taboret beside the bed. She bent over and kissed Leland on the cheek. There was a somnolent murmur, and she smiled and kissed his eyebrows and finally the tip of his nose.

This time, he awoke, his eyes widening to see her bending over him. "Laure! What a wonderful way to wake up to a new day!"

"In the fairy tale, as I recall," his honey-haired wife said, tongue-in-cheek, her green eyes sparkling with merriment, "it was the prince who kissed the sleeping beauty and wakened her from the spell that the wicked queen had placed upon her. But since you were the one who was sleeping, my handsome prince, it was only logical that I should waken you. Now please eat your breakfast while it's nice and hot. I'll have mine with you, and we can chat. It will be quite some while, alas, before we can do this again."

"You're absolutely marvelous, my darling!" He glanced down at the tray and grinned boyishly. "You've prepared a breakfast of my very favorites. No one could ask for better than that. Only I hope that Mrs. Emmons won't be put out because you've usurped her place in the kitchen."

"I don't think so. Besides, she's still sleeping," Laure said with a grin. And then, turning serious, she went on, "What is your final schedule, dearest?"

"Last night, when I went over my reports, I discovered that I'd quite forgotten that the *Aurania* will put in at the Irish port of Cobh. So, I'm now planning to go from there by train into Dublin, and I'm looking forward to having a good, long visit with our Lucien. Then I'll go over to London for some business, and from there to Paris and possibly Berlin. I'd like to get German goods and some of the goods from Austria-Hungary, too; I might just stay a week in Vienna, as well. So, with any luck, I should be back at the most in two months, assuming I can get good connections all the way through.''

"My, that sounds like a crowded itinerary," Laure said softly, a note of admiration in her voice.

"Not at all, my dear. It's quite a normal schedule for someone who's serious about his business." He paused, then went on, his voice taking on a more serious tone. "You know, dearest, I am determined to see that you have the best of everything—as I've often told you. I hope you understand, too, how much work has to go into accomplishing this. I'm the equal of any man when it comes to doing what's necessary—I hope you realize that. And if it takes me weeks and weeks of traveling and working twelve hours a day, why, then, I'll just do it. It's nothing for an entrepreneur of my ingenuity. Don't let anyone underestimate—"

His voice unexpectedly rose in a crescendo, and Laure, puzzled, broke in. "Dear Leland, please. No one is underestimating your abilities. I was just concerned that you not overtax yourself. I am grateful for all you do—I appreciate it, believe me I do. And I love you all the more for it." She paused and smiled coquettishly at him. "I must say, sometimes I think you've spent too much time kissing the Blarney Stone, the way you go on about yourself!"

This gentle jest had an unexpected result, and Leland suddenly turned on his wife. "Are you implying that we Irish are nothing but bags of hot air? Do you think I can't accomplish what I set out to?"

Laure struggled to respond to her husband's unexpected pique. "But surely, darling, you know I'm only teasing you. Why, of course I know you're an astute businessman; I didn't mean to insult you or hurt you. Please forgive me, my dearest.''

Leland sat silently, his face a stony mask.

Laure put her arms around his shoulders and snuggled close to him. "I'll certainly miss you," she whispered. "Two months will seem almost an eternity, when we're separated." She stepped off the bed and rose, supple and fluid. Unbelting her robe, she let it fall in a heap at her feet, and then she

26

moved toward Leland in her negligee. He swiftly lifted the tray and placed it on the taboret at the side of the bed and held out his arms to her.

And then, once again, time stood still for them, and there was sweetness and fire and beauty in the early morning as they said their farewells.

Chapter Two

After Laure had bathed, she returned to her bedroom and dressed. She joined Leland in the dining room about an hour and a half later, since both of them wanted to be with the children on this morning, to mark Leland's leavetaking of his family. Clarabelle Hendry graciously insisted on dining in the kitchen so that the family's farewells would be private.

As Leland and Laure ate a token second breakfast of fruit and coffee, Laure's fourteen-year-old son, Paul, plied his stepfather with earnest questions. It was obvious that he would have given anything to have gone along across the Atlantic to be reunited with his older brother, Lucien. Leland sensed this and remarked, "One of these days, Paul, it's quite possible I'll take you along with me. Let another year go by, and we'll see how things are then."

Laure looked at her husband; their eyes met, and they both smiled, as much from the delicious memories of their love-filled morning as from the knowledge that Paul's envy had been gently assuaged.

She was glad that, even with his mind preoccupied as it was over his business affairs, Leland thought enough of the children to say now, casually, as he finished a second cup of coffee, "How would all of you like to go down to see me off on the *Aurania* this afternoon? Boarding time is four o'clock, and it sails on the tide about quarter to five, I'm told. That will give us time for a quick inspection of the ship. It's said to be an extremely luxurious vessel."

"That would be wonderful!" Paul Bouchard eagerly spoke up.

Celestine, who was now nearly twelve, and Clarissa, ten, enthusiastically chorused: "Oh, yes, please take us! Please!"

The youngest child, John, going on six—though enjoying his breakfast cocoa—was intrigued enough at the prospect of an outing to put down his spoon and call out, "Me, too!"

After breakfast, Leland went off to his office, but not before leaving word that he wished that afternoon to speak with Kerry Dugan, the amiable Irishman who for a number of months had been the Kennistons' coachman. Following his return from Hong Kong, Leland had decided that they needed a private carriage driver, a man whose sole responsibility would be to take the members of the family wherever they wished to go in New York and, when it was required, could also transport Leland quickly to his midtown office. Such a step seemed prudent as the city became more and more crowded, the streets more jammed with humanity. And, too, in bad weather such as New York was experiencing this winter, Leland believed it to be a wise precaution to have an able driver in charge of the reins so that there would be no danger of Laure's risking any accident, especially if she had the children with her. Accordingly, he had hired Kerry, a personable young man in his late twenties whom Leland had met quite by chance one day as he was leaving his office and was attempting to hail a hansom cab to drive him downtown to Gramercy Park. Standing on the curb outside his office, Leland had noticed that across the street a carriage driver was having difficulty with an aging brown gelding that had slipped and was trying to recover its footing on the slippery, icy cobblestones. Furious at the animal's floundering, the driver had seized his whip and was preparing to flog the unfortunate beast when suddenly a young man pushed his way through the crowd that had gathered and, with an indignant shout of "Don't you dare!" wrested the whip from the stocky drayman's hand. Then, quieting the animal, he had soothingly urged it to its feet. It had finally regained its balance and stood snorting and whinnying in its fright. Then the young man had turned to the driver and said in a thick brogue, "You're not fit to drive a horse!"

The driver had uttered an oath and, retrieving his carriage whip, mounted his vehicle and driven off, looking back and shaking his fist at the cheerful young Irishman.

Leland Kenniston had watched the entire episode with growing amusement and admiration, and when it was over,

29

he hailed the young Irishman: "Over here, my good lad, if you please. I'd like to have a word with you."

After introducing himself as a fellow Irishman and extolling the young man's kindness, Leland had taken Kerry Dugan to a nearby saloon. There he watched the young Irishman voraciously attack the free lunch that went with a single beer. "It's been a long while since you've eaten, I'd judge from the looks of it," he had hazarded.

"And you'd be right," had been the flippant answer.

Kerry Dugan had been a stockman back in Ireland before leaving for New York two years before to seek his fortune—and to follow his pretty second cousin, in the high hopes of marrying her. He had taken odd jobs all over the city, trying to save enough money to be in a position to propose to his pretty colleen. But she had proved fickle and had married a phlegmatic, forty-year-old butcher because he could offer her the security that assuredly her younger suitor could not. Then, to top things off, Kerry had lost his job.

Leland had earnestly questioned the young Irishman, and when he had determined for himself that Kerry was a good driver and experienced in the care of horses, he had brought the man back to the brownstone and introduced him to Laure. Then he had taken the man along to show him the small but comfortably furnished rooms at the top of the winding staircase above the stable that was behind the house. These were to be the man's living quarters, and for the struggling young Irish immigrant, the rooms looked to be a virtual haven. He readily shook Leland's proferred hand and accepted the entrepreneur's terms for employment. Then, with an ingratiating wink at little John, who by this time had crept up behind his stepfather and was peering round his knees at the stranger, Kerry Dugan politely took his leave, to go and fetch his meager belongings and bring them back to his new home.

And so it was that in the afternoon of this January day, about an hour before his departure, Leland returned home from the office and called the young driver into his study for some final instructions. Looking now at his pocket watch, the older man stood up from his desk and came around to where Kerry sat.

"Well, Kerry, my man, it's almost time for you to load my trunk onto the carriage. While I'm away, I'm counting on you to look after my family. See that the children get plenty of outings, and that Mrs. Kenniston avails herself of every opportunity to visit the shops on the Ladies' Mile!''

"I'll do me best, sir. You have me word on that—and a Dugan never goes back on his word,'' was the amiable Kerry's quick reply.

"Good. I'm sure everything will go well while I'm gone. And now''—Leland glanced at his pocket watch—"I think we have just time enough for a wee bit of my best Irish whiskey. Can I offer you some, then?''

"Well, sir, I wouldn't ordinarily, seeing as how I'm on duty, but I'll not say no on such a cold day as this.''

"And I'm sure a dram won't hurt you, Kerry,'' Leland replied, lifting a decanter from the desk in front of him and pouring a small amount of whiskey into two crystal tumblers.

About an hour later, the entire Kenniston family excitedly boarded their spacious carriage, and with a crack of his whip, Kerry Dugan started the horses along. The carriage rounded Gramercy Park and turned west, heading toward the Hudson River and the Cunard pier. It was a bright, sunny afternoon, and the children laughed and talked in their excitement over the adventure of seeing Leland off.

As they were approaching the pier, they were forced to slow their progress in the increasing congestion of fashionable carriages, buses, hansom cabs, and conveyances of every description that were converging on the pier, bringing passengers to the ship. When they finally reached the curb in front of the loading area, they all climbed down while Kerry unloaded the trunk and suitcases that Leland had packed for the journey and found a porter to carry them aboard ship. Then they all entered the loading shed—a huge three-sided building that extended along the length of the ship moored at one side. It was thronging with people: Porters were pushing handcarts piled high with luggage, while nearby, three stevedores, bending their backs, their faces contorted with exertion and dripping with sweat, shoved forward a huge wagon laden with cargo that they maneuvered into the Cunard liner's hold. The steel-framed shed of the steamship company reverberated with the magnified grunts and cries of stevedores, the buzz of conversation, the calls of a visitor to a passenger, till it sounded like a veritable Tower of Babel.

Leland noted at once the striking contrast between the rough American dock personnel and the polished, almost courtly manners of the Cunard staff. Clearly, his journey in the first-class section of the ship promised to be the height of luxury and convenience.

After Kerry had seen to the loading of the luggage, and Leland had confirmed with the ticket agents the location of his stateroom, the entrepreneur led his family up the gangplank, following behind many other passengers. They then proceeded along the upper deck, and as they came round to the starboard side of the ship, they could see out into the harbor. "Look there, Laure," Leland exclaimed. "You can see Bedloe's Island. Next year, I'm told, they'll start erecting the Statue of Liberty there. It'll be one of the wonders of the world, from what I read about it the other day. A man named Bartholdi has designed it from copper sheets. It will be in the form of a woman with an uplifted arm holding a torch and will stand over a hundred fifty feet high. It's to commemorate the French and American revolutions, you know." He nodded his head and smiled. "How appropriate that it will stand at the very opening of the harbor to greet all those immigrants who will be coming to our shores in search of the freedom all of us hold so dear and so many of us take so lightly." Leland remained silent for a moment as he gazed out toward the island. "Well now, that's enough philosophizing. Let's go find my cabin. Take my hand, John."

He led the way farther along the already crowded deck, where some of the passengers were standing at the rail to catch their last glimpse of New York harbor. "I was lucky to get a cabin on the upper deck," Leland commented. "According to the Cunard people, incidentally, this is one of the finest ocean liners ever built. Its latest feature is an increased beam that makes for greater stability in rough weather. That also allows for increased speed, although the ship weighs over seven thousand tons. Why, do you know we'll be traveling at over fifteen knots, so we'll reach Ireland in a mere seven days? That, needless to say, has made the *Aurania* a most popular vessel. I understand from the ticket agent that it's totally occupied—some four hundred eighty cabin passengers and seven hundred others traveling in steerage. It's really a majestic ship."

"It won't sink, will it?" Clarissa asked with concern on her pretty face.

"Bless you, honey, no, I don't think so. The engineers

who designed it saw to that. And even in the roughest weather, I'm told, it won't be too uncomfortable. Of course, there are some folks who would get seasick in a rowboat in Central Park, but, happily, I'm not one of them,'' Leland genially observed. ''Ah! Here we go. In this door and then down the hall. Good afternoon, Purser. My name is Leland Kenniston.''

''Good afternoon, Mr. Kenniston.'' The purser, a spade-bearded man in his late forties, resplendent in a new uniform, with braid and gold buttons, respectfully inclined his head. ''Cabin 3-A is the second door to your left, sir.''

Opening the door of the cabin, he ushered them all in. Clarissa and Celestine simultaneously gasped with admiration, and even Paul was impressed. ''It's really roomy and very comfortable looking, isn't it, Father?''

''That it is, Paul. According to the informational brochure I received when I purchased my ticket, these private cabins are called 'bridal suites.' They have all the latest conveniences, like incandescent electric lamps, which of course are not only in the cabins but also in the public saloon. Also, when I want the steward, to order some wine or perhaps a snack, I can press this button''—he suited action to word, walking over to a wall and gesturing to a gray metal button—''and the steward will come. There's central heating, and in the bathroom, there's running water from taps. Well, that's enough of my cabin; now let me take you into the main saloon. By the way, the English meaning of that word isn't a place where you drink, but rather a large assembly room where you could practically hold a convention. Come along this way, my dears.''

The main salon, or, in the English version, saloon, drew concerted gasps of excited surprise from everyone—except obdurate little John, who frowned and began to suck his thumb, indicating that he was thoroughly bored with the proceedings. There were straightbacked, overstuffed loveseats and elegant tapestry-backed antique chairs throughout the enormous room. Its vaulted ceiling made the saloon seem even more spacious, and the ingenious arch directly in the middle was elaborately ornate with stained-glass patterns and mosaics. The upright posts throughout the saloon were of the finest dark walnut, glossy with polish, and the windows were tall, giving the overall impression of an enormous gentlemen's club. As Leland pointed out, ''These days, the steamship

33

companies think that passengers will be much more comfortable if they can be led to believe they're still on dry land, and that's why we have this lavish rococo display of furniture. On that raised platform to the right, they'll have musicians playing classical music during the dinner hours, and in the afternoon—when tea is served—a potpourri of popular tunes. Nothing has been spared to make everyone aboard—that is, of course, those of us in the cabins—feel like sybarites."

"What's syb'rite?" John suddenly piped up, fixing a questioning stare on his stepfather.

Leland chuckled, gave Laure an amused glance, then squatted down. Putting his hands on the little boy's shoulders, he gravely explained, "Why, John, it means someone who likes to have things just so—nice and comfy—just the way you want cocoa all the time and lots of it, isn't that right?"

This quip completely dispersed John's temporary petulance, and he burst into a peal of laughter and nodded, indicating that he thoroughly understood.

"We'll take a quick look at the dining room, and then I think they'll come along beating small gongs to let visitors know it's time to go back on shore and wave good-bye."

After they had made a quick inspection of the enormous dining room and marveled at its superb tables and the chinaware, the sound of the hand gong was heard, followed by the polite voice of the steward, announcing that all visitors were to go ashore. Leland herded his flock out onto the deck and moved toward the gangplank. He kissed and hugged Celestine and Clarissa, shook hands with Paul and with John, and then he took Laure in his arms and gave her a long and passionate kiss. "That's till I come back to you, my darling. However, I shall leave with a memory to cherish during the nights when you won't be beside me," he whispered for only her to hear.

Reluctantly, Laure ended the embrace. "Take care of yourself, please, darling. And do give my love to Lucien, and tell him his brothers and sisters wish him well. Perhaps you can induce him to write letters to them, and not just to me."

"I promise, my dearest one. And I'll conclude my business swiftly because I want to come back to you as soon as possible."

She put her arms around him and savored a last lingering

kiss as the sound of the gong, repeated now at short intervals, urged visitors ashore.

When they were down on the pier again, Laure looked up and saw him standing at the rail. She blew him a kiss, as did the girls, and John and Paul waved good-bye. The gangplank was drawn up, and there sounded the long steamship whistle. Slowly, the liner moved away from its moorings, nudged by three tugboats out into the upper bay of New York, before heading past Bedloe's Island and on into the Atlantic.

She stared after the ship, the smoke from its smokestacks lofting like little fleecy clouds into the blue, chilly sky. From time to time, little John pulled at her skirts, as if to plead with his mother to be taken home, and the older children grew restive, too. Finally, when the ship had disappeared from view, she declared with a sigh, "Now we'll go home, children."

When the postman delivered the mail next morning, Laure uttered a cry of delight to find a letter from Mara Bouchard—Luke's eldest daughter—in amongst the bills and circulars. Eagerly slitting open the envelope, Laure walked quickly into the drawing room, sat down on the green and pink striped silk settee, and began to read Mara's words:

Dear Laure and Leland:

Thank you for your lovely letter, wishing all of us a joyous Christmas. It was wonderful having our family reunited for this special holiday, and it seemed to give Christmas a new meaning. I think we all felt closer to one another and felt, too, that the spirit of God's compassion is something we should practice more often—as Ramón learned to do with Rhea Penrock. You know, I often ask myself if, had I been in my husband's place, I would have acted so generously toward her—this woman who, after all, *did* kidnap our child. Even though her motivation was—in the end—understandable, there is still the fact that what she did caused us all tremendous grief and pain. As you may be able to ascertain, I still experience anger over the situation, although I hold no grudge against Rhea.

At any rate, our unity has been restored, and Gatita seems to have suffered no ill effects of her separation from us—even though it was of more than two years duration. Indeed, I think that she bears less of a scar than any of us from the ordeal.

Unfortunately, though, I can't say that Windhaven Range is faring nearly as well as we are personally. All the while that Ramón was gone searching for Gatita throughout Mexico, where we believed she had been taken, the daily business of the ranch fell off somewhat without his needed leadership. Lucien Edmond, of course, kept things running as smoothly as he could—and my brother is, thank God, a very astute businessman—but without Ramón, he couldn't leave as often as he might have done to investigate new markets for the cattle.

Well, we have come to discover that during the last year, the northern Texas cattle ranchers have gained an enormous advantage over us southern Texas dwellers because of the presence of the railroad lines that have been laid up there. We recently got a feeder line through to Carrizo Springs, but I'm afraid that it has come to us a bit too late. You see, the northern Texas ranchers have formed a syndicate among themselves, and all the members cooperate with one another regarding water rights, rights of way, etc., thereby lowering their expenses and increasing their efficiency. This, in turn, has enabled them to offer their beef at significantly lower prices than we can to all the buyers from the Midwest and the East. Needless to say, this has had a drastic effect on our own income. Thank goodness we still have a substantial amount of money left from the old silver mine, for without it, I dread to think how we could continue to operate. We have so many, many families dependent upon us for their livelihood—not to mention Catayuna and her school and the Catholic nuns who help her run it.

Oh, dear! I certainly didn't mean to go on in such a pessimistic vein, dear Laure and Leland. But you are family, of course, and I've always felt that one should be able to share the bad as well as the good with kin.

And speaking of family, Lucien Edmond and Maxine received letters from their far-flung children just before Christmas. Hugo and his wife, Cecily, are firmly established in their medical practice out in Wyoming. Apparently what initial animosity they experienced from the long-time residents has long since dissipated, and they are now both well liked and respected by their neighbors and patients. Carla, however continues to vex us all, because she persists in living out of wedlock with her fellow American artist, James Turner. Their Parisian friends don't bat an eye at this arrangement—more's the pity. Still, Carla is establishing herself as a painter of no little talent, apparently—or so it seems from the newspaper accounts of her gallery showings. I suppose one must keep up with the times and try to accept the younger generation's mores—but I must confess, I have a hard time doing so. And Lucien Edmond and Maxine are having an even *harder* time accepting the arrangement, of course, because she's their daughter.

Well, it is nearly dinnertime, so I'd best begin cooking for my hungry family and end this letter. Again, thank you for all of your good wishes. Perhaps one of these days we'll be able to take a vacation and visit New York. Your town house as you've described it sounds so very lovely that I'd just adore being able to accept your invitation to stay with you.

> Most fondly,
> Mara Bouchard Hernandez

Laure smiled as she tucked the long letter back into its envelope. She was pleased that Mara once again displayed her old indomitable spirit—although Maxine Bouchard had indicated in her last letter that her sister-in-law had aged considerably in the two years that Gatita had been missing. Then, recalling Mara's reference to Windhaven Range's financial difficulties, Laure frowned. Perhaps when Leland returned from his European business trip, if things went as well as he expected they would, they could extend an offer of a loan, should the financial situation at the range worsen.

She sighed. Time would tell, she decided, and there was no point in dwelling upon it now.

Chapter Three

It was just past seven o'clock the next morning, a Friday, when Clarabelle Hendry apologetically knocked at Laure's bedroom door with the news that a telegram courier had just come to the front door of the house with a dispatch addressed to her. Puzzled, and not a little perturbed, Laure hastily put on her robe, drew on her slippers, and hurried downstairs.

"Are you Mrs. Leland Kenniston, ma'am?" the gawky, red-haired young courier demanded.

"Yes, I'm she," Laure said after a moment's hesitation, fearful that—like most telegrams—this one contained bad news. Taking up her purse, she extracted a coin. "Here you are—for your trouble. My, it's a very chilly morning, isn't it?"

"Thank you, ma'am. Yes, it sure is. Well, hope it's good news." The courier grinned and went down the front steps, walking off swiftly with an amiable wave of his hand.

Laure inhaled the crisp, cold January air and noted how the trees seemed more beautiful with their icy glaze. The sky was cloudless, but the sun seemed to cast no warmth whatsoever.

Laure fixed her gaze on the sky and on the trees, even though every impulse within her urged her to tear open the telegram and learn the news. Finally, she closed the door and walked into the parlor. She opened the envelope and read the lines, and then her eyes widened, and she uttered a stifled gasp. It was from Benjamin Franklin Brown.

We were attacked by a dozen men who dynamited
the dam and burned some of the cottages and sheds.
Marius Thornton severely wounded. However, Dr.

38

Kennery has hope that Marius will live. We are
rebuilding, repairing all damages. No one knows why
we were attacked.

"Oh, my God!" Laure cried out, clutching the edge of the
sofa. "This is horrible, just horrible! Why would anyone
attack us? Why do we still have enemies?"

She sat down heavily, the telegram crumpled in her hand.
Clarabelle Hendry came into the room and realized that her
friend had some intensely disturbing news. But feeling that it
would be best not to disturb her, she turned and went back up
the stairs to check on the children.

The news could not have come at a worse time. With
Leland away, Laure knew she must make all decisions. She
wished that she could see for herself what damage had been
done, and she would like to make certain that Marius Thornton received the best possible care after the inexplicable
attempt on his life. He had always meant so much to both
Luke and herself. His gentle and kindly ways, as well as his
devotion and his hard work, had made him seem like more of
a friend than an employee. She had mourned along with him
the death of his beloved Clemmie, knowing what a burden
her loss placed on him. Yet bereaved though he was, he never
faltered in the carrying out of his responsibilities toward the
Bouchards or Windhaven Plantation.

She sat for a moment longer, irresolute. She wished now
that she had read the telegram immediately, had told the
courier to wait for a reply, for the message was something
that must be answered at once, something that demanded an
immediate decision.

Once again, she read the telegram and tightened her lips,
shaking her head with deep concern. The wording of it was
ominous indeed, but with her usual optimism, she hoped that
Marius would recover from his wound. It would be good, she
decided, if she were there to nurse him back to health, for she
felt she owed it to him. Even more than that, it would be wise
for her to reestablish the presence of the actual owner on
Windhaven Plantation. The attack, the unexpected violence,
was something she personally had to reckon with; Marius and
Benjamin were there as foremen, and they should not be
expected to bear the consequences by themselves.

No, the issue was clear: She must return to Windhaven at

once. If there was danger at the plantation, she wanted to confront it herself. She had sworn to uphold Luke's concept of a commune that would provide for white and black men alike, without discrimination or prejudice. She was bound to the continuation of this dream; it was her duty, a burden that she had assumed when she had married Luke Bouchard. She could not gainsay it, nor would she ever.

Slowly, biting her lip, she walked up the stairs to her bedroom. She pondered the further implications of the telegram. To leave now would mean that the children would be entirely dependent upon Clarabelle Hendry. Happily, Laure knew that she could rely upon the gracious, gentle woman to take care of them in her absence. She would be absolutely reliable, and the children would lack no comfort nor affection when they returned from school each day.

She sat down at her dressing table and, closing her eyes, began to speculate on what problems she might have to deal with when she arrived in Alabama. She was so absorbed in her thoughts that she did not even hear Clarabelle's knock on the open door.

Clarabelle had halted, halfway in and out of the room. When she saw the honey-haired matron's face, creased with worry, the forehead lined, the eyes intent and yet unseeing, she exclaimed, "Laure, may I ask what is wrong?"

"Oh—Clarabelle! You startled me. My mind was a million miles away—or, more accurately, about a thousand miles away. Back in Alabama." She paused, then declared, "I'm going to ask a big favor of you. I—I have to go back to Windhaven at once, Clarabelle."

"Oh? My gracious! Please tell me how I can help."

Laure patted her friend's hand. "Bless you. You see, I've had a telegram from Benjamin Franklin Brown, the assistant foreman on the plantation. . . ." Laure then explained to the governess the few details she knew regarding the attack.

"So you see," Laure concluded, "I must go back there at once. No one else can handle this, Clarabelle. And I have to ask you to look after my children until I can get back."

"But of course I'll do that! You don't even have to ask me."

"Thank you. You'll never know how much it means to me, Clarabelle. I'll make it up to you, I promise."

"You needn't do anything of the sort!" Clarabelle responded.

"And the only thing you should have on your mind right now is what you're going to pack. Now I want *you* to promise that you'll try not to worry about the children while you're away."

Laure brightened. "You're so dear. I have such confidence in you, Clarabelle. And now I've got to hurry. As I remember, there's a train that leaves Grand Central Station at twelve-thirty. Speed is of the essence, and that's why I'm not taking the steamer."

"Can I do anything to save time for you, Laure?" the governess helpfully inquired.

Laure halted a moment, frowned, closed her eyes, then suddenly exclaimed, "Why, yes you can, now that you mention it, Clarabelle! Would you kindly go down to the telegraph office on Fourteenth Street? I want to send a wire to Lopasuta and ask him to meet me in Montgomery. I need his help, and I'm sure he'll respond to the crisis."

"I'll be glad to send the wire. Don't you fret."

"Thank you, and God bless you, Clarabelle. Here . . ." Laure seized a piece of paper and, dipping her pen in the inkwell, jotted down a few words. "I'll give you Lopasuta's address on Greenley Street in New Orleans. In my wire I'll just tell him what has happened and say I'm leaving this afternoon for Montgomery on the train. I'll ask that he please meet me, as it's of the utmost importance." She finished writing and handed the paper to Clarabelle.

"I'll send it right away, Laure. Are you sure I can't help you pack?" the governess asked.

Laure shook her head. "No, thank you. That wire to Lopasuta is far more important. And I'll use the time while I pack to make up a good story for the children. . . ."

It was shortly after noon when Geraldine Bouchard received Laure's telegram at the house on Greenley Street. She tipped the messenger and then stood hesitating a moment, wondering whether she should open it, since it was addressed to her husband, Lopasuta. Luke Bouchard's adoptive son was at the Kenniston & Co. office—where he served as legal counsel for the New Orleans branch—and the young Comanche would not be home for hours. The telegram might well contain some message that demanded an immediate response, which would certainly excuse her having read it, Geraldine rationalized.

She quickly opened the telegram. When she read it, she uttered a cry of dismay and called to her nursemaid, Willie Mae Thompson, to look after the children. "I have to go at once to my husband's office," she explained. Then quickly donning her bonnet, she hurried out into the street to hail a passing calash.

Ten minutes later, she arrived at the storefront offices that housed the Kenniston & Co. import-export firm as well as a legal clinic, which Lopasuta and his new law associate, Eugene DuBois, ran for the impoverished of New Orleans. The tall Comanche, seeing the concern on her face, came quickly forward to her. "Geraldine, darling, something's wrong! I can tell by the way you look—"

"Yes—forgive me, but a telegram came for you. It's from Laure. I wasn't certain if I should open it, but then I thought that perhaps it was news you must have. . . ."

"There's no need to apologize, sweetheart. Telegrams are usually important. Here, let me see."

She handed him the folded yellow sheet, which he opened and examined, frowning as he read the contents. He looked at her and said, in a grave voice, "I must go at once to meet her in Montgomery, as she requests. If she leaves New York this afternoon, which is what she planned, she should arrive in Montgomery by Sunday morning."

"Perhaps I should go with you, darling." Geraldine looked anxiously at him, but Lopasuta shook his head.

"I think it wouldn't be wise, dearest Geraldine. Understand, I'm grateful for your offer to come with me and to help, but this attack on the plantation was carried out by malcontents, or perhaps people who have a grudge against the Bouchards or Laure. I suspect I know one of the reasons it could have taken place—bigotry. You've read, I know, of the incidents of racial violence that have been occurring more and more frequently throughout the South." He sighed and shook his head. "It seems some people just have to create turmoil and hardship—reacting to differences among people exactly the opposite from the way the Bouchards do. Before the Civil War, when the entire South seemed bent on keeping the black race in chains, the Bouchards stood almost alone in their defense of the black man's dignity and right to a place in society. They've been true to that ideal. That's why they've survived and have accomplished so much, Geraldine. But it has also gained them enemies.''

"I can't imagine anyone hating the Bouchards," Geraldine replied.

"They do, my dear. I remember during Reconstruction—even afterwards—people used to call Luke a scalawag, a Northern sympathizer, a traitor to his class. And now we're faced with people who resort to violence and the most scurrilous and cowardly kind of raiding. So I must say no, my dear, to your offer to come with me; there's far too much danger.''

He looked up at the clock on the far wall of the office as he pondered his schedule. "I'll catch the train to Montgomery and be there to meet Laure Sunday morning. Then, of course, we'll have to go immediately to the plantation to see what has been done.

A look of desolation came over Geraldine's face.

"Don't worry," Lopasuta said, seeing the look. "I'll take every precaution. The proper authorities will be called in. . . . Ah, here's Eugene!"

A tall, well-dressed Creole had entered the office, and upon seeing Geraldine, his face broke into a smile.

"Well, what a pleasant surprise, Geraldine!" Eugene offered his hand with a radiant smile. "Mei Luong was just saying last night that she'd like to have you and Lopasuta over for dinner again soon.''

"There now, darling," Lopasuta airily put in as he circled his wife's shoulders with his left arm. "You've an invitation you mustn't refuse. Eugene and Mei Luong's company will take your mind off my trip.''

When he saw Eugene look questioningly at him, he handed the Creole the telegram Geraldine had just brought. His junior partner scanned it, shook his head, and scowled. "That's damnable!"

"It *is* that and more. I'm going to go back with Laure Bouchard to Windhaven Plantation and see what I can learn about those skulking cowards who attacked the plantation and wounded poor Marius Thornton. Perhaps by making some inquiries in town I can get to the bottom of things faster and more easily than Laure could do. However, this means that you'll have to take my place and handle anything that might come up. As far as current business goes, all we have are

43

those two actions against the Ace Shipping Company for loss, and I'm sure the judge will give us an extension if we request it. I'm not yet ready to come to a settlement, and perhaps if we hold them off for a month or two, they'll come around to our way of thinking.''

"I agree with you, Lopasuta. Don't worry. I'll handle everything. And what I can't manage, I'm sure Judith will be able to. You can be sure the office will run smoothly—at least as well as it can without you.''

"And that's saying a lot,'' Lopasuta concluded with a hearty laugh, and clapped Eugene on the shoulder. Turning back to his wife, he said, "Geraldine, if there's anything really important that you should know right away, I'll send a telegram.''

"All right, darling. But please take care of yourself.''

"I promise I won't get into trouble, and I'll be very careful.'' Lopasuta spoke like a husband who was used to his wife's anxiety. "I'll come back safe and sound—and I'll bring you a present for being such a good girl,'' he said jokingly, trying to tease her fears away.

"Just bring *yourself* back safely, Lopasuta, darling,'' Geraldine retorted. "Don't let yourself be shanghaied again.''

He chuckled and kissed her. "No chance of that,'' he said, although inwardly he cringed at the still-painful memories.

Six years earlier, shortly after Laure had become a widow, a New Orleans gambler—who was also seeking to ruin Laure Bouchard's financial standing—had arranged to have Lopasuta drugged and taken to Hong Kong and there abandoned. The abducted man's life had been saved by a goodhearted, uneducated sampan girl, Lu Choy, who had found him lying unconscious in an alley. During a terrible storm, the two had become lovers, clinging to each other in need—and nine months later Lu Choy had died giving birth to a boy. When at last Lopasuta had gained his freedom, he had prayed that Geraldine would forgive him for his infidelity. And forgive him she had, and their love for each other and for this child whom he had named after his adoptive father, Luke Bouchard, served even more to unite them in the strongest of all possible bonds.

Luke was now five. His half brother and sister, Dennis and Marta, now five and four—were Lopasuta and Geraldine's children. They were unfortunately the only ones they could have together, for a doctor had told them that for Geraldine to have another would cost her her life. That knowledge had brought the couple even closer together than before.

Lopasuta roused himself from his reverie. "Well then, since you're here and I haven't had lunch—and I don't think Eugene has, either—why don't we go out together? It'll be the last meal the three of us will be able to share for at least a few weeks."

"I'd like that," Geraldine exclaimed, forcing herself to brush aside her concern for Lopasuta and respond favorably to his proposal. She gazed up at her handsome husband and gave him a resigned look. "I won't make any more fuss about your going off without me. Just remember," she warned, "if you do need a woman's touch there, you send for me, and I'll come at once."

"Now that I'll promise." He smiled down at her and brushed her cheek with his fingertips. "All right then, let's go. Judith, you'll hold down the fort until we come back?" Lopasuta called out.

Judith Branshaw Marquard, Lopasuta's highly skilled secretary, emerged from her cubicle at the back of the office to greet Geraldine and to answer Lopasuta's query. "Yes, I'll manage very nicely, sir. By the way, I was able to get some information on that lost shipment of Mr. Kenniston's goods. It appears that the captain made a stupid mistake and had his stevedores unload at a Florida port, instead of at New Orleans. The shipping line has admitted that their man was at fault, so I think that you can expect a settlement pretty soon."

"That's fine news, Judith. All right, then, we'll try not to delay your own lunch hour too much," Lopasuta assured her. "Later this afternoon, you, Eugene, and I will sit down and resolve some of the more immediate concerns. I must confess, I'm worried enough about the situation at Windhaven; I don't even want to have to think about business for the next few weeks."

Chapter Four

Riding the train up to Montgomery, Lopasuta found himself practically alone in the parlor car, and the time by himself gave him the opportunity to reflect on how much his life had altered since he had first come upriver in the middle of May, thirteen years before. He smiled to himself at the memory of staring openmouthed at the imposing red-brick chateau with its twin towers—and how odd he must have looked in return: a coppery-skinned young man wearing a buckskin jacket with gaudy green trousers (which a New Orleans storekeeper had craftily persuaded Lopasuta to buy) and shiny new black shoes obviously pinching his feet, hitherto accustomed only to moccasins.

Lopasuta had made that long journey to Windhaven from the Comanche stronghold in Mexico, where he had been reared. His adoptive father, Luke Bouchard, had provided him with an opportunity to make a new life for himself. When he had first arrived at Windhaven, he had wondered what his future might be with Luke Bouchard—a man whom he had never seen, yet of whom he had heard so much. And now he knew. His mind went back to the graves atop that towering bluff where his adoptive father lay in the eternal sleep that united him with his beloved grandfather, Lucien. . . . Lopasuta shook his head, trying to clear away the sadness he still felt whenever he thought of Luke's untimely death six years before.

Gazing out the window, he was suddenly confronted with his own reflection as the train went into a tunnel and the interior lights created a mirror out of the glass. He stared intently at his image, trying to get a measure of himself, and he thought of how he must have looked to Geraldine when they first met in Montgomery seven years earlier.

She had sat in the courtroom and had been enthralled by his impassioned speech on behalf of a black client who had been cheated by his boss, a wealthy white man. After the trial, Geraldine had gone up to Lopasuta and expressed her admiration. When they had announced their intentions to wed, her parents had been scandalized, and they had reserved for Lopasuta—a man of half-Comanche, half-Mexican blood—the same scorn that they frequently showed to blacks. But by now they had come to admire and even to love him, and this had contributed much to the serenity of Geraldine and Lopasuta's married life.

As the train finally pulled into the Montgomery station, Lopasuta's thoughts were again of Windhaven Plantation. He would do everything in his power to see that justice was done and that the Bouchard heritage could continue without further incident. He owed this much to the memory of the man who had given him a new impetus and purpose for his life and who had let him prove that the strains of mixed blood in no way hampered his own God-given ability and talents.

The train from New York reached Montgomery late that morning. As Laure descended the steps from the railway car, Lopasuta hailed her. At once recognizing the tall, handsome Comanche lawyer, Laure excitedly responded to his wave with one of her own. A porter carried her large valise down behind her, allowing her to rush unimpeded over to Lopasuta. "God bless you for coming, Lopasuta," she said in a husky voice filled with emotion. "I'm sure it's a terrible imposition on my part to take you away from your work—your own as well as that which you do for Leland—but I didn't know who else to turn to. You see, Leland went abroad on business only four days ago, and Lucien Edmond is off on business, as well. . . ."

"Please, Laure, you needn't apologize. I'm glad you called upon me to help. It's the least I can do," Lopasuta assured her.

"Dear Lopasuta," she murmured, as she drew him to one side, away from the center of the crowded platform. "I hope that my telegram didn't upset Geraldine."

"No, not really. Indeed, she wanted to come along, but I

47

dissuaded her. From what you told me in your wire, I don't think Windhaven is any place for a woman right now—and that includes you. I don't want you to fight such battles—and certainly not alone. I'm here to determine just what is behind all this, and I'm at your service for as long as Eugene DuBois can manage things at the office. I'm hoping I can stay until we ferret out the reason for this dreadful attack upon your peaceful community."

Laure took a deep breath before she blurted, all in a rush, "The worst of it is Marius's wound. Though I'm sure he's getting the very best of care, I'm extremely worried about him. As you may know, Lopasuta, he never was the same after his Clemmie died three years ago. I just hope he still has the will to live."

"And you haven't the slightest inkling of who might have been responsible for the attack?" Lopasuta pursued.

"No, Lopasuta. A few years ago, I might have said that perhaps it was some of your own enemies. But you've been in New Orleans for so long now that people in Montgomery have practically forgotten you. I've racked my brains to think of someone who might have been responsible for this, but I can't think of anyone."

"I swear to you that I'll do everything in my power to find that out for you. And now, if we could go home . . ."

She smiled at him and said in a soft murmur, "I don't know if you used that word on purpose to make me feel more at ease, but whatever the reason, it thrilled me to hear you say it—more than I would have thought. I guess Windhaven will always be the place I most think of as home."

She sighed, tucked her arm in Lopasuta's, and stared steadfastly at him. "Would you think it foolish of me to wait and leave for Windhaven tomorrow morning? My thought is that we should get a good night's sleep, and we can be fresh for the problems we'll meet when we arrive there. Let's have dinner and talk a while," she said. with a sad smile, "and tomorrow we'll return to Windhaven Plantation."

"Hot damn, Jed, I got myself a big one!" Bud Corley exulted. Tall, sullen-faced, the forty-six-year-old sharecropper worked a small, rundown plot of farmland six miles northeast of Lowndesboro for its owner, Jed Durfry. The latter, ten years older than his tenant, was short and stocky and walked with a discernible limp, which he had had ever since he had taken a ball in his hip at the Battle of Bull Run. He owned a rundown little store in the poorest section of the town, at the southeast boundary of Lowndesboro, and the back room of the store had long been a meeting place for the disgruntled poor whites of the area, where they voiced their resentment against now-free blacks.

It was nearly sundown, and Corley, Durfry, and their friends, Tobias Hennicott, Sam Arlen, Bevis Marley, and Jake Elmore, had met for a snake hunt. They had chosen a swampy site near a stagnant creek, not far from Hennicott's whiskey still. All of them wore overalls and heavy leather boots up to the knee and carried gunnysacks and long-handled steel clamps. The clamp on the end of a six-foot-long ashwood handle was activated by a spring just under the top, which could be pressed with the thumb to open the steel jaws. Bevis Marley, whom Magnus Borden had hired as an embalmer in his Lowndesboro funeral parlor, was a balding, stocky man in his late thirties who had lost nearly all his teeth in drunken brawls. He had a few hours earlier caught the first water moccasin of the hunt. It measured only three feet, and it was nowhere near the size of the snake Bud Corley had just caught. Earlier, Corley had been so sure of his prowess that he had told Jake Elmore—a scrawny man in his forties, only five feet four inches in height, with an unkempt shock of greasy black hair—that he would catch the largest snake this evening, and was willing to bet ten dollars to back up his claim.

Corley had moved around the edge of the creek and spied the water moccasin coiled atop a log protruding from the water and, holding his breath, had tiptoed as close as he dared. Pressing the lever under the top of the long handle and darting the steel jaws at the snake's neck, he snapped them shut, just as the water moccasin sought to uncoil and strike. Now, lifting it up on high, he exulted, "Boy, that wins my bet; it's a good six feet, if it's an inch!"

"They ain't never been water moccasins that big 'round here," Tobias Hennicott complained.

"Figger it out: Just holding it up like this shows me it's as tall as you are, and you're five-ten, ain't you?" Corley jibed.

"Guess you're right," Hennicott sorrowfully nodded. "It sure is a whopper, I'll give you that!"

49

"Well, boys," Corley expansively declared as he deftly dropped the snake into his gunnysack and shook it to make sure that the snake would stay at the bottom, "we've got about another half hour of light left, and unless one of you fellers comes up with a bigger one, I've won me the ten bucks, and I want cash on the barrelhead."

"Now, wait a minute," Hennicott protested. "You didn't bet with all of us, just with Jake here."

"Oh, no, I said loud and clear I bet all you fellers ten bucks—and that means if I win, all of you shell out. That'll be fifty smackers! Wowie, with that sort of cash I can buy me one hot time with Suzy Davis over at Ma Trent's place."

"Well, I ain't got that kind of cash," Hennicott grumbled, "but I'll give you four jugs of my corn whiskey."

"Your whiskey ain't worth ten bucks for four jugs. Make it six," Corley haggled.

"All right, all right. I've had enough of hunting snakes. I never liked the critters to start with," Hennicott continued to grumble.

"You know, if you keep up talk like that and spoil our sport, Tobias boy"—Corley grinned and winked at his cronies— "I'll just have you kill 'em all. Now that's a messy job somebody's gotta do."

"Not me! Lordy no." Hennicott backed away, his eyes wide as saucers. "I never killed me a water moccasin, and I'm not about to try now—why hell, it'd bite me and kill me."

"Well, then Bevis could lay you out nice and peaceful-like in the parlor," Corley jested.

"Don't say things like that; it ain't healthy," Hennicott whined.

"Hell, he's a yellow-livered whiskeymaker—what do you expect from him? I'll kill the snakes," Jake Elmore volunteered.

"You do it, and I'll give you ten bucks for the job," Corley replied. "Well, the rest of you want to give up, or do you think you can catch you a bigger one?"

"Hell, it's too damp around here for me," Sam Arlen spoke up. He was a forty-seven-year-old farmer whose pudgy face was topped by a shock of gray hair.

"All right, then, I'm the winner. Pay up, you fellers," Corley chuckled. "Then we'll go over to my farm and have ourselves some food and some of Tobias's whiskey. Jake, I'll save you some food and whiskey for when you get done with your chore. Here's your ten bucks."

"Thanks." Elmore pocketed the money and gingerly seized the gunnysacks that the others passed to him. In all, the six had caught ten water moccasins, but it was obvious that Corley's catch was the winner by at least a foot-and-a-half.

"I'll go get the whiskey," Hennicott volunteered.

"Think you can carry all six jugs?" Corley asked him.

"I'll bring two. It's a mighty long walk over to your farm from my still. And I don't feel like hitching up horse and buggy on a muggy day like this. I'll owe you the other four."

"We got witnesses here to prove you're in debt to me, Tobias boy," Corley good-naturedly answered. "Just hurry up and get that whiskey over there by the time we're ready for it."

Hennicott nodded, glowering, then stalked away through the woods.

"He's a sore loser. And I wish he'd get himself a new still, so he could make some decent whiskey," Corley commented to his cronies. "I been tellin' him for six months he needs some copper tubin', but no, he's too miserly to spend a nickel. Hell, he could sell his stuff in Montgomery, as well as here in town, if he'd only come up with better stuff."

"As long as he keeps sellin' Sheriff Brennaman the jugs reg'lar, he'll do just fine," Bevis Marley joked.

"Well, old Tom Brennaman's a good man—best sheriff Montgomery ever had—even if he does go a mite heavy on the booze. He knows when to keep his nose out of other people's business—and just like us, he don't think much of niggers running around lordin' it over us whites," Corley vehemently declared.

An hour later, the six men lolled at their ease in rickety chairs on and in front of the sagging front porch of Bud Corley's one-story white-frame farmhouse—though age and lack of paint had turned the wood a grayish hue. The men had placed their chairs so that they were all in a ragged circle and could easily swap yarns and boasts.

Tobias Hennicott had hurried over with two jugs, and one of them was now passed around. A few minutes later, Jake Elmore shuffled up, a broad grin on his homely face. "Well, no two ways about it, Bud. You won the money fair and

51

square. Your snake was the biggest of all of them, and that's a fact. Messy critters to kill—but you could sleep with them all tonight and not have to worry, and I'm here to tell you so," he affably declared.

"Hell, who wants to sleep with snakes? Me, I go fer some sweet poontang in that Montgomery house Mrs. Westin runs," Sam Arlen averred.

"I don't like black meat, even if it's for free," Corley scowled as he reached for the jug and took a healthy swig. "Though I will say, from what I hear tell, over at the Bouchard place they got some mighty fine-lookin' nigger gals so light they could almost pass for white—like that octoroon who married up with that feller Burt Coleman."

Bevis Marley grunted and spat. "He's a damn disgrace to the whole white race, that Coleman bastard is. But I'm with you; I wouldn't mind pokin' his gal. You ever see her in town?"

"Sure, over to Sattersfield's store," Arlen agreed. "All the same, in the dark they're all alike, and that's a fact."

"Now I ain't so sure 'bout that," Corley bawdily winked. He took another swing from the jug and then spat it out. "Crissake, Tobias, when you gonna learn how to make real corn likker? If you get rid of that old sloppy still of yours, you might put out some good-tastin' brew!"

"Now you just wait a second," Hennicott declared. "Don't knock what's free. I never charged you boys a cent for any of my whiskey, and you all know it. Anyhow, Sheriff Brennaman likes it."

"Hell, he'd like anything that gets him drunk," Corley spoke up again.

There was a squeaking noise as the front door of the rickety farmhouse was pushed open, and Sally Corley, Bud's fourteen-year-old daughter, came out to join the men. She wore a dirty cotton dress, which had once been white but now, graying from so much wear and the strong lye she used during the washings, almost matched the dilapidated wood of the house itself. Barefooted, her dark-brown hair tousled and hiding one cheek, she was ripely developed for her years. Her breasts were almost unnaturally large, and they boldly stretched the thin material of the dress, so much so that the prod of her nipples was plainly discernible. Her hips were lushly rounded, as were her thighs, and as she saw the men's eyes turn to her as if magnetized, she shyly drawled, "Good evenin', y'all."

"Gosh now, Sally gal," Sam Arlen grinned, "you're growin' up real fast. Gettin' to be a right purty piece."

"That she is, Sam boy," Jake Elmore agreed. "Hey now, Bud, you'll have to marry Sally off real soon—unless she runs away from home first. From what I hear tell, there's a strappin' feller over on the Anderson farm that's got his eye pegged on our Sally here."

At this, the teenaged girl simpered, then giggled and hid her face in the crook of her elbow to feign affected modesty, while the other men guffawed.

But Corley didn't join in the laughter. He took another swig from the jug, set it down hard on the floor with a thud, and squirmed in his chair as he broke into the conversation with, "Look, when are we gonna see Tom Brennaman again? I hear tell them Bouchards are all upset about what's happened over at their place and might put on some extra help so there won't be any more trouble."

"Do you have to talk about it with Sally around, Bud?" Jed Durfry reprimanded him with a scowl. "Nobody in Lowndesboro's supposed to know that Tom's on our side. Even though the sheriff says he doesn't have any 'thority over here in Lowndes County—so that's his out in terms of helpin' them folks—we don't talk about it."

"Yeah, guess you're right," Corley grudgingly admitted.

But before he could expand on the theme, Tobias Hennicott piped up with, "How come you never got married again, Bud? Lots of the fellers around here have lost their wives, but they replaced 'em soon enough. Your wife, Jake, didn't she die from river fever, or sump'in like that? And you married again right smart after."

"Yeah, sure did." Jake Elmore grinned and winked. "Got me a live one this time. Amy's almost as purty as Sally here, though 'course she's twice Sally's age. You see, Bud, some of us fellers got smart and married again. How come you didn't?"

"None of your goddamn business!" Corley gruffly brushed the query aside.

At this moment, Sally moved over to Bevis Marley, who had lost his own wife just a month before. She touched the back of his head and bent over to whisper something to him.

53

Marley chuckled and nodded, then put his hand behind the girl and pressed it against her right hip. "I sure would like that, Sally honey," he muttered.

Bud Corley heard that reply and, springing up from his chair, strode over to his daughter and cuffed her on the side of the head, sending her sprawling on the rough, uneven floorboards.

"That's the way to treat a bitch that gets out of line," Durfry guffawed.

But Hennicott shook his head and peevishly complained, "Bud, ain't you got nothin' better to do 'n beat on your own flesh and blood that way?"

Corley put his hands on his hips and stared daggers at Hennicott. "Look, Tobias, that's my business. Sally's a bad girl, always has been. She needs the back of my hand to keep her in line, just like her ma did."

"Yeah, Bud, but sometimes you hit harder 'n you intend," Arlen said.

Corley did not deign to answer this insinuating remark, but instead just walked back over to his chair, picked up the jug, and took another swig before passing it on to Durfry. Sally, who had risen from the floor and sidled away from her father with a fearful glance at him, now went down the porch and began to talk to Arlen in a low whisper. "Now you watch yourself, Sally," Corley shouted. "If you don't, you'll get something you don't like, and you know what it is. Leather, gal . . . on the bare!"

"That's no way to talk to a sweet young thing like our Sally here," Arlen tried to propitiate the sharecropper.

"She's my daughter, not yours, Sam Arlen, and I'll thank you kindly to keep out of my family affairs," was the huffy answer.

"Come on, Mr. Arlen, let's take a little walk. Pa's awful mean this evening," Sally taunted her father by putting her arm around Arlen's neck.

"Now that's an invitation no Southern gentleman can refuse, honey child," Arlen lewdly chuckled as he rose from his chair and put his arm around Sally's waist.

"Let go of my daughter, you son of a bitch!" Corley snarled. Once again springing up from his chair, he leaped down from the porch, his fists clenched, and took a swing at Arlen, who ducked just in time.

The tension in the air seemed to have exploded with this one violent action. Now, a first-rate brawl broke out. Even Tobias Hennicott, who appeared all piety and docile disposition, picked up a broken floorboard on the ground and swung it at Jake Elmore's posterior. Bevis Marley and Jed Durfry, who had both imbibed more corn liquor than was good for them, squared off and began to fight, each of them landing some glancing blows on the other man's jaw.

Arlen fought back, but he was no match for the enraged Bud Corley, who floored him with a right hook to the jaw and then stomped back to the porch. He thrust the door open, reached inside, and pulled down his shotgun from the wall. Firing a barrel into the air, he shouted, "Now all of you can get off of my property!"

"Look, you bastard," Durfry exclaimed, "you're forgettin' that I own this place, not you. You're just my sharecroppin' tenant."

"Is that so?" Corley snarled. Quickly lifting the shotgun to his shoulder, he let fly a second volley from the other barrel, this one aimed at the branch of a live-oak tree some ten feet above Durfry's head.

The branch came down near his head, and Durfry uttered an oath and backed away. "All right, put down that shotgun and we'll call it a draw right here."

"Don't you ever call me a bastard again, Jed Durfry, you understand me?" Corley shouted, brandishing the empty shotgun. "I do a hard day's work, and I turn over my profits to you like I should. I know you got eyes for Sally here, and I'm warnin' you! You just leave my gal alone."

"All right, all right, so maybe we had a little too much of Tobias's lousy corn likker," Durfry mumbled in apology. "Come on, fellers, we oughta know when we're not wanted around here. Besides, we've finished the jugs, and there ain't nothin' more to drink."

Gradually, one by one, the men moved off, chatting among themselves, glancing back at Bud Corley and his daughter.

Sally now stood at the other end of the porch, both hands on the rail, but careful not to press down too hard lest the rotten wood give way. From time to time she sent apprehensive glances at her surly father, who had replaced the shotgun on the wall and come back out to puff at his corncob pipe. Her face was flushed, and her eyes were sparkling. She had seldom been the center of so much male attention, and frankly she would have wished it to continue. The thought that these men were fighting over her—as she interpreted it—was extremely flattering. As for Hank Anderson, all he wanted to do was get her in the hayloft, and he hadn't even so much as talked about giving her a ring. Not that he wasn't good-looking and strong, but just the same, a girl had to be careful. If she gave it away before he popped the ring on her finger, she'd never land him.

Bud Corley was silent for a long moment, then shifted his chair so that he faced Sally. "You know, Sally, you really had a hell of a lot of nerve actin' the way you did in front of all those fellers. You made me out like a fool, gal."

"Didn't mean to, though, Pa." Suddenly she was whiningly contrite, little-girl-like.

"Yeah, but you did, just the same. Seems like I gotta learn you all the time. I guess the back of my hand ain't the best lesson. I think maybe you're forgettin' what I got that's a lot better for teachin' you manners."

"Pa—honest I—I—please, Pa, I didn't mean no harm!" Now she cringed and regarded him with widened eyes.

"I think maybe you need a good dose of that leather strap right about now, Sally."

"Oh, no, please, not that, Pa. I'll be awful good. Please, Pa, I didn't mean to make you out bad in front of all those fellers. Please don't use it on me, Pa!" she begged.

He moved toward her. "Well now, we'll see. If you're real nice to me tonight—*real* nice, I mean, Sally gal—I might just let you off. Let's see how good you can be. But right now it's gettin' late, 'n I'm hungry. You fix me a mess of vittles, then we'll talk about the whuppin' you git or don't git."

Chapter Five

Young Lucien Bouchard was busy tidying up his room in the dormitory of St. Timothy's Academy in Dublin, Ireland, making ready for the opening of the spring term. Now in his seventeenth year, the tall, good-looking youth considered himself to be quite mature, and indeed, if one were to judge by his deportment during the past few months, one would be forced to concur. For by now Lucien was almost unrecognizable to those who had known him the previous year as a hothead and firebrand, and his friends often remarked on the change. A year ago, during his sixth term at St. Timothy's, he had allowed himself to be overly impressed by his stepfather's support of a free, independent Irish republic, as well as by the discussions he had had with his favorite instructor, Sean Flannery, on what freedom would mean for Ireland. As a result, he had incurred the wrath of the headmaster of the school, Father O'Mara, as well as that of his own family, by engaging in physical demonstrations against English troops, whom he had condemned for harassing decent, law-abiding Irish citizens.

Several of these escapades, in the company of his two closest friends, Edward Cordovan and Ned Riordan, had brought him to the suspicious attention of Dublin magistrates. The headmaster had finally given Lucien a scathing lecture over the consequences of his attempting to take on the entire British army for the cause of Irish freedom, not the least of which was expulsion. Additionally, Sean Flannery had cautioned him about attempting singlehandedly to strike a blow for the Irish cause, saying that by so doing Lucien could only blacken his reputation, harm his glowing future, and when all was said and done, achieve very little more than what a tiny pebble does when it is flung into a pond and causes only a few ripples on the surface.

But, even beyond this, it was undeniably the influence of lovely Mary Eileen Brennert—a beautiful young girl with whom Lucien was, by now, convinced he was very deeply in love—that had finally convinced the youth that the obstinate pursuit of rebellious defiance had to end.

When the news of Lucien's involvements with the authorities had come to the ears of Mary Eileen's father, the games master at St. Timothy's, the man had forbidden her to be seen in the young man's company—until such time as the teenager ceased his folly.

And that was why, in his final year at St. Timothy's, Lucien had resolved to work assiduously at his studies, and at the end of the fall term, he had taken honors in English, history, and philosophy. Father O'Mara had complimented the youth on his acumen and concentration, telling him that he was sure to graduate with honors if he continued on his present course.

"I shall do my best to keep out of trouble, Father O'Mara," Lucien had answered with a straight face and lowered eyes. His new attitude of humility became him, and the strict head of St. Timothy's permitted himself a fleeting little smile, as he remembered how angry he had been with the handsome young American youth who had come across the seas and immediately sought to take up the sword like a knight of old, ready to slay the English dragon.

Among his other courses, this semester Lucien intended to continue his study of French, knowing that would please Leland Kenniston. It was, his stepfather had told him aboard ship when first bringing him to St. Timothy's, the business language of all of Europe. More than that, it was one rich in tradition and great literature and drama.

Lucien's schedule was a full, even exhausting, one. Together with the athletic events in which Lucien was determined to participate, it provided a nose-to-the-grindstone existence, and this period between semesters was a much-needed break.

As he finished tidying his room, Lucien smiled to himself and sat down at his desk. Taking pen and paper, he wrote Mary Eileen a note, for tomorrow, he had decided, he would go to the secret place where they always met and where they also left messages for each other in the little hollow of an oak tree. There he would leave the note in which he requested her company the following Sunday afternoon.

This done, Lucien sat back and stared dreamily at the ceiling. Then, suddenly, he remembered the unopened letter he had received from his mother. He removed it from the desk drawer and quickly read it. Mailed the second of January, the letter contained bits of news about the family—what they had done for Christmas, what presents the children had received. Laure specifically did not mention that Leland was intending to visit Lucien during the course of a business trip. She and Leland had discussed this: "Now that Lucien seems to be on an even keel," the entrepreneur had said, "I don't want him to think that I'm checking into how he's behaving. I think it would be much better if I just appeared on the scene, as if, finding myself near Dublin, I had impulsively decided to stop off and visit him. In that way, he won't feel that he's on trial and has to make a special show of good behavior in my presence."

Finishing his mother's letter, Lucien sighed and returned it to his desk drawer. Her words had been so full of cheer, full of the busy comings and goings of her life in New York; and yet he had detected a note of sadness, even of loneliness, in the lines in which she had asked him to write often. At least he could take satisfaction that his own new attitude had not only improved his marks, but put at ease the mind of his concerned mother.

Rubbing his eyes, he stood up, moved to the window, and stared out onto the barren brown lawn. Winter had been harsh in Ireland, and Sean Flannery had told him that hundreds of tenant farmers who had been subsisting on scarcely more than a potato a day were in arrears on their rents to their English landlords. Many had died or, giving up their strong pride of holding onto land, had abandoned the farms and had gone instead to cities in search of any kind of work, even the most menial. Now, although sobered by his knowledge that any more flamboyant gestures against the tyrannical English authorities—as he still privately characterized them—would mean the irreparable loss of his young sweetheart, Lucien had also forced himself to acknowledge that in New York, too, there were wretched slums where thousands of men, women, and children lived in abject poverty in areas like the lower

East Side. He recalled what he knew of Jacob Cohen and his family, Russian Jews who had lived in such squalid conditions as scarcely could be imagined, until his stepfather had offered Jacob the post in his firm that enabled the family to escape the ghetto forever. No, poverty was not merely an Irish problem; his own nation had much to answer for, too. He also had begun to recognize the fact that if he wanted some day in the future to be able to help anyone—whether here in Ireland or at home in America—he would first need to complete his education.

He smiled to himself when he thought of his schooling. Now that Mary Eileen's father had relented and accepted him—thanks to Father O'Mara's tacit intervention—he knew that he wanted nothing more than to finish his studies here, be awarded the highest possible honors, and then seriously talk to Mary Eileen's father to propose himself as a suitor for her hand in marriage. Of course, they were both as yet too young; but she gave promise of being a sweet, helpful, and loving woman who would make him the ideal wife.

There were depths to her that he had not suspected when their friendship had begun. She had a profound feeling for goodness and honesty, but at the same time—most delightfully—she demonstrated a wonderful sense of humor and had permitted herself, as their relationship developed, to poke gentle fun at him, with the hope of getting him to mend some of the ways she still found somewhat abrasive to her. Also, she loved the out-of-doors, and she could identify many birds, flowers, shrubs, and trees. Gradually, hardly knowing it, Lucien began to see the hills and meadows of Ireland through her own eyes and to appreciate the country more, to savor its imperishable beauty.

He was interrupted during his musing by a knock at the door and called, "Come in!"

It was Edward Cordovan. He, along with Ned Riordan, had felt the weight of Father O'Mara's displeasure during the preceding year, and like Lucien and Ned, he too had profited from the lesson they had learned. Indeed, the trio seemed more inseparable than ever, and a friendly rivalry had developed among them, with each boy determined to lead his class and to win the appreciation of his teachers and tutors. Moreover, with the new semester, each of them had a girl—from the same nearby school in which Mary Eileen Brennert was enrolled. Ned was extremely fond of a black-haired, green-eyed sixteen year old named Peggy O'Rourke, while Edward Cordovan shyly admitted that he had fallen desperately in love with Mavis Dailey, who would celebrate her sixteenth birthday this coming Sunday. Mavis was a tall, intellectual-looking blond girl who excelled in Greek and Latin, but for all her studiousness, she had already won the attention of her games mistress by her skill at field hockey and badminton.

"How are you, Edward?" Lucien cheerfully inquired.

"Just fine. And yourself?"

"Couldn't be better—except for this foul weather. I'm going to wait until next Sunday before I take Mary Eileen to Dublin again—weather permitting," Lucien declared.

"I'm taking Mavis tomorrow after mass, no matter what the weather is," Edward proudly retorted, then blushed as Lucien gave him a long, searching look. "What's wrong with that? Do you think you're the only fellow here at St. Timothy's who has a sweetheart?"

"Oh, no, Edward, not in the least. I'm very happy for you—although, at first glance Mavis is just a bit formidable. I mean, she hits the books a lot."

"And what's so bad about that?" his friend defiantly countered. "Look how much better you're doing because you've given the books a spell, instead of trying to be a hero."

"I guess you're right. Anyway, this isn't the weather for battling the constabulary, or the soldiers," Lucien chuckled. "When you see Mavis, give her my best."

"Of course I will. Ned might take Peggy, too, and then we'd have a foursome. You're sure you don't want to take Mary Eileen and come along with us?" Edward hopefully asked as he headed for the door.

Lucien shook his head. "No. I'm doing an essay for Mr. Flannery on the Irish kings, and I'd just as soon stay indoors and work on it." He suddenly grinned broadly and admitted, "Anyway, I'm at the stage where I'd like to be alone when I take Mary Eileen out."

"So that's the way the wind blows, is it?" Edward stopped on the threshold and eyed his friend. "You're that serious about her?"

"Yes. When this semester's over, I—well, I'm going to discuss it with her father first, to make sure he approves of

61

me. If he does, I'm going to tell him that I'm going to marry her and take her back to America with me."

Edward uttered a long whistle and shook his head. Then he teasingly murmured, "Who's going to be your best man, Ned or me?"

"It should be 'Ned or I,' idiot, and if you want to get a first in English, you'd better remember that grammatical rule," Lucien twitted him back.

"You'll wind up being a schoolteacher yet, you mark my words," was Edward's parting shot as he left the room and went down the hall whistling "Erin go bragh."

Once ensconced in his stateroom aboard the *Aurania,* Leland Kenniston had intended to unpack his baggage, until he reminded himself that he was, after all, in a first-class cabin. Accordingly, he summoned the room steward, a mild-mannered little man who was deferential to a fault.

"It'll be my pleasure to put your garments away, sir, I assure you." He neatly hung up Leland's business suits and a newly custom-tailored dinner jacket and trousers, patting them to make sure that not a single wrinkle appeared once they were draped over the wooden hangers. "If you'll excuse my boldness, sir," the steward remarked, "your sense of style is excellent. These are as finely tailored garments as one would find on Saville Row."

"You think so?" Leland was smiling, amused at the steward's flattery.

"Indeed I do, sir."

Leland chuckled again, hugely pleased with his initiation into the luxurious and solicitous comforts that the crack new steamship provided for its patrons. He lounged back in his easy chair, watching the steward efficiently put away socks, shirts, and underwear into different drawers, then stash the empty suitcases themselves neatly out of sight at the back of the closet. A feeling of satisfaction and well-being settled over him as he watched the steward bustling about. Of course, such service was his due. He was already widely known, and contractors, suppliers, and shippers alike knew his name. *Leland Kenniston.* It was an unusual name, with a ring of authority to it. And soon it would be as well-established in Europe as it was in New York, San Francisco, New Orleans, and Hong Kong. Who could say—perhaps one day the newspapers would be filled with accounts of his business acumen.

A feeling of euphoria had filled him ever since last night, when Laure had sought him out and proved the fervor of her love. He had everything in the world he wanted—except more success, but that was material, and it would come. One did not even have to think of such things because anyone whose judgment mattered could see how much he had already accomplished in so short a time! And he had a beautiful wife, who was passionate and devoted to him; he had her children, who already idolized him, a fine house, good friends, loyal, industrious employees—as the saying goes, the world was his oyster.

The steward turned and inquired if there was anything else that might be done.

Leland shook his head but beckoned to the man to approach, and then gave him a five-dollar tip.

"Thank you, sir!" the steward gasped. "You are most generous. I shall be at your service until we reach Cobh, sir; don't hesitate to inform me of your needs. And may I ask if there is anything else I can do for you at the moment?"

"Yes, my good fellow, you can tell me if the seating arrangements have been made for dinner this evening," Leland requested.

"Indeed they have been, Mr. Kenniston. I have the seating plan right here." The steward drew a folded sheet of paper out of his gold-braided and brass-buttoned jacket, then he unfolded it and located the name of his generous passenger. "Ah, here you are, sir. You are down for the second sitting, at eight o'clock. You're at a table with Mrs. Gwendolyn Meredith, Mr. and Mrs. Lionel Jefferson, Miss Astrid Fuller— she has an amazing variety act, I'm told, sir—and finally Henry Cadwallader, our first mate."

"You mean I'm not at the captain's table?" Leland suddenly erupted, frowning.

"I'm sorry, Mr. Kenniston. I'm sure you'll find your dining companions most enjoyable. I'm sure no slight was intended—indeed, Captain Ellerton only occasionally puts in an appearance at the table. He generally dines alone on the bridge. I'm sure, sir, you'll find Mr. Cadwallader a charming gentleman with a vast knowledge of sea lore," the steward volunteered.

"I see. Oh, very well. No doubt I'll have a delightful evening. Thank you, steward."

"Thank *you*, sir. And, sir, my name is William Hazeltine. May I reiterate that if there's the least little thing you need, no matter what time of day or night, simply ring for me. I'll leave you now so you may freshen up. By the way, the first sitting for dinner is not full. If you were to wish an early meal, you would need only to go to the dining room at six-thirty, and the headwaiter would be glad to seat you." With another deferential bow, the steward left the stateroom.

Leland lay down on the bed and closed his eyes. The trip was starting out most satisfactorily—certainly this kind of luxury was no more than what he deserved after all his years of hard work. He realized that after the fortunate meeting with Lopasuta Bouchard—who had saved his life on the voyage back from Hong Kong—everything he had touched had turned to gold, almost literally. As the culmination of it all, he had found a wife of divine beauty and tenderness, a woman who could be as ardent a mistress as she was a faithful, loving and devoted mother. Such women were rare—but, of course, it took a man of wisdom to select her from all the other aspirants.

A smile grew on his handsome face. He had never before felt so purposeful, so certain of his destiny and the inevitable success of it. Nothing could hold him back from becoming, one day, the most important importer-exporter in all the world. Once he had established these various links of his business in the leading cities of Europe, it would almost be a fait accompli.

It was certainly a goal to seek out and to plan for; there was no room in the mind of a successful entrepreneur for misgivings. Uncertainty, doubts, fears, these were the things that plunged one down into failure. No, it was essential that one should think with the greatest optimism and the certain, even smug assurance that what one planned, one would accomplish. Then it was simply a matter of doing it—and he knew that he could.

He suddenly put his hand to his forehead. There had been a slight twinge like that of a headache, and it was highly inappropriate to his mood. No doubt a good meal would restore him to perfect fitness.

He stretched, then rose and removed his clothes. As he

washed up and changed into evening dress, he hummed softly to himself. In two and a half hours it would be time for dinner. He would go at the second call, and he would see who was at the captain's table this evening. Surely before the voyage was over, the captain would invite him to dine, perhaps even offering him the post of guest of honor. And, if that happened, it would be an important sign that his star was truly in its ascendency!

Chapter Six

The dinner offered the first-class travelers aboard the *Aurania* was even more lavish than the fare at fine New York restaurants like Delmonico's. Passengers could, if they chose, order at least ten courses, with generous portions and many side dishes. Venison, grouse, ptarmigan, mallard duck, smoked or roasted Virginia hams, beef Wellington, Maine lobster, and jumbo shrimp from the Gulf Coast—even sirloin of buffalo—were only a few of the major entrées on the dinner menu. A choice of at least a dozen soups, and as many appetizers, ranging from *coquilles* St. Jacques to the chef's own excellent pâté, were complemented by an enormous assortment of fresh vegetables. The dessert menu was equally abundant and imaginative, and all of this was accompanied by at least five different wines, beginning with a pale, dry sherry from Lisbon as aperitif.

In a thoroughly convivial mood, Leland Kenniston partook of the rich viands and helped himself liberally to the wines, which made him more loquacious than ever, but not in the least tipsy. It was true that from time to time he enviously glanced over at the captain's table, where, as pointed out by Henry Cadwallader—the plump, thickly mustached first mate who sat to Leland's right at one end of the table—there were such famous guests as the brothers Curie, Pierre and Jacques. According to the first mate, who prided himself on being au courant with everything that was happening on shipboard, the Curies had just discovered piezoelectricity, a form of electric polarity, in crystals.

Nonetheless, Leland was greatly mollified by the attention paid to him by his companions at the table, notably Astrid Fuller, the comic vaudevillean, who turned out to be a roguishly attractive woman in her mid-thirties, with flaming red hair that owed nothing to any artificial coloring. When Henry Cadwallader had first presented Leland to the others at the table, Astrid had boldly run her eyes up and down him, taking his measure. As he had seated himself, she had leaned over from his left to announce, in a voice slightly mellowed by wine, "I am most delighted to meet you, Mr. Kenniston."

Though English-born and having admitted, during the course of the meal, that she had been raised very strictly, Astrid had a startlingly bold streak to her nature. Midway through dinner, she caused Leland to raise his eyebrows when, glancing around to make certain that no one else could hear her, she huskily whispered, "I must remember to thank the person responsible for putting us together at this table, my dear Mr. Kenniston. I do hope you will grant me the pleasure of your company and join me in a nightcap later. My cabin is 12-C."

He goggled at her, not quite certain what the invitation implied.

She laughed softly at his apparent confusion and added *sotto voce*, "You obviously are a most cultured gentleman— someone who would be good company. And I would enjoy some good company, because my friend of the last two years has decided to stray to greener pastures, you see."

He mumbled something inarticulate, gave her a warm smile, and in order to recover his poise, took a long sip of his wine, which accompanied an excellently prepared serving of shrimp with a garlic-flavored sauce.

Mrs. Gwendolyn Meredith was, by contrast, a somewhat desiccated, dowdy, vulgarly bejeweled dowager. When prompted by the first mate to make herself known to her table companions, she drew out a lorgnette from her reticule, eyed everyone at the table, and then, sniffing slightly, said in an affectatiously high-pitched voice, "There really isn't much to tell. After my third husband—peace to his memory—died two months ago, I went over to the United States to see the sights. Frankly, I shall be most happy to get back to my native heath in Warwickshire after my duty call on an elderly aunt in Dublin."

The older couple who completed the roster at the first mate's table were extremely aloof and diffident, and when the couple had left the table—after dessert, save for a glass of port—Henry Cadwallader conspiratorially whispered to Leland,

"They're filthy rich folks from Manchester who made their money by bottling mineral water and advertising it as a cure-all for everything from dyspepsia to carbuncles. Wealth, alas, does breed a certain amount of social snobbery."

"I should consider that an understatement, Mr. Cadwallader," Leland declared, delighted that the first mate recognized him as a man of the world in whom one could confide. All in all, it was not quite so bad as he had thought it might be. Certainly the attention of the vaudevillean had proved a most interesting diversion. Leland found himself looking forward to spending time with the attractive and undoubtedly talented Englishwoman. Surely even Laure couldn't truly object to his having a drink or two and a chat with a lonely woman traveling by herself. And besides, Astrid obviously enjoyed meeting worldly and cultured people—and he obviously filled that bill nicely.

He sighed contentedly. He felt that a lucky star shone down on him this evening, on the first night of the Atlantic run. Perhaps it would be well to take a turn in the saloon; there he might find some congenial partners for a game of cards. The way he felt right now, he could win against all odds. Everything smiled at him, from his happy domestic life, to an innocent flirtation, to the thriving amplification of his business enterprises. Why, then, should he not believe that he would be equally fortunate with a deck of cards? The happy thing about it was that he could afford to lose—and that was when a man could win. It was only when he had a fixed stake, and was fearful that he might lose it, that he actually did lose. Yes, the goddess of good fortune would certainly smile on him tonight.

Accordingly, he rose from the table. He tended his apologies to Astrid Fuller and requested the honor of her company the following evening. Then, with a small bow, he thanked the first mate for being so gracious a host and walked out past the captain's table. The two Curie brothers remained seated, the only passengers still with the captain, who had called for the wine steward to bring a bottle of tawny port and a box of the finest Havana cigars for his famous guests. Yet, he would bet a dozen guineas here and now that if he were to take a megaphone and announce his name to all the diners in this elegant room, it would be better known than theirs. After all, was he not one of the leading entrepreneurs in the United

States, with foreign affiliations that would soon span the globe? He gave himself a satisfied little shake and aimed a condescending smile at the two Curie brothers. Then he walked slowly beyond the tables into the main saloon, with the huge, vaulted ceiling, the paintings and tapestries, the overstuffed chairs with their antimacassars and soft pillows, the elegant ottomans and couches. He stood watching, his eyes roving slowly around the enormous room, which in no way suggested that he was aboard an ocean-going vessel. What he wanted now was to meet some extremely important people and then, by dint of skillful card-playing, show them that he was at least their equal, and perhaps even their superior.

Thoughtfully, he patted the wallet in his inner coat pocket, filled with greenbacks and a substantial letter of credit, which he had procured at his New York bank the day before departure. There was much more money where that came from, and from now on there would be an endless flow of it from all his enterprises, particularly when he established new subsidiary headquarters in the greatest cities of modern Europe!

Three men at a table in one corner were playing cards, and for a moment Leland was tempted to go directly to them, introduce himself, and suggest that he take part in their game. But upon further examination he decided that these were not the most affluent or well-dressed passengers, and that if he wished to make his importance known aboard the *Aurania*, it would be far wiser to seek out the most elegantly dressed and obviously well-to-do men frequenting the enormous saloon.

He looked slowly around, hands on his hips, his head tilted back, his bright eyes sparkling with animation and enthusiasm. Never before had he felt so much the master of things, so much the organizer and creator. In his present mood, he felt that he could overcome any adversary, any danger, any odds against his chances of success. It was exactly the sort of outlook a man of his ability should and must have for success; that went without saying.

Even as he thought this, he told himself, with a knowing, secret little smile, "There's so much that Laure doesn't yet know about me. It will be a surprise to her, when she finds that her trust in me is truly justified. When she learns that I shall undoubtedly be the most important businessman in the United States before much longer, she'll respect and love me even more. But before I can prove myself to her, I must prove myself to strangers, since she already loves me and accepts me and understands that I am bound for success. These strangers, to be sure, know nothing about me as yet. So let us see what we can do about rectifying that situation.''

His eyes glowed with vitality, and he exhaled a long, energetic sigh. He felt himself imbued once again with the strange new euphoria in which everything was roseate; in which a mood of anticipation, growing stronger from moment to moment, made him certain of triumph no matter what he assayed.

He saw three men, off to his left just back of the center of the enormous saloon. Two of them were on a richly upholstered settee; the third man—a nearly bald fellow with a noticeable paunch—was leaning forward, his elbows on his knees, supporting his chin with both hands in a deep, low armchair facing them. All three men were animatedly conversing. The two men on the settee were of vastly divergent types: The man nearest him, elegantly groomed in evening dress, was about forty and had the ruddy, healthy look of an outdoorsman about his clean-shaven, handsome face. His companion, at his left—also, of course, in white tie—was wiry and pale, with high-set cheekbones and a short Vandyke beard, which made his face seem Mephistophelian.

Leland walked slowly toward them and overheard the man with the beard speaking in French. After waiting for a moment when he could break in, he cleared his throat and importantly declared, in French, ''*Messieurs, je suis votre voisin de voyage. Voulez-vous peut-être jouer une petite partie des cartes?*''

The three men looked at one another, then glanced up at him. The nearly bald man in the armchair eyed him with an amused look, then, shrugging, answered, ''*Ça m'est égal, m'sieu.*''

Leland introduced himself, adding that he was an importerexporter with offices throughout the world. Since, in his judgment of the moment, this was very nearly the truth, he had no qualms about boasting of his achievements. The three men looked suitably impressed, and the man with the beard rose and introduced himself. ''I am, m'sieu, Henri Courvalier. I am from Bordeaux, and I have a vineyard with fine grapes and sell my wine in your United States.''

"I am enchanted to meet you, M'sieu Courvalier," Leland replied, and extended his hand.

The bearded man gingerly took it and then, with a mechanical smile, shook it and nodded. "Perhaps we can find a more private place for our little game, eh, m'sieu?"

"But of course. And I shall have a steward bring us some brandy to cement our new friendship," Leland declared with a smile.

The two other men now rose, each making a brisk, almost military bow toward the newcomer. The nearly bald man in the armchair tucked his right hand under the left lapel of his coat and haughtily declared, "M'sieu, I am Boris Vendrikoff, born in Odessa but now residing in Paris, where I manage a private investment company."

"Most interesting," Leland beamed, quite pleased with himself for having come across such unconventional types.

The elegantly groomed third man, with a supercilious gesture of his right hand, declared in a distant, coolly impersonal voice, "And I, M'sieu Kenniston, am Remy DuClos, from Le Havre, where I am owner of a transport service. All of us have been friends for some few years now, m'sieu. We have just concluded our business affairs in New York, and all three of us are going to stay with an Irish friend and do some fishing in the lakes of northern Ireland. I trust that now you are edified as to our identities?"

"Decidedly, M'sieu DuClos. Perhaps I'll see you, as well as M'sieu Henri Courvalier, in Paris, for I plan to open a branch of my importing and exporting firm there shortly."

"Most interesting," Remy DuClos indifferently murmured, eyeing his two friends, as if to wonder why this intruder had foisted himself upon them.

"Gentlemen, it will be an exciting evening, I promise you," Leland enthusiastically declared, oblivious to the discomfiture of the other man. He gestured with a vigorous wave of his right arm toward an unoccupied corner in the huge, high-ceilinged saloon. "I think we can play there; there aren't very many people around, and we can be at our ease. Do you agree, gentlemen?"

Again the three men eyed one another, then simultaneously nodded. The French vintner declared, "It will do as well as any, M'sieu Kenniston. *Allons-y!*"

There was a table with four chairs ideally suited for the

71

group, and Leland at once plunked himself down in the largest, most comfortable chair, leaving his three new acquaintances to shift for themselves. Then, with a grandiose flourish of his arm, he beckoned a passing steward. "The best brandy on shipboard, steward, if you please. Double portions for my friends and myself—and do please bring them quickly!"

"At once, sir," the steward nodded, and then, recognizing the three men with whom this brash Irish-American entrepreneur had allied himself, gave each of them a deferential nod. He then went to the bar to procure the ordered brandies.

"I forgot to ask you for a deck of cards, a brand-new deck, steward," Leland exclaimed when the man returned. He drew out his wallet and tendered a pound note to the efficient employee. He had kept a good deal of British currency from his trip last year, and it was a handsome tip.

The steward at once smiled his thanks as he pocketed the note, and his manner became more obsequious, and even humble. "That's most generous of you, sir. I'll see that you're not disturbed here, all of you. If there's anything else you need, you've only to ring for me—you'll find an electric button just to the right of your chair, on the wall, sir."

"Why yes, I see it. Thank you, steward." Leland leaned back with an expansive smile on his handsome face. To him, all of this seemed preordained, as if it had been intended to be since the very dawn of time, as if he knew in advance that he could not possibly lose, no matter what the skills of these three strangers.

The steward returned with two decks of cards, and Leland again took out his wallet, tipping him another pound note. Then the steward hurried back with a rack of chips. After the man departed, Leland regarded his new acquaintances and declared, "I daresay all of you know how to play poker?"

Again the three men exchanged a questioning look among themselves, and Remy DuClos responded, "As it happens, M'sieu Kenniston, we are indeed familiar with that game."

"Excellent! And, of course, to make it more interesting, even though it's certainly a friendly game, I'm sure you'll want to agree to a stake."

"If you mean play for money, to be sure," the Frenchman replied, after both his friends had signified their willingness with a simultaneous nod. "What stakes do you propose, *mon ami*?"

Leland was busy opening one of the decks of cards. Shuffling them, he buoyantly declared, "Let's start with a hundred dollars to open, if you've no objection."

"That is a bit high, M'sieu Kenniston, but if that is your pleasure, we shall do our best to accommodate you." Remy DuClos gave him a polite nod.

"Then it's settled! Now, let's see—the blue chips will represent a hundred dollars, the red fifty, the white twenty-five. Is that acceptable, gentlemen?"

The other men murmured in the affirmative, curiously eyeing the bluff Irish entrepreneur. They all settled back as—having passed the deck over to DuClos, who promptly cut it with a flourish—Leland began to deal.

"Do you wish to play the variation known as draw poker, M'sieu Kenniston?" DuClos gently interposed.

"Of course! Just good, straight poker; no nonsense about deuces wild, and that sort of thing," the Irishman jauntily averred. "And, since we're playing by standard rules, gentlemen, one must have jacks or better to open. I trust you have no objection to that?"

"None at all, M'sieu Kenniston. Well now, let us see, *mes amis,* whom fortune will favor in this game." The elegant DuClos fanned his cards in his left hand and lifted his snifter of brandy in his right, toasting Leland, then took an appreciative and lingering sip. "Superb brandy; excellent body and a fine bouquet!"

The play began, while, beyond these four men, the buzz of conversation of the other guests formed a pleasant background. The first hand did not begin too auspiciously for Leland; he found himself with only a pair of eights, an ace, a five, and a ten. Nonetheless, determined to prove that he would win, despite all odds, he took four cards when it was his time to draw, retaining only the ace. Then he frowned slightly to find that he had acquired only a pair of queens and nothing else. The winner was the vintner, who chuckled as he gathered in the chips and commiserated, "Do not be downhearted, *mon ami;* the cards are still cold. We have hours ahead of us, and your enthusiasm will make the evening an entertaining one."

"Of course. The first hand means nothing, gentlemen." Leland snapped his fingers in the air and shrugged. "And, as you say, the cards are cold to start with. But never fear, they'll come around to my side in good time. Your deal, I believe, M'sieu DuClos. Shall we now say two hundred dollars to open, just to make things more interesting?''

The three Frenchmen again exchanged a wondering look, and then Remy DuClos nodded in agreement. "It shall be as you say, M'sieu Kenniston. Two hundred dollars to open."

Leland had caught the exchange of glances between the three men, and leaning forward while taking his wallet out of his coat pocket and putting it down on the table before him, he almost truculently declared, "Gentlemen, don't for a moment have any fears that I can't afford to pay for my pleasures— though, of course I expect to fatten this wallet before I leave here this evening. I have a letter of credit in the amount of ten thousand dollars and cash in this wallet representing at least that sum. And my business in New York and my bank account there add up to ten times that amount and more."

"Rest assured, M'sieu Kenniston," DuClos courteously answered, "my friends and I have not the least doubt that you are a gentleman of means. And to set *your* mind at rest, we ourselves are equally able to pay our debts as we incur them. Now, let us get down to the serious business of playing this poker game you seem to find so important."

Once again, Leland frowned. He felt it incumbent upon himself to explain exactly why a man of his stature needed just such a stimulating diversion. "You must understand, gentlemen," he said in an almost patronizing tone, "that tonight is most important to me. It is the beginning of a journey that will lift me into the top flight of the business world, and every European capital will soon know my name and respect it. Thus, this evening is a kind of celebration, if you please. And when I saw you chatting there, I told myself that here were three intelligent, cultured men who would recognize a man of prominent affairs when they saw one." His pronouncement thus delivered, Leland turned his attention to his almost-forgotten glass of brandy and took a second small sip. His spirits were high enough, he felt, not to need bolstering from alcoholic spirits.

Leland proceeded to win the second hand, but he lost the next two so that by the end of the fourth hand, he had lost over eight hundred dollars. Undaunted, he paused now to sip again at his brandy and to light a cigar.

Boris Vendrikoff inquired, "Sir, you have the air of a man who is enjoying a vacation—perhaps much needed after the duties of business and family. Isn't that so?"

"Why, in a sense you happen to be right," Leland chuckled, his good humor returning at this obvious acceptance of him, by his new acquaintances, as a social equal. "However, I am married, as it happens, to a very beautiful woman, and I shall visit my oldest son in Dublin when we land, since he's going to school there, you see."

"Then you are, in a sense, a bachelor for the time being," Henri Courvalier ventured. He smiled and revealed, "In that case, you must certainly visit Paris, where you will find many *belles poules*, so that you may amuse yourself during your newly found freedom."

"Perhaps I shall," Leland airily agreed. "I believe it's my deal. Shall we say three hundred dollars, now, for openers?"

Remy DuClos was intrigued by Leland's behavior. "You have told us, I believe, that you are in the importing and exporting business, and that you are one of the most prominent in that field. But, if I may be permitted to say so, your constant increase of the stakes might lead one to believe that you take risks that surely you would not take in the conduct of your own business."

Leland studied the remark for a moment and then decided to reply to it. "Perhaps not. But then, among friends, one can be more daring—isn't that so? Come now, let's play cards!"

After another hour, Leland was on a first-name basis with his three companions. By then, as well, he had lost half the cash that was in his wallet, but it did not seem to concern him. Pausing long enough to order brandies for all around and two new decks of cards from the attentive steward—giving him two one-pound notes as a tip for his service—Leland declared, "I feel that my luck is going to change for the better, *mes amis*. Indeed, perhaps this is a fortuitous meeting for all of us. I can, through my business—just as an example— sell your wines," addressing himself to the vintner, "and I can do as well for you two others. We must talk of this—after we have finished our card game."

"I, for one," the vintner chuckled with a wink at his two companions, "would be most happy to have more people drink my wine in the United States. I know that in such places as New Orleans and in the better restaurants of New

York, fine wines are drunk. But my impression is that Americans drink mostly whiskey.''

''Not always,'' Leland countered. ''In my country, we have many cultured people who appreciate the bouquet of a fine wine. You must send me a case, and if I like it, I shall certainly make arrangements to import your wines and merchandise them in all the cities where I have offices.''

Henri glanced at his two companions and made a covert wink to indicate that he was taking this with a grain of salt.

It was well past midnight, and although the ebullient Irishman had won a few more hands, he had lost many more overall.

Remy DuClos yawned and glanced at his watch, which he drew out of his vest pocket on a solid gold chain. ''It is really past my bedtime, M'sieu Kenniston,'' he apologetically declared. ''Shall we have one last hand?''

''What a pity. I was just beginning to warm up,'' the entrepreneur cheerfully responded. ''But so be it. However, to finish the evening with a flourish, let's make the opening ante five hundred dollars.''

''Very well, if that's your pleasure.''

After the deal, Leland drew three cards, hoping to build a flush. But he was unlucky, as he had been throughout the evening. It was Remy DuClos who won the final hand, and when he raked in the chips, he eyed Leland and murmured, ''I do not wish to press you, Leland, but if you wish to settle this little debt of honor . . .''

The handsome Irishman nodded and took out his wallet. His face fell when he opened it. He had lost over nine thousand dollars. Paying them now would wipe out his cash, leaving him with just a letter of credit for the entire European trip. The three men stared intently at the hesitant Irishman, then exchanged a significant glance. Finally, aware of the heavy silence that had suddenly fallen, Leland put his wallet back into his pocket after extracting three of his business cards. ''If you don't mind, gentlemen, I am somewhat short of cash—though I again assure you that I have ample credit and many financial contacts throughout the world. What I propose to do, if you will be willing, is to write each of you an I.O.U. on these cards, signing them, of course, so that my bookkeeper will pay you or your representatives whenever you wish to collect. You can, of course, send a letter to my office and enclose the card. It will be just as good as money, I assure you."

"This is really somewhat irregular, Leland," Henri mildly protested, and both Boris and Remy nodded their confirmation of this attitude.

"If it were not for the fact that this trip is so important to me and that I plan to open offices in the major cities of Europe, gentlemen, I should settle with you here and now," Leland boasted. "But, you can see from this card and also from this letter of credit . . . here it is; examine it, gentlemen—" Here, he unfolded it and put it out on the table for all of them to see. "There is absolutely no question as to my solvency and my ability to pay my debts."

"Oh, very well," Remy DuClos wearily declared with another glance at his watch. "I am certain that you will not go back on your word. Besides, it has been a most amiable evening, and it has been a pleasure for me to make your acquaintance, Leland."

In turn, as each man told him the amount he was owed, Leland wrote the figure on the back of the card with the date. On the front he wrote, "Payable upon demand to either the principal or his representative," and then he signed his name with a flourish.

"There you are, gentlemen." He abruptly rose from the table, rubbing his forehead, for he found that his headache had returned. The euphoria of the evening had worn off a bit, and fatigue had set in. He had begun to blink almost constantly, and during the last two or three hands, he had discovered that his powers of concentration were flagging. "I daresay that I am in as much need of sleep as you are, Remy. Well then, of course I shall see you during the rest of the voyage. Thank you for a most enjoyable evening."

With this, giving each of the three men a quick bow, he turned and walked back to his stateroom.

Remy DuClos stared after him, then shrugged and turned to his two companions. "I cannot say for certain," he said, "but I do believe that man is quite mad."

"As for me," Boris Vendrikoff muttered, "I find him quite boorish. What airs he gives himself, and how splendidly he makes a case for himself as to his importance! Until this evening, I had never heard of his name or that of his firm."

"Nor I," Henri Courvalier chimed in. "One has only to

hope that these I.O.U.'s will be honored. The moment I leave ship, I shall send this to my secretary in New York and instruct him to forward it at once to the office of this curious man.''

Chapter Seven

When he went back to his stateroom that first evening out, Leland Kenniston rang persistently for his steward, despite the lateness of the hour. About five minutes later, hastily dressed and yawning, his eyes blurry with sleep, William Hazeltine softly knocked at the cabin door and was told to enter. "Is anything wrong, sir?" he solicitously asked. "You aren't feeling ill?"

"No, of course not," the Irish entrepreneur impatiently cut him off with a wave of his hand. "I'm just thirsty. Will you get a double brandy? The best brandy you have on board—make sure of it."

The steward did not show his annoyance at being wakened for so relatively unimportant an errand, but instead respectfully inclined his head and, in a noncommittal tone of voice, responded, "I'll bring it at once, sir. Is there anything else I can get you? Perhaps some black coffee?"

"Are you implying that I'm not sober?" Leland indignantly asked. "If I wanted coffee, I would have said so. Just get the brandy. I want to do some thinking before I go to sleep."

"I'll do the best I can, sir. The bar is closed, you know. . . ."

"I've perfect confidence in you, Hazeltine." Now Leland's tone was ingratiating, accompanied by a warm smile. "You'll find a way to get it, I'm sure. Just be quick about it, if you please. I'll take care of you; you know that."

"That's not at all the question, sir. I assure you."

"I'd like the brandy at once!"

Leland slowly seated himself in the deepest stuffed chair of his cabin, wincing as a wave of pain throbbed in his temples.

He probably *had* drunk rather more than he should have; certainly he had played many hours, and fatigue was claiming him. In spite of this, he felt exhilarated. So what if he had lost all that money tonight? Tomorrow was another day, and once he got to London and Paris and Berlin and Vienna, he'd make a fortune as soon as he concluded trade agreements with the leading fabricators of those great European cities. What he had spent tonight could be put down as entertainment, a form of diversion to occupy him until the *Aurania* dropped anchor in the port of Cobh.

About ten minutes later, the steward knocked at the door and brought in a large snifter nearly a third full. "It's from my own private stock, if you don't mind, sir," he apologized as he set the glass down on the night table beside his importunate passenger. "Is it all right for me to leave you now, sir? You won't be requiring anything more tonight, will you?"

"No, no, Hazeltine, I'm fine." Leland made a lordly gesture with his hand in the air, waving it in an irregular circle as if to indicate that such minor details were better left unmentioned. His mind was on more important things—the future global recognition of his trading company. That was what tonight was all about, really.

The steward looked at him obliquely, then shook his head as he slipped quietly out of the stateroom.

The Irish entrepreneur reached for the snifter and, blinking his eyes, took a long swallow. Then he went over to his bed and stretched himself out, luxuriating in its comfort. "I've made some important friends tonight," he told himself, half aloud. "What I've lost over the card table, I'll more than make up for in profits. I'll handle Henri's wine, certainly. And I'm sure I'll do business with his friends. Yes, I'm on my way along the road of international success!"

He downed the rest of the brandy, belched, and winced as a bitterish surge of fiery alcohol was regurgitated. Swallowing, he lay back on the pillows and closed his eyes again. The snifter dropped from his nerveless hand, and he slept dreamlessly, soundly.

It was not until half an hour past noon of the next day that he wakened, his mouth and throat dry, his stomach nauseated from all the brandy. Unsteadily getting out of bed, he hastened to the lavatory to make his ablutions. The splashing of cold water on his face revived him, and he stared at himself

in the mirror. There were faint dark circles under his eyes
. . . but then he grinned at himself and felt young again. It
was a minor setback—all great men had their share. The
greatness lay in their being able to cast off the past with its
retrogressions and to go steadily forward.

Leland did not again play cards, though the three gentlemen he had met on the first night out were often in the saloon
and amiably nodded to him. On the third evening out, Remy
DuClos bought him a drink and conversed with him at some
length on how his own firm might be able to transport goods
from France to New Orleans and New York. No mention was
made of the large debt that Leland owed to him, as well as to
his two friends.

For the remainder of the voyage, Leland sought to make
sparkling conversation at the dinner table. He was particularly
amused by Astrid Fuller's growing efforts to offer him a night
of love, but with the utmost discretion. Each evening, their
repartee became a fencing match in which each strived to
score off the other; there were times when he made her blush
with sly, though poetic, references to the carnal passions that
brought strangers together and made them ardent lovers for all
time. Once again, he was exhilarated by the sound of his own
voice; and as he listened—almost as a stranger will listen to
someone whose voice is mellifluous and catches his ear—
Leland found himself pausing to choose words that would
have greater imagistic color and, hence, create an even more
conquering effect on this sensual, mature beauty of the English stage.

That was as far as things went, however, for he felt it
would be too indiscreet to accept Astrid's by now blatantly
open invitation to come to her stateroom at night; nonetheless,
it flattered his ego. But once in Paris or London—or Berlin or
Vienna—where no one would know him, there was no reason
why he could not indulge in a tiny little affair—just to prove
that he could conquer and triumph at anything he set out to
do.

Laure Kenniston and Lopasuta Bouchard sat side by side in
the spacious carriage they had hired at their Montgomery
hotel to take them to Windhaven Plantation.

Despite her anxiety over the fate of Windhaven Plantation,
Laure looked serenely beautiful in her tailored gray wool suit,

81

pleated and draped, and a matching fur-trimmed cape. The Alabama weather in January was damp and chilly, although a far cry from the New York cold she had left.

The ride to the plantation would take about two hours, and then she would at last be back at the red-brick chateau. She realized how much she had changed in the few years she had been away, living a life of luxury in New York, pedestaled like a goddess by her attentive husband. Now she was faced with problems so weighty that they would tax even a strong man like Leland—and yet the task of facing them befell her. She had already decided not to cable Leland informing him of the trouble, nor would she urge him to return, because in her view, Windhaven was her responsibility and hers alone. She had assumed the trust of maintaining the Bouchard estate when she had married Luke.

She remained silent for a long while, and Lopasuta, understanding her feelings, was silent also, waiting for her to speak. He couldn't tell whether she was even aware of the moss-laden old oaks whose lacy tendrils occasionally reached down and tickled the window frame of the passing carriage. He wasn't sure if her eyes, which stared so fixedly out the window, noticed the rushing waters of the Alabama River or if all they saw were old memories.

Finally, she sighed audibly and then turned to Lopasuta. "I was just thinking how Luke's grandfather made this same journey over ninety years ago. All the way from the Gulf Coast, with only a packhorse and his musket and perhaps a hunting knife, taking his water from the river, making his bed on a grassy knoll after making certain there were no snakes or wild beasts in the offing. What courage he had, and how it was rewarded!"

"Yes, it was Sangrodo, in the stronghold, who first told me of old Lucien and the good he had done, and the love he bore for the Creeks. Luke, too, was a man with vision and without the slightest suspicion or hatred in his heart for those who were not like himself. What a pity it is that not all men can be like him. Then, of course," he began, adding a whimsical note to the somber conversation, "there would be no need for lawyers like myself. Things would be settled in an amicable manner, without resorting to the courts and to time-consuming and money-wasting litigation."

"If that were the case, dear Lopasuta, you might be a tiller of land, or perhaps a merchant, but you would still uphold the rights of the weak against the strong. That is your nature and your creed. And now, I begin to see what mine is, and I see I have neglected it since I went to New York with Leland.''

"But you mustn't reproach yourself!" he quickly interposed, taking her hand and squeezing it gently to reassure her. "You left the plantation in good hands, with Marius and that young, imaginative Benjamin Brown."

"Yes, Lopasuta, but Marius and Ben are blacks, and I'm afraid I've put them in a dangerous position. Even the New York newspapers have been reporting how some whites are trying to abolish all the rights of the blacks that Lincoln hoped he set forth in perpetuity. The attack proves that I have reason to be concerned. It is a bad time in the South. There are still those in the North who hate us because we seceded from the Union, and there are those in the South who still hate the North—and themselves, too, for having lost the war. People like that take out their anger on the defenseless and the innocent. Oh, I would to God such wounds would be healed for once and for all time!"

Laure looked out the carriage window again. Trees shivered in the chill wind from the northeast, bowing toward the river. The bleakness of the scene—with the dull, leaden-hued sky and the wind that occasionally lashed the carriage so hard that the isinglass windows shook in their mountings—seemed a logical and inevitable part of the gloominess of her errand. Overshadowing everything was her deep concern for Marius Thornton, whom, with his dear Clemmie, Laure had learned to love for the dedication and concern they had shown for Windhaven.

"So many friends we knew are gone," she now reminisced, "like your teacher, Jedidiah Danforth. What a wonderful, salty character he was, full of courage and vitality."

"Yes, indeed. I'll never forget how he mustered out in the dead of night, when the Ku Klux Klan had come to burn me out. While I was trapped inside my burning house, he drove his buggy at breakneck speed to bring help. He saved my life; thank God he didn't lose his in the process. I had another year to learn from him before he died—that was ten years ago. How much I loved him, even when he made me pour over the law books in his library! He could be so sardonic and irascible at times, and yet I knew that that was his way of challenging me, of forcing me out of myself, so that I would develop all that was in me and one day be a credit to my people. Yes, we have wonderful memories, Laure."

"But we still have some good friends back there, like Mitzi and Dalbert Sattersfield. He's still mayor of Lowndesboro, you know," Laure said, smiling at the tall Comanche lawyer. "They can't find anyone better, so they've reelected him many times now. He's kind and good, and Mitzi is so happy with him. Ah, I wonder what might have happened if Luke had lived, if we could have lived out our days on Windhaven Plantation, watching our children grow up. . . ."

"But, surely you must realize how well your life has been going since those first awful months after Luke died and before you met Leland. You were so anguished and so vulnerable then—"

"Yes, vulnerable to the likes of that scheming gambler who had you shanghaied, and who sought to destroy the good name of the Bouchards."

"That's true. But he is forgotten now, and his evil will not live after him. And yet, after what's just happened at the plantation, I'm greatly concerned over these current enemies. My feeling is that they may be old ones, and that I must trace back those who hated me, to see if their friends or relatives or associates took up that vendetta against me. I should feel horribly guilty, dear Laure, if that were the case, because then I would say to myself that it was I who had brought this suffering and sorrow to you—and you surely do not deserve it."

"Oh, no, Lopasuta, please don't think that!" she quickly answered, putting her hand on his wrist and steadfastly looking into his eyes. "It was against the Bouchard name that all those deeds of violence were aimed; you bore the name, and so you were a target for them. But remember, we have always been able to overcome their schemes."

"And we shall again this time, Laure; that's why I'm coming with you, to see if I can't ferret out the real identity of those nameless riders who shot Marius and tried to destroy the plantation," the Comanche lawyer avowed.

The mournful whistle of a nearby steamboat sounded as they rounded a bend in the river road. The vessel had veered toward the near shore, in an effort to avoid the shoals on the farther side of the river. On the afterdeck, two hands could be seen coiling lines, while above, on the promenade, two hardy passengers—a man and a woman—took the air, holding their coats tightly around their necks and hunching their shoulders against the raw wind.

Lopasuta saw Laure's gaze following the ship's progress, a sad smile growing on her face. Once again he waited for her to speak. When she did so, there was a note of wistfulness in her voice.

"Lucien and Paul used to watch the riverboats for hours at a time, when they were little," she said. "Lucien would sit in the crook of a tree, pretending he was the captain on the bridge. He'd shout down orders to Paul to 'get up more steam.' After a while, Paul would tire of playing the fireman—he'd want to be captain. But Lucien would say no, he was the elder, and he was captain by rights. Then they'd argue. Oh, I knew they adored each other, even then, in spite of their brotherly spats." She gave Lopasuta a wry smile. "Things change so quickly, Lopasuta. Now, I suppose, small boys dream of being engineers on the railroad."

Lopasuta smiled. "I know my boy Dennis does. And I suppose we must resign ourselves to certain kinds of change. When I was a boy in the Comanche stronghold, I dreamed of being a great warrior. But Sangrodo told me that those days were gone forever. So here I am now, a respectable lawyer, working in an office, and fortunate to be in your husband's employ. . . . Will he be coming here when he returns, do you think?"

"I'm not sure. He did say he'd be gone about two months. By then—God willing and with your help, Lopasuta dear—we can solve the mystery of the attack and present a stronger front so that this violence will not be repeated. That's at least what I hope for, and pray for, as well. So I shan't send him a cable unless I'm absolutely certain that we can't settle this with the help of those loyal people who still live on the land."

Lopasuta took her hands in his and smiled at her. "We shall work together, you and I, Laure. The land is eternal; evil men do not leave their mark upon it long, and it remembers those who respect it and work with it and let it grow stronger by not abusing it."

"Yes, that's true, dear Lopasuta." She sighed; the two

85

looked at each other, and each understood what the other was thinking.

And then, very gently, putting his arm around Laure's shoulders, Lopasuta murmured, "You mustn't worry, Laure. When we get to Windhaven Plantation, you'll be able to set matters right once again, as they should be."

She sighed again and nodded in silent reply, and as they continued along the river road they could see the steamboat just slipping from view around the bend.

Chapter Eight

Leland Kenniston had left the ship at Cobh and had at once boarded the train that would take him to Dublin. Though it was already dusk and the light was fading fast, the sight of the Irish countryside stirred him, and he leaned back and sighed, recalling his boyhood. How far he had come since then! The world was definitely within his grasp now.

The railway carriage swayed slightly, and the motion was hypnotic and comforting. He closed his eyes for a moment and pretended that he was a pasha, with a stately palace and scores of servants to attend his every whim. His beautiful Laure, the green-eyed, honey-haired goddess, would of course be his favorite wife—but, in such a palace, he might have hidden chambers where beautiful, enticing concubines would await him for the servicing of his sudden, capricious yearnings. He would eat from a solid gold service, and his cutlery would be made from the finest silver mined in all the world. There would be baubles and jewels for most of his minions, but for Laure there would be star emeralds and necklaces of diamonds, jades, and topazes.

A rush of memories surged upon him now. The lights in the tiny houses that dotted the landscape outside his window made him think of his own boyhood hearth, his dear mother sewing on a chilly evening by the light of a dim lamp, his father seated comfortably before a peat fire in their snug cottage. It had been too long since he had thought of those days, now so long gone, and the reminiscences of those times kept him company as his train passed through Counties Cork, Limerick, Tipperary, and Kildare before finally completing its journey to Dublin.

It was early dawn when the train reached the city. Stepping

from the train into the cold mist of the Irish morning, Leland tipped a porter to help him with his bags, then he secured a hansom cab to take him to the best hotel. There, he flung himself down on the bed and slept dreamlessly, waking at about noon. When he sat up, he blinked his eyes and went over to the window and drew the shutters. The sky was a chilly blue, and even the sun seemed bleak. He hurriedly dressed and tugged the bellpull hanging by the bed, deciding a hot cup of tea was definitely called for on such a cold morning.

A pretty, rosy-cheeked Irish maid, not more than nineteen, came to his ring. She curtsied, smiling shyly at him, for he had a warm smile on his face and was at his most personable.

"My colleen, mavourneen, would you be so kind as to bring me a substantial breakfast? It will be my first in our beautiful Eire in many a day."

"Oh, faith, sir! You're Irish, too?" she naively asked.

He was standing over by the window, drinking in his fill of the Dublin streets. He turned to her with another warm smile. "Indeed I am. I was born in County Mayo, mavourneen. I've come home, now, to visit a fine boy at St. Timothy's, where I sent him. It's the best education in the world. And not only because the school is excellent, but also because Ireland has the loveliest women—of which you yourself are one, my pretty colleen."

"Faith, sir, and I think ye've kissed the Blarney Stone!" she giggled, and then, very red in the face, apologetically gasped, "Oh, sir, forgive me. I spoke out of turn—"

"There's no offense taken," he hastily answered her. "What's your name, lass?"

"Kitty O'Toole, your lordship." Again she made him a curtsy.

"It's a pleasure to meet you, Kitty O'Toole. Do you think I might have some scones with butter melted into them—plus a rasher of bacon, some scrambled eggs, and some Irish breakfast tea? Ah, yes—and let's not forget porridge, with plenty of cream and sugar!"

"I'll get it for you directly, your lordship!" Kitty O'Toole gave him another curtsy and then, still blushing, hurried out of the room.

Half an hour later, Leland Kenniston attacked his ample breakfast and ate with relish. It amused him to see the attentive way the pretty, young maid hovered about him to make certain that he had every comfort he desired. This he interpreted as yet another sign that all the auspices of his European journey foretold an unequivocal triumph at whatever endeavor he would undertake.

Only briefly did he think back to the huge sum he had lost in gambling aboard the *Aurania;* this he shrugged off, telling himself that Jacob Cohen would see to it that all bills were paid and the debt of honor expunged so that his reputation would remain unsullied. Besides, had he not already promised himself that the three men who had taken the money from him would one day—and very soon at that—become his customers? What he had lost was thus merely an investment for the future, a wise investment in the Biblical sense—as enjoined in the proverb that teaches that when one casts one's bread upon the waters, it comes back a thousandfold.

Finishing up his breakfast, he wiped his chin and washed his hands. Then he went to the wardrobe and pulled out his topcoat. Whistling as he fairly ran down the stairs, he hailed a carriage to take him to St. Timothy's Academy. He had told the innkeeper that he would probably remain one more night, since pressing business required him to take the ferry over to Liverpool the next day and, from there, an express train down to London. He would spend the day with Lucien, and then he would write a letter to Laure to reassure her that all was well with their son.

Their son. A momentary twinge of regret pricked him as he recalled with a frown that Laure would never be able to give him a child of his own. Perhaps it was time for him to induce her to let him adopt her children, so they would at least bear the Kenniston name. He was the last of his line, and it was a line that had gone back centuries—even to the Irish kings, he was certain.

Unfortunately, he knew how fondly Laure clung to the name of Bouchard. He wondered, with some envy, if he could not himself achieve the almost legendary reputation old Lucien Bouchard had had so long ago. Then the feeling of certainty and determination returned to drive away these few lingering doubts. The entire world would soon know the name of Kenniston. Perhaps that was more important than a child of one's loins.

* * *

Just before two o'clock that afternoon, the carriage driver halted his vehicle in front of the main entrance to St. Timothy's Academy. Turning in his perch, he called out, "We've come to yer destination, mister."

"Thank you; you've made good time. Here's for your trouble," Leland said.

"Thank ye, sir! Would ye wish me to wait for ye?"

"No, I think not; but thank you for asking."

"Not at all, sir," the wizened Irish carriage driver declared. Then, tipping his black stovepipe hat and giving Leland a respectful nod, he clucked to his horse and drove off.

The handsome entrepreneur strode toward the doorway of the Gothic central building of the academy and rang the bell. A white-haired old man answered, eyeing him up and down.

"I wish to see Father O'Mara, if you please. Tell him Leland Kenniston from America is here."

"I'll tell Father directly, sir. You just come in out of the cold, sir!" Now the elderly man was all smiles and deference. He ushered Leland into a small anteroom and bade him take a comfortable chair opposite the door to the headmaster's office, then hurried to find Father O'Mara.

A few moments later, the elderly priest strode down the hallway. He was dressed in his black cassock; a rosary hung about his waist, and it bobbed with every step. His face was beaming as he extended his hand. "Mr. Kenniston! A real pleasure to see you again! It has been too many years since you've been back to the old sod to pay a visit to your friends. But, I've been grateful for your letters, and I must say your stepson has been a real credit to the school this year—a fine broth of a lad indeed. . . ."

Leland's face clouded for an instant. Here was a reminder, once again, that this "fine broth" of a lad was not his, not even by adoption. But his engaging smile swiftly returned, and he held the headmaster's hand in his strong grip and jovially remarked, "That's indeed kind of you to say, Father. Although I must say privately, for your ears alone, that I'm greatly relieved that he's no longer trying to be the hot-blooded hero he set out to be during his third year."

"I share that feeling, Mr. Kenniston. Please—come into my office. I'll have my houseman brew us a pot of tea."

"Thank you, I should like that." Leland seated himself before the priest's desk and leaned back in his chair, waiting for the conversation to resume. Father O'Mara shoved some papers to one side, then settled himself and leaned back, his hands folded and his thumbs twiddling in his lap. With an expansive smile, he remarked, "I trust you'll be wanting to see young Lucien."

"Yes, I had the notion of taking him to a first-rate Dublin restaurant for dinner this evening."

"I'm sure he'll enjoy that. His classes are over for today, and I think I know where you can find him."

"With Mary Eileen Brennert?" Leland smiled as he hazarded an educated guess.

"The very same thought I had. As you know, Mr. Kenniston, that girl has had a very sobering influence on your stepson. Frankly, despite his brilliant mind and quick grasp of essentials and his adapting to our Old World ways, I was worried about him for a while. He was getting into nothing but trouble when he and his two friends, Ned Riordan and Edward Cordovan, went into Dublin and tried to take on the entire British army. Since then, happily, they've seen the error of their ways."

"I know. I was ready to take a trip here last year to intercede and lecture him about acceptance of one's responsibilities," Leland soberly replied.

"Well, fortunately that trip wasn't necessary, and now you've come at an excellent time. He's done very well at his studies—and, as I said before, the charming daughter of our games master has steadied him. She's a sweet, gentle girl, with a great sense of responsibility and filial obligation, the sort of thing one reads about in novels, but does not often see."

"I've gathered that from his letters to his mother, Father O'Mara. I must say, I'm relieved to find that all is still going well." Leland smiled at the old priest, then declared, "Well now, you apparently know where to find them, and as long as he is with Miss Brennert, I should like to meet her, as well."

"I'll send my houseman out to get them and bring them both to you here, Mr. Kenniston," Father O'Mara proposed.

About a quarter of an hour later, Lucien Bouchard and Mary Eileen Brennert were ushered into Father O'Mara's office. Lucien's eyes widened. Leland laughed and rose from his chair and came toward him. "Father! Goodness gracious, what on earth are you doing here? I had no idea you were coming!'' Lucien blurted.

"I know. It was my surprise. You see, Lucien, I'm on a very important business trip—and since I found that the *Aurania* sailed directly to Cobh, I said to myself, why shouldn't I come visit my favorite son as well?'' He shook hands with Lucien and then turned to Mary Eileen Brennert. "And you, my very beautiful colleen, are, I take it, my son's true inspiration.''

Lucien blushed at his stepfather's florid compliment and observed that Mary Eileen had lowered her eyes and was also blushing violently. In a soft, quavering voice, she responded, "I—I'm a good friend of his.''

"And, I hope, one of these days, something a good deal more,'' Leland brashly went on with a beaming smile. He brought her hand to his lips and kissed it, and even Father O'Mara raised his eyebrows in surprise at the flamboyant gesture toward the teenage girl. "I wonder, Miss Brennert, if you would give me the pleasure of dining with Lucien and me this evening?''

"I—I think I could. But I don't want to intrude upon a family reunion—''

"Miss Brennert, it's no intrusion whatsoever. I am most happy to have this occasion to get to know you.''

"All right, then, thank you. I'd be pleased to come,'' she timidly responded.

"Well, that's settled! Meanwhile, shall we go for a walk—or, is it too cold for you, Lucien, Miss Brennert?'' Leland suggested. He was feeling most energetic, and the prospect of a brisk walk was suddenly an attractive thought.

"Well, it's very wet out there on the campus,'' Lucien dubiously began. "Maybe we could just talk for a bit in one of the public rooms—if that's all right with you, Father O'Mara.''

"Of course, Lucien,'' the priest responded benignly.

"Good. Come, Father, I'll show you the way.'' Lucien turned and, taking hold of Mary Eileen's elbow, guided her out of Father O'Mara's office. Leland turned to look at the headmaster of the academy, then smiled broadly and quickly followed his stepson and the boy's sweetheart.

Lucien led his stepfather to an unoccupied lounge, waiting for Leland to sink into a large brown leather chair before taking a seat himself. Mary Eileen followed Lucien's lead. Indeed, the young girl was so obviously embarrassed by this unexpected encounter and still more so by Leland Kenniston's effusive greeting, that she automatically gravitated to a hard-seated straight-backed chair; sitting stiffly upright and clasping her hands in her lap, she demurely looked down at the floor, trying to efface herself as much as possible.

"Well now, son, it's awfully good to see you again—and to see you looking so well!"

"I—I'm very glad you came, Father. How is Mother?" Lucien was still a little dazed by the unexpected appearance of his stepfather.

"She's fine. And your brothers and sisters are fine, too. As a matter of fact, I took them all to see the ship when I embarked. I'm afraid that John didn't really appreciate the tour, however—he'd have been much happier left at home with a huge pot of cocoa," Leland airily jested.

Lucien let a brief smile cross his face and then looked at his stepfather. "You—you're no longer angry with me for my past behavior in Dublin?" he ventured.

"Absolutely not!" Leland waved the suggestion away with a flourish of his hand. "When your mother and I read your letters, we were well aware that you'd decided to take the path of discretion, an obvious change of heart most reassuring to us." He turned to smile at Mary Eileen. "I think, unless I'm absolutely wrong in my judgment, that this charming young lady was mainly responsible for that change of heart— isn't that so, Lucien?"

Now it was Lucien's turn to blush, and he stammered, "I . . . well, yes—I think I told you that Mr. Brennert didn't want me to see her because I was getting into trouble . . . and so—"

"And so," his stepfather finished, "you decided to be wise and discreet. There'll be plenty of time to decide what causes you want to champion when you're older. I'm afraid that perhaps I did lead you a bit into extreme action by talking so much about the freedom of Ireland. But that's over and done with; there's no need to talk about anything unpleasant. What I do want to talk about is where to take you both to dinner this evening in Dublin. I trust, Mary Eileen, your father will have no objection to your joining us?"

"I—I'm sure not, sir, when I tell him that you've come all the way from America."

"Good! I'll tell you what—I want to go back into Dublin because I want to do some shopping for gifts. I'll come back for you at about six—that'll give you both time to freshen up and dress—and while I'm gone I want you to think of a really posh restaurant, the best in Dublin that I can take you to." He paused a moment and stared at Mary Eileen. "You know, Lucien, I really envy you. If I were your age and falling in love for the first time, I couldn't have picked a more beautiful girl."

Mary Eileen blushed even more hotly now, averting her eyes from the brash, handsome, mature man who paid her such effusive compliments. Indeed, out of sheer helplessness, she glanced rather poignantly at her young sweetheart, who was not looking at her, but rather was staring openmouthed at his stepfather.

"Well, I'm afraid I'm talking too much," the Irishman went on, "but that's understandable, seeing as how I've been looking forward so much to this trip. I'm going to achieve great things, Lucien; you and your mother will be proud of me. I hope to establish offices in London, Paris, Vienna, and Berlin, among other cities. When you're of age, I'll be able to set you up in whatever situation you want—mark my words. Well then, I'll leave you two for the time being, and I'll be back here at six." He rose from the chair and walked slowly toward Mary Eileen Brennert. "I hope we'll be great friends, my dear," he said gently, as he extended his hand to her.

The young girl tentatively accepted his hand and mumbled something inaudible.

"Until later, my dear," he heartily exclaimed, as he gave her a quick bow and left the room.

Faithful to his word, Leland Kenniston came back with a carriage promptly at six to take Lucien Bouchard and Mary Eileen Brennert to McCafferty's, then the ranking restaurant of Dublin. Though the restaurant was unusually crowded for a Thursday evening, by dint of giving the headwaiter a pound note, Leland managed to secure a comfortable table at the rear, one that would insure privacy of conversation.

As they made their way to the back of the restaurant,

Lucien found himself admiring Mary Eileen's trim figure in the midnight blue wool dress she wore. The rush of warm air that had hit them the moment they had stepped indoors caused Mary Eileen to remove her heavy serge coat immediately and carry it over her arm.

Her own father had been enthusiastic about the dinner, saying, "I want Mr. Kenniston to see what sort of fine, decent Irish girl his stepson is enamored of." When she had blushed and protested, Mr. Brennert had laughed heartily. "Well, me darlin', of course it *could* be your wonderful scones is the reason the boy keeps comin' around—but you and I both know better. I wonder if it's too soon to tell him that when the time comes that he's old enough and he has something solid to offer you, I wouldn't object to him coming to me, man to man, and asking for your hand in marriage. Nothing less, mind you." Then he added, with a grin, "And even that I'll take under advisement." He had given her a kiss on the cheek and murmured, "Have a good time, me darlin'!"

Now, as Mary Eileen and Lucien sat down at the table in the restaurant, Leland turned to them and said, "You must let me order dinner for all of us!" He beckoned to the elderly waiter, who approached attentively, a napkin draped over his left arm, his shrewd eyes contemplating the elegantly dressed entrepreneur. He suspected that this customer was not the kind to stint and might very well order the most expensive items on the menu. He was not wrong; Leland promptly ordered lobster bisque, salmon in Hollandaise sauce, sirloin of beef with stuffed mushrooms, roast snipe, and capons served with asparagus and melted butter, to be followed by petit fours. The dinner was to be accompanied by the finest French Bordeaux—red and white, according to the course.

As he dipped his spoon into his lobster bisque, Leland eyed Mary Eileen and, with a man-of-the-world wink at his stepson, declared, "I must say, Lucien, your taste is impeccable. I couldn't have found a more delectable colleen than Miss Brennert."

Mary Eileen kept her eyes lowered and fixed her attention on her soup, while Lucien shifted nervously in his seat, hugely embarrassed by the intimate compliment. "Th-thank you, Father. We're very fond of each other," he finally

95

vouchsafed. At the same time, he sent his stepfather a pleading glance.

"Come now, Lucien, you mustn't be too shy; that's the role a girl plays because of her innocence and inexperience. You, on the other hand, with a keenly intelligent mind—not to mention with a father like me to back you to any financial success you're after in this world—why, you needn't take a back seat to anyone. Yes, indeed, you could have your pick of eligible women, when it comes time for you to marry. But I will say that I myself will gladly give you my permission to marry this charmingly modest and yet exceptionally beautiful young woman."

Lucien Bouchard sighed loudly in exasperation. "You— you really mustn't say such things, Father. . . ." he hesitantly began.

But Leland was no longer involved with this topic of conversation. Instead, he took a few more spoonfuls of his soup then pushed the bowl aside. With a shrug, he declared, "This isn't too bad, but we'd get much better in Paris, I can assure you. And that reminds me, I've a surprise for you. I'm sure you'll be free this summer, and it's high time you visited the Continent. A young man should sow his wild oats before he thinks of settling down, and certainly he must see Paris and Vienna and Berlin."

"I—I was wondering whether I shouldn't go back home to see Mother and my brothers and sisters," Lucien hazarded.

"Well, if you wish, but I personally believe—and I'm sure Laure will agree with me—that you should spend at least a few weeks in those great cities in order to be exposed to all their tradition and culture. After all, I am going to them for the purpose of establishing new business headquarters there. Ah, I shall become as famous throughout Europe as I am already in the United States, Lucien. And I expect my son—I think of you that way, you know—to make a good impression and to carry on the business image that I myself have established. You're very personable, and you're very good-looking. I'm sure that you will impress the business associates I shall undoubtedly make on the continent. One thing's certain: When you do visit the rest of Europe this summer, you'll find all my new offices ready and their staffs eager to look after you and to give you the grand tour."

"I—I'm most grateful, F-Father." Lucien glanced covertly

at Mary Eileen, who remained steadily eating with her eyes downcast, not wishing to interfere in this family discussion. Surreptitiously, Lucien reached for her hand under the tablecloth and was rewarded by a quick little squeeze and the sight of her deepening blush. She coughed, then reached for a glass of water and quickly sipped it, pretending that she had swallowed something the wrong way.

With the snipe, which was garnished with browned potatoes and beautifully served on a silver salver, Leland waxed expansive. "Now this is more like it. It surely is every bit as good as Simpson's-on-the-Strand in London. They've braised the meat properly, and it's firm yet tender. Excellent!" To the waiter, with a wave of his hand, he proclaimed, "Tell the chef that he has my full compliments!"

"Very good of you, sir." The elderly waiter inclined his head and scurried off to the kitchen.

Leland filled the glasses with the red Bordeaux, and then, lifting his glass, he proposed, "A toast to one of the loveliest girls I've ever seen on either side of the Atlantic—and to my fine stepson, Lucien, who has had the wisdom to select her as his wife—"

"Please, Father!" Lucien anxiously interjected. "We— we're much too young to think of marriage, yet!"

"Oh, pshaw," his stepfather chuckled with a wave of his glass. "This girl is a treasure, and of course you have only the most honorable intentions toward her—which necessarily means marriage eventually. As a matter of fact, if you wish, I'll be happy to talk to her father on your behalf, Lucien—"

"Oh, no!" Mary Eileen gasped, crimsoning to her temples at this and regarding Leland with a look of utter incredulity.

"Please, I wish you wouldn't, Father! I first want to finish my schooling, so that's at least four more years. Then it'll be time enough to think of such things. . . . if she— Oh, Father, please let's not talk about such things!" Lucien was almost in tears at the way the conversation was going. He felt absolutely helpless at the way his stepfather seemed so oblivious to his and Mary Eileen's sensitive feelings.

"All right, then. When you both feel the time has come, you may be certain I'll give you an excellent reference to Miss Brennert's father," his stepfather chuckled. "You see, Miss Brennert—dash it all, I'd really rather call you Mary Eileen, because obviously before too long you'll be one of the family. Besides, it's difficult to call one as lovely as you—the very flower of Irish beauty—''

"Oh, no," Mary Eileen burst in. "You—you mustn't say these things to me! You—you'll quite turn my head, Mr. K-Kenniston." Mary Eileen's voice quavered, and she glanced frantically at Lucien as if seeking help from her young escort.

"But I do say it—as a connoisseur and as an expert who's traveled the world over. The fact is, Mary Eileen, if I were Lucien's age, I'd see to it that nobody else could ever have the chance to win you!"

Mary Eileen's blushes, which had already been furious, were now so violent that she took up her napkin and hid her face in it, pretending to wipe a morsel off her chin. Lucien merely dug his nails into his palms. For the life of him, he could not understand why Leland so obstinately continued with this topic of conversation when it surely must be obvious that it was embarrassing Mary Eileen.

"Well now," Leland finally pushed his plate to one side, "I think I'd best leave some room for the sweet. I hope their petit fours are up to standards. And, of course, we'll have coffee and a cordial—Mary Eileen, allow me to order something special for you. Perhaps an apricot liqueur. And you, Lucien, I think that on such an occasion as this you'll join me with a brandy."

"No—no, thank you, Father. Just coffee."

"Well, at least Mary Eileen will have the cordial, won't you? And I'll have a brandy, then," Leland decided, as he beckoned to the waiter.

The dessert met with the Irish entrepreneur's approval, as it did with Lucien and Mary Eileen's. The young people dug into their sweets, as did Leland, and his concentration was at last diverted, halting the flow of his loquacity.

After the supper, Leland took out his wallet and paid the bill with an overly generous tip to the elderly waiter. He then sauntered out to the sidewalk, trailed by a nervous Lucien and a hesitant Mary Eileen, both of whom were bracing themselves for the worst. However, once they were seated in the carriage the doorman had secured for them, Leland's mood seemed much more subdued. Indeed, he barely acknowledged the young woman when Lucien suggested dropping Mary Eileen off at her cottage on the grounds of the academy rather than at the school itself.

"We'll drop her off at home, by all means," Leland offhandedly agreed. "By the bye, Lucien, I promised you a surprise." He reached into his coat pocket and produced a slip of paper. "I had it drawn in New York just before I left. It's for your Continental tour of Europe this summer."

Lucien stared at the bank draft, which was in the amount of two thousand dollars. "I—Father, this is very generous. But it's so much! I could pay for my trip and my next year's tuition. . . ." he faltered.

"Nonsense!" Leland clapped his stepson on the back. "I'm going to pay the tuition directly to the school; this draft is all yours, to spend as you will. You've earned it. Father O'Mara has told me how you've buckled down and behaved yourself this past semester. Oh, yes, I was worried about you, and so was your mother. But today Father O'Mara took away the last doubts. So you spend it as you see fit."

Lucien was mystified by Leland's unusual generosity, as well as by his behavior all during the evening. His affability and almost garrulous good humor was in marked contrast to his sternness the previous year, when he was angry over Lucien's involvement in Irish politics. Equally puzzling was Leland's insensitivity on the subject of his stepson's relationship with Mary Eileen: He seemed totally unaware that his comments had caused both of the young people acute embarrassment. Decidedly, it was a most mystifying evening. His stepfather seemed in full possession of his senses, being not the least tipsy. . . . Lucien did not quite know what to make of it. However, there being nothing else to do, he folded the check, put it into the pocket of his jacket, and said, "Well, Father, it's most kind and generous of you. I shan't waste it, you can be sure of that. Thank you again—and thank you for the dinner."

"Oh, yes, Mr. Kenniston," Mary Eileen at last spoke up. "It—it was very kind of you to invite me along. It was indeed a lovely dinner."

"Think nothing of it," Leland replied, again in a tone of complete indifference that contrasted so sharply with his earlier effusiveness.

By now, they had reached the cottage of the games master. Lucien proposed, "I'll see you to your door, Mary Eileen." He took her hand and led her up the pathway. "Good night," he whispered. "I hope tonight wasn't too upsetting for you.

I'm sure my stepfather didn't mean to embarrass you. He must be overly tired after a difficult trip, and so he just isn't thinking too clearly about what he's saying.''

"Oh, my! Please, you—you mustn't be so upset. And don't say anything to your father that would hurt his feelings. Well, I'm getting awfully cold, Lucien. I've got to go in.'' She hastily kissed him on the cheek, then turned and opened the front door.

"Good night, Mary Eileen,'' Lucien called after her as he walked back to the carriage. There was a despairing tone in his voice.

"Good night, dear Lucien. I'll see you tomorrow afternoon after classes.'' At this point, the door of the cottage opened wider and the games master stood there. He took in the carriage and the two men in it, then nodded and waved a good night to them before closing the door behind his daughter.

Lucien's attention was redirected when Leland suddenly declared, "Well, now, let's go back to St. Timothy's. Though I'll leave for London first thing in the morning, you'll be hearing from me. And remember, spend that money any way you like—but I strongly advise your touring Europe this summer.''

"I—I'll remember what you said, Father. Thank you very much for a—for a lovely evening.''

Chapter Nine

Laure Kenniston felt her pulse quicken as the tall twin towers of the red-brick chateau came plainly into view. Over near the river, high on the bluff, were the graves of her martyred husband Luke, old Lucien, and Dimarte. These were hallowed shrines, to which, on each December 18, the birthday of the founder of Windhaven, she had gone with Luke to pay tribute to a man whose deathless, indomitable, spirit had guided generations of Bouchards as well as those who had been joined to the family by marriage or had become their loyal employees and aides.

There were tears in her eyes as the carriage came closer to the chateau, the stately house where she had come to live with Luke and had shared his life. And now she had returned alone, save for her adoptive son, to come to grips with a new malevolence that threatened Windhaven and its inhabitants, as well as the Bouchard name and those who lived in the community of the Bouchards.

She started and gestured with her hand toward the demolished dam. There were men working there, repairing it, and she said to Lopasuta, "Now I can see the extent of the damage; it's even worse than I expected!" She looked around sadly, then declared, "We must find out quickly who these marauders were and have them punished. But first things first. I must reassume the stewardship of Windhaven Plantation, after having been away for so long."

By now the carriage had rolled up the drive and come to a stop before the entrance to the red-brick chateau. As it did so, Laure gave a cry of joy, for the front door of the chateau had opened, and descending the veranda steps now were Dalbert

Sattersfield, the one-armed mayor of nearby Lowndesboro, and his charming wife, Mitzi, whose friendship with Laure went back so many years.

"Mitzi darling! How wonderful it is to see you! And you're still looking as young as ever. . . ." Laure called, as she hurried forward to embrace Mitzi. Dalbert, now gray at the temples, but still distinguished and still as handsome, stood with his one arm outstretched to welcome them.

Laure kissed them both, then asked, "But what are you two doing here? Surely, Dalbert, you're taking time away from your business. . . ."

"Buford Phelps is doing a wonderful job running one of my Lowndesboro stores, and I have a perfectly able assistant at the other one. So Mitzi and I decided, especially after we found out how badly hurt poor Marius Thornton was, that we'd stay here and watch over things until you could come down and see for yourself. I'm sorry that Leland could not come with you."

"I know dear Leland will regret that he was unable to accompany me when he learns this, but, you see, he sailed for Europe the day before I had that telegram, Dalbert, and there wasn't any way of getting him back. Besides, there wasn't any need, for Lopasuta is here with me—and this is really *my* duty because I was Luke's wife and a Bouchard, before I met Leland," Laure solemnly replied.

"Well it's sure good to have you back. I only wish the circumstances that brought you were more fortuitous." Dalbert Sattersfield turned and shook hands with Lopasuta. "It's good to see you again, too. Do you know, Lopasuta, now that you're here, maybe you and I can ride into Montgomery, to see if we can get some protection from the sheriff. Lowndesboro doesn't have a sheriff of its own anymore, so we've had to call on the Montgomery official whenever we've needed help down here. But whenever we've done so, the man's been pretty intractable. Your legal expertise will be useful, I think. Perhaps we should go as soon as you've unpacked and perhaps had a bite to eat."

"I agree that that would be a good idea," Lopasuta replied. "It's only two-thirty, so there's plenty of time."

"Good, let's do it. While we're gone, Laure can confer with Benjamin Brown—and, of course, spend time with Marius.

102

Mitzi has been helping to nurse him, incidentally, and he seems to be making some progress.''

Indeed, Laure had already drawn Mitzi to one side, and the two lovely women were discussing the best course of action to take over Marius's wound.

"I'm going to look in on Marius right now," Laure told Mitzi. "I'm so worried about him; you know, of course, that he's like family to us.''

"Yes, I know. He's a very dear man. It's been upsetting to see how he's aged since Clemmie's death. I don't think he'll ever get over it. . . . I suppose his being so distraught depleted some of his strength, making this bullet wound more serious than it otherwise would have been," Mitzi dolefully remarked. "Abel Kennery has been out to see him every day, and he's not terribly optimistic, I'm afraid.''

"All we can do is hope and pray, I suppose," Laure said. "Do you know if he's awake now?''

"Yes, but his mind seems to be wandering. Perhaps it's the medication Dr. Kennery gave him to soothe him, so he could get some rest," Mitzi explained.

Laure nodded and went to the room where Marius Thornton was quartered. At Dr. Kennery's suggestion, he had been moved to the most spacious of the guest rooms—one with a large four-postered double bed—so that he could rest in utter comfort.

Through the partly open door, Laure could see a woman sitting at Marius's bedside. This was Tess Gregory, who had also volunteered to be his nurse.

A low faltering murmur indicated that Windhaven Plantation's foreman was awake—but his voice was feeble, without energy, and Laure hesitated a moment, almost fearful of seeing him so stricken. A wave of guilt surged in her, for she told herself that if she had come back more frequently to Windhaven Plantation, if she had taken more direct control and not been absent so much, perhaps this terrible thing wouldn't have happened.

She came in slowly. Tess, who had seen her and beckoned for her to come in, deferentially rose from the chair she had drawn up alongside Marius's bed. Bending to the recumbent figure, Tess whispered, "It's Miz Kenniston, Marius, come to see you.''

"Oh, please, don't move; don't try to move, dear Marius!" Laure cried out in alarm, as she saw the tall, wiry black man try to lift his head from the pillows, his eyes widening, his lips trembling as he tried to form words of greeting. "You lie still. I just wanted you to know I came the moment I heard, my poor Marius. But you're going to get well, I know you are, and so you must rest and do everything Dr. Kennery tells you to!"

Marius forced a wan smile to his face. "Awful good of you . . . . to come . . . . to see me, Miz Laure," he said in a faint, unsteady voice. "Got myself shot like a damn fool . . . . oughta have been more careful—"

"Now, you stop that sort of talk, Marius Thornton!" Laure scolded, frowning in order to belie the urge to weep. "The very idea, thinking that it's your fault, when a group of savages, for no reason at all, raid the plantation. Thank God you weren't killed. What you have to do now—and this is an order, Marius Thornton—is rest and get well, do you hear me?"

He smiled faintly and nodded. "I'll try my best, Miz Laure. I sure want to be up and around—Ben can't handle everything. Oh, he's a smart boy—but, I've been here a whole lot longer, so I know what this place truly needs, Miz Laure."

Now she could no longer control her tears, and they stung her eyes and trickled down her cheeks as she leaned to him, took one of his rough, callused hands between hers, and insisted, "There isn't anybody else in all this world who can do a better job than you, Marius! That's why we all need you so much; that's why you have to get well."

"You're mighty sweet to fuss about an old fool like me, Miz Laure," he murmured.

"You're not an old fool, and you know it, Marius. Why, you're barely in your forties; you've got a long life ahead of you, if you behave yourself and obey doctor's orders!" Laure scolded. "And now, *I've* talked too much. You're going to take a long nap, and when you wake up, Amelia will give you good and nourishing chicken soup, and you're going to eat it all. Incidentally, Marius, Lopasuta came back with me, and we're going to see that everything that needs to be done, will be, and also make certain that nothing like this ever happens again on Windhaven Plantation. And then, when you're well, you can go back to managing this place and making it the finest in all the South! I'll see you later, dear Marius. Sleep now."

Laure turned, nodded to Tess Gregory, and left the room before she lost complete control of her emotions. Her tears fell fast, for inwardly she had a dreadful apprehension: For all his comparative youth, Marius looked feeble and listless, and she was deeply concerned. She did not even want to think what would happen, if he should die as a result of that wound—no, it mustn't happen! She also told herself that she would have to arrange her domestic life with Leland to be able to make at least six trips a year back to Alabama, instead of just one or two, and stay a few weeks each time, to make certain that all was going smoothly. But the first thing, the most important thing of all, to be sure, was finding out the cause of that sudden, inexplicable attack on decent people, who asked no more of life than to work hard and to produce crops for the community and for themselves.

Lopasuta and Dalbert had gone out to the stable, mounted geldings, and ridden into Montgomery. It was about four-thirty when they arrived, and they tethered their horses in front of the sheriff's office on the main street near the capitol building.

"There's a new sheriff, elected just last year," Dalbert explained to Lopasuta. "His name is Tom Brennaman, and he used to be an overseer of a pretty large estate in southeastern Alabama before the war. He saved some money and bought some land east of here."

"You said he's a hard man, Dalbert?" Lopasuta reiterated.

"Not the kind to get too excited about what happened to Windhaven Plantation, I'm afraid. I hope the two of us can convince him to take a more active role. We had our own sheriff in Lowndes County till about a year ago—old Carl Fernstrom. When he died, three fellows ran in the election to complete his term as sheriff; when there was no clear majority, we had a run-off election—but then the ballot boxes were stolen. The state courts stepped in and gave the sheriff of Montgomery County—that's Brennaman—*pro tem* jurisdiction in Lowndes. So far Brennaman has ignored the order—

says the people of Montgomery didn't elect him to keep law and order for a bunch of farmers and country gentlemen. But as the peace officer, duly appointed, it's up to him to enforce the law."

They entered the office together, and Tom Brennaman emerged from his cubicle. He was a burly man, weighing almost two hundred fifty pounds, with thick sidewhiskers, dark-brown hair, blue eyes, and a thin mouth. He wore the star of his office, and he had a leather holster around his portly middle with two pistols, rather than the more usual one. Brennaman fancied himself as a crack shot and an outstanding law enforcer, but he was actually lazy by nature and sought to have as many creature comforts as were made possible by the bribes and gifts that affluent citizens made to him to insure his support in the event of need.

"Well, gentlemen, I was just about to close the office for today. What can I do for you?" he greeted them in a gruff, condescending voice.

"My name is Lopasuta Bouchard. I'm a lawyer in New Orleans, Mr. Brennaman. And this is Dalbert Sattersfield, mayor of Lowndesboro," the tall Comanche said, introducing himself and his companion.

"I know the mayor." Tom Brennaman gave Dalbert a curt nod, then squinted at Lopasuta. "What brings you gents all the way to Montgomery?"

"Well, Sheriff Brennaman," Dalbert calmly replied, "as you may have heard, a group of men wearing hoods made a raid on Windhaven Plantation about a week ago. In the process, they shot and seriously wounded the foreman, Marius Thornton, and they needlessly and cruelly killed a pet dog. We're here to ask you for protection. We think that it's serious enough that at least one of your deputies should be assigned to the area to see that these scoundrels don't come back and repeat their marauding. They burned the sheds, tried to burn the house itself, and destroyed a lot of the crops, as well as dynamited the irrigation dam."

"Yeah, seems to me I heard tell of a little ruckus downriver, but I figured that it was a personal thing—and besides, from what I heard, the people working on the land had every chance to defend themselves," the sheriff airily replied.

"Sheriff Brennaman," Lopasuta now spoke up, "I'm the

adopted son of Luke Bouchard, who, you may know, gave up his life to save Governor Houston. His widow remarried and has been in New York for the last few years, but she's come all the way down here to see if things can be put to rights. Her husband unfortunately is in Europe on business, so I've come along with her because I think she shouldn't have to handle this alone.''

"And just what do you expect of me, lawyer?" Brennaman's tone was arrogant and insulting.

"To do your simple duty, nothing more, nothing less. Mayor Sattersfield asked you if we couldn't have some protection.''

"You haven't shown me a need yet, fellow." Again, Brennaman sneeringly denigrated the Comanche lawyer. "You got any notion why people would try to rampage on your property?"

"I can't say for sure, but I suspect it's because there are black tenant-workers there," Lopasuta indignantly responded.

"Yeah, I've heard tell there's plenty of niggers there, and they're all acting like white folks. Now then, Mr. Bouchard—didn't you say that was your name?—Mr. Bouchard, you can't rightly expect folks in these parts to take kindly to uppity niggers. We've had them forced down our throats ever since the war ended. Why, dammit, we've even had them sitting in the state legislature. . . .''

"You mean you aren't going to do a thing about this attack? There has been an attempted murder, after all. They shot Marius Thornton," Dalbert angrily intervened.

"Look, Mister Mayor, you stick to your bailiwick, and I'll stick to mine. I got no proof of anything. All I heard was rumors. Old Jim Peevey came by the day after the thing happened and told me what he knew, which wasn't too much. Nobody pressed charges or filed a complaint in my office, so what was I supposed to do? And what would I find out, if I went down there now, can you tell me that?" Brennaman glowered at them. "If you'll excuse me, I want to close the office. I'm going to have dinner with one of my Montgomery constituents, just as soon you fellows finish your business.''

"You seem to have finished it already, without even looking into it," Lopasuta fiercely countered.

"That's your opinion, mister. All I'm saying is I don't take kindly to people waltzing in here, telling me what my job is.''

"I take it, then, Sheriff Brennaman, you expect us to shift for ourselves,'' Dalbert stared incredulously at the burly law officer.

Tom Brennaman shrugged. ''Makes me no mind what you do, Mister Mayor. Like I said, this ain't your neck of the woods, it's mine. And I don't like outsiders meddling in my business. Oh, sure, I heard there was a ruckus up there, like I said. You say a fellow named Marius Thornton was wounded, that right?''

"Yes, shot for no reason at all. He's in serious condition right now, and if he dies, it'll be murder,'' Lopasuta angrily declared.

"Well, when it comes down to that, if he dies, then of course I'll have to look into it officially. He's a white man, isn't he?''

"No, Sheriff Brennaman. He's black.'' Lopasuta had all he could do to maintain his self-control, and his tone was icy.

"Well, then, what do you expect? I tell you, it's amazing that there are still folks who haven't learned their lesson and insist on keeping niggers around and treat them like they were born white. Not many people are gonna stand for that, Mister Lawyer. Now you'll kindly excuse me. I'll be late if I dally around any more with you. I hope you find out who messed up your land there. We don't like to see that sort of thing happen—but I'll remind you there's usually a reason for something like that. Good evening to both of you gentlemen.''

With this, the sheriff clapped his hat on his head, strode past Lopasuta and Dalbert, opened the office door, and went out.

The two men turned to each other, and the expression on their faces was one of disgust.

"I'm waiting for you to clear out, gentlemen, so I can lock the office,'' Brennaman called, from outside.

"We've wasted our time, Lopasuta,'' Dalbert murmured. "Maybe we can find help elsewhere. Let's give this terribly accommodating sheriff a chance to close his offices and go off to his dinner.''

When Lopasuta and Dalbert returned to the plantation, they told Laure of their useless call upon Sheriff Tom Brennaman.

"I've decided," the Comanche lawyer told Laure, "that tomorrow I'll take the train to Tuscaloosa to see Andy Haskins. With his influence as a former representative and state senator, it's quite possible he might be able to help us. The sheriff is as violent a racist as any man I've met in all of Montgomery during the days when I was apprentice to old Jedidiah Danforth. You'll get no help from him, and if anything, he'll just be smugly satisfied if more blacks are hurt."

"That's dreadful! I don't suppose we can force him to do his job?" Laure inquired, her face filled with worry.

Lopasuta shook his head, and Dalbert chimed in, "With all due respect, Laure, you'll get absolutely nowhere with him. And if you tried to go to court to get him to perform his duty, you'd probably get hedging there. The whole trend of events in this country—it's true even in Washington—is to take away the civil rights that blacks gained after Lincoln set them free. It's an understandable reaction, I'm afraid. There are still enough die-hard Confederates who will never accept the theory that a black man can have any intelligence or humanity. And, of course, Alabamans feel the carpetbaggers used blacks for their own profiteering purposes, so that's another thing that galls a lot of natives. They just want to get even for what they think they've been done out of." He sighed and shook his head. "The question of race is certainly a very troublesome issue again. Well, Lopasuta, good luck to you with Andy Haskins. Give him my best, and Mitzi's, too, if you will."

"I'll certainly do that. I should be back from Tuscaloosa by the day after tomorrow. I'm sure I'll have some good ideas to report from Andy."

Andy Haskins, now director of the Tuscaloosa Sanatorium, was leaner and grayer than the last time Lopasuta had met him, but the warm and amiable one-armed Confederate veteran had, if anything, mellowed. "It's good to see you, Lopasuta. Mighty good of you to call on me all the way from New Orleans. But what brings you here? I read in the paper about the dastardly attack on Windhaven. Did you come up from New Orleans in that connection, by any chance?"

Quickly, Lopasuta detailed the events of Tuesday night, and Andy scowled and shook his head. "Utterly damnable!

And you say Sheriff Brennaman won't do anything about it?"

"Not in the slightest."

"Lopasuta, I've heard about that sheriff. Everybody knows that he's one of those rednecked Southerners who can't get over the war. And now that the Supreme Court seems to be swinging to the opposite side when it come to civil rights, I think we're in for some bad times. The Ku Klux Klan could very easily be riding again, to pay the blacks back—in their moronic way of thinking—for even having gained freedom. As to equality, that doesn't exist, no matter how idealistic Lincoln was. You know yourself, Lopasuta, that after a century or more of slavery, it's difficult to condition folks' minds to accepting people as their equals—people they've been putting down as inferiors for so long."

"Yes, and I'm afraid that, just as you say, if the Supreme Court should reverse itself and say that blacks have no civil rights, it's going to be harder and harder for me to defend black clients in the Louisiana courts. There's prejudice enough, without adding the opinion of the highest legal body in our country to that racist side," Lopasuta sadly avowed. Then, leaning forward, he proposed, "I came here to ask if—because of the former political connections you had, Andy—you might see your way clear to getting done what Sheriff Brennaman won't," Lopasuta earnestly entreated.

Andy scowled, scratched his head, and hesitated a moment. "I've made some good friends at the capitol, there's no doubt about it, Lopasuta," he finally declared. "Every politician has debts owed him, and perhaps I should try to collect. Those debts, incidentally, were for support of bills that I believed to be right for the state; they had nothing to do with patronage or spoils."

"I know that, Andy. Your record is unblemished, and it's only a pity you didn't go on to become governor."

"You're much too flattering, Lopasuta." Andy permitted himself a mild chuckle. "Maybe if I'd had you as my campaign manager, feeling as you do and with some influence yourself, I might have tried for that high office. Of course"—he winked at Lopasuta—"there's always the future. But seriously, I'm happy here, and so are Jessica and the children. I feel that I'm doing a good deal of worthwhile, beneficial work with

110

people who, for all intents and purposes, have become unable to fend for themselves. Of course, I have a fine staff of excellent doctors, and you know yourself that we're only just beginning to explore the human mind. It's by no means a science, though I've sent away for European journals for the doctors, and I've read them myself, trying to improve my own knowledge of what we do know and how people can be influenced by tragedies or suffering.''

"Laure has told me how much you've done already, and how you've helped people, Andy. But going back to your political influence, do you think it's worthwhile to pursue it?''

"I'll talk to William Blount—he was the one who wanted me to run for governor. But, first of all, I'd suggest you'd be well advised to hire some trustworthy private guards for at least a month or so. You'd be able to control things that way, and you wouldn't have to rely on outside sources.''

"That's not a bad idea. Thanks, Andy.''

"Anyway, getting back to old William Blount, he still has plenty of connections in the legislature. Won't do any harm to talk to him, that's for sure. Meanwhile, I hope you'll stay over this evening. Jessica will cook you a mess of the best vittles you ever tasted.''

Lopasuta gladly agreed to this invitation, and Andy asked one of the orderlies to ride over to William Blount's house and ask him to come for dinner, also.

White-haired, bluff, and hearty of manner, William Blount had lost about forty pounds and looked younger than his seventy-one years. He shook hands warmly with Lopasuta, and then turned to Andy Haskins and said, "Andy boy, I understand you have a little problem. You did a lot for me and the boys, and you did it honest and square. If I can do anything to help you or your friend here, you just name it.''

Andy gestured to Lopasuta to explain, and the young lawyer related the details of the attack on Windhaven Plantation and their subsequent meeting with Sheriff Tom Brennaman. He also relayed Andy's suggestion of hiring guards.

William Blount grunted and shook his head. "Brennaman's a mean critter, lower 'n a polecat with a mangy hide. He got the job because nobody else wanted it, but he thinks he's a god, with his little tin badge. Trouble is, what he says is gospel, more or less. Andy's idea is a good one to counteract the sheriff's do-nothing attitude, and I'll tell you what I can do for you: I know a few trustworthy men who are crack shots, and they've been down on their luck ever since the war. They would look after the land and the buildings and such for you, and they wouldn't charge too much.''

"That sounds great, Mr. Blount.''

"You see, if you try and get the law to take your side, then whoever is behind this business is going to get the wind up and maybe hold off a while, so you won't ever see who did it. You'll be tipping your hand, so to speak. But with plain folks on the payroll, nobody knowing what they're really there for, the fellows who thought up this nonsense might come back for another try—and then you can catch them redhanded.''

"It makes sense,'' Lopasuta admitted.

"Yes, I think so too, William,'' Andy agreed.

"Can you stay over here another day or so, Lopasuta?'' William Blount asked.

"Yes, I can. Our friend, Mayor Dalbert Sattersfield, is with Laure now, watching out for things; besides, I don't think they'll try anything so soon again.''

"Good. Because tomorrow I can bring around these fellows I told you about. Three reliable men. I've known them quite a spell, and I'll vouch for them,'' William Blount said.

"I'd like to meet them.''

The next day at noon, William Blount brought three men with him to the sanatorium, to meet with Lopasuta and Andy. They were John Hornung, Frank Connery, and Sydney Berndorf. As William had indicated, all three men had served in the Confederacy before being wounded and mustered out.

Berndorf, the oldest at forty-seven, had immigrated from Düsseldorf with his parents some ten years before the Civil War. He had risen to the rank of sergeant and been personally decorated by Jefferson Davis for valor during the Battle of Bull Run. He and the other two men remained bachelors. Hornung, now forty-five, and forty-year-old Connery had been jilted when they had been sent off to fight for the Confederacy. Berndorf had been engaged to a young milliner, who had died of fever shortly after Appomattox. And all three of them were now barely making a living at odd jobs.

After talking with each of them, Lopasuta hired them on, giving them an advance in salary and their train fare. He bade them report to Windhaven Plantation as soon as possible. Thanking both William Blount and Andy Haskins, Lopasuta then took the next train back to Montgomery.

Chapter Ten

Leland Kenniston did not know that one of the three men upon whom he had forced himself for a game of cards had also stayed in Dublin for a day, planning the next day to catch up with his two friends for the fishing in northern Ireland. Remy DuClos had made this stopover in Dublin in order to buy his beautiful wife a set of the finest Irish table linen, which was to be shipped to her directly. It was to mark the tenth anniversary of their marriage, and it was to be a surprise, since Eugenie DuClos had chanced to mention that she had always longed to have the very finest lace-edged cloths when she served dinner to her friends and acquaintances. Such a mission was well worth the loss of a day's fishing, though his companions, Henri Courvalier and Boris Vendrikoff, made affable sport of the way he doted on his wife.

Before he went to sleep in his Dublin hotel, DuClos sat down and wrote Eugenie a very long letter, which he planned to have the bellman post the next morning in the main post office. After many items of news and expressions of endearment, the letter continued:

> I have not forgotten our anniversary, my dearest one, and if the shipment arrives as I hope it will, you will shortly have a token of my undying love for you.
>
> And now, before I forget, my dearest, I must tell you of one curious episode on the voyage to Ireland. The very first night out of New York, Boris, Henri, and I were talking about our business affairs when, out of nowhere, there appeared a well-dressed and effusive American of Irish descent. He insisted that we play poker with him. I may say that what I won from him,

and which he acknowledged in an I.O.U. as a debt of honor, will pay for my entire trip.

This man is extremely interesting. He is handsome, I should say in his mid-forties. From the very outset, he boasted of his prowess as a businessman—it appears that he is in the business of importing and exporting. But he seems to regard himself as the most prominent entrepreneur in the entire world, which of course is a mild exaggeration, to say the least.

I take it that he is wealthy, married, and with a family, and my first impression was that he was on perhaps his first trip to Europe and eager, therefore, to cast off for a time his conjugal bonds, which kept him not only faithful but also occupied with his commerce. For he seemed to me to be seeking a kind of escape from reality. He fancied himself to be an eminent card player, which he assuredly was not, for he could not keep from his face the secrets of when he had a good hand and when his hand was execrable.

What struck me as singular, my sweet Eugenie, was that he reminded me a little of my poor cousin, Theophile, who for some years was confined in the Hospice d'Aleines in Bourges. You did not know him, but as early as his fifteenth year, he began to suffer delusions, fancying himself almost the reborn son of God. He was exalted and arrogant; his speech was flowery, and his manner was affectatious as if he were an actor at the Comédie Française. Boris and Henri were not sure whether to be amused or to rebuke Monsieur Kenniston for his boastfulness—but, at any rate, dearest Eugenie, he did provide us with a most unusual kind of diversion . . . to say nothing of the delightful profit he contributed to our coffers.

I look forward to returning home to you, my beloved, and I hope that what will precede me will meet with your fondest approval.

Your loving husband,
Remy

David Voohries was the director of a small but enterprising new exporting firm whose chief investors intended to do business in the United States, as well as in Canada and some of the major South American ports.

Several months earlier, Voorhies had made a week-long visit to New York and, quite by accident, had met Leland Kenniston while the Irishman was lunching at one of his favorite restaurants. The place had been crowded, and the headwaiter had apologetically asked Leland whether he would permit someone else to be seated at his table, for which he had made an earlier reservation. When Leland agreed, the waiter had brought over a tall, gangling, towheaded man—David Voorhies. The chance meeting had led to an interesting conversation, and Voorhies promised to correspond with the Irish entrepreneur with a view to seeing if each could help the other.

Shortly before departing for Europe, Leland had received from the exporter a letter indicating that he would be interested in forming an alliance with Leland's company and diverting part of his cargo shipments to New York or New Orleans—or anywhere else that Leland proposed—allowing direct sales to be made, profiting those on both sides of the Atlantic.

In his reply, Laure's husband had written that he planned a European business trip and that he would call on David Voorhies when he arrived in London. And thus it was that, two afternoons after arriving on British soil, Leland Kenniston took the lift to the fourth floor of a building in the City, the financial heart of London.

The efficient office clerk ushered Leland in at once to David Voorhies's office, where the tall Englishman energetically rose to shake hands with him. "It's dashing good of you to pay me a visit, though I hadn't expected you quite so soon, Mr. Kenniston!" he exclaimed in a broad Devonshire accent. "How can I be of service to you?"

"I'd like to have your latest offering sheet to see if you have any wares I'd be interested in at this time," Leland declared cheerfully.

"Well now, we're constantly expanding, Mr. Kenniston. As you know, my primary dealings are with farm products as well as textiles—from fine fabrics and linens to hemp."

"And are you taking on other items to offer the United States, Mr. Voorhies?"

"Well, I also represent a small firm that makes lovely

116

porcelains, for use as elegant decoration in homes. The artist this firm has contracted to design the more expensive items is quite a gifted man. As it happens, I have something that was sent to me by this firm; its name is Jesand Ltd., by the way.'' He reached down to his lower desk drawer, opened it, and took out a small statuette, not more than a foot tall, of a Pekingese dog sitting on a cushion. He gestured with his left forefinger. "You'll notice, Mr. Kenniston, that when I press down the cushion while pushing back on the dog, the two sections pull away from each other, revealing a hidden chamber. You could put a box of lucifers in there, or a couple going out for the evening and wanting to hide valuables might actually put bracelets in here, or rings, or even necklaces. I don't think a burglar would think of looking for such treasures in this statuette.''

"It's a fascinating item. What's the prevailing price for it?''

"A few London shops, in the better areas, have it selling for fifteen shillings. In wholesale lots, I could let you have, say, a thousand of these at six shillings each. In your currency, Mr. Kenniston, that would be about one dollar and fifty cents. You could price it at three dollars and thus make a one hundred-percent profit.''

"Very good, indeed! That's the way to make money—in volume! Mr. Voorhies, I'd like to give you an order for twenty thousand of those statuettes.''

"That's most generous of you! Where shall I have them shipped?'' Already, David Voorhies was taking out an order pad and beginning to write down the sizable order.

"You can ship them to my New York office, and here's my card, Mr. Voorhies. Send the bill first, under separate cover, and I'll instruct my bookkeeper to pay it the moment it is received.''

"Mr. Kenniston, I'm flattered that you've come all the way across the Atlantic to see me, and I trust this is the beginning of a mutually profitable association. Is there anything else I can interest you in?''

"Not at the moment—however, you may be able to help me,'' the Irish entrepreneur declared. "I'm rather pressed for time, you see, and I'd like to establish an office here in London. Since our two firms are already associated, could I ask you to assume the further responsibility of hiring a small staff for me? I would of course offer you the post of London factor for my company. I could also offer you a reasonable salary, above commissions, and the work would not interfere with what you are doing for the firms you represent.''

''I think that could be arranged,'' Voorhies nodded. ''What sort of staff would you need?''

Leland thought a moment. ''Well, first of all, a reliable person who could handle correspondence and do the book-keeping, too. Then, a second individual, preferably a middle-aged man with a family—that would mean he would be serious about his job and work harder at it because of his domestic responsibilities; he would make contacts here in London and try to arouse interest in some of the products that I would offer in my own prospectus. You, of course, as factor, would supervise his work. Yes, two good people would be fine, and the office needn't be too large to start— although as my success here will assuredly increase, the quarters should lend themselves to expansion.''

''Leave that to me. I'll tell you what, Mr. Kenniston. Along with the invoice I'll be sending you for the statuettes, I'll send you a receipt detailing the outlay of wages for these two persons and, of course, the rental on a decent office.''

''Fine. The bookkeeper at my home office will then immediately send you a draft for the amount due, Mr. Voorhies. And that, I think, concludes our business.'' Leland rose to take his leave. ''It has been a distinct pleasure meeting you and doing business with you.''

''The feeling is mutual, Mr. Kenniston. I look forward to a very long association for both of us. By the bye, we must get together socially sometime. My wife would like it very much. Are you traveling with your family, by chance?''

''No, I've not been accompanied by my beautiful wife and children—hers by previous marriage, regrettably. . . .'' Suddenly, Leland Kenniston's smile vanished, and a frown replaced his exuberant look—but only for a fleeting moment. Then, once again, he showed Voorhies his buoyant smile of utter self-confidence. ''I've a wonderful family, and I'm very proud of them!'' he declared.

''Well, if your family should ever join you in your business in London, I would love to have you out to my country house near Nottingham. My wife and I could show you a very good time, with cricket and lawn tennis and badminton and the

118

like. Spring is most delightful there, if you could manage it, Mr. Kenniston.''

''We'll see. Thank you for the invitation. And again, I'm glad that we settled all this. Now I can go off to Paris feeling much easier in my mind, and I have every confidence that you will represent me very ably and get me the staff I need to gain a foothold here in London. You know, Mr. Voorhies, before I finish, I intend to be the head of the greatest importing and exporting firm in all the world.''

With this, not waiting for an answer, he turned and left the office. David Voorhies stared after him, then uttered a low whistle and shook his head. ''The blighter has confidence in himself, and that never hurts. And if he can actually manage to unload those twenty thousand porcelain dogs, he's certainly halfway to proving he is indeed the greatest importer-exporter in the world.'' He chuckled to himself as he sat down and selected a cigar from a nearby teakwood box. He took a cigar cutter and neatly cut off the tip, then lighted it, drew in until it was going well, then leaned back and exhaled a smoke ring, a look of total satisfaction on his lean face.

During the next six weeks, Leland Kenniston continued his peregrinations on to Paris, Berlin, and then Austria, changing his itinerary as the mood struck him. On his second day in Paris, he went to the Bourse to inquire of its director whom the Frenchman might suggest as a factor to represent his American firm, and he was graciously recommended to an Edouard Villefranche, a dapper little man, fussy and given to flowery diction, who was manager of a small exporting firm dealing in fine Bordeaux and Burgundies.

Leland, with his fluent French, charmed the man, who recognized in the Irish entrepreneur a kindred spirit. Villefranche invited Leland to spend two weeks at his country estate some thirty miles outside Paris, where the Irishman was lavishly entertained and fêted on sumptuous gourmet luncheons and dinners. Villefranche's cook was a chef who had given up his own restaurant to work for the dapper exporter at a munificent wage.

Before he left for Berlin, Leland had appointed Edouard Villefranche as his factor and instructed him to ship a thousand cases of his finest wines to the New York address, adding that his bookkeeper would pay the invoice upon receipt.

119

*   *   *

In Berlin, he sought out the American consul. The diplomat referred Leland to Herr Emil von Bittersdorf, a huge man with a porcine face who, the consul told him, was one of the shrewdest of German businessmen. Von Bittersdorf wined and dined Laure's husband and, impressed by Leland's boasting about his expanding business and increasing affluence, agreed to be his factor.

On the ninth day of Leland's stay in Berlin, Von Bittersdorf introduced him to a scholarly cousin, Kurt von Orfing, who dabbled in his own private workshop, which he had built in the cellar of his luxurious town house in the wealthiest section of the city. He had inherited the house and a fortune from his father—but was in the process of frittering his capital away on worthless inventions and grandiose schemes of trying to corner the European market on silver and gold. Von Orfing warmed to the Irishman and, sensing that here was a man who could further his own ambitions to reknown through the marketing of his inventions, induced the entrepreneur to back him with an advance of three thousand dollars for a water-repellent cape. Von Orfing had treated the fabric with chemicals and demonstrated to Leland the efficacy of this formula by pouring buckets of water over a piece of cloth that had been thus treated. The inner surface did indeed remain dry for a time, but after Leland had left, the material became soaked through. However, before saying his good-byes, Leland—as he had done in London and aboard the *Aurania*—scribbled on his card an authorization to his bookkeeper to advance Von Orfing the agreed-upon sum for his invention.

He proceeded at last to Vienna, and he was equally speculative and buoyantly optimistic there, for his unconquerable mood remained with him and, indeed, grew from day to day. By the end of his first week in the Austrian capital, he was certain that, on this trip, he had assured at least the doubling of his personal fortune. As a result, he decided to extend his stay in Vienna, and in addition visit several other cities not previously on his itinerary. His additional efforts, he was certain, would mean greater comforts and luxury for his beloved Laure and the children.

Chapter Eleven

Jacob Cohen, though usually managing only the jewelry department of Leland Kenniston's importing-exporting firm, had been given the authority to take charge of the entire business during Leland's absence on his European trip. The Irish entrepreneur had given him a signed and notarized power of attorney two weeks before his departure, which caused Jacob to confide to his wife, Miriam, "The way he trusts me is very rewarding, my dearest, but it involves a heavy burden of responsibility that I should rather have not had."

"You are always a prophet of doom, my dearest husband," she had responded with a smile. "But it's good that you're so conscientious and so anxious, because that's exactly why Leland gave you that responsibility. Be complimented; don't worry, and don't *kvetch*."

This had made Jacob chuckle in spite of himself. He had shrugged and nodded, "You're always right, sweet Miriam. All right—I will not *complain*. You've never been wrong—so, I shall take your advice, but I'll still *worry* because it's my nature."

On the next-to-last day of February of this year of 1883, shortly before noon, a portly, black-haired man with thick side-whiskers sent word through the Kenniston & Co. receptionist that he wished to see the "person in charge of paying the bills."

The receptionist directed the man to the bookkeeper, who politely inquired how he could be of help. It took only a moment for the bookkeeper to realize that the matter was not routine, and he excused himself and hurried into Jacob's office and informed him that he should see the visitor. The name, Charles Morley, did not register with Jacob, but shrugging, he declared, "Please show him into my office, Mr. Johnson."

"Very good, Mr. Cohen." He returned to the by-now impatient visitor and, with his most engaging smile, averred, "If you'll come with me, I'll have you see our Mr. Cohen."

"Very good."

"Here you are," Mr. Johnson agilely stepped out of the way, as the visitor strode into Jacob's private office.

"May I help you, sir?" Jacob patiently demanded.

"Why, yes, I do believe you can, if you're in charge of the finances here. It involves, ah, a certain debt that must be discharged. You see, it appears that your employer engaged in a game of cards aboard the *Aurania,* and he lost a good deal of money. I represent Henri Courvalier. Upon landing in Europe, he forwarded to me a personal card, a business card, which your Mr. Kenniston had signed. If you will look on the back, you will see that it attests to all this, and it states the amount of the debt."

"A game of cards? Aboard ship?" Jacob scratched his head and echoed, at a loss for words. When he had been a passenger in steerage, coming to America as an immigrant from Eastern Europe, Jacob had heard stories of life in the first-class section of the ship, where, in the course of an evening, a rich man would gamble away a fortune on which a poor family could live for a year. He had never seen such a game, of course, nor could he imagine his ordinarily prudent employer being involved in one. This was the last thing in the world he would have expected from Leland Kenniston—to saddle him with paying a personal debt that should never come out of company funds. "Excuse me if I keep you waiting a bit. I want to verify the signature," he told his visitor.

"That's fine with me. You can be sure it's legitimate, but go ahead and take your time. Satisfy yourself it was indeed Mr. Kenniston who signed that card," the man avowed.

Jacob Cohen stared again at the card. It looked exactly like the cards he had seen his employer ordering several months previously—the same stock, same engraving. And there could be little doubt that the signature was Leland Kenniston's; the surname was executed with the same decorative capital *K* that had always been the entrepreneur's hallmark. Of course, it could have been a skillful forgery, but Jacob had no reason-

122

able basis for believing this, nor could he attempt to assert it to this stranger. Naturally, his employer had the right to order the firm to pay out money to whomever he chose, for whatever purpose, and while it was unusual to cover a gambling loss out of the operating budget of a business, Jacob saw no alternative but to honor the debt.

"I—I'll write you a check at once. If you'll just have a seat for a moment, I'll go into the accounting room and draw it up for you," Jacob wearily declared.

Having withdrawn to the room where the firm's accounts were kept, Jacob opened the safe and took out the Kenniston & Co. checkbook. He shook his head and mumbled to himself, "I just don't understand this. It's not like him at all. If he took along cash and a letter of credit, why couldn't he have paid this out of his own personal money, instead of drawing upon company funds? Well, there's no use asking questions when he isn't here to answer them. I'll just have to write the check; that's all there is to it."

Young Lucien Bouchard had worked diligently all this week, having manfully given up the previous weekend's outing with Mary Eileen in favor of completing a particularly important essay. Today, the bright sun of this early Sunday morning and the warming temperature seemed to be rewarding him for his work and assuring him of a delightful excursion.

The thought of a trip into Dublin took his mind back to his meeting some six weeks before with Leland. How singularly his stepfather had acted, particularly in his exaggerated compliments to Mary Eileen. Although she had said nothing about it in all this time, Lucien knew that she had been flustered by so much close attention from a man whom she was meeting for the first time and who, although he was obviously standing in the relationship of stepfather to Lucien, had almost talked as if he himself were a suitor for her hand. That behavior was so uncharacteristic of his stepfather that Lucien mulled it over for days after Leland's departure for London.

Still and all, he was content. The size of the draft that his stepfather had given him for a summer tour of Europe was comfortable assurance that he could still have plenty left, whenever he wished, to buy Mary Eileen a gift.

Lucien was happy, too, that he continued to be on good terms with Mary Eileen's father. The games master was a blunt, outspoken man, and three weeks earlier, Lucien had chanced to meet him tramping across the expansive campus on his way to the gymnasium. Lucien, boyishly grinning, had avowed, "Mr. Brennert, I just want you to know that I respect your daughter very much. I'm extremely fond of her, and I have some long-range ideas—"

"Tush, man!" The games master had held up a hand to fend off Lucien's potentially embarrassing declarations. "Don't start talking about your youthful aspirations when the weather's touching the freezing mark. This is neither the time nor the place, besides which, you lack the wherewithal, as yet, to make any kind of promises to me regarding Mary Eileen. When that time comes, and if you're still an upstanding citizen and I approve of you, it will be for my daughter to make up her own mind. Good day to you!"

That statement, gruff though it was, had been a definite step forward, Lucien told himself. That night, as he fell asleep, he dreamed of walking down a church aisle with a radiant Mary Eileen on his arm, dressed in white satin, shyly eyeing him with all her love and devotion, and he felt himself exalted among men as he took her in his arms after the priest had wed them and kissed her with tenderness and adoration. . . .

One of the instructors who went into Dublin regularly had very kindly helped young Lucien open a bank account, and so Laure's oldest son had a passbook showing a sizable deposit. He had kept back some twenty pounds that he intended to use for Sunday outings—such as the one today. He chose his very best suit and cravat and, the day before, had taken the unusual step—now that he could afford the luxury—of engaging a carriage to call for Mary Eileen and himself at about noon. He hoped that this would make a good impression on both her and—most especially—her father. The couple would go to Jarlie's for a noontime meal, and in the evening, after walking down to the waterfront and enjoying the sights of the seaport, they would dine at McCafferty's. Lucien hoped to make *this* meal at that superb restaurant a far more pleasant event for Mary Eileen than the last one with Leland had been.

Accordingly, a little after the appointed hour, he climbed into the carriage and bade the driver take him to the Brennert house. Mary Eileen was already waiting for him, specially dressed in a hunter-green wool suit with velvet collar and cuffs—out of which peeked delicate lace. The nipped waist and the modified bustle accentuated her delicately curved figure, and Lucien caught his breath at the sight of her.

Mary Eileen's father received him at the door, eyed him, then chuckled. "My, don't you look handsome! You're a regular toff, Mr. Bouchard. Mary Eileen's been waiting expectantly, so I hope the two of you have a most pleasant Sunday. Don't bring her back too late now, mind you!"

"I shan't, Mr. Brennert. We'll lunch at Jarlie's, then stroll around the city. Then directly after dinner at McCafferty's, I'll have the carriage bring us right home. We shouldn't be later than eight-thirty or nine, at the most," Lucien explained.

The games master nodded. "That's fine. McCafferty's, is it? 'Tis a grand place, and quite dear, I'm told." He chuckled again, this time with greater humor. "Mary Eileen, lass, this fine gentleman has a carriage waiting to take you on a gastronomic tour of Dublin, from the sound of it. Now don't eat too much—and I don't have to tell you, my girl, go easy on the spirits."

"Father!" Mary Eileen murmured, as she sent him a long, reproachful look. Then, turning to Lucien, her eyes sparkling, she declared, "Ever since your father took us to McCafferty's in a fine carriage, everyone in school has envied me. I can just imagine what the girls will be saying tomorrow."

"If they don't want the nuns to rap them on the knuckles for talking in class, they'd better not say anything," her father jested. "Off with the both of you, now! You'll have to pay the carriage driver for all this waiting time, no doubt, so save your talking for when you're on your way. And have a good time, both of you!"

Proudly, yet shyly, Lucien Bouchard took Mary Eileen's arm and led her out to the curb, helped her into the carriage, then seated himself beside her and bade the driver proceed to Jarlie's.

"Father thinks very highly of you now, Lucien," Mary Eileen vouchsafed as the carriage was rolling in the direction of Dublin, about two miles away. "I'm so glad, for I should have been heartbroken if he'd told me last year that I couldn't see you again."

He turned to her, his heart beating faster. "Do you—do you really care for me that much, Mary Eileen?" There was a lump in his throat as he spoke, and his voice was unsteady.

She looked down and blushed, then shyly nodded.

"Oh, Mary Eileen!" he breathed, unable to speak further in his rapture. Lucien felt that this Sunday would be the epitome of all that he had dreamed of, ever since he had first seen her and been smitten by her gentle, serene beauty.

He could see her lips curve in that exquisite tremulous smile that so characterized her, and he knew that what he said had pleased her, even though he had not put into words the full thought. But she could not be unaware of his esteem for her, and his ultimate desire to make her his wife when he came of age. If only his stepfather hadn't spilled the beans by blurting it all out there at McCafferty's!

Nevertheless, she in no way seemed to hold that unexpected confrontation against him. His resentment against Leland began to wane, and he excused it now, being in a magnanimous mood. He ascribed Leland's excessive behavior to unaccustomed solicitude for his new family. There was no doubt that he was very much in love with Laure and that was all to his credit. No harm was really done, and this time he would have Mary Eileen all to himself through the afternoon and evening. If all went well, their intimacy together for all these hours might mean that he would be permitted to kiss her—and then express what he really desired: her pledge of troth to him, her promise that one day they could be married. Yes, he would do it. Leland had, in a sense, paved the way, by his forthright declaration, and now that it was out in the open, it would be only logical for Lucien to follow it up with his own avowal. He would tell her exactly how much he loved her and describe his plans for their future together.

"You're very quiet, Lucien," she timidly murmured, but he caught the faint trace of a smile at the corners of her sweet mouth. He had an almost overwhelming desire to kiss her lips, but he naturally restrained himself. Such a move would be premature, too brash, and too obvious. Besides, what he felt for her was too fine, too noble to allow him even to think of offending her with any gesture that might suggest he was willing to take advantage of her feelings for him.

"I—I was just thinking about—things, Mary Eileen," he lamely managed, after a pause. She had turned to him now, looking at him quizzically. How beautiful her gray-green eyes were, so lustrous. And that exquisite mouth with its hint of trembling that came and went as her moods changed! It was the kind of face that inspired poetry, rhapsodic sonnets such

126

as Shakespeare had written about his "dark lady." Each moment near her strengthened his desire to marry her, to contribute to her life as she would to his, to share and to give, and he felt the purest of motives in this love.

"What sort of things, dear Lucien?" her voice came gently, as the carriage clattered over the cobblestones, entering now the outskirts of Dublin.

"I—well—I'm so glad you could spend this Sunday with me, Mary Eileen," he blurted. "You see, you mustn't think I'm insincere, because I—I mean whatever I say to you, Mary Eileen. You see, I—I'm in love with you."

"Oh, Lucien!"

"It's true. I want to marry you some day. And when I finish at St. Timothy's, I'd like to ask you to be engaged to me, Mary Eileen. Of course, I'll ask your father for his permission first, so he won't think I'm doing anything behind his back. . . ."

She turned away to look out the window and did not speak; he reached for her hand and gently pressed it between both of his. He intently watched her, waiting for her answer, and saw the rosy blush suffuse her soft, pink cheeks. His heart was beating like a trip-hammer now, and he had never felt so ecstatic. The gentle, soft scent of her hair wafted to his nostrils, and it seemed to him, as her fingers quivered in his grasp, that he was close to paradise at this moment.

Mary Eileen did not dare to look at him, but for her, too, the moment was one of trembling emotion. Her own heart was beating fast, and she knew that she was blushing—yet she could not suppress it. There was so much she admired about the tall boy from America, who loved her country and had been willing to fight for it. Yes, even when her father had angrily spoken out against the brash, headstrong newcomer from across the Atlantic, who thought that he could accomplish single-handedly what long years of struggle by an oppressed populace had failed to do, Mary Eileen had secretly admired Lucien's bravado and élan.

He began again, trying to steady his voice and releasing a little the pressure of his hands against hers. "I know I'm too young to speak of it now, but I—I want to marry you as soon as I've settled in whatever profession I choose as my livelihood. Now I want you to understand that a promise to become engaged doesn't place any obligation on you. You don't owe me anything—I mean— Oh, the devil take it. I'm getting it all wrong. . . ."

"No, Lucien," she softly interposed, still without looking at him, but she put her other hand atop his and pressed it gently, to let him know that she was thoroughly sympathetic. "I understand exactly what you're trying to say. I'm very fond of you too—and, although I'm too young to think of marriage now, as Father would say to me, there's no one else. And if you and I still feel the same way about each other when your schooling's done, if marriage is what you really want—"

"Oh, yes, Mary Eileen, I do. I want it with all my heart! I love you so, and I won't ever love anyone else! I swear it to you—"

"Hush, dear Lucien." She took away her hand and put a finger to her lips, then whispered, "The carriage driver will hear you, and he'll think us so silly and so young—"

"Never mind! He was young once himself, and I'll bet he's been in love. Oh, Mary Eileen, you've made me so happy! I do understand you, don't I? We're engaged, unofficially, aren't we?"

Shyly, at last, she turned to look at him, still blushing, and she gave him a tiny little nod, and he uttered a long sigh and then, since he could no longer control himself, leaned forward and kissed her ever so briefly on her soft, tremulous mouth. She gasped softly, but her smile was exquisite.

The carriage was passing down Turton Lane, about half a mile from the pleasant little restaurant where Lucien and Mary Eileen were going for luncheon—but it in fact amounted to a belated breakfast. The crisp air had given them both an appetite, but they had both promised themselves not to eat too much so as to spoil their appetites when dinnertime came at McCafferty's. However, when one is young, one's appetite is boundless, and one feels oneself immortal—and surely, on this beautiful Sunday afternoon, with the blue sky filled with soft cumulus overhead in fleecy sheeplike forms moving slowly across the sky, Lucien felt keenly alive and radiantly happy.

As they neared the end of Turton Lane, prior to turning right onto Rhys Street, where they would proceed several blocks east to Jarlie's, Lucien heard angry cries, catcalls, and hoarse shouting. Puzzled, he peered out the carriage window and saw ahead a group of men, shabbily dressed, brandishing sticks and shillelaghs. Anxiously, he pulled down a little panel ahead of him to call up to the coachman, "What's all this, driver?"

"Near as I can tell, sir, it's the Fenian lads gettin' ready to march on the British troop garrison. There's been real bad blood the last week here in Dublin, sir—perhaps you haven't heard about it. I didn't think they'd be down this way, though, for the garrison's a mile off to the west. I guess this is a show of strength. I'll get you to Jarlie's as quick as I can, sir!"

"Thank you, driver." Lucien closed the panel and turned to Mary Eileen. "I certainly didn't count on anything like this happening—"

"I'm not worried, Lucien," Mary Eileen hastily assured him. "I'm with you, and you don't take part in this sort of thing anymore, do you?" Her gray-green eyes were wide and questioning.

"You have my word of honor on that. I'm sympathetic with the Irish, you know that, and I'll always be. But I don't have any illusions anymore that I can change things all by myself. And I won't get into trouble ever again."

"Then I've nothing to worry about," she declared with a tender smile.

They went on without incident, and in a few minutes they arrived at Jarlie's and were ushered to a table in a corner.

When the food arrived, Mary Eileen exclaimed over it, saying to Lucien, "I'll probably have no appetite for dinner tonight at McCafferty's, but this is so good, and I'm so hungry. . . . You must think me a proper pig!"

"Never in the world, Mary Eileen! Just enjoy it. And don't worry, we'll go for a brisk walk, maybe down to the waterfront, and five hours from now, we'll surely be hungry again."

"Do you think it's safe to go for a walk after what we saw down Turton Lane?" she anxiously inquired.

"I'm sure it'll be all right. The driver said they were marching on the garrison, and that's off in the opposite direction from the port. Let's not worry about it. If it looks like there might be trouble, we'll just come right back here. We can go to that lovely park that's a few blocks away from here—the one with the duck pond—and just sit on a bench and look at the sky. Sometimes I love just sitting, don't you?"

"Oh, yes! I can just sit for hours, watching the clouds roll overhead."

Lucien found this simple conversation absolutely enchanting. It was, he thought, a foretaste of the sort of conversation they would be making once they were husband and wife, over their own breakfast table, perhaps in New York, or wherever else his work would take him. It was such a delicious picture that he could not help putting down his fork and staring avidly at Mary Eileen. Catching his gaze, she turned scarlet again and whispered, "You're embarrassing me; you mustn't look at me like that, as if you'd seen me for the first time—"

"But I feel that way every time I look at you, dear Mary Eileen," he whispered back.

It was almost two o'clock when they finished, and the bill came to only nine shillings threepence. After leaving a generous tip, Lucien took Mary Eileen's elbow and guided her to the cashier's counter, where he paid; then, holding open the door for her, they walked out into the bright sunlight.

A sharp breeze was coming in from the waterfront, and Lucien suggested that they forego walking to the harbor and instead go directly to the park. Mary Eileen was quick to agree with this idea, and after she boldly linked her arm in Lucien's—which brought a smile of delight to his handsome face—they strolled slowly toward their destination.

Mary Eileen did most of the talking, chatting happily about an upcoming field hockey match between her school, St. Eulalie's, and its longstanding rival, St. Mary's. Lucien barely heard her words; rather, he found himself distracted by the tone of her voice and her tinkling laughter—so delightful that he basked in them, heedless of everything except the knowledge that she was truly his girl and nothing else on earth mattered at that moment.

". . . will you, Lucien? Lucien?"

Suddenly her words broke in upon his thoughts, and he realized that he hadn't been listening. He gave her a sheepish grin, and confessed as much, begging her indulgence—after explaining why she should be so forgiving—and asking her to repeat what she had asked.

Mary Eileen giggled at his consternation. "I said, will you be attending the hockey match to see me play?"

"I wouldn't miss it for the world," was Lucien's reply.

As they rounded the corner of the street across from the park, Mary Eileen exclaimed, "Look! Over there. It's a parade of some sort. I love parades. Can we go watch, do you think?"

"I don't think it's a parade, Mary Eileen," Lucien declared, shaking his head. "I'd say it's those men we saw earlier when we rode into town—and if that's the case, we'd best get away from here quickly." The anxious look on his face was replaced by quick look of amusement as he declared, "With my luck, I'd get arrested this time just for being an innocent bystander—and Father O'Mara would never believe I wasn't involved in trouble again. Nor, come to think of it, would your father. They'd undoubtedly make some solemn pronouncement about 'where there's smoke, there's fire,' and I'd be declared guilty without a chance to defend myself. So come on, my girl, let's go find a quieter place to stroll. . . ."

But Mary Eileen obstinately stood her ground. "No, I want to watch," she declared. "If those men are marching for Irish freedom, it would be unpatriotic to walk away," she earnestly avowed. "Besides, they won't do any harm. They're just letting off steam, the way my father says they do when there's no other avenue open to them for expressing their feelings," Mary Eileen compassionately explained.

By now, the group of marching men—who numbered nearly a hundred—had quickened their pace, and they were not more than a block and a half away, advancing toward Lucien and Mary Eileen. The sight of so many angry men suddenly had its intended effect, and Mary Eileen felt fearful.

"Well, perhaps we had best go somewhere else," she reluctantly agreed.

"I'd say it would definitely be best." But as he led her away to his right, he saw three platoons of Dublin policemen, supplemented by a small contingent of smartly uniformed British soldiers, armed with rifles to which they had already affixed bayonets. A portly captain with a walrus mustache marched at their head and held up his hand, barking a command for the men to stop. The police and the soldiers had come out of a street half a block to the teenagers' right, appearing almost without warning, and suddenly Mary Eileen and Lucien were caught between the mob and the uniformed ranks. As the policemen spread out as if to surround the oncoming mob as much as possible, the British soldiers took the lead in advancing on the marchers.

Frantically, Lucien took Mary Eileen's wrist and gasped, "Oh, my God! Let's get out of here! There's going to be trouble if they've already fixed their bayonets. They're determined to rout the marchers any way they can!"

"Oh, dear! It's all so senseless! Why can't they let them march and sing and have their say without bloodshed?" Mary Eileen pathetically asked. But Lucien did not answer. He was far too worried after observing that the marchers had not fled, but instead were now slowly and grimly advancing toward the armed soldiers.

"Men, I order you to disperse! What you are doing is unlawful, and we are prepared to deal sternly with you, if you continue your march," the captain bawled through a megaphone to make his voice heard to the last marcher.

There was a tall, gaunt, gray-haired man in the front row of the marchers, brandishing a club. He uttered an oath and cried out, "We'd sooner give in to the devil! We're fed up with your slaughtering innocent Irish lads and taking over a city you've no right to! We're marching on! Let us pass!"

"You advance at your peril, men!" the captain warned. Then, turning to his soldiers, he exclaimed, "Have your rifles at the ready."

Still the mob continued its advance, and now the captain called to a soldier behind him, "Corporal, raise your rifle, and fire a warning shot. Above their heads, mind you—we'll not be accused of firing on men armed only with clubs and sticks."

The corporal raised his gun and fired up at the sky. To the soldier's surprise, from the group of marchers there came answering gunfire—shots of a pistol and an old musket. The captain uttered a cry and clapped a hand to his left shoulder, staggering back, hit by the pistol ball. A cheer came from the marching contingent, and more shots rang out.

"Give it back to them, men! Give it back to those dirty rebels!" the captain cried, taking away his hand and staring at the blood that dripped from his fingers.

At the first sound of gunfire, Lucien and Mary Eileen had begun to run toward a huge oak tree across the street in the park. The massive trunk would provide ample protection for the two terrified teenagers. Then came a second volley of shots, and suddenly Mary Eileen stumbled, uttering a strangled little, "Oh . . . oh, I—I'm hurt. . . ."

"Oh, dear God, no!" Lucien groaned aloud. Mary Eileen began to sink down on her knees. He caught her in his arms and lifted her up and bore her over toward the oak tree. "Oh, please!" he sobbed. "Tell me—where does it hurt? I—I'll go for help! I'll run and get the ambulance to take you to the hospital—"

"No! Oh, no—please, please—Lucien! Don't leave me! It—it's my back . . . it went right through my back—and . . . oh, Lucien, I feel so weak. . . ."

He was sobbing, his eyes nearly blinded with tears, as he carefully unbuttoned her jacket and then saw the hideous blotch of blood staining her white blouse. "Mary Eileen, I've got to get a doctor or an ambulance—" he sobbed.

"No . . . don't leave me, oh—dear Lucien—why did this have to happen? I—I do love you so. . . . I wanted to marry you. Oh, Lucien, I'm getting so cold—so very cold. Hold me—hold me. I'm so afraid. . . ."

"Oh, no! Oh, please, God, no! Don't let this happen to her! Oh, God, in Your justice, don't let her die!" Lucien screamed out in his frenzy. He stared down at her. Her eyes were blinking, and she seemed to be straining to say something to him. Then a trickle of blood emerged from the corners of her mouth, and her eyes closed. He felt her shudder in his arms, and he uttered a maddened cry. "No, no, don't die! I love you. I need you! Oh, Mary Eileen—don't leave me!"

She was still. Beyond him, there were shouts, curses, the crackle of gunfire. But he was oblivious to all that. He could only stare at her, tears running down his cheeks, digging his fingernails into his palms until they bled, helpless and hopelessly unable to move from the place that had been her rude, harsh deathbed. Suddenly the sun disappeared behind a cloud, and it was symbolic—for indeed the life had gone out of Lucien Bouchard's soul.

"Dear God! Dear God in Heaven, why, why, why?" he sobbed aloud. He stooped then, gently lifting her up in his arms, her head lolling onto her breast, and he moved away from the oak and into the street that had suddenly become a battleground. The soldiers and civilians were fighting brutally. As he watched in stricken anguish, one of the privates rammed

133

his bayonet into the belly of a youth who could not have been much older than himself, in ragged clothes; and he heard the boy scream, saw the bayonet wrenched out, bright with blood . . . the color that now stained his own clothes, the color of Mary Eileen's blood that had marked him.

All at once, realizing they were badly outnumbered, the marchers had turned and fled, disorganized rabble leaving at least a dozen of their number dead or badly wounded in the street. Two British soldiers lay sprawled in death, and another was sobbing as he clapped both hands over his belly where a musket ball had penetrated. The captain was getting first-aid from a sergeant, and he was foully cursing the demonstrators.

Lucien walked slowly by them all with his terrible burden. The wind dried his tears even as he shed them. "You dirty, filthy, goddamn butchers! You've killed my girl! All we wanted to do was be married and be happy—and you killed her, just to put down men who wanted their freedom from butchers like you!" he shouted, beside himself, not caring what happened now.

The captain slowly turned, his face contorted with pain. He saw the youth standing there, and he observed the lifeless body of Mary Eileen Brennert in Lucien Bouchard's arms.

Then he shook his head and called out, "I'm sorry . . . I couldn't know— I don't know if my men did it or maybe it was one of them. . . . Forgive me, forgive all of us. It's duty we don't like, but we have to do—"

"Oh, yes, it's your duty to murder innocent men and women and children in the name of English rule! May you all rot in hell! You sent *me* there with your fine killings!" Lucien shrieked at the top of his voice.

Then, turning his back on them, conscious only of Mary Eileen's body in his arms, Lucien walked away from the scene of carnage that, in a single horrifying, accidental moment, had blighted all his hopes and dreams.

He did not know where he was going as he walked aimlessly. Her body seemed light, and from time to time he stared down at her lovely face, as gentle in death as she had been in life. And he wept, hoarsely, his body shaking with great sobs. As he moved down a side street, an elderly man and his young granddaughter came out of a dingy flat and saw him and his burden; and the old man crossed himself and whispered to the child, "Pray for the poor soul. Pray for all the innocents who die in this cruel world of ours, so many of them in the hope of making Ireland free. You may live to see that day, girl, but not I.''

Lucien neither heard nor saw them, so their pity and compassion did not touch him. The entire world was fixed into this timeless, horrific instant of brutality and needless death. Perhaps, vaguely, as he prayed and wept, he had the lingering, faint illusion that she would come to life in his arms—but he knew she would not. He also knew that, with her death, the most vital phase of his young life had ended, snuffed out by that random bullet.

Chapter Twelve

Lucien Bouchard did not know how he could bear to face Mary Eileen Brennert's father. As he walked aimlessly down the Dublin streets, carrying her in his arms, his soul was black with guilt, as if the Furies had singled him out, determined to pursue him with all the relentless and vindictive hatred of their vengeful nature.

The air had grown colder, and his tears dried on his cheeks. Over and over his mind replayed the same crushing thought: Why had he not more forcibly led her away from the park at the first sight and sound of the marchers? This lashed at him like a steel-tipped whip, and each time he looked down into her cameolike face, he uttered a groan out of the utmost agony of soul.

After about ten minutes of walking, a plump, thickly bearded constable came up to him and hailed him. "Say there, laddie, what's the trouble here?"

Lucien blinked his eyes, staring at the man as if he were an apparition out of some phantasmagoria. Finally, in a hoarse, shaking voice, he averred, "My girl—my girl's been killed. We were over by the park . . . and the marchers came, and then the soldiers . . . and there was a stray shot—"

"Oh, poor laddie! Poor lass—here now, my name's Constable McFee. You let me take you to the station—it's just around the corner—and we'll take care of things for ye. You say she's your lass—and your name, young sir?"

"I—I'm Lucien Bouchard, and—"

"Never mind the rest for now, lad. I'll need more information, but it can wait." Then, solicitously, recognizing the state of exhaustion that Lucien was in, the constable volunteered, "Would you let me carry the lass, young sir? I'll be real gentle with her, as if she were me own daughter, I promise." Constable McFee looked down at Mary Eileen's peaceful face and could not suppress a sigh. "Ah, 'tis a sorry day! When will these troubles end? Why do these things happen?" he asked rhetorically.

Suddenly Lucien started to wail aloud and shout: "Oh, my God! Why didn't I take her away before they came—"

The constable put a comforting hand on his shoulder. "Now, now, young sir, you mustn't blame yourself! 'Twasn't your fault, God knows that. You come along with me, now. I'll see to everything."

Such kindness burst the dam of Lucien Bouchard's tormented reserve. He broke down and wept like a child, and he allowed the constable to carry Mary Eileen's body the half-block around the corner to the station.

Lucien buried his face in his hands and started to weep again when the solicitous constable eased Mary Eileen's body onto a bench at the side of the constabulary duty room. Then, reverently, he covered her face with his large white handkerchief, and as Lucien watched this, his tears increased and his sobs redoubled. With that symbolic gesture, he knew she was gone forever, and he was here alone, and suddenly Ireland had become an alien, terrifying, and hostile place.

Constable McFee had given Lucien time to compose himself before asking him all the necessary questions. Meanwhile, a young policeman was sent to fetch the undertaker, Connors McCarthy.

McCarthy, a solemn-faced man in his early fifties, arrived with his assistant; both wore the black coat and top hat of their profession. They quickly and silently took charge. Lucien, still dazed and sobbing, watched them as they lifted Mary Eileen's lifeless body with great care, placed it in a pinewood box, and carried the box out to the hearse. McCarthy then approached Lucien and said that after transporting Mary Eileen's body to the funeral home, he himself would come back to take Lucien out to Mary Eileen's father's house.

It was not more than twenty minutes later when McCarthy returned, this time without his assistant—who had stayed behind to supervise preparation of Mary Eileen's body for the wake—but still driving the now-empty hearse.

Constable McFee, who had also volunteered to accompany

Lucien out of the city, stepped over to the youth. "You'll be telling us the way, young sir, and we'll go along directly. Please, you mustn't feel you're responsible. It's that cursed trouble we're having with the English, and it might have been you instead of her."

"I would to God it had been," Lucien cried out, as he walked slowly to the front of the hearse and climbed into the seat beside the funeral director. The constable rode along on the other side, and the clack-clack-clack of the two horses' hooves on the cobblestone streets was a lugubrious and torturous sound to Laure's oldest son. He felt, as the horses drew nearer and nearer to the games master's little house, that Henry Brennert would be well within his rights to kill him on sight.

Then his mind went back over the conversation he and Mary Eileen had had that very noon—which now seemed to have been a hundred years before. To think that he would never see her again, never see that tremulous sweet smile, those clear, gray-green eyes, never hear her soft, gentle voice saying his name—it was too much to endure. *Oh, God— why . . . why?* Into his mind the lament of self-condemnation ran like a perpetual engine that gathered power and momentum until his brain was filled to the point where it was ready to explode. He absolutely could not shake the feeling of responsibility for the snuffing out of her beautiful young life.

They reached the Brennert cottage, and Lucien unsteadily got down from the hearse and walked slowly up the front path. At that moment, the door opened, and Henry Brennert, tall, wiry, his gray hair cropped close, emerged. His eyes widened as he saw the hearse, the undertaker in his long, black coat and high top hat, and then the constable. "What is it? What is it, Lucien?" he hoarsely cried out.

"I—oh, God forgive me! Mr. Brennert—I'd give my life to bring her back—"

"To bring her back? What are you saying? Mary Eileen? What has happened? Oh, sweet Jesus, tell me!" His eyes were wild and already glazed with the start of tears.

Lucien Bouchard sank down on his knees and clasped his hands as in prayer. "We'd had lunch at Jarlie's, you see, and we headed to the park . . . and there were marchers . . . and I told Mary Eileen that we ought to go away because I'd heard there might be trouble—"

138

"What then? Tell me; tell me everything!"

"Yes—yes, s-sir. I—I took her hand, and we started to leave, and then all of a sudden from a dead-end street some soldiers came, and their captain challenged the marchers, and there were gunshots . . . and then Mary Eileen was hit. . . . Oh, please, please forgive me! I wanted to marry her—I wanted to be her husband. I loved her! For nothing in the world would I have endangered her—you must believe it! Forgive me, forgive me!" Lucien sobbed.

Henry Brennert stiffened, raising his clenched fists like hammers above Lucien's head. "Why did you let it happen?" the father railed, waving his fists as if to strike Lucien.

But Constable McFee came forward and soothingly interposed, "Sir, you mustn't blame this young man. I've never seen one carry on so. . . . He loved her—it's God's own truth. We knew of the trouble, but these young folk, they couldn't know what was planned. He did the best he could—the bullet might have hit him instead; indeed, he'd have given his life for her! You should have seen him carrying her body in the street, when I came upon him, sir—it would have broken your heart, it fair would have! Don't blame him, Mr. Brennert, by all the saints; he loved her, and he's a good lad. . . ."

Then Henry Brennert lowered his hands and helplessly opened his palms. He began to weep, and then he sank down on his knees and put his hands on Lucien's shoulders, and the two rocked back and forth as the games master groaned, "My sweet lass! All I had left in the world! First my Meg died, died just six months after giving Mary Eileen birth—and now she's gone from me, too! Ah, I've nothing! Oh, God, God, how much longer must innocent people die for Ireland's sake?"

The constable turned aside and dabbed at his eyes with his handkerchief. Even the undertaker was moved. And there, as the dusk fell on the wintry scene outside Dublin, Lucien Bouchard and Henry Brennert clung to each other, as if seeking what tiny consolation might be gleaned in the sharing of their communal sorrow.

Like one drawn by an irresistible magnet, Lucien felt himself compelled to attend the wake for Mary Eileen Brennert on Monday evening. Earlier that day, Father O'Mara had called Lucien into his study to hear the account of what had taken place on that tragic Sunday afternoon, and he had told the tortured youth, "I know it must seem to you the most unjust and heartless thing in all the world. And I know that you feel totally guilty and believe that you caused her death. No, son, you did not. It was God's will, and we are not to question what He plans for us mortals." He paused and studied Lucien's drawn face. "Are you going to the wake tonight?"

"I am, Father O'Mara. I want to—to see her one more time. I've prayed in chapel for her forgiveness. I've also tried to understand—but I still don't." Lucien's eyes were hollow and bloodshot from his weeping and sleeplessness.

"I know how deep and honest and sincere your feelings were, my son. I truly believe that you intended to marry her one day, and she would have made you a good wife. I know, too, that you will never forget her. Console yourself that at least she had little pain and she is with her Maker. May the memory of her goodness remain with you always, guiding you in all that you do."

"Th-thank you, Father O'Mara," Lucien quavered.

"What are your plans? Do you think that you might want to take off a few weeks, possibly even to go back home to your mother and stepfather?"

"I—I haven't had time to think, not really, Father O'Mara. But I feel so lost now, so helpless, so out of place."

The headmaster of St. Timothy's gravely nodded. "I sympathize very deeply with you. You must do what you think best. Happily, you're very young, and time will soften this hurt. But Lucien, you must believe that you are not guilty of her death. You cannot go through the rest of your life with that cloud over you. It was merely a tragic circumstance; we must accept what our dear Lord has in store for us. That is the price we pay for our lives, Lucien. I will give you my blessing and pray that your sorrow will be eased and that you can resume the richness of your own life before too long."

"Thank you, Father O'Mara."

Though Lucien had gone fortified of soul from Father O'Mara's gentle words, it seemed to him that the wake was even more terrible than the reality of Mary Eileen's death. Her body, brought out from the funeral home, lay in state in

140

the darkened parlor; a single candle was burning at the head of the coffin and another at the foot. Her elderly aunt, a woman in her seventies, was constantly weeping and referring to incidents of Mary Eileen's childhood; her cousin, a stout woman in her thirties, looked askance at Lucien, as if to intimate that she regarded the sturdy young man as the male-factor responsible for this scene of grief.

But at last Henry Brennert asked his relatives to adjourn from their vigil, and taking Lucien by the elbow, the games master led him into the parlor. "Go see her for the last time, lad," he whispered. Then he drew back and closed the door.

Lucien stood watching the flickering candles at the head and the foot of the coffin. Tears began to run down his cheeks as he moved toward the casket, compelled by a force he could not understand, which drove him toward what he did not wish to see, yet knew he must. He stared down at the cold oval face, the eyes closed in repose, the sweet lips silent. With a choking cry, he bent forward and kissed her on the mouth and murmured, "Forgive me, Mary Eileen! I loved you! I'll love you all my days!" Lifting his eyes to the ceiling, he said softly, "God, be kind to her soul; she was sweet and good."

He turned, half blinded by his tears, and made his way out of the parlor and closed the door. Henry Brennert stood there, and he also was weeping, holding out his hand to Lucien. "I'll pray for you, too, laddie," he said in a choked voice. "I would to God you could have married her one day and taken her back to America with you."

"Oh, please, Mr. Brennert, for God's sake! I feel so useless and at fault! I don't know how you can bear to look at me, much less tell me you wanted us to marry. How can you ever forgive me—"

"I can easily, lad. She died young and innocent, before the world had a chance to corrupt her. Maybe that's as well. Maybe it's true what they say: The good die young and are saved the knowledge of evil. Yes, laddie, I'll pray for you. And if you go back to America, think of me now and again and write me how you're doing—will you promise me that?"

Lucien Bouchard could not speak, but only nodded and squeezed Mr. Brennert's hand the harder. He made his choking, hardly audible good-byes, then left the cottage, numb and agon-ized, not knowing what to do. Tomorrow morning, the funeral would be held in the little graveyard near the church, a quarter of a mile from the girl's school. . . .

A gentle rain had begun to fall, and it was as if the heavens wept to receive the soul of Mary Eileen Brennert, Lucien thought to himself, as he stood near the gravesite. He listened to the young priest intone the mass for the dead and saw Mary Eileen's father toss a handful of dirt onto the box as it was carefully lowered into the grave. Then he himself stooped, plunged his hand into the moist sod, and tossed a handful as his own requiem, even as the priest intoned the words, *"Requiescat in pace."*

Immediately after the funeral, Lucien headed back to St. Timothy's. He had been excused from classes all this day, but now he desperately needed advice, so he went to Sean Flannery's private study on the second floor of the academy building. The instructor was seated at his desk, reading essays that his pupils had submitted the previous week, scribbling marginal notes and placing the already-read papers in a neat pile as Lucien halted by the half-open door and then hesitantly knocked.

"Come in, come in!" Sean Flannery said impatiently without looking up. Then he turned and raised his eyes, which widened and softened, as he lay down his pen. "Oh, Lucien, it's you. Come in, my boy, and close the door. I can guess that you want to talk, and I want to help, if I can."

"Thank you, Mr. Flannery."

"I assume you went to the funeral? No need to answer. I can see from your face you did. I'm sure it meant a good deal to poor Mr. Brennert to have you there."

"I hope so."

"Lucien, I think I know what you're going through right now, and when I heard about it, I was thunderstruck. It's a real tragedy. But you mustn't regard it as a punishment of some kind—because it's not. You've changed so much for the better, in the past year or so. You're coping with problems in a constructive way, not in the rebellious way you used to follow. No, my lad, this is no punishment—though I think you could regard it as a test . . . a big one. A lot now depends on how you meet it."

"I know, Mr. Flannery. But all I can think of is that it was

142

all my fault. If only I'd made her come away more quickly, she'd be alive today.''

"You can't know that. If you'd gone somewhere else, another stray bullet might have found her, if it was so destined. For your information, there were three or four riots in various sections of Dublin on Sunday. At least a dozen civilians were killed, as well as five soldiers, and God knows how many more were wounded. No one can predict or control the course of these uprisings. The British are sending more and more troops into Dublin and Belfast because a lot of hotheads seem to want to play the role of martyr.''

"She was a martyr, too, Mr. Flannery," Lucien observed as he slumped in the chair to which the instructor had gestured him. He bowed his head and twisted his fingers restlessly. "Oh, Mr. Flannery," he suddenly cried out, "I loved her so much!''

"I know you did," the young instructor said softly. "And always keep her memory green within your heart; don't let it die. She was your first and everlasting love. I don't think you'll want to judge all women by her in the future—that wouldn't be right—but her memory may serve to guide you in the years to come.''

"Perhaps. All I know is that I really did want to marry her. I wanted to live all my life with her, to have children by her—" Lucien broke down again at this point, and he began to weep softly, covering his face with his hands.

Sean Flannery stared at him a moment with a compassionate look on his handsome face, then he abruptly rose, walked over to a sideboard, opened the door, and took out a bottle of old Irish whiskey. Uncorking it, he poured two stiff shots into jigger glasses and brought one to Lucien. "Here, drink this down. I don't ordinarily do this, but I think you could use a dose of whiskey just now. It'll help calm you.''

Slowly, young Lucien raised his moist eyes to Flannery's earnest face and accepted the jigger. He put it to his lips and swallowed a little, then grimaced.

"Good! Take it slowly, and don't waste a drop of it. It's one of Ireland's chief contributions to this world of sorrow and suffering," his instructor quipped, as he took a draught from his own glass. "But tell me, what are your plans now, lad?''

After a long pause, Lucien finally observed, "I don't really

143

care if I finish school or not, Mr. Flannery.'' There was such an aching hollowness to him, and he did not care a fig for his studies, or his high marks, or his future at St. Timothy's. He knew only that somehow he had to leave at once, perhaps go back home, where time alone would heal the bleeding wound of his suffering.

"That's understandable, too. And you might be right about not wanting to stay here. There are many places where you can continue your education—and you *should* do so, eventually. But right now, I know you're at loose ends. I imagine that even your friends, Ned and Edward, don't mean a thing to you. I presume you want to get back to your family as fast as you can, where you'll find the love, comfort, and consolation that you need. Isn't that about it?''

Wordlessly, Lucien nodded, than sipped more of his whiskey and again grimaced. He set the glass down on a little taboret beside him.

"I've always believed that when one is young, one should obey the dictates of one's heart. And if you want to go home now, I think you should.''

"You honestly do, Mr. Flannery?'' Lucien anxiously looked up at his instructor.

"Decidedly. You'll do nothing except mope around here; you'll tackle your books and your homework listlessly, and you'll be of no use to anyone, least of all to us who try to guide you into becoming a really fine scholar. You've already got the basis for acquiring knowledge; you've got a keen mind, and discounting some of your understandable youthful emotion, I'm sure you're going to be a good, worthwhile man in a very few years. You've only a few credits lacking to earn your certificate, and perhaps they won't even be necessary at many colleges. Right now, my advice to you is to go back home and think about continuing your studies in one of the higher institutions of learning in your country—there are plenty of good ones, like Harvard and Yale, to mention only two. I must confess that I myself have often been attracted by the idea of going to America and teaching there because it's a young country untainted by our Old World notions. No doubt about it, it's the land of the future. But I've a secure post here at St. Timothy's, and then there's my Irish background, which I can't shake off so easily. So, I'll probably stay on here as a teacher, telling young Irish lads—not unlike yourself, really—to pray, to think about Irish independence, and yet not to do anything rash about it. You had a taste of the radical life, and you know how dangerous it can be. That's exactly why you feel the way you do now about poor Miss Brennert.''

''Yes.'' Lucien nodded, unable to formulate any words, for his mind was still oppressed by the cloud of remorse that had haunted him since Sunday afternoon. He had not slept well either Sunday or Monday night, and he felt as physically fatigued as one who had been through a battle. Fortunately, he was a survivor—even though the one he loved most in all this world, yes, even more than his mother, was gone forever.

''Have you given any thought to what you might eventually do for a livelihood, Lucien?'' Sean Flannery prompted, as he went over to the sideboard to procure the bottle again and replenish Lucien's glass. ''No, don't say no to it; a little more won't hurt you. Drink it down, I tell you. Good lad. Now then, what do you envision as your possible career?''

''I—I've never really thought about it, Mr. Flannery. I suppose I was simply coming here to finish secondary school and then see what my stepfather had planned for me. He's in importing and exporting, you know. He mentioned, when Mary Eileen and I dined with him some six weeks ago, that he hoped I'd prepare myself to take over his business. But I'm not sure I want to do that.''

''You're still very young. You've your whole life ahead of you. You may become a writer, even a poet—or again, possibly a man of affairs. But, whatever you do, Lucien, you'll bring imagination and sensitivity to it; I can foresee that. Go back to America, then, but don't take with you the burden of guilt over Mary Eileen Brennert. Promise me that. Let your heart be easy and free in the months and years ahead . . . to find another woman, perhaps—''

''Oh, no, I couldn't think of any other girl. Not now, not ever again.''

''But you will,'' the instructor gently interposed. ''And because of the sweetness and the tenderness of your relationship with Mary Eileen, you'll be the better man, the better lover, the better husband for it. Be certain of it. Lucien, of all the students I've had the last few years, you've been the brightest and the most promising. I want you to keep in touch with me. And if ever I can help you, please write to me and tell me. My happiest moment will be when I hear that you've

145

finally found a purpose to life and channeled all your potential into what's best for you."

"I—I'm very grateful. You've been wonderful to me. I've always valued your friendship and your advice and your teaching, Mr. Flannery."

"Good! And I've respected you as a worthy pupil, with your own sometimes obstinate and opposite ideas, but always with logic to them. That's good, Lucien. Always question what you're not sure of, and don't accept facts simply because they're told to you or printed in black and white. Always be ready to question all facts, until you're sure of them. Then see how they relate to your own way of life. Persevere and look to the future and believe in yourself. That's the advice I have for you. That and my prayer that God will bless you in your endeavors."

Lucien rose, and the two men firmly clasped hands. Then, deeply moved, Lucien Bouchard nodded a farewell and left the room.

Chapter Thirteen

That Wednesday morning, Lucien went into Dublin to withdraw the substantial bank draft that his stepfather had given him. Next to the bank was a travel office, and Lucien ascertained that, fortuitously, the Cunard steamship *Servia* would leave from Cobh two days later. He at once booked passage on it in a first-class cabin. Next he took a carriage back to St. Timothy's, where he swiftly packed his things and made arrangements with the kindly school porter to have his trunk shipped separately—generously tipping the old man for this as well as all past kindnesses. Finally, he went and said his last farewells to Father O'Mara, Sean Flannery, and his two best friends, Edward Cordovan and Ned Riordan.

The sky was heavy with a cold rain on this day, and the grounds of the school, behind which loomed the tenement buildings of Dublin, evoked a feeling of utter melancholy and gloom in Lucien as he trudged across the campus for the last time, carrying his valise. He was impatient to leave, for there was nothing more to hold him here in Ireland. He knew now that he did not want to continue his European education, even if it meant giving up the idea of visiting Paris, Berlin, Vienna, London, and even colorful Rome. He felt suddenly, desperately, the need to reestablish his own identity and to find his roots, so that he knew that he existed for a purpose. All his hopes and dreams of marriage, of establishing a career that would make Mary Eileen proud of him, of having children by her and watching them grow up to maturity, with families of their own—all this was now finished. Only the memories of her sweetness and her kindness to him were left to crowd in upon his conscious moments, exacerbating his anguish over the brutal fact that he would never see her again upon this earth.

He had thought briefly of telegraphing his mother, to inform her of his arrival. That would have been the logical thing to do. But having found himself unable, up to now, to write to her about Mary Eileen's death, he did not want suddenly to alarm her by a telegram, which would only give her seven anxious days of waiting while the *Servia* made its long journey across the Atlantic. No, it would be far kinder, he reasoned, to arrive home unannounced.

It was Friday, March 8, a gray morning, when Lucien was escorted to his first-class cabin. The deferential, soft-spoken steward saw at once that his young passenger was morose and certainly out of sorts, not at all the mood one would expect of a youth about to embark on an Atlantic crossing. Impeccably trained in the Cunard tradition, he had brought Lucien's valise into the stateroom and begun to unpack it, then had solicitously inquired, "Is there anything I can do to make your voyage more pleasant, Mr. Bouchard?"

The youth turned, his eyes dull and listless, but he saw at last the kindly face of the steward. A surge of emotion welled up in him at this manifestation of compassion, even though it was from a stranger. He drew a deep breath and shook his head. "No, thank you, steward. All I want is to get back home to New York to my parents, you see, and you certainly can't do anything to help speed the voyage," Lucien replied with a sad smile.

"That's true, sir." The steward hesitated a moment. "My name's Albert Pinckney, Mr. Bouchard. If you need me, all you have to do is to ring that buzzer. I'll be at your disposal night and day. Could I perhaps get you some small refreshment? We won't be serving luncheon, you see, till we're out of port and on our way, which I should estimate will be a good two hours from now."

"I—perhaps some hot tea and buttered scones, if it isn't too much trouble."

"Why, bless you, Mr. Bouchard, no trouble at all! I'll be happy to bring them to you directly. Now then, I've put away the empty valise that contained your traveling clothes. I've placed your things in the drawers—you'll find them most conveniently laid out. By the way, dinner will be about seven this evening, and I'll see to it that you have a place at a good table—with some young people, if I can arrange it. I imagine

148

you'd like a little companionship, for since we'll take just over a week to make the crossing to New York, it will be nice to have some friends to talk to; at least I've always found that to be true.''

"You're very kind, Mr. Pinckney. Thank you. I—I'll just rest a little now.''

"Certainly, sir. I'll see to your refreshment directly.'' The steward bowed, excused himself, and quietly closed the door behind him. He thought to himself, *That young man has something on his mind—and it's not just going home to see his parents*. He wished there were something he could do for Lucien to brighten him up. He made up his mind to ask the purser if Mr. Bouchard could be placed at a table with a family that included some pretty young daughters. . . .

The *Servia* was about a hundred tons heavier than the *Aurania*, but slightly longer and narrower. Like the *Aurania*, it carried masts for sails, so that when there was a fair, brisk wind, fuel might be saved. It was not quite so luxurious as the ship on which Leland Kenniston had sailed to Cobh, but that made absolutely no difference to Lucien. If anything, he wished only that it were faster than the steward had told him it would be, for he was impatient to reach home. Symbolically, he felt that the sooner he crossed the Atlantic, the farther he would be from the agonizing events of that fatal Sunday afternoon, when all the joy of his life had suddenly been obliterated by a stray bullet.

There was a knock at the stateroom door, and Lucien turned to see the steward entering with a tray of scones and a pot of the finest Ceylon tea. Lucien had been staring desolately out through the porthole at the choppy dark-blue water, for the wintry weather hardly augured an entirely smooth crossing. Still and all, when Lucien had originally enrolled at St. Timothy's, making his first Atlantic crossing in the company of Leland Kenniston, he had found himself to be a passable sailor with no trace of seasickness. The rolling and pitching of the stateroom on this second voyage was not too unpleasant, and so long as the crossing was swift, he anticipated that he could easily endure it.

"I'll place it here on this coffee table, Mr. Bouchard,'' Albert Pinckney's voice broke in on his somber thoughts, and Lucien smiled wearily at the steward.

149

"That will be fine, Mr. Pinckney," he said congenially. "And thank you. I'm sure the refreshments will tide me over till lunch."

"Yes, sir. Remember, if there's anything else you'll need, just ring the buzzer. A good day to you, Mr. Bouchard."

Warmed by the steward's attentive interest, Lucien discovered that he was, indeed, ravenously hungry and devoured the scones and drank all the tea. Then, enormously refreshed, he went back to the porthole to look out over the choppy Atlantic once more.

In the dining salon that evening, Lucien found that the steward had managed to seat him at the second mate's table, with a priest, a married couple in their late twenties, two teenaged girls traveling with their sternly imposing dowager mother, and a personable man in his early thirties who was returning from a vacation in Ireland—his native land—to go back to work as a reporter on the *New York Times*.

The second mate, a gruff-voiced, good-hearted, stocky man in his late forties, made the introductions, and the priest looked over with considerable interest at young Lucien. "I understand from your steward that you've been in school in Dublin, Mr. Bouchard," he pleasantly offered.

"That's true, Father. At St. Timothy's."

"Oh, yes, good old Father O'Mara—you couldn't ask for a better school or a better headmaster. But the spring semester has just recently started, hasn't it? I'm surprised he allowed you a break—"

"I—you see, Father Cassidy, a—a close friend of mine died . . . and I—and I wanted to go home to my parents," Lucien falteringly explained, blushing and self-consciously looking down at his plate.

"My sincerest condolences, my son. Perhaps after dinner, it would do you good to chat with me a bit. You might find that I have something to offer you."

"I—I'd like that very much, Father Cassidy."

"Good. But now, let's attack this excellent brisket of beef. The Cunard line is famous for its cuisine, and I confess that the one sin of which I am consistently guilty is that of gluttony," the portly priest chuckled.

After dinner, since the weather had calmed and the sea was

smooth again, Father Cassidy suggested that the two of them take a walk around the deck, and Lucien eagerly assented. The priest was kind without being probing. His first remark was only, "How long were you at the school, my son?"

"Nearly four years, Father Cassidy. I'd planned to finish there, until this—this terrible thing happened."

"Would it help if you told me about it, my son?"

Lucien found himself suddenly eager to explain what had happened, his own participation in it, and his own inordinate feeling of guilt. When he had finished, Father Cassidy sighed and shook his head. "You are far more sensitive than I expected of a boy your age. No, not a boy—you're a man, in truth, for the way you express yourself and the feelings you have for Mary Eileen show you to be capable of very mature sentiments and emotions. First, I would say to you, as others surely have, you must never believe that you caused the death of your sweetheart. If we know anything about God, it's that He disposes of us according to His divine purpose. And Mary Eileen would certainly not want you to suffer such tortures as of the damned in hell, my son. She loved you, after all, didn't she?"

Lucien could not control the tears that poured down his cheeks. The priest put his arm around the youth's shoulders and let him regain his control, compassionately silent, until Lucien was again able to speak. "I shall never love anyone else, Father Cassidy."

"All of us owe God a death, my son. It is collected when He deems the time due. And I am sure that He has ordained that you will find, one day, a woman whom you can love. Take comfort in this, as well as in the fact that Mary Eileen's soul is among the angels."

Lucien wept again, but these were purging tears, and they gave him strength. "Thank you, Father, for hearing me out. You've helped me a good deal."

"May God bless you, my son, and keep you in His holy ways. Never fear, He knows what is in your heart, and He is mindful of your decency. Persevere, find your way in life, obey the precepts of our Lord, and you will be rewarded." The priest made the sign of the cross over Lucien's bowed head, and then he gently touched him on the shoulder. "Be at rest and in peace, my son, and accept my humble blessing as His

151

servant. I'll see you often during the voyage. If ever you wish to talk to me again, come to my stateroom. Your steward will tell you where it is. Good night to you, my son."

During his subsequent meals in the dining salon, Lucien Bouchard found himself the cynosure of two pairs of eyes at his table, these belonging to the two girls in their teens who sat primly beside their mother. Her austere presence obviated any flirtatious conversation—nor, for that matter, would Lucien have been willing to indulge in it. But the older of the girls, about sixteen, with bold features, high-set cheekbones, and blond hair set in tiny curls along the top of her head, sent him roguish glances from time to time to intimate that she would be not averse to his striking up a conversation with her out on deck. However hard she tried, though, Lucien did not respond to her bait.

Apparently Father Cassidy had occasion to speak to the girls' mother and had doubtless informed her of Lucien's bereavement. Thereafter, the looks cast upon him by these young sylphs were tinged with deep compassion and not a little wonder, for he had become in their eyes a sort of hero-martyr. They had been weaned on the sentimental novels of Mrs. E.D.E.N. Southworth—which their mother did not know they read—and they saw in the handsome, poised, reticent young man at their table a fascinating, dashing fellow akin to the kind that novelist had created.

Lucien did take as much exercise as he could during the voyage, walking around and around the deck each morning, pausing at eleven to take bouillon and crackers from the friendly steward who followed him like a faithful dog at almost every occasion. Albert Pinckney, too, had been informed by Father Cassidy of his young passenger's great loss, and he wished to hearten him in every possible way, without overstepping the bonds of propriety expected of a well-trained Cunard employee.

After a day or two of this regime of exercise and good food, followed by nights of exhausted sleep, Lucien felt his strength returning and, inevitably, his spirits recovering from the deep gloom that had held him in thrall when he had arrived aboard ship. Recalling now Father Cassidy's words about persevering and finding one's own way in life, he decided to go to the ship's library for at least an hour every afternoon, to peruse books on commerce, geography, history, and the sciences, to see whether any subject struck a responsive chord in his mind. He did not yet know to what profession he wished to aspire, for his education in Dublin had been that of a young gentleman of means and leisure—to be erudite and knowledgeable about most things, but not a specialist in any one field. However, Lucien strongly felt that it was vitally important to learn to do one thing particularly well, to master it, so that he might earn his livelihood and feel that he was contributing to the society in which he would find himself.

On the third day of the voyage, he was in the library, reading passages from a recently published volume on new American industry, when a vibrant contralto voice with just a note of pleasant laughter in it suddenly drew him from his intense study.

"It must be a fascinating book."

He blinked his eyes and looked up, to see a tall, slim girl, with raven hair flowing nearly to her waist and tied loosely with a long green silk scarf. Her face was heart-shaped, her eyes were a deep, dark blue, very wide and well spaced to either side of a dainty Grecian nose, and her mouth was full and sensuous.

"Why—er—yes, yes it is. It's a very interesting book."

"What's it about?" she almost playfully asked him.

Remembering his manners, Lucien slid out of his chair and stood up, holding the book with his left hand, his forefinger marking the page he had just been reading. "It—it's about the expanding industrial horizons of America, miss," he explained somewhat pedantically, flushing hotly under her scrutiny.

Her eyes fixed him with an amused, but not at all depreciatory look. Sensing that he was somewhat nonplussed, she hastened to explain her forwardness and at the same time introduce herself. "Forgive me. I suppose I shouldn't have burst in on you like that, like a storm at sea. My name's Eleanor Martinson. I'm a dancer, with a troupe on the way to the United States. I'm looking forward to it; it'll be my first time in your country—I assume you're an American?"

"Oh, yes, Miss—Miss Martinson. My name is Lucien Bouchard."

"I'm most pleased to know you—and I do hope you'll forgive my interrupting you. But I couldn't resist because you looked so serious and so lost in thought," she said with a laugh. With this, she thrust out her hand as a man might, and Lucien found himself holding it and shaking it, while smiling rather fatuously at her.

Strangely, her voice reminded him in a way of Mary Eileen's, but this girl seemed so totally different, so free and blithe.

"A dancer," he finally managed to say. "I've never met a professional entertainer before. I presume your parents are in the theater, then?"

"No, not at all. Actually, my mother and father decided to go their separate ways—even though it's sort of against the Church of England—so I was sent to a very stuffy private finishing school in Switzerland. However, I always liked dancing, and so I started investigating it, took lessons, and by a great stroke of luck got a chance to go to Paris, where I auditioned for the troupe."

Lucien stared at her, his eyes wide. "Do your parents know that you're engaged in such an occupation?"

"Are you suggesting, Mr. Lucien Bouchard, that because I am a dancer, I'm not respectable?"

"Oh, no! It's just that I've never known anyone from a decent background . . . that is to say . . . oh, dear—"

"Never mind, never mind. Now then, what about you? You know practically all there is to know about me at the very first meeting, so I think it's only fair that you tell me something about yourself, Mr. Lucien Bouchard," she finished with another soft, merry laugh.

"There—there's really not much to tell, Miss Martinson," he began.

"Oh, for heaven's sake, please don't call me that; it makes me feel so old. I'll bet I'm not much older than you are—I've just turned twenty."

"I—I'm just seventeen," Lucien somewhat sheepishly confessed.

"Don't look down at it; you're probably at least as much a man as some men I know twice your age, Lucien. I presume you don't mind me addressing you familiarly. I insist you call me Eleanor. Do you dance, by the way?"

"Oh, no! I mean, I never took any lessons."

"Well, it's never too late to learn, and you're certainly graceful looking. Besides, dancing is a wonderful excuse to take a woman in your arms. Or, from the woman's viewpoint, a man."

Lucien was left breathless by this rapid exchange of commentaries, but he perceived that Eleanor Martinson was completely at her ease.

She laughed again, a heartening laugh, the laugh of one who had no problem coping with the most unexpected situations that life might offer. "You know, you're a very serious young man, Lucien Bouchard." She was seated now at his left and stared intently at him.

Thrown on the defensive, he tried to justify himself, almost protesting, "But I'm not really that way—I like a good time as much as anyone! Really, I do."

"I'm sorry. I didn't mean to twit you like that." Instantly, she was contrite, leaning back in her chair and smiling frankly at him. "I guess it's just because, when I meet someone whose looks I like, I want to know everything about him as fast as I can. Maybe that's wrong—but it does save so much time, you know. There are so many dreadful people in this world who pose and aren't themselves and want to show you a false picture. I really don't have time to waste on them. But you seem real, Lucien Bouchard. I mean it."

"Th-thank you, Eleanor," he quavered. He did not know what tack to use. This young woman was like a breath of ocean air, suddenly gusting, then soft and lulling, and again forthright and swift and penetrating. It kept him scrambling for the right answer. And suddenly, without reasoning, he told himself that here was a young woman whose friendship he might enjoy cultivating. She was so vastly different from anyone he had ever met before.

"You promised you were going to tell me about yourself, Lucien Bouchard," she now prompted.

"Well, I'm going home. I was in Dublin—I went to St. Timothy's Academy there—and I decided to go back home to New York."

"Didn't you like your studies there? And why did you go to Ireland, of all places, if you're an American? Weren't the schools good in New York?"

"My—my stepfather is Irish, you see, Eleanor, and, well,

he told my mother that an education abroad would give me a wider concept of things and that I could learn much more. Oh, yes, New York has very good schools, but my mother agreed with him, and that's why I went."

"I see. But now you're going back—have you finished school?"

Lucien could not understand why he felt compelled to tell this free-spirited, beautiful young woman all the reasons for his actions, although ordinarily he would have been too shy to dwell upon his own life. But the words of Father Cassidy seemed still to ring in his ears, to encourage him to go forward in life and not to look back too much. That was why he said, "I—I knew someone there. She—she was killed. . . . I just didn't want to stay there any more. . . . It was too lonely, too awful—"

"You mean, you were in love with her? That's very tragic, Lucien. Yes, you're the sort of young man who would feel very deeply—I can sense that about you already."

He turned crimson to his earlobes. No girl had ever talked to him so frankly before; far from being offended, he found himself responding, as if he had been encased in a glacier and suddenly a warm ray of sun had begun to thaw him out. "I—I was in love. She was the first girl I ever really loved—and she died for no reason at all."

"Do you want to tell me about it? Please forgive me, if I'm touching on something that's painful to you, Lucien. But I'm really interested. I'm not just prying, you must believe that!" Eleanor told him, putting a hand on his wrist.

Her touch was electrifying, and he trembled. He began to tell her his story, haltingly at first and then with greater ease. When he had finished, he abruptly buried his face in his hands and his shoulders shook with muffled weeping.

"Poor Lucien," she exclaimed. Suddenly, she gathered him into her arms and held him to her while he sobbed. Embarrassed by his behavior, however, he tried to pull away. "It's all right, Lucien. You don't have to feel ashamed of being sensitive. There is nothing unmanly about expressing yourself."

Finally regaining self-control, he looked at her through tear-blurred eyes.

There was an enormous sympathy in her widened eyes, and

her lips trembled as she said gently, "Please promise me that you won't be hard on yourself for this."

"I—I'll try."

"Good." Impulsively, suddenly, she leaned forward, put her left hand on his shoulder, and kissed him tenderly on the cheek. Then, lithely springing up from her chair, she left the library.

The next afternoon, Lucien went to the ship's library again, and he chose a book on American history. Twenty minutes after he had begun the book, the door opened and Eleanor Martinson came in, this time wearing her raven hair in a thick bun piled at the back of her neck. A scarf of dark-blue silk tossed casually around her neck floated in the air as the door swung behind her.

"And what's the book this time, Lucien?" she airily demanded.

"Oh—Eleanor! How—how are you?" He looked up from the book to greet her, then stumbled to his feet, turning the book upside down.

"I'm fine. Do you know what it's like outside? It's just wonderful. There's a brisk breeze, and the sun's shining, and you shouldn't be a bookworm at a time like this. Come out and stroll around the deck with me, Lucien. It'll do you good. I need the exercise, too. I've had to spend a very dreary luncheon with an old lady who insisted on telling me all about her ancestors in Wales—and I had to try to seem polite, though honestly there were times when I wanted to throttle her."

"Eleanor—what a thing to say!" he found himself gasping out, then burst into laughter.

"Now that's the first time I've heard you laugh! It does wonders for you, Lucien. You should do it more often. Come on, now." She extended her hand to his and drew him, not entirely unwillingly, out of the library and onto the deck.

The cool sea wind struck them full in the face as they turned and walked hand in hand toward the prow of the ship. Lucien found the salt air salutary, and the sound of Eleanor's voice was soothing as she prattled on about her life with the dance troupe, the cities she had visited, as well as the coming tour of America, which would take the troupe all through the East and the South.

A few minutes later, while she still retained hold of his hand, Lucien violently blushed as he saw Father Cassidy coming toward them in his black cassock and hat, with his rosary about his neck, counting the beads and murmuring a prayer. "Good afternoon, Father," Eleanor called gaily to the priest.

Father Cassidy looked up, nodded, and then halted a moment, the sea wind tugging at his cassock. He observed Lucien's blushing face, smiled, and replied, "And a good afternoon to you, to both of you. How are you, Mr. Bouchard?"

"Very—very well, F-Father," Lucien stammered.

"May God be with you both." He gave them another gentle smile and continued his leisurely walk aft.

Nonplussed by this sudden encounter, over scarcely before it had begun, Lucien felt his heart beating as a wave of anxiety passed through him. He hoped that Father Cassidy did not think he was so fickle or shallow as to be able to shift his emotions from grief to happiness overnight. And then he calmed himself, telling himself that the good Father surely approved of the way he was behaving. For hadn't Father Cassidy said one must go forward in life, and not look back? And hadn't he smiled, just now, when they met him? Yes, surely that was the case. With a relieved sigh, Lucien became conscious of the fact that Eleanor was squeezing his hand gently and looking into his eyes, as if to read his thoughts. With a contented sigh of relief, he returned the pressure of her hand and smiled at her, as they continued their walk along the wind-swept deck.

The lovely young dancer began to speak animatedly about her profession. Her face glowed as she described the feelings she had when she danced—the enormous pleasure it gave her, for example, to execute a difficult move; or the feeling of emotional freedom that dancing imparted; or how when she was dancing, she felt that the music was almost a part of her body, the voice of her soul.

"But being a dancer certainly isn't a bed of roses, you understand," she told Lucien. "No, indeed! It takes a great deal of physical discipline—as well as physical stamina. The members of the corps de ballet are on stage almost throughout the entire performance, and even when standing still, we must, of course, maintain a strict balletic position." She smiled wryly. "That's something that doesn't concern us too often, unfortunately, for we're not at rest all that much."

She stopped and suddenly grinned. "Actually I do believe that many members of our audiences come just to see our relatively unclothed bodies— Why, Lucien, you're blushing!"

Embarrassed, he looked down at his feet. After a moment, he raised his head slightly, and said, "Never mind. Please go on. I didn't mean that you should stop telling me about your life as a dancer."

She looked at him through partly closed eyes, a smile lifting the corner of her mouth. Patting his shoulder, she fondly told him, "I'll try to temper my words so that they don't disturb you."

"They don't disturb me," he somewhat hotly retorted. "It's just that . . . well, I'm not used to hearing a woman speak the way you do, that's all. I'm *not* a prude!"

"I'm sorry," she responded, taking his arm once again, and leading him on. "I didn't mean to upset you—and I didn't mean to imply that you're prudish. I realize that most people don't feel the way we dancers do about the human body. You see, we don't believe that there's anything lewd or immodest about the unclothed human form—which was, after all, created by God in His own image, according to the Bible. So as far as I'm concerned, it's much more natural for the body to be unclothed than it is to be clothed. Not that we go about dancing naked, mind you—" She noticed that Lucien appeared to be struggling with himself to keep from blushing as he listened to her words, but she refrained from commenting on his discomfiture. Instead she blithely continued, "Surely you've seen pictures of ladies in dancing costumes, so you know that quite a bit of us is up for public view. The usual length of my tutu is considerably above my knees, and, of course, we've only got flesh-colored tights on under those filmy gauze skirts, so the men—especially those who've chosen orchestra seats—get quite an eyeful!"

Lucien cleared his throat, then managed to blurt out, "Tell me about the touring, Eleanor. What's it like, going from place to place? Does the entire troupe go on tour, or only some of the members?"

Eleanor turned her face away, hoping that her new friend wouldn't see her smiling at his obvious attempt to change the subject. Looking back at Lucien, she said, "Well, the troupe that I perform with is something of an oddity insofar as the corps de ballet—which is to say, the nonsoloists in the troupe—is the same one in every place we perform. Usually, in fact, a new corps is assembled by an advance ballet master in each new area. For example, our troupe will eventually perform in San Francisco. What is normally done is that an advertisement would be placed in the local newspaper out there telling of the need to assemble fifty so-called ballet girls, and anyone from factory workers to housemaids would be hired—not needing to know anything at all about dance, mind you. They just stand there—or walk across the stage—showing off their limbs. Indeed, many of these young women have given us legitimate dancers a rather lurid reputation because they frequently aren't terribly respectable and are often for hire by their gentlemen admirers. But that's only the case with the troupes that travel in your homeland, not in Europe. With us, you see, ballet has a great deal of tradition, and our audiences wouldn't put up with poor performances or performers."

"I see," Lucien said thoughtfully. "So what you are essentially doing is bringing some culture to the hinterlands."

"Essentially, yes. Although the choices of what we perform are also somewhat different from what we would put on in European capitals and cities. For example, we've mounted what are called touring spectacles, which are great sumptuous extravaganzas, and not just ballets. We'll be performing two separate spectacles: 'Enchantment,' which consists of four acts and twenty tableaux, and 'Excelsior,' which has six acts and twelve scenes. And, of course, we've got to haul around whole rooms full of scenery and props wherever we go—things like gilded chariots and the like."

Lucien looked at her pensively. Finally, he said, "It sounds like a whole different world—certainly it's like nothing *I've* ever seen, nor have ever heard my mother talk about having seen."

"No, she probably didn't. Oh, there were tours made by many of the most memorable European ballerinas back in the forties and fifties—wonderful dancers like Fanny Elssler—but they performed only classical routines, not theatrical dancing."

Eleanor fell silent and looked dreamily into space. "Someday," she mused, pushing back a strand of windswept hair, "I, too, will be a soloist. Indeed, someday, I will have my own troupe." She looked at Lucien, who was staring at her, intrigued by her remarkable determination, then laughed at her own audaciousness. "Everyone should have a dream—don't you agree?"

With that, she impetuously kissed him on the cheek, dropped his arm, and walked quickly away in the direction of her cabin, leaving Lucien staring after her.

Chapter Fourteen

Lucien Bouchard and Eleanor Martinson met twice more before the voyage to New York came to an end, and by their second meeting, Lucien felt himself more at ease in Eleanor's company, and less guilty about his growing attachment for her—although he still found it necessary to explain his feelings away by viewing them as a reaction to her compassion and the fresh perspective she afforded him on his situation.

On their last night at sea, Lucien and Eleanor were able to dine together when one of the regulars at the young American's table came down with a stomach ailment and remained in his cabin. As they sat side by side, Lucien found himself startled when Eleanor subtly but distinctly kept pressing her leg against his. At first he thought he must be mistaken—it surely was the result of the swaying of the ship—and even whispered his profuse apologies to her for such outrageous familiarity, albeit unintentional as it was. However, when the action kept repeating itself—indeed, even growing more and more intimate as she ran her foot up and down his leg—he finally realized that far from finding it unacceptable, Eleanor was actually instigating such physical communication.

He turned to her, his mouth agape, about to speak his mind, but she put a finger to her lips and bade him remain silent. His heart began to pound and his palms started to grow moist, making it difficult for him to hold onto his dessert spoon. His hand was shaking a little as he lifted a bite of peach sherbet to his mouth and, fearful that he would make a fool of himself by dropping some in his lap, he placed his spoon on the saucer—with more of a clatter then he had intended—and forsook the remainder of his dessert.

He dimly heard the conversation of the other passengers at

his table and was somewhat embarrassed when he realized his name had been spoken twice before he heard it. Stammering, "I—I'm sorry. I'm afraid my mind was—uh—elsewhere. . . ." he requested the question be repeated and then answered it as quickly as he could without appearing rude. Glancing sideways at Eleanor, he could make out a lively gleam in her eye, and her lips twitched in such a way as to make him aware that she was amused by his discomfiture.

Finally, dinner came to a close and everyone filed out of the dining salon, some in search of other amusements—such as a last evening of card playing—and others to return to their cabins to pack their clothes in preparation for their arrival in New York the next day. Eleanor brazenly put her arm around Lucien's waist—an act that was rewarded with hostile looks from the two teenage girls who had shared Lucien's table during the entire voyage—and she propelled the handsome young man out of the salon.

She seemed serenely unaware—or unconcerned—of the curious glances of other passengers, many of whom by now had heard of Lucien's bereavement over Mary Eileen. Indeed, not a few of these travelers commented on the apparent closeness of Lucien and Eleanor. One or two of the men made sly remarks about the couple, saying the best way to overcome the loss of one woman is quickly to replace her—preferably in bed—with another, while the women chastised and censured the pair—Lucien for being able to overcome his grief so easily, and Eleanor for leading an impressionable, sensitive lad astray.

"Eleanor . . ." Lucien started to protest, as he felt his self-control being sorely tested, "I must get back to my cabin and pack."

"Nonsense. You've plenty of time to do that," she quickly countered. "I would like you to come with me now. Back to my cabin. I think it's time we were . . . alone together. After all, we may never see each other again."

Lucien felt his heart sink as the truth of her final words hit him. He felt himself close to tears at the thought of losing yet another close friend, and he stopped in his tracks and turned to look at Eleanor. "I—I hadn't thought about that," he quavered. "But of course you're probably right. After all, it's highly unlikely that our paths will ever cross, since we travel in such different circles." He sighed deeply, then declared,

"I shall always treasure the memories of our friendship and the things we shared—"

"I want to share even more with you, Lucien," the beautiful young dancer broke in, stroking his face lightly with her fingertips as she gazed into his eyes. "Please come back with me to my cabin," she whispered huskily.

He groaned at the full realization of her words, and he reddened as he felt his manhood stir at her proposal. Desperately trying to ignore this physical response, he started backing away from her, protesting, "Eleanor, I c-can't . . . please . . . I want to be true to Mary Eileen. . . . Besides, I don't—" he gulped, "I don't love you, and it's always been my intention to remain . . . chaste . . . for my bride."

"First of all, Lucien," Eleanor softly replied, "I'm sure Mary Eileen wouldn't have wanted you to give up your life just because she gave up hers—however tragic the circumstances. And as for not being in love with me"—she sidled up to him and put her hands on his shoulders—"it isn't necessary for a man and a woman to love each other in order for them to be lovers." She cupped his head in her hands and brought his face down to hers, then kissed him tenderly yet firmly on his mouth.

"Oh, Eleanor . . ." Lucien said hoarsely. "This isn't right. . . ."

"Is there anyone standing here telling us it's wrong?" she asked him mockingly. "If it's all right with me, I should think that's all that matters. Don't worry," she teased him, "I won't hurt you."

He became indignant at this, feeling that she was taunting his virility. "I'm not *afraid* of . . . fornication," he said, almost spitting out the word as if it burned his tongue. "A man can have morals, you know!"

"Of course you can, and I'm sorry if I upset you. I certainly didn't mean to cast aspersions on your . . . physical abilities. I assure you I thought nothing of the kind," she said as she took his arm once again and slowly walked down the ship's corridor that led to the staterooms.

They didn't speak again until Eleanor suddenly stopped and turned toward Lucien, saying, "This is my cabin. Will you at least come in for a glass of wine? I have some chilling. It's quite delicious. We can make a farewell toast to each other. What do you say?"

He hesitated briefly, then acquiesced. "All right. But only for a few minutes. I really am quite tired."

"I understand," she replied evenly.

She unlocked her door and glided inside the small but ample cabin, holding the door open for Lucien and then closing it behind him. She walked over to the wine cooler and lifted a bottle of white Bordeaux from its bed of ice shavings. She deftly uncorked it, then poured two generous glasses and handed one to Lucien. She sat down on the edge of her bed and patted it, indicating that Lucien should do the same.

The youth hesitated briefly, then followed her example. Sipping the wine, he declared, "Umm, it's quite good, isn't it? I'm afraid I don't know much about wines. I've seldom had the opportunity to drink them, you see—when I left home for school, I was still quite young, and, of course, at St. Timothy's they hardly served wine with the meals."

Eleanor laughed with Lucien at the comical notion of a stern Catholic school passing bottles of wine down the long refectory tables, and the tension that had been building between them relaxed. Indeed, Lucien was enjoying himself so much that he quite forgot that he had told her he was tired and had to get back to his room, and helped himself to another glass of the dry wine.

Both of them were getting mildly intoxicated, and when Eleanor kicked off her shoes, Lucien didn't hesitate in joining her. The lovely dancer started giggling when she realized Lucien was staring at her feet, and demanded to know what he was looking at.

"I was just trying to see if your feet are any different from a nondancer's," he seriously told her, then began laughing at the absurdity of his statement.

Eleanor laughed along with him, then told him, "No, my feet aren't any different, but my legs are much more muscular."

Lucien immediately began to blush at her bold use of the word "legs," for in polite society, no mention of such parts of human anatomy was ever made, and he had never heard legs referred to except euphemistically, as "limbs."

Eleanor started to giggle again when she realized why he had reddened, but rather than drop the subject, she brashly pursued it. "Really, they're quite muscular. Probably more so than yours. What do you say we compare them?"

Before he could protest, she unbuttoned her skirt and let it fall to the floor, so that all that covered her from the waist down was her short chemise, for unlike most women of the day, Eleanor eschewed the constraints of fashion and wore neither corsets nor heavy petticoats. She then slowly removed her jacket and then her blouse, exposing the top of the filmy garment, leaving her standing there almost naked.

Lucien sat like one transfixed, unable to take his eyes from her luscious body. Slowly, gracefully, she began to dance for him, humming softly for musical accompaniment. Her body was lithe, strong, her movements sure and precise yet fluid and unrestrained. She obviously had difficulty limiting her actions to the confines of the small cabin, but Lucien could easily imagine her dancing on a large stage. Although there was nothing intrinsically erotic to her routine, he found himself once again becoming aroused, this time quite uncontrollably, by the sight of her almost-nude body, by her closeness, and by the musky scent that emanated from her as she began to sweat in the confines of the little room. Her obvious desire of him, and, of course, the fact that the wine had done much to numb his inhibitions, only lessened his self-control.

He groaned and said her name, and she stopped dancing and came over to him. Kneeling down in front of him, she kissed him passionately on the mouth, at the same time unbuttoning first his jacket and then—very slowly—his shirt.

"No, we mustn't . . ." he started to protest, but she silenced him with another kiss, and he gave in to her ministrations. When she had removed his jacket and shirt, he felt terribly exposed and asked her to please turn out the gas lamp that still burned brightly overhead.

She did as she was bid, more or less—leaving the lamp turned very low so that they could still see each other, although the degree of darkness was so nearly complete that they almost seemed like illusions to one another. Eleanor then started to unbutton Lucien's trousers, but he pushed her hand away and fumbled to do it himself—although whether it was from the need to be assertive or because he was too embarrassed to have her hand brush his swollen manhood even Lucien couldn't have determined at that moment.

When at last they were lying naked together side by side, Eleanor took Lucien's hand and moved it over her own body.

166

She smiled in the darkness when she realized after a few seconds that he no longer needed her guidance and let her hands do some exploration of their own on his well-muscled body. He moaned with pleasure, keenly aware of his heightened sensitivity, feeling that he wanted this experience to last forever.

Suddenly, Eleanor began nibbling his earlobe, and the sensation was almost overwhelmingly exciting. Then, apparently realizing that this was, indeed, his initiation into the realm of carnal love and that his ardor wouldn't be contained much longer, she guided him into her moist body. The effect was electrifying, and within seconds his body began to arch and spasm, and he climaxed explosively.

As he lay in her arms, depleted, she gently stroked his back. After a few minutes, he tried to raise himself up, but she pressed him back to her. "Eleanor," he said finally, "I must go. I—this shouldn't have happened. I don't know what came over me."

She said nothing, merely continuing to stroke his back with her fingertips, then letting her hands wander onto his buttocks and thighs.

He gulped hard, then continued, "Please, Eleanor, I've got to get back to my room. I—damn it all! What kind of a man can I be, that I could have intercourse with another woman so soon after the death of the woman I loved? What kind of a monster am I?"

He began to sob, and Eleanor stopped fondling him and wrapped her arms tightly around his shoulders. "Oh, Lucien, Lucien," she whispered, "you aren't a monster! Don't you see? What we have done is an affirmation—a confirmation—of life. Yes, you loved Mary Eileen, and you would have been faithful to her, I'm sure, had she lived. But she's dead, Lucien. She's dead. And you're very much alive. Don't hate yourself for needing to experience all the joys of life! And don't hate me for having introduced you."

He stopped crying then, and let the impact of her words reach him. "Oh, Eleanor," he told her, "I couldn't ever hate you."

She smiled and kissed his forehead. "I'm glad. I wouldn't want you to have bad memories of me. You see, Lucien, despite what you may be thinking of me—that I'm a very worldly woman who has known many lovers—I've only known two other men. One was the man I was briefly

167

engaged to—until I found out that he was a drunkard—and the other man was someone I was very fond of, and very attracted to, but who wanted a commitment from me that I couldn't give because I very much want a career for a few more years. However, just because I didn't want to marry him didn't mean that I couldn't be his lover—which I was, until the troupe sailed for America. I miss him very much, and so you see, you have helped me with *my* loneliness as much as I've helped you with yours. Indeed, I've become very, very fond of you," she said, her voice becoming throaty.

Lucien took the initiative this time, taking her into his arms and kissing her fervently. Soon they were transported once again into the heights of ecstasy, and the real world and all of its cares ceased to exist. . . .

When Lucien woke early the next morning, finding himself lying naked in bed next to Eleanor, his first impulse was to dress hurriedly and run to find Father Cassidy, to ask the kindhearted priest to hear his confession. However, when he turned his head to gaze upon his still-sleeping companion, Lucien changed his mind. Propping himself up on one elbow, he stared down at the dancer, whose uncovered bosom rose and fell steadily with her deep breathing. Her porcelain skin was set off by her long raven hair, which was fanned out on the pillow, framing her striking face, with its prominent cheekbones. Her face was quite serene—indeed, a small smile seemed to play about her lips—and Lucien wondered why it was that he should feel so guilty about their night of lovemaking when she appeared so completely untroubled.

He sighed. She was so incredibly beautiful, so warm and generous, so much more mature than any woman her age he had ever met—not that he had met many, of course. He thought about Mary Eileen. True, she was only a few years younger than Eleanor, but in comparison, she was like a young child, she—

The impact of Mary Eileen's terrible death suddenly returned once again with tremendous force, and he began to sob uncontrollably. Eleanor immediately woke up and, correctly guessing what saddened Lucien so, said nothing but just wrapped her long arms around the youth. They lay there locked in each other's arms, rocking back and forth slightly as would a mother and child, until Lucien sniffed heavily and pushed himself back from her.

Embarrassed, he began to stammer, "I—I'm sorry, Eleanor. You must think me an awful baby, crying all the time."

"Nonsense! You have every reason to feel sad—and when I'm sad, I certainly cry, so why shouldn't you?" She smiled at him and kissed the tip of his nose, reddened from crying. "And if you're at all like me, crying makes you ravenous. What do you say to getting dressed and having an enormous breakfast?"

But Lucien shook his head to this suggestion. "No, I couldn't eat now, really I couldn't. I . . . I guess I—" He stopped, unable to express his thoughts, fearful that he would hurt her somehow.

"Go on, please, Lucien," Eleanor prompted.

"Oh, Eleanor! You've been so good to me! But I just want to be alone right now. You've made me all confused about so many things. I feel like half my judgments and values have been suddenly turned upside down, and I need time to myself to think things through."

"I understand," she said simply. "Well, go on, then. Perhaps we'll see each other to say good-bye before we dock in New York."

"I hope so," Lucien declared, as he reached down to the floor for his crumpled trousers and underclothes, pulling them on under the sheet. Somehow, he couldn't bear the thought of standing naked before her in the bright light of day. Then he jumped off the bed and quickly pulled on and buttoned his shirt, then his jacket. He was about to leave the cabin when he realized he was barefoot and—grinning in embarrassment— he rummaged around until he found his shoes and socks and jammed them on his feet.

He started out the door, but he turned and came back into the room. Striding to the bed, he looked down at Eleanor and softly told her, "I'll never forget you. . . ." Then, fighting back the lump in his throat, he retraced his steps and left the cabin, closing the door firmly behind him.

Lucien wandered up to the deck, and he was pleased to find himself quite alone. He presumed all the other passengers were either at breakfast or were—as he himself should be doing—packing their belongings.

He walked up to the rail and leaned against it, enjoying the bracing cold and the salt-tanged wind on his face. It helped clear away the dullness that lingered from the wine he had drunk the night before. It also, he admitted to himself, acted like a cold bath in reducing his ardor—which threatened to resurface whenever he thought about Eleanor.

He stood there for a long time, needing to come up with a rational justification for his actions. An emotional one just wouldn't do—he now prided himself on having become a sober, thoughtful, reasoning man who had outgrown his impetuous behavior of the year before. It was this aspect almost more than any other that disturbed him, and when he finally realized it, the feeling that he had sinned against his church was suddenly vastly diminished. After all, his father had been a passionate man—indeed, he had once overheard his parents talking, when they hadn't realized he was there, and they were reminiscing about how they had met. He recalled how upset and shocked he had been at the time to learn that they had known each other, in the Biblical sense, before their marriage. And, of course, many of the other students at St. Timothy's had boasted of their sexual prowess with some of the harlots in Dublin. He admitted to himself that had it not been for the fear of contracting some terrible disease, he, too, might have been initiated into carnal knowledge by one of these ladies for hire.

No, he now told himself with some relief, there was nothing wrong with what he and Eleanor had done last night. Of course, he still would have preferred that his first time would have been with Mary Eileen—he had loved her so!—but since that wasn't meant to be, he couldn't think of anyone he would rather have lain with than the beautiful young dancer.

He decided to seek her out, and smartly turning on his heel, he left the deck and went in search of her.

It was a very disappointed Lucien Bouchard who returned to his cabin. He had looked all over the ship for Eleanor but to his dismay couldn't find her anywhere. Finally, reluctantly, he decided he had best do his packing, and walked slowly down the corridor to his stateroom.

170

As he opened the door, something on the floor caught his eye. He was surprised to find a letter addressed to him on scented lilac-colored notepaper, apparently slipped under the door. Carefully opening the envelope with his thumbnail, Lucien was delighted to find it was from Eleanor. He began slowly to read.

My dearest Lucien:

As soon as you left me, I decided to pack my things and then spend the remainder of the voyage with a fellow dancer in her cabin. You see, I realized it would be best if we didn't meet again before we docked, despite what I had said earlier.

Lucien, as I told you, I have grown very fond of you—much too fond of you for my own good. For as I also told you, I want to pursue my career for a few years yet, and getting involved with a man at this time would be detrimental to my goals. Not only that, as you said yourself, we belong to two different worlds, and I'm sure your family would be quite dismayed if they thought you were becoming seriously attached to an entertainer. I'm quite aware that despite my antecedents, because I am a dancer, I am looked upon as little better than a whore—because, unfortunately, many ballet girls have done much to deserve that sobriquet.

There is another reason I prefer not to see you again as of now: I know you are a terribly decent young man, and as such, you are probably feeling that you are obligated to me. You may protest, when you read these words, that this just isn't the case, that your feelings for me are true and real. Well, dear Lucien, this may in fact be the case—but I believe that you are too ethical, and too much absorbed in the aftermath of our love-making, to be able to see the truth, should it be otherwise.

Therefore, I will stand by my decision. I will say my good-bye through this letter, rather than in person. I hope you will carry good memories of me and of our time together. Some day, if you find yourself in England—or if you wish to write to me, after I return home in about six months' time—my address is:

#12, Macclesfield Street
London, England

In the meanwhile, do take care of yourself, my dear Lucien. May you always find everything you seek.

Eleanor

Lucien stared numbly at the paper. Her flowery handwriting began to swim as tears came to his eyes.

"Good-bye, Eleanor," he finally whispered.

At the wharf in New York, Lucien—unencumbered except by his valise, for his trunk was coming by a later vessel—pushed his way through the disembarking throng to be among the first to reach a customs official. As a consequence, a few minutes later he was hailing a hansom cab and giving the driver the address of the brownstone on Gramercy Park.

It was drizzling, and the chill wind from the northeast reminded him of Dublin at its worst. All the same, it was wonderful to be back home, and he did not mind the weather. However, the rain began to fall in torrents when they were halfway to their destination, and the coachman drove the hansom cab under a viaduct and peered inside the carriage. "We'd best stay here for a spell, until the rain lets up. I can't see ten feet in front of me. I hope you don't mind the wait."

"No, I guess it can't be helped, though I do want to get home quickly."

Twenty minutes later, the rain abated, and the coachman started the horse at a trot. Shortly after nine o'clock that evening, he stopped his vehicle in front of the brownstone. Lucien jumped down to the ground and took his valise. Then, his eyes sparkling with eagerness, he resolutely strode toward the door.

Clarabelle Hendry opened it to him and uttered a startled cry. "Oh, my heavens! Why—Lucien—is it really you? I didn't know you were coming back from Dublin—"

"I—I had to, Clarabelle. Is Mother home? I don't suppose Father's back yet from Europe." He entered the foyer of the brownstone, set down his baggage, and looked around intently. How good it was to be back home; he'd almost forgotten how comfortable the house was, how spacious and cheerful. Outside, the weather was dreary even though the rain had slackened, but in here it was warm and snug and it was home.

"Oh, of course you don't know, Lucien—your mother had

to go back to Alabama. Something terrible happened there—there was an attack on the plantation, and poor Marius Thornton was shot and very seriously hurt," Clarabelle explained. "And no, your father isn't back yet from Europe; no one's had any word yet as to when he will be."

"Oh, my God!" Lucien exclaimed. "That's terrible news! Poor Mother—all by herself. I—I ought to go to Alabama and be with her; maybe I can help. What actually happened? Do you know, Clarabelle?"

Clarabelle reiterated all that she knew—which was little more than she and Laure had heard initially. She explained that Laure had written several letters, giving a few more details, but they were only sketchy. "So you see, so far they don't know who the men were, or what reason they had for doing what they did. Your mother asked me to look after the children while she was there. She was going to be met by Lopasuta."

"That's good. He's a fine lawyer, and perhaps his legal background will be of help. Besides, he used to live in that area, and he'll know what to look for." Lucien nodded, as if to himself. "Well, Clarabelle, I think I'd better get a good night's sleep and then see to making arrangements tomorrow to go to Alabama. Is Paul still up, do you know?"

"Yes, he is, Lucien. His friend David Cohen came over to do some homework with him, and they're both upstairs in Paul's room. But the girls and little John are all asleep."

"Good. I'll just go upstairs and say hello to Paul and David, then."

"Can I get you something to eat? You look so tired. . . . What did happen to make you come back, Lucien, if you don't mind my asking, and if I'm not prying into your affairs?" the kindly woman urged.

Lucien bit his lips and was silent for a moment. Then, with a philosophical shrug, he declared, "Well, Clarabelle, I may as well tell you. I'd fallen in love with a very sweet girl there, Mary Eileen Brennert—perhaps Mother mentioned her to you, from my letters."

"Oh, yes, I recall. Your mother was so happy that you'd found someone nice."

"She was wonderful." Then, as swiftly and painlessly as he could, Lucien recounted all the tragic events that led to his decision to come home.

"Oh, you poor lad, how horrible! I'm so sorry for you, Lucien—how terrible it must have been. I certainly understand now why you wanted to come home. . . . You must have felt so lost. . . ."

"Yes, lost and empty, Clarabelle. I did meet some nice people on the voyage home—that was a comfort. But now that I know that Mother has some trouble on her hands, I definitely want to try to help; it might also get my mind off my own problems. As for food—well," he grinned, "John's not the only one who likes your cocoa. I remember that you always made the best cocoa in the world, Clarabelle."

She brightened, although there was a suspicious moisture in her eyes as she patted his arm. "You go ahead and see Paul and David, Lucien, and I'll come up with a tray of cocoa and some slices of cake I baked just this noon."

"Thank you, Clarabelle. You don't know how good it is to be home again!"

"And it's good to have you here, Lucien," Clarabelle warmly replied. "Now you go on up, and I'll be there presently."

"Thanks, I really appreciate your concern."

"But it's my duty—and besides, you know how I love your mother and all of you," the kindhearted widow exclaimed, almost as if indignant at being praised for work that she found intensely gratifying and fulfilling.

Lucien could not trust himself to speak, but smiled and nodded to her and then went up the stairs.

He knocked at Paul's door and was eagerly told, "Come in, come in!" When he opened the door, both Paul and David turned, and Paul let out a joyous cry as he rushed forward to take Lucien's hand, before yielding to the impulse to give his elder brother a hug. "Lucien! We never in the world expected you to come back so soon! Is school over?"

"Well—it is for me. I had to come." He turned to Paul's companion. "Good to see you again, David." Lucien thrust out his hand, and David Cohen warmly shook it. Then Lucien turned back to his younger brother.

"You know, I remember how anxious you were to follow me over the ocean and go to school in Ireland the way I did. Well, I'm here to tell you that, while the school is wonderful, you'll be much happier right here at home."

174

"But why do you say that, Lucien?" Paul was mystified.

"Well, when you make some close friends and something happens to them, no matter how much at home you thought you were, you suddenly feel yourself a stranger in that place. That's what happened to me. I'll tell you more about it when I'm rested," Lucien laconically responded. Then, turning to David, he asked, "How're your father and mother and Rachel?"

"They're just great, thanks," David smiled and answered. He gave Paul a quizzical glance, then turned back to Lucien. "By the way, did you see your stepfather in Europe? You know, the other night I overheard my father telling my mother about some peculiar bills from abroad. Naturally, I wondered—"

"I did see Father. He took the *Aurania* and disembarked at Cobh. He came to visit Mary Eileen and me, took us to dinner, and then he went on. He said he was going to London, Berlin, Paris, and Vienna. Clarabelle said no one's heard from him."

"No, no one has. And my father sounded a little worried," David replied.

"I see." Lucien frowned, not knowing exactly what to make of this remark. "Well, tomorrow morning I'll go see your father at the office. Besides, I've got to make plans to go on to Alabama to see Mother."

"I wish I could go with you," Paul replied. "I know there's been some trouble at the plantation. Clarabelle told us about it after Mother had to leave so suddenly."

"Well, it sounds a bit dangerous. I'm going down there to try to help Mother, essentially—but it will give me something to do and think about. The way I feel right now . . . I—I need that."

David eyed the older youth and sympathetically asked, "Do you want to tell us? I can see from your face you aren't at all happy. . . ."

"No, I'm not." Once more, Lucien had to dredge up the courage to overcome the pain caused by detailing the events of that fateful day in Dublin. When he finished telling his story, the two younger boys remained quiet for a long moment, staring down at their feet.

Finally David groaned, "How horrible for you! Poor Lucien!"

"That's awful!" Paul helplessly shook his head. "I know words don't mean very much, but I'm so terribly sorry."

Lucien sighed, then put his hand on his younger brother's shoulder. "Thanks, Paul, I appreciate your feelings. . . . I think I hear Clarabelle." There was a knock at the door, and Lucien hurried to open it. The governess entered with a tray on which were placed three cups of steaming cocoa and three slices of chocolate cake. And for the moment, all the problems and pain were forgotten.

Chapter Fifteen

Lucien Bouchard did not sleep well that night, despite the fatigue that assailed him. His mind was tortured not only by recollections of Mary Eileen Brennert, but now by a fresh and new burning wound, which had opened with the thought that his mother might be facing the terrors of men as unscrupulous and criminal as the Ku Klux Klan. Even though Lopasuta was there to help her, Lucien felt that as her son, as a member of the family, he himself should be on hand. If there was anything that his experience with Mary Eileen had left him with, it was a fervent desire and need to go to the aid of those he loved.

At dawn, he flung aside the covers, made his ablutions, and quickly dressed, then went down to the kitchen to prepare his own breakfast. He had learned from Paul the night before about Kerry Dugan's having been hired as a coachman, and he intended to ask the man to drive him to his stepfather's office. He felt it was important that he talk to Jacob Cohen before making arrangements to leave for Alabama.

He had not bothered to unpack, and that, as it turned out, would be an advantage. Once he determined to join his mother, there would be little time for dallying. He did not know the train schedule, but he estimated that it would take at least two full days to reach Montgomery.

Impatiently, he waited until about eight-thirty, when he assumed that the coachman would be awake and have had his breakfast, and then went to the coach house and knocked at the door of his upstairs rooms. The genial young Irishman opened the door at once. Lucien explained who he was, and the man exclaimed, "Mr. Lucien, is it? I thought you were supposed to be in Ireland!"

"I was, Mr. Dugan; I just got home last night. I wonder if I could ask you to drive me uptown to my father's office as soon as possible."

"Sure, and it'll be me pleasure, Mr. Lucien. Just wait till I get me suspenders on—there now. And me top coat. Okay, then, let's be off."

Lucien followed the coachman down the stairs and into the stable. Kerry Dugan quickly hitched the gelding to the carriage, and Lucien was about to climb inside when he realized that his sisters and brothers would be up by now. He bade Kerry wait while he reentered the kitchen, where he found all four of them at the table, with Clarabelle Hendry serving bacon and eggs to them. Briefly, he explained that he was going to Leland's office, and if all went well, he would go directly from there to the train station, to embark for Alabama as quickly as he could. With a cry of protest, little John got down from his chair and ran to hug his eldest brother's knees, while Celestine and Clarissa came to give him a farewell kiss. Then, shaking hands with Paul, Lucien swiftly turned and went to the waiting carriage.

He had taken with him the cash from the bank draft, carefully concealed in a section of his valise with only a moderate amount in his wallet. It would have to be converted to American money again, of course, but Jacob Cohen could probably arrange for that quickly enough. It would also be a good idea to buy an extra suit of clothes or two and some underwear and shirts. And perhaps he should have another valise to carry them in. The fact was that he had really outgrown a good deal of his old attire, and he had not taken pains to replace his wardrobe while in Dublin.

Kerry Dugan deposited him in front of the building where Leland had his suite of offices, and asked if he should wait. "No, thank you, Mr. Dugan. I'll spend some time here with Mr. Cohen, and then, after taking a short time to buy some clothes, I'll go right to the train station. It's not too far from here, I know. There's no sense in your waiting around for me."

"Well, then, I'll be wishing you the best—and give me regards to your dear mother. What a wonderful woman she is!"

Lucien brightened at the compliment and nodded. "I'll tell her, Mr. Dugan; she'll be happy to hear from you. Yes, she is wonderful—and I have to go to her and help her because things are very bad in Alabama. Please look after my brothers and sisters—and Clarabelle and Mrs. Emmons.''

"I certainly will, you can count on it. Well, then, I'll be seeing you when I see you—isn't that about right, Mr. Lucien?''

Lucien nodded and waved, and then he went into the building.

Jacob Cohen had come to work early this morning and was already busy in his office. When he heard the front door open, he hurried out of his office to greet the visitor, assuming that it would be the woman whom he had just hired to act as receptionist and secretary and who was to start this very morning. He stopped short when he saw Lucien Bouchard and uttered a shout of welcome. "*Boychik!* When my David told me this morning that you were home, I could scarce believe my ears. It is so good to see you—but I understand there has been trouble with you, and for that I am sorry.''

"Thank you, Mr. Cohen, I appreciate that. . . . And I wonder if I might talk with you in private. I'll tell you all about it, but I'm going to leave for Alabama as soon as I can. I want to be with Mother—you know about the trouble she's having down there, the attack and all.''

"I do know,'' Jacob reflectively rubbed his chin, "but I wonder whether it's any place for a young lad like yourself.''

"After the past couple of weeks, I think I feel equal to it, Mr. Cohen.''

"Yes, after what has happened, I think it's right that you should go, if only to see your mother again. It has been a long time. But you will be careful, won't you? Let Lopasuta handle matters, and you concentrate on taking care of your mother.''

"I will.''

"Good. Now, come into my office, *boychik*,'' Jacob affectionately said. With an arm around the youth's shoulders, he led him into his office and closed the door. "Tell me the story in your own way, if you've a mind to.''

Lucien sank into the chair that Jacob held out for him and briefly related the episode of Mary Eileen's tragic death. Jacob, seated across from the sad youth, sighed and closed his eyes. After a pause, he said slowly, "It was dreadful that you had to endure something like that, for someone you

179

loved. These senseless riots, this bloodshed—*Gottenyu*, Miriam and I knew what that was back in Kiev, when the Czar sent his Cossacks out in pogroms against our people. There was such terror and fear, and one never knew where they would strike next. *Boychik*, I understand why you came back now, and why you don't shrink from going to Windhaven. Do you need any money?''

"No, you see, Father visited me in Dublin some weeks back, and he gave me a very large draft. That reminds me—Mr. Cohen, most of my money is in English pounds. Could you take me to the bank and get an exchange for me?''

"Of course. We'll go directly, before it gets too crowded.''

"And I think I'd better buy some new clothes because I only have my heavy winter suits, and my trunk from Dublin hasn't yet arrived. I also need a sturdy pair of work shoes. Then I have to go over to Grand Central Station and see what train I can take.''

"Now, don't fret. I'll handle everything for you. In fact, I'm really glad you've come.'' Jacob shook his head and placed his fingertips together, pressing them firmly and staring at them for a moment. "Lucien—may I ask you a question? You saw your father when he was abroad. Did he—was he acting at all . . . strangely? I don't mean to alarm you; there's nothing really wrong, I'm sure. But I was just wondering—''

"Well, if you want to know the truth, Mr. Cohen,'' Lucien replied, "he *was* very strange when he took Mary Eileen and me to dinner at a fine place in Dublin. I thought perhaps he was a little—well, tipsy. But, he wasn't. And then he gave me all this money, telling me I should spend the summer in Europe. Well, the money came in very handy when I decided to come back home after what happened, it's true, but . . .''

"Yes, I can imagine it would. And speaking of money, as long as you're here, I'd like to be frank with you. Running the risk of overstepping my bounds, I'll tell you in confidence that Leland has done a few strange things I really don't understand. For example, when he went on the *Aurania*, he got into a card game, and he lost quite a bit of money. He signed I.O.U.'s on the backs of his business cards, and already the representatives of those three men to whom he lost the money have come in here and demanded payment. Of course, I had to honor the debts, but I don't understand why he would let them come out of business expenses. I thought

180

he had enough cash with him. Well, I just don't understand it. And he sent me a cable last week, telling me some of the purchases he's made. *Heiliger Gott!* Some of the things he's bought I don't know that we can sell at all here in this country. I hope he'll be back soon to explain, because he's spent so much money, and not too much has come in lately. Forgive me for speaking this way, my boy. I'm sure you understand it's out of concern.''

"Yes. But I'm as much in the dark as you are, Mr. Cohen.''

"Well, we won't get any answers by sitting here, *boychik*. Let me take you to the bank, and then we'll go over to the Douglas Department Store. Leland thinks highly of the place. Before he left, he sent me over there and insisted I buy a very expensive new suit, coat, and hat and charge it to the firm. He's a very generous man, perhaps too generous. But, I'm sure there must be an explanation, and when he comes back we'll work it out. Don't you trouble yourself about that. First things first. We've got to get you off in style to Alabama. And once we find out about the trains, maybe you can have lunch with me.''

"I'd like that very much, Mr. Cohen.''

"Wait'll I put my coat and hat on,'' he said, rising from his chair. "Then we'll go attend to our chores. Don't worry, *boychik*, we'll have you with your mother in no time.''

They exchanged the currency at the bank and then walked to the Douglas Department Store, where Lucien was completely outfitted for his journey. Then Jacob and Lucien took a hansom cab to Grand Central Station, where they learned that a train bound for Montgomery via Washington and points south would leave at four that afternoon and would arrive two days later. Once again, he considered sending a wire to his mother, but realized that it could only raise more questions than it would answer. She had enough to concern her at the plantation, without his adding to her burden. He would appear at Windhaven in two days' time, when he could explain everything.

"Good!'' Jacob declared, when all the arrangements had been made. "I think we have time now for lunch. I know a nice kosher restaurant that serves good food—''

181

"That would be nice, but I insist that you be my guest," Lucien firmly declared.

"I'd rather make it Dutch treat." David's father grinned.

"Oh, no, Mr. Cohen. I owe you a good lunch and then some for all you've done for me. Incidentally, I hope you won't mind, but I want to ask you more about these bills of my father's, the ones you mentioned this morning when I came in."

"I understand. They're very troubling. I'm really at a loss to comprehend why he's bought some of the things he has in Europe, because I don't think there's any market for them here." Jacob had a worried look on his face as he hailed a hansom cab and directed the driver to take them to his favorite restaurant.

Lucien Bouchard was grateful for this opportunity to spend some time with David's father. He found the elder Cohen a warmhearted, concerned, and interested friend, and he was certain that the business could not be in better hands. The man was as wise as he was levelheaded. Midway through lunch, Lucien asked, "What do you make of Father's behavior? I've told you about how he behaved toward Mary Eileen and me. He really embarrassed us both. And I know he wasn't drunk."

"No, Leland isn't a heavy drinker at all. I don't know what it is. Maybe it's nothing more than overwork. I know that he's been driving himself to expand his business ever since he married your mother. I also know that that's perfectly understandable—your mother is a wonderful woman, so he would naturally try to do the very best he could for her. That is certainly normal behavior. As for his purchases for the business—well, I think he'll be able to explain how he plans to sell them—even though I cannot see their value at all. Those statuettes, for instance. At this point I don't even know where I will store them when I get them!" Jacob shook his head and uttered a doleful sigh.

"Well, maybe when he returns home, the sea voyage will calm him down and give him a chance to rest," Lucien hazarded.

"I certainly hope so." Jacob sighed again. "You see, Mr. Bouchard—"

"Is it Mr. Bouchard all of a sudden?" Lucien smiled. "To

what do I own the honor of that mode of address, which makes me feel older than I really am?''

"*Boychik,*" David Cohen's father looked steadily at the handsome youth across the table from him, "you have aged, whether you know it or not. What's happened to you in Ireland has made you a *Mensch,* and though it's been a terrible sorrow for you, it has given you courage and heart and strength, which you couldn't have had if you'd been tucked away in some private school in America and kept away from all that's going on in the world. There's some good to be found in everything, even when you think it's all evil. I feel badly about the loss of your Mary Eileen. I'm sure she was a wonderful girl, or you wouldn't have been attracted to her. But even in this tragedy, there is the hand of the Almighty, there is His purpose, and this is a test for you. This is the only way you must look at it, Lucien. I talk to you as I would to my David.''

"I'm very grateful. I like you very much, Mr. Cohen. And your David has been a wonderful friend to Paul."

"*Ach,* the way we talk, you would think we were two old women. Stop it, now. Let's be sensible,'' Jacob blew his nose with a handkerchief, then tried to put on a stern frown to show that he had not the least sentiment in the world. "I like you too, *boychik.* I think you will have a wonderful future. Well now,'' he said, taking out his watch and scowling at it as if he were angry at the time it told, "it's nearly three o'clock. We'd best get you down to the station so you'll have plenty of time to settle into your train before it leaves. And when you come back, I'd be very pleased to have you over for dinner—a dinner in your honor!''

"I promise you I'll let you know when I'm home. I only hope I can do Mother some good down there."

Jacob accompanied Laure's son to Grand Central Station and saw him aboard the train. Then, walking slowly out of the station on his way back to the offices of Kenniston & Co., he shook his head and said gloomily to himself, "I only pray that everything will be all right—that he will come through all this, and so will his mother, and I hope, Leland, too. May the Almighty bless them all and keep them safe from harm!''

Lopasuta Bouchard sat on the veranda at Windhaven Plantation, deep in thought. It felt good to be back at the place that held so many special, happy memories for him . . . but it troubled him deeply that his visit should have been necessitated by something as tragic as the attack on this beloved plantation.

It was an inauspicious welcome back to Lowndesboro, he thought, as he treated himself to a cigar while he sat on the stone steps. He was only in shirt sleeves, for while it was cool, the sun was shining, and it was the kind of weather he enjoyed. Finally, when he had finished his cigar and felt he had revived all the memories he cared to of his work as a lawyer in these parts, he rose and started to go back inside.

Just as he was about to open the door, however, Dalbert Sattersfield rode up the gravel drive, dismounted, and tethered his brown mare to the hitching post. The two men greeted each other warmly, and Lopasuta invited Dalbert to join him in some coffee.

"I could definitely stand a cup, and a bit of conversation, too, Lopasuta," Dalbert said as he climbed the steps of the veranda. "I've been doing a lot of thinking, and Mitzi's been talking to me, too. She's concerned for Laure, as am I, so I figure it wouldn't do any harm for me to stay around here for a short spell, till we see what's going to happen. Even though I've only got one arm, I'm still a crack shot. By the way, are there any weapons in the chateau? Do the workers have any?"

"Not too many. There are a couple of rifles in the cotton gin shed, hidden away there, and some ammunition. There are also two rifles in the study closet on the first floor, and enough ammunition for those. As a matter of fact, just yesterday I asked some of the tenant-workers here if they had any weapons on hand to protect themselves, and there isn't much. Ezekiel West has only an old Confederate saber that he got from his former master, and Doug Larson has just a pistol and a hunting knife. That's not exactly a match for a dozen men who might be armed and bent on mischief, but it'll have to do for the time being."

"Perhaps you ought to go into town and get some more rifles and ammunition from my store, Lopasuta," Dalbert suggested. "By the way, what about those three men you hired?"

"They're due to arrive here this afternoon sometime. There's an empty cottage at the southeast corner of the estate, and the three of them can bunk there. Fortunately it's been quiet ever since we got here.''

"Thank God for that,'' Dalbert exhaled with a sigh of relief. ''How's Marius?''

Lopasuta shook his head, a glum expression on his face. "Not good at all. Dr. Kennery was here last night, and he doesn't like the looks of that wound. The bullet entered in a bad place, and Marius lost a lot of blood. He's still very weak. Apparently because he'd been overworking himself before he was injured, he wasn't in the best physical condition, and so the wound is more serious than it would normally be. I'm really concerned about it, and so is Laure. He had a very restless night—in fact, I guess he was delirious, because he kept calling for his Clemmie.''

Dalbert sympathetically shook his head. "It's no wonder. They had such a happy life together with all the children.'' He fell silent a moment, then said, ''I don't even like to think such things, but if he should die, which pray God he won't, what will become of his children?''

"I've already discussed that with Laure, although she doesn't want to think about it either. Still, it's best to face reality,'' Lopasuta gravely replied. "Ezekiel West and his wife, Marva, say they'd be glad to look after them—actually, they've been doing so ever since poor Marius suffered that wound. West has two grown ones of his own, and they both like the children and get along with them fine.''

"That's a blessing. But let's hope it doesn't come to that. Well now, I'll go in and see Marius shortly, but I think I'll take that cup of coffee first.''

"Let's go into the kitchen. Laure's there discussing things with Benjamin Brown while Amelia cooks him some breakfast.''

When the two men entered the kitchen, Laure rose from the table. "What a nice surprise, Dalbert! I didn't expect to see you again so soon.''

"I got to thinking, Laure, that because I know this area pretty well and also a lot of the folks who live in Montgomery, I might just latch on to something that'll help solve this nasty business.''

"Do you think anything more is going to happen?'' Her voice was low and unsteady.

"I shouldn't be surprised. I don't want to alarm you or get you to worrying, Laure, believe me. But I'm a realist,'' he

185

said, and shrugged. Then his face became grave. "I hear Marius is doing poorly."

Laure turned away and bit her lip. "He doesn't look at all good, I'm afraid. I'm beginning to expect the worst. He's so very feverish, and he keeps calling for Clemmie. Dr. Kennery gave him another sedative last night and some medicine besides, but he's very worried, too." She paused and sighed. "Perhaps he'll respond to you, Dalbert."

"Let's hope so," Dalbert replied, and he quickly downed the cup of coffee. Then he rose and went to Marius's room, where Marius lay on a sweat-soaked bed. Laure, ill at ease, twisting her hands nervously, followed Dalbert as the one-armed mayor gently opened the door and entered.

Elinor Larson was seated by the bedside, applying a cold, wet cloth to Marius's forehead. She looked up at Laure and Dalbert and explained, "I thought I'd take over from Tess Gregory, nursing him a spell. I feel it's the least I can do, since he was willing to risk his life to protect all of us," she said in a soft but urgent whisper.

"That's very thoughtful of you, Mrs. Larson," Laure murmured back with a pallid smile. "But I'll stay with him, now. I'm sure your family needs you."

"Thank you, ma'am. But I'll come back and spell you again later." She rose and quietly left the room.

Laure took the vacated chair, then leaned forward and took one of Marius's thin, callused hands between hers. "Dear Marius," she murmured, "we're all praying for you. You must get well and come back to us. You're family to us, Marius."

Slowly, laboriously, his eyes opened. His gaze wandered first to Laure and then to Dalbert, who stood at the foot of the bed, grasping one of the posts with his hand, trying to muster a smile that would cheer the critically wounded foreman.

"Clemmie, I can't hardly see you! You're so far away. . . ." Marius murmured in a weak, halting voice. He tried to turn his head, and Laure at once squeezed his hand and anxiously declared, "Please do rest, Marius; don't fret yourself so. You have to give yourself time to get well, you know."

"Clemmie! I love you so! You're so far away now. . . . Clemmie—the children are fine, but we miss you so very much. . . ."

Laure uttered a stifled groan of anguish and turned to

Dalbert, whispering, "He's delirious again. It's just dreadful! I wish Dr. Kennery were here—"

"There's not much he could do, Laure," Dalbert gently said. "If, as you say, he's been this way for a whole week now, it's clear he's certainly not improving any. He just doesn't seem to have the will to fight. Poor fellow . . . it's a shame. I've always respected him and admired him."

Laure suddenly burst into tears. "Oh, Marius, don't you recognize me? It's Laure—Laure Kenniston! Please look at me, dear Marius!" she plaintively entreated.

Marius Thornton sighed, and his head turned slowly toward Laure. Then his eyes seemed to clear, and he saw her as if for the first time. "Miz Laure! My, it's good to see you. I was just thinking . . . 'bout Clemmie, you know."

"Yes—yes, dear Marius. I—I know." Laure's voice was choked with tears.

He closed his eyes again for a moment, and then, his voice fainter than ever, he falteringly said, "Tried my best . . . shouldn't have had trash like them coming here burning and shooting and scaring folks to death . . . I tried so hard . . . tried to drive them away when they came . . . got in the way— in the way of a . . . bullet. Didn't mean to . . . sorry, Miz Laure—"

"Oh, Marius, please don't! Don't try to talk about it. It wasn't your fault; everybody knows that. You've made Windhaven what it is now, and you can be proud of it—just as Luke is proud of you and watches down over you. Please rest and get well, dear Marius!" Laure's tears streaked her anguished face. Dalbert Sattersfield, deeply moved, stood behind her and stared at the suddenly frail-looking black man who had given so many of his years to the cultivation of Windhaven's soil.

"My chill'in . . . are they here now? Haven't seen them for days . . . I think. . . ." Marius's voice was growing progressively fainter. His strength was flagging, and Laure gripped both his hands in hers and stared at him, willing him to live with all her strength as the tears rolled unchecked down her cheeks.

"Clemmie's chill'in . . . sweetest there ever was . . . 'cause she was so sweet . . . herself. . . . Things gettin' dark now, Miz Laure. I think my Clemmie . . . I think she's— yes, she's—she's . . . waitin'. . . ."

187

He uttered a long sigh; his eyes closed, and his head turned slightly to one side.

Laure bowed her head and sobbed. Dalbert came forward quickly to put his arm around her shoulders and to stare at the serene face of the man whose life Luke Bouchard had saved so many years before and who had paid him back so many times over by his diligent stewardship of the land entrusted to his charge.

"He'll see his Clemmie in heaven, Laure," Dalbert consolingly murmured. "We'll bury him next to her, over on that easy stretch of land leading up to the bluff."

"Yes, Dalbert—that would be perfect. And pray God that his gentle spirit, like those of Lucien and Dimarte and my Luke, will watch over Windhaven Plantation in the long years to come, even when you and I have gone to join them," Laure whispered, as she released Marius's hands and slowly rose, crushed in grief.

Chapter Sixteen

It was a dreary late afternoon in mid-March when the train bearing Lucien Bouchard from New York pulled into the Montgomery station. During the two days he had ridden the train, he had had ample time to mull over all the events he had experienced during the past month—the happy memories overshadowed by the irrevocable loss of his first love. He was almost grateful that he was now embarked upon a mission to bring what solace and help he could to his beloved mother, for he realized that this alone could distract him from the morbid anguish that had stricken him at the very moment the stray bullet had pierced Mary Eileen Brennert's body. When he had held her in his arms, he had believed that his own life, too, was coming to an end—or at least changing in a direction so unpredictably new and dolorous that he could not even bear to think of it. Now, however, in the aftermath of the tragedy, reality had set in. The long train trip had forced his attention again on what was taking place around him. And instead of continuing his self-absorption, he found himself wondering how he might contribute to his family's welfare.

He was carrying his valise and a new suitcase containing the clothes he had purchased at the Douglas Department Store. Wearing his new topcoat, he looked the latest word in fashion. He stood gazing around the station, trying to acclimate himself. Some of the passengers who had got off with him were mounting horses or climbing into buggies, or simply meeting relatives—embracing and kissing them, with the excited conversation that always comes with family reunions. No one was expecting him, and it was a gray day with the prospect of rain—yet because he knew he would soon be reunited with his mother, he felt more cheerful than he had been since the day of Mary Eileen's death.

Rousing himself from his reverie, Lucien realized that the other passengers had driven off by now; it was a quarter of an hour after he had descended from the train car. The friendly stationmaster, seeing him still standing there, his luggage at his side, solicitously asked, "Mister, ain't you got no one comin' for you?"

"No, I'm not expected. Is there a horse and buggy for hire that'll drive me to Lowndesboro?"

"That's a mighty far trip, but over there—that there driver seems to be asleep on his seat. Can't say I think much of the old horse he's got, but it might get you there, if you're not in a hurry."

"Thank you. I'll go ask him." Lucien stooped to retrieve his bags and walked slowly off toward the waiting horse and buggy. The driver—a man in his late forties, wizened and with a straggly, gray beard—was indeed asleep. Lucien cleared his throat. "Er . . . excuse me, driver. Would you like a fare, driver?"

The man came to with a start, looked wildly about, then glanced down and sheepishly grinned. "Guess I must have been taking a little catnap. Sure, I'd like one. Where're you bound for, mister?"

"Do you know Windhaven Plantation—it's that tall, red-brick house near Lowndesboro, along the Alabama River?" Lucien inquired.

"Sure do. But, it'll cost you . . . hmm, three dollars."

"That's a fair price. All right, I'm for it," Lucien cheerfully exclaimed as he put his luggage inside, then clambered in and settled back with a contented sigh. He knew the journey would take about two hours, or perhaps as many as three, since after all the horse did look old and none too sturdy. If it had not been for his luggage, he would have enjoyed riding a horse to the plantation—feeling the solid earth beneath the horse's hooves, enjoying air that was still cool, but redolent with just a hint of the spring to come. He would definitely have to ride, once he was settled at the plantation, for he had not done so in a long time. But for now, he was glad to relax, and he leaned back in the comfortable seat of the buggy, his back well supported by the padding.

The driver had kept up the carriage and seen that it was spotlessly clean and polished.

"We'll take the main street, mister, and then head southward at the edge of town," the man called back to him.

"That sounds about right. I'd like to see the city—I've been away from it for a few years."

"That so? You visitin' the folks at that place you mentioned? That's where the Bouchards are, you know."

"I know. I'm a Bouchard. I'm coming to see my mother, who's here now. She came down from New York—that's where we've been living lately." Somehow, this friendly exchange of confidences helped momentarily ease the nagging desolation of Lucien's thoughts.

"Well now, I'll be bound!" The driver looked back again with a friendly nod. "Seems to me I recall your daddy. Drove him a couple of times. Wasn't the name Luke Bouchard?"

"You knew my father?" Lucien eagerly leaned forward.

"'Deed I did! Fact is, though he rode horseback himself a lot, once in a while he needed my services here in town, when he was off on an errand for something. He was a fine man. He was the one took the bullet meant for the governor. . . ."

"Yes."

"So you're his son! It's a small world, ain't it? Well now, if I don't get you home inside of two and a half hours, my name ain't Jethro Elderberry," the man grinned. "You just settle back and be comfy now."

They headed down the main street, and suddenly a horse and buggy came at them from the intersection at the right. Jethro, muttering an oath under his breath, reined in his horse, then grumbled, "Road hog! Fancy new rig 'n all, showin' off! Sorry if I jostled you, Mr. Bouchard."

"It's all right."

They were stopped in front of a small hotel, which was opposite the large general store. Two men were seated in chairs on the hotel's porch. One of them was Bodine Evans—whose duties as hotel clerk were hardly onerous these days, and who took every advantage of the slack trade to lounge about and see what was going on outside. The man next to him was gaunt-faced Cyrus Williams, the barber. His new assistant was doing so well that he had decided to grant himself an extra day off every week, and this was the day. He

191

and Evans were drinking buddies, and they had already tucked away three or four small whiskeys at a saloon farther down the street.

"Look what we got here." Evans pointed to the buggy carrying Lucien Bouchard. "A real dandy!" Then, raising his voice, he called out, "Where're you bound for, sonny?"

"To Windhaven, down near Lowndesboro," Lucien replied, a friendly smile on his face.

Evans scowled, turning to Cyrus Williams. "You hear that, Cy? Goin' to see them nigger-lovin' Bouchards. Wonder if they've learned a lesson—"

"Keep your voice down, you fool!" Cyrus Williams muttered to him. "You want it spread all over town that we know what happened last month?"

Jethro was about to shake the reins and urge his horse to continue the journey, but Lucien had heard the clerk's scurrilous remark and bade the driver wait. Irritated, he turned to stare at the towheaded, lanky Evans and called back, "What do you mean by that remark? My name's Lucien Bouchard, and I don't like what you're saying about my family."

"Oh, don't you now, sonny?" Evans sneered as he rose from his chair. He put his hands on his hips and strutted like a pouter pigeon up and down the plank porch. Peering intently at Lucien, he said, "And just what is your relation to them folks, sonny?"

"Luke Bouchard was my father, God rest his soul."

"Oh," the man laughed, "the biggest nigger-lover of them all!"

Lucien turned pale with rage. Glancing at Jethro Elderberry, he snapped, "Just stop here a few minutes. I can't let that man get away with such talk."

"Now take it easy, Mr. Bouchard; you don't want any trouble your first day back." The driver tried to placate the angry youth, but Lucien was having none of it. Climbing down out of the buggy, he advanced toward Bodine Evans. "You'll take it back about my father."

"Like hell, I will, you young punk. Everybody in town knows how them niggers live there easy as you please, payin' no rent, livin' high off the hog, maybe even eatin' at the same table with all them Bouchards. . . . God-fearing white folks don't really cotton to that sort of thing here in Montgomery,

Mister Bouchard.'' Evans sarcastically emphasized the title with a mocking sneer.

All the pent-up anguish and resentment that Lucien had felt over the unjust death of Mary Eileen now burst within him like a broken blood vessel. Clenching his right fist, he swung at Evans and connected on the clerk's jaw, felling him.

"Hey, now!" Cyrus Williams got up from his chair, his eyes wide with alarm. He quickly stepped forward to try to act as peacemaker. "You've got no cause to do that to my friend Bodine!"

"You keep out of this, or you'll get some of the same!" Lucien panted.

"Lord-a-mercy!" Jethro Elderberry groaned, as he steered the horse over to the curb and then leaned forward to watch the fracas.

Bodine Evans had righted himself and now, snarling angrily, came at Lucien, with both fists clenched. He lunged out with his left and, in a moment of blind rage, was able to drive his right fist against Lucien's left cheekbone, momentarily staggering the youth. But this pain served only to incite Lucien to even more furious retaliation: With a flurry of punches, he sent Evans sprawling and rolling over on the ground, groaning and panting, "I had enough! All right, I had enough!"

"Let him be!" Williams whined. "You got no call to pick a fight like that—"

"I told you, if you want some too, come ahead!" Lucien waved his right fist and glared at the gaunt-faced barber.

"Hell, I ain't gettin' myself involved with Bodine's fight, I reckon,'' Williams finally shrugged. Then he stooped to help the disheveled, semi-conscious clerk to his feet.

As he did so, Lucien angrily exclaimed, "I don't ever want to hear any more talk from either of you about the Bouchards! Just because we happen to treat people fairly and decently, it gives you no cause to make slurs and slanders on our name. You remember that. If I hear anything like that again, you and your friend will get a lot worse."

"Hell, I didn't say a word, mister," Williams whined again. "Come on, Bodine, let's get you some whiskey. You took an awful lickin' there."

"I'll get even with him," Evans muttered for only his friend to hear. He shot Lucien Bouchard a look of venomous

hatred as the youth got back into the buggy and gestured to
Jethro to resume the journey.

"Here you be, Mr. Bouchard," Jethro Elderberry enthusiastically exclaimed as he drew the horse to a halt in front of the
Windhaven chateau. "I'll give you a hand with your bags."

"Thank you, that's nice of you. Only, really, I can manage—
they're not too heavy, just clothes," Lucien said with a
smile.

But Jethro had already gotten down from his perch and,
opening the buggy door, reached in for the nearest piece of
luggage, then grabbed the suitcase that the youth had bought
at the Douglas Department Store. "It's my pleasure, Mr.
Bouchard," he said quietly. "Did me a heap of good to see
you tackle that redneck white trash with his insults to your
dad. Now I knew your dad, like I told you, and he was a fine
man, and if there were more men like him in this world, we
wouldn't have all this hate and wars and stuff like that. No,
sir, it did my heart good to see you stretch him on the ground
there."

"I—that's kind of you to say, Mr. Elderberry. I'm grateful
to you."

"No, sir, it's the other way around," the buggy driver
insisted, as he walked with Lucien toward the stately oak
door, with its gleaming brass knocker.

"Mr. Elderberry, you've given me something much more
than a ride; you've given me wonderful knowledge I can be
proud of: that other people who knew my father loved him as
I did."

Jethro Elderberry set down the suitcases and turned to the
youth. He put out his hand, and Lucien shook it. "I'm proud
to know you, too, Lucien Bouchard, mighty proud. There're
some people around Montgomery who might not like the
Bouchards, but you can count me among those who do—and
I'll bet there're lots more like me. A privilege, Mr. Bouchard.
Hope I'll be seeing you again. You made the sun shine for me
today, I don't mind telling you." With a wave of his hand,
the wizened driver went back to the buggy, climbed onto the
perch, took up the reins, and started back to Montgomery.

Lucien, deeply touched, watched him disappear down the
road they had taken, and then, blinking his eyes quickly, for
there were tears in them, he took a deep breath, reached for

the brass knocker, and struck three times, feeling that even though it was his home—indeed, that Windhaven Plantation was legally his as his legacy from Luke—it had been so long since he had been here, he almost felt like an intruder. He remembered the story his father had told him about the history of the knocker and how they had replaced it after the Yankees had set fire to this building during the last week of the Civil War. How good it was to be home again, and he was glad that he'd met Jethro Elderberry. There were good people around, all over the world; one had only to find them. It was a heartening thing, and he felt the better for it.

The door was opened by Amelia Coleman, who uttered a gasp and then beamed. "Mr. Lucien! For heaven's sake, what in the world are you doing here? Come in, come in! My, how happy your mother will be to see you!"

"Thank you, Amelia. I'm glad to be back; I truly am. And you're as lovely as ever."

"Oh, I'm sure you're just being flattering to an old married woman, but it's nice to hear, all the same. You're looking fit, and my how you've changed! You're a grown man now—but here I am prattling away like an old magpie, and you're eager to see your mother." Then she giggled, and added, "Your timing's just perfect—I'm making dinner right now, it just so happens. And you seem a mite thin, so I'll see to it that you get well fed, now that you're back."

"I remember what a wonderful cook you were. Yes, it'll be like old times, won't it?" Lucien entered the foyer and set down his valise and suitcase.

Lopasuta was just coming down the winding stairway, and at the sight of Lucien, he cried out, "By all that's holy! What on earth—?"

"Lopasuta! It's good to see you!" Lucien exclaimed, grasping his adoptive brother's hand.

"I thought you were in Ireland. What brings you here, boy?"

"That's a long story. I'll tell you about it later, but first I'd best see my mother."

"She's with Dalbert Sattersfield in your father's old study. She'll be happy to see you. Come along!"

Lopasuta, his arm around Lucien's shoulders, led the way to the study and knocked on the door. Laure, looking pale and drawn, opened the door and stopped dead in her tracks.

195

"Oh, Lucien—Lucien—what ever in the world? What has happened—what about school? Why are you here, darling?"

"So much has happened to all of us, Mother. What's happening here, anyway? When I got back to New York, Clarabelle told me that there'd been an attack on the plantation, and that you'd come here. I felt I just had to see you and see if I could be of any help."

"Oh, my darling, you don't know how glad I am to see you—and to have you with me right now, especially. Poor Marius has just died. It's broken my heart. . . ."

"Oh, dear God! He was such a fine man! What will become of all his children?"

"Fortunately, Ezekiel West and his sweet wife, Marva, are going to care for them. Marius himself hired them—I'm sure you'll like them when you meet them. And there are others, too, you'll have to meet. Oh dear, so much has happened. But we'll have time to talk later, when you've rested and eaten. Dalbert, Lopasuta, it's just about time for dinner, so why don't we all go into the dining room? After dinner we can fill Lucien in on all our plans," Laure proposed. She put her hands on Lucien's shoulders. "You're so tall, so manly—I almost didn't recognize you! Oh, darling, it's so good to see you! But why did you leave school? And why didn't you tell us you were coming?"

"There was no time to write, Mother, and I didn't want to alarm you with a telegram. And . . . I'll tell you all about it at dinner. I don't—well, anyway, I had a good reason for coming, Mother." Lucien found that he could hardly bring himself to discuss once again the events that precipitated his determination to leave Dublin and come back home.

They were seated around the dining table, taking coffee after dinner, when Lucien finally managed to relate the incidents of that fatal Sunday in Dublin. Laure put down her cup with a clatter. "Oh, my poor darling! How terrible for you!" She reached for her son's hand and squeezed it. "I knew how much you loved her; I could tell that from your letters and when you visited us last year in New York. But please, darling, you mustn't feel that you were in any way responsible for her death—that simply isn't true."

"I've thought a good deal about it, Mother, and I know

now that I'm not at fault," Lucien said slowly. Dalbert and Lopasuta silently looked at the poised youth, then exchanged a compassionate glance between them. "Still, when I got back to New York, when I learned that you'd come here, I knew I had to come. If I can be of some help here, it'll help me forget."

"That's very thoughtful of you. You don't know how much I've missed you. I did feel so alone when I had to come all by myself, because, of course, as you know, your stepfather departed for Europe just two days before I got that terrible telegram from Benjamin Brown," Laure answered.

"Who would want to do such a thing, Mother?"

"We're not sure, but we suspect it's people who hate us because of what we stand for—what the Bouchards have always stood for since your great namesake first came to Alabama."

"I—maybe I shouldn't mention this, Mother, but when I left the railroad and took a buggy here . . . Well, there were two men on a hotel porch we were momentarily stopped in front of, and one of them called out to me to ask me where I was going and—well, when I told him, he said something about 'nigger-loving Bouchards.' I'm afraid—well, I lost my temper, and I got out of the buggy and knockèd him down."

"Good for you, Lucien!" Dalbert chortled, slapping his knee and winking at Lopasuta.

"You might have been hurt, darling! You shouldn't be so impulsive. You know how Leland and I worried about you, when you tried to pick fights with British soldiers in Dublin," Laure said.

"This was something else, Mother. I couldn't just sit there and let him insult us. Worst of all, he attacked Father. I just saw red, and I lost my temper—"

"That's very understandable," Lopasuta put in. "I think I would have been tempted to do the same thing. Dalbert, what Lucien has just told us gives me an idea. Maybe these two men were responsible for some of what happened last month."

"It could very well be. I'll see if I can find out anything about them. At any rate, Lucien," he said, turning to the youth, "we're all glad to have you back here."

Lucien solemnly nodded. "I've had enough classical education for a while, anyway. I'm pretty sure of that. I want to learn more about the land. I want to be useful. After all, I'm seventeen, so it's high time I take a lot of the responsibility for Windhaven on my shoulders.''

"Lucien," Lopasuta gently said, "we're certainly glad to have you back here on the team. And now, Dalbert, let's you and I go have a cigar and a little brandy. I imagine that Lucien and his mother would like to be alone for a spell.''

Chapter Seventeen

It was Wednesday night, two nights after Lucien had arrived from New York, and it had rained heavily just before sunset. Off to the east the distant rumble of thunder was heard from time to time, and the three-quarter moon was obscured behind thick, dark clouds. From the towering bluff, there had come at midnight the sound of the screech owl, disturbed by the inclement weather, seeking its roost for the long night, waiting for birds or rodents to come within its view that it might feed. An hour passed, and then two more. There were no lights in the red-brick chateau, nor in any of the tenants' houses on the rich, rolling land of Windhaven Plantation. In the cottage at the far southeast boundary, the three guards whom Lopasuta had hired were playing cards; soon after one o'clock in the morning, they yawned and agreed to take shifts. They cut cards to see who would stand guard for the first two hours, then the next two, and finally the last. Sidney Berndorf, the German, oldest of the trio, drew the lowest card, and his two companions—chuckling at his woebegone expression—went off to their beds to sleep, bidding him keep his eyes open and wake them if there were any sign of trespassers.

Berndorf nodded, grunted something in his native tongue, and then, armed with a rifle he had loaded earlier that afternoon, emerged from the cottage and seated himself on the heavy, low footstool. The rifle cradled over his lap, his hands resting lightly on it, he stared out into the dull, damp night. A faint, yet chilly wind gusted from the river, which was at crest. More rain, and there would assuredly be a flood—he had already pointed this out to John Hornung and Frank Connery. They had shrugged, and Connery had said, ''That's not our bother; we're being paid to guard, not to worry about the river or the crops. You worry too much, Dutchie.''

Berndorf scowled as he sat there on the stool. He did not really like either Hornung or Connery, but all three of them were in the same boat—broke, without jobs—and they had been glad to leave Tuscaloosa for the prospect of a livelier life near the capital of Alabama. Connery had heard that there was a house on the outskirts of Montgomery with fancy girls who could be had for a modest fee. Hornung was anxious to check out this rumor, but Berndorf had shaken his head and growled, "I don't sleep with *Dirnen* anymore. There's no pleasure in it, and you might catch something from them.''

He knew the other men did not much like him, yet this was a job; the pay was good, and he hoped that it would last a while. His dream was one day to go to New Orleans and see his second cousin, who might have a better opportunity for him. But he'd been dreaming that same dream for almost twenty years now.

He sat there listening, waiting, for almost an hour. Then he thought he heard something. At the southwestern edge of the towering bluff, there seemed to be a stirring in a clump of live-oak trees that fringed the base of the bluff and extended almost to the bank of the river. Carefully rising from the stool, crouching low to make himself as small a target as possible, he moved stealthily toward the clump of trees, the rifle already cocked. He heard nothing. But the sound of the river at crest was alarming, as the waters rushed downstream. Vaguely, he could perceive the outline of the rebuilt dam, which Lopasuta had explained to him had been dynamited last month when the unknown attackers struck.

Berndorf was prepared to fight, for he was not a coward—he had, after all, been decorated for bravery during the Civil War, and he had never run from a battle. But by nature, he was mild-mannered and soft-spoken, and of late he had become somewhat dour and withdrawn, for life had begun to seem to him something of a sour joke. He was nearing fifty, alone in life—though he would have liked a young woman by his side to comfort him. But he was very homely, and no woman would look at him twice. On the few occasions when he had gone to a brothel, the girls had been diffident and too quick to suit him, showing him no tenderness at all. In a way, he wished he were back in the old country, where a woman knew that a man was the master, and that her place was predetermined by the rule of *Kinder, Kirche, und Küche.*

He sighed, scratched his head, and was about to turn his back on the clump of live-oak trees and return to the stool and resume his place of guard, when suddenly an arm clamped over his mouth and nose, cutting off his breathing. He felt the sharp, cold edge of a knife blade pressed against the side of his neck, and his eyes goggled as he dropped the rifle. Then he heard a sibilant voice in his ear: "If you yell, I'll cut your throat, you hear me? Nod your head, if you understand."

Swiftly, Berndorf nodded; the sweat of fear was already rank on his body, and in his terror he felt the urge to urinate.

"That's bein' smart. Okay, fella, I want you to tell me what you know about the people over in the big house—how many there are, and who they are. Got me?"

"Y-yes," Berndorf stammered. "There are altogether five people: the lady of the house, Mrs. Kenniston; her son, Lucien; Lopasuta Bouchard, who is the adopted son of Mrs. Kenniston's former husband; the cook, Amelia Coleman; and the cook's husband, Burt, who lives there but works downriver."

"That's the lot of them?" the harsh voice asked. At the same time, the man pressed the knife point harder against Berndorf's throat. "You're sure?"

"As God is my witness, I am telling the truth!" Berndorf squawked.

"Well now . . ." the raider mused. "That's mighty interesting. I think we'll have a bit more fun than we originally planned, seein' as how there's so few people around to object. Yes, indeedy, there ain't no point in overlookin' a golden opportunity, that's for sure."

Berndorf felt his knees weaken, certain that his time had come and this hooded man intended to kill him then and there, that being the "fun" the man talked about. But to the German's surprise, the knife blade was removed from his throat.

The voice was mocking, now, as well as sibilant: "You've got a choice, fella. Keep your mouth shut and turn around fast and go back to where you were and don't see anything, get me? If you do like you're told, I'll spare your life. You don't know who we are, and you won't ever know, understand? Otherwise, you'll wind up dead right now. If you're gonna go along with me, nod three times. . . ."

Berndorf shuddered and frantically nodded three times.

"That's a smart fella. Don't look back when I let go of you. Just march straight over to that stool of yours and sit down. And look off to the east. It's a nice view, and you can almost see the moon if you stare hard enough."

Again, he nodded, stricken with terror.

"We've got friends all 'round here, fella. If you blab, I'll find out about it, and I'll come back and do you in—and it won't be an easy death. Nod again, if you get the message."

Berndorf lost no time in nodding, and then he felt the arm release his mouth. He closed his eyes and kept his head turned away from his assailant.

"You're playin' it smart. Good! Get on back to your post. Remember what I told you: Just one word to anybody about what you might hear tonight, and you won't live much longer. Now get goin'!"

Sidney Berndorf was about to stoop to retrieve his rifle when he again felt the point of the knife, this time digging into him so that it drew blood. He automatically started to cry out, and at once a hand was clapped over his mouth. "Leave the rifle. You won't be needin' it. If your friends ask, tell them that you got scared by an owl or something and dropped it into the river. Make up a story—I don't care what you say. Now, get goin', before I change my mind and cut you up nice and slow!"

Stumbling, he ran more than walked back to the stool. Now he could no longer control himself, and he felt the warm trickle of urine run down his leg. Grimacing with disgust, almost ready to sob in frustration and shame, he seated himself solidly on the stool, facing the east, with his back to the rolling fields of Windhaven Plantation.

The man who had accosted Sidney Berndorf ran over to a clump of trees and was now whispering to three other men. "Jed, you take care of the dam so that they won't rebuild it quite so easily. There's lots of dynamite, and if you use a long fuse, you'll be well away from it when it blows. Bodine, you go set a charge under the stable—but not too much dynamite there, hear? 'Cause I want Bevis to go on up to the big house and give them folks a good scare, which I reckon he can do just after the stable starts firin' up. Way I figure it, the menfolk'll hightail it over to the stable right quick to put out the flames. While they're distracted, Bevis can do some damage to the mansion—heave a mess o' rocks through the windows and stuff like that.''

"Suits me fine," Bevis Marley wickedly laughed, his three remaining teeth exposed by a grin that was more a sneer than anything else. "But what about you, Magnus? What're you gonna be up to?"

"I'll stay here and guard the horses—hell, we can't risk them runnin' off when the excitement starts, can we? Besides, all that fast movin' that needs to be done—well, let's face it, my size don't let me move all that quick," the fat undertaker confessed. "Okay, men, you git goin'. And make sure there ain't any hitches!"

The three men started off, but they were halted by Borden's loudly whispered, "Bevis!"

The stocky funeral parlor worker stopped in his tracks. "What is it, Magnus?" he sullenly asked.

"I want you to come straight back here as soon as you've done your job, you got me? I know how much you like to look for extra trouble—hell, that's why you ain't got but three lousy teeth left in your stupid head—but don't go lookin' for it tonight. That's an order!"

"I hear you, Magnus."

"You better. 'Cause if you mess things up for the rest of us, you'll find yourself lookin' for another job. There's plenty o' men in Lowndesboro who'd jump at the chance to work in my funeral home there, and you know it."

"Don't worry, Magnus," Marley assured his boss. "Everything'll be just fine." With that, he turned and hurried away into the trees, heading straight for the red-brick chateau.

As he watched his men run off to do their nefarious deeds, Magnus Borden chuckled softly to himself. "I'd say in about ten minutes, them folks is gonna have one doozy of a rude awakenin'!"

Just as he predicted, in ten minutes' time there was a muffled explosion from upriver, followed closely by a second, less powerful explosion from over by the chateau. "That'll be the stable, for sure," Borden said aloud. He took out his pocket watch and consulted it by the light of the faint moon. "I'd say Bevis'll start heavin' them rocks in another couple o' minutes—just as long as it takes them two Bouchard fellas to haul themselves out o' their nice, cozy featherbeds. Yep, they ain't likely to forget tonight none too soon!"

*   *   *

Lucien Bouchard was thrown out of bed by the force of the explosion and stumbled to his feet, dazed and trembling. Then, realizing what had happened, he threw his clothes over his nightshirt and ran out of his bedroom and down the stairs.

Lopasuta also was wakened by the explosion, and he, too, wasted no time in dragging on his trousers and hurrying out of his room, stopping just long enough to grab a new rifle he had purchased that morning at Dalbert Sattersfield's store.

The two men met Laure Kenniston in the hallway, looking stunned and distraught. "Oh, my God!" she screamed. "They're attacking us again, aren't they? That's what's happening, isn't it?"

"I'm afraid so, Laure," Lopasuta murmured. "You stay here; don't go out. Lucien and I will do whatever has to be done. Ah—I hear Burt downstairs. He'll help us, too, of course. Come on, Lucien. Let's get moving."

They ran out of the chateau and stood on the front lawn for a moment, exchanging glances. Then the three men hurried around the side of the mansion to the stable. There, they stopped short, appalled at the sight. The building had suffered a considerable amount of damage from the blast—for, in his haste, the inexperienced Bodine Evans had set much too large a charge—and the south wall was engulfed in flames. Two of the horses had been badly hurt, and their agonized whinnies filled the night.

Lucien, now sobbing and swearing aloud upon seeing the plight of the two beasts, asked for Lopasuta's rifle so that he could mercifully put them out of their misery with quick shots to their heads. Rejoining Lopasuta and Burt, who were trying to beat out the flames, Lucien angrily shouted, "The bastards! Why are they doing this, Lopasuta? Who's behind all this? Damn them to hell! Why are they doing this? Why?"

There was no time for a reply, for just then several of the workers dashed up, breathless and shouting. Doug Larson and Elmer Gregory were among them, and immediately they took the lead, organizing the men into a bucket brigade of two lines—one to bring full pails from the well to the stable, the other to return the emptied pails. Lopasuta, Lucien, and Burt joined the line of panting, heaving men who were passing the full buckets to the site of the fire. After several minutes of unremitting labor, punctuated by the curses and groans of the straining fire fighters, the blaze was contained and, finally, extinguished.

"I think we've done it, men," Doug Larson called out. "We've lost most of the stable, but we've kept the fire away from the main house."

"Thank God," Lopasuta cried out. "Fellows, that was superb teamwork."

Lucien, released from the exertions of the moment, exhausted and nearly sobbing with emotion, staggered and stumbled in the dark. "Damn them, Lopasuta!" he moaned. "What do they want from us? Why can't they leave us alone?"

Lopasuta hugged the sobbing youth to his chest, trying to comfort him. He realized that the boy was feeling not only the torment of the immediate situation but also his pain over Mary Eileen's death, which had once again been brought to the surface. "I don't know why they are attacking us, Lucien . . . at least, not for sure. I know it doesn't seem to make any sense, but apparently—from what I have been able to find out—groups like the old Ku Klux Klan are very much on the rise again, and they are randomly attacking people like us, like your family, who treat blacks as equals. It is despicable, it is cowardly, it is a threat to all the tenets we hold dear—but we will fight them . . . and we will win." Lopasuta's voice was hard as stone, his mouth was a thin, angry slash in his face.

Lucien shuddered a little when he felt the depth of his adoptive brother's anger and realized the fury that had been aroused in the Comanche. For a fleeting moment, he was very, very glad that it was not he who had aroused Lopasuta's enmity.

"Come, my brother," Lopasuta finally said after a long silence. "Let us see what else those bastards have done. I have a terrible feeling that the other charge was set over by the dam. It seems to be a favorite target of theirs."

What they saw there was nightmarish. The dam had been entirely demolished, and the cresting Alabama River had flooded a good portion of the southwestern fields. When Burt, Lopasuta, and Lucien arrived on the scene, they found Benjamin Brown had taken charge and was urging the other workers to prepare an improvised dike against the flood waters that, if not kept in check, would wash away all the newly sown seed that had been planted the previous week.

Lopasuta hoarsely said to Lucien and Burt, "They blew up the dam but good, this time." He looked at the terrible scene all around them and softly cursed. "Those bastards!"

"But where were the guards that you hired?" Burt wanted to know.

"I'll find out. I'll go out there right now and see what happened." Lopasuta strode out toward the distant cottage where the three new guards were quartered and found that Frank Connery and John Hornung were already dressed and hurrying out to aid Ben Brown. Sidney Berndorf, however, was just sitting at the table, pale and trembling, and he shook his head as Lopasuta approached him. "Mr. Bouchard, I never encountered anything like this. . . . I'm scared silly . . . dynamite . . . my God, we all could have been blown up to kingdom come!"

"But you were on guard, weren't you? Frank Connery just told me that you took the first shift. Didn't you see or hear anything?"

Berndorf inwardly winced, but he had his answer ready. "Not a sound, as God's my witness, Mr. Bouchard. I'm sorry as hell—"

"Well, I can't hold you accountable for it, Berndorf. Anyhow, I'd like you to give the men a hand there—the Alabama's at flood stage, and this rain didn't help one damn bit. I still wish to God I knew who was responsible for all this—but I'll find out, so help me!"

As soon as he had seen the three men—Lucien, Lopasuta, and Burt—hurry off to the stable, Bevis Marley pulled on his burlap hood, ensuring him anonymity, and began his own dirty work. One by one, he carefully aimed and hurled the large rocks he had gathered into a neat pile at his feet. His first target was the window just to the right of the door, and it smashed into hundreds of pieces. Next, he aimed for the two parlor windows, and they, too, fell before his assault. Methodically, he broke every window in the front of the house, laughing gleefully as each one surrendered to its fate.

Inside the house, Laure Kenniston was both terrified and angered. Shouting at a distraught Amelia Coleman to stay in the center of the house, away from any windows, Laure ran into Luke's old study. She grabbed the ancient musket hanging over the fireplace—not knowing the first thing about weapons and therefore unaware of its uselessness—and ran out the front door, heedless of any danger.

When Bevis Marley saw the beautiful matron appear at the top of the veranda steps, he blinked his eyes at first, disbelieving this vision. But the vision was real indeed, for the woman began to move, slowly descending the front steps, her bare feet hesitating slightly as they touched the cold stone. The slight breeze caught her shift and lifted the hem, briefly revealing her silken calves.

Marley licked his lips and felt his manhood become aroused. "Holy shit!" he hoarsely whispered. "Magnus, my good man, you're jist gonna have to forgive me. This here's one opportunity that's too damn good to pass up."

Laure, in her haste to protect her home, had ignored the fact that she was only lightly clad in her silk nightgown, and now, as she cautiously stepped onto the carriageway, the moonlight illuminating her from behind exposed her luscious contours almost as clearly as if she were completely naked.

Tossing aside the rock he had been about to throw, Marley ran up behind Laure as she moved onto the lawn and stood looking around for her tormentors. "Lookin' for me, ma'am?" Marley sarcastically asked, grabbing the old musket as she started to turn toward him. "Now, now, that ain't no way to behave toward a friend," he told her, throwing the weapon down, an evil grin splitting his ugly face. "And I'm your friend, ma'am—your *real good* friend. You're gonna know me as well as any woman ever knows a man," he panted, pulling her to his chest and running his hands hungrily over her body. He groaned with desire as he lifted her filmy nightdress up over her buttocks.

Laure fought furiously, biting and scratching and kicking. Desperately, she tried to knee her attacker in the groin, but Marley anticipated her attempt and, with a vile oath, backhanded her viciously across the mouth. Stunned and weakened, her fury was no match against his strength, and as she choked back her sobs, she felt herself being forced to the ground. His hands were all over her then, forcing her legs apart and stroking the inside of her thighs. One hand began roughly to caress her left breast, and he suddenly cursed and looped his fingers around the neck of her nightdress, exposing her heaving bosom as the thin fabric ripped away under his tugging.

Lust glazed his eyes as he stared down at her almost-naked body. "My, my," he breathed, "you sure are one beautiful bitch." He held her down with one hand while, with the other, he fumbled clumsily to get his trouser buttons undone.

"You goddamned fool, what the hell do you think you're doin'?" A voice suddenly split the silence that had fallen upon the scene, save for the attacker's panting. "I told you we didn't have time for your foolin' around, damn your hide! Her menfolk'll be comin' back any minute, you stupid idiot!"

"Hell, boss, I got time to give this here beauty a right good pokin', and that's a fact. You might call it a souvenir of this night of fun," Marley petulantly declared.

"Get off of her—right now!" Magnus Borden shouted. "And get up on this here horse of yours pronto or I swear I'll leave you high and dry to fend for yourself."

Reluctantly, Marley drew himself up off of Laure, making certain that his hood was still firmly in place so she couldn't identify him. He still held onto her wrist, however, cruelly digging his fingers into her flesh and forcing her to her feet. "I'm gonna come back for you one of these days, missy. You watch and see if I don't," he growled. "Meanwhile, I'll just take me a reminder of what I almost had . . . an' what I *will* have, right soon." He reached out and tore off the pendant she wore around her neck, a gold locket that had belonged to Luke's stepmother and that Laure never removed. It gleamed in the moonlight as Marley held it briefly up for her inspection before he tucked it into his pocket. "Next time you see this, ma'am, you and I are gonna have one nice long time together . . . and that's a promise."

With that, he swiftly mounted the horse that Borden had brought for him, and the two men rode off into the night.

Laure sank back down to her knees and began to sob. She clenched and unclenched her fists, the anger and humiliation rising with every moment. She picked up one of the rocks Bevis Marley had dropped and flung it with all her might at a nearby tree. Then she put her hands over her eyes and wept.

When Lopasuta and Lucien returned to the chateau twenty minutes later, they found Laure still kneeling on the front lawn, which was wet with dew, clutching her torn nightgown about her, barely covering her body. She was too upset by her ordeal to feel any shame at inadvertent exposure. Lucien ran over to his mother, and wrapping his shirt around her, he solicitously began to tend her as she told them, in a voice now cold and dispassionate, what had happened.

Raising her tearstained face to Lopasuta, she avowed, "Tomorrow morning, right after breakfast, I want you to teach me to shoot. I want to be able to fire a rifle correctly and accurately. And another thing—I want to go to the general store and buy a pistol. For as long as I live here, I'm always going to be armed. No one will ever again do to me what that man did. Never."

Chapter Eighteen

On the twenty-sixth of March, the day on which William K. Vanderbilt gave a fancy dress ball in New York City, the most sumptuous entertainment yet seen in these young United States, Leland Kenniston boarded a Cunard steamship in Southampton to return home. He had concluded his whirlwind tour of Europe's major cities, buying some items that were not known in this country, but that he believed would make him a considerable profit. He had gone back to London for the final leg of his journey, in order to confer with his new factor there, David Voorhies.

By now the almost frantically exuberant entrepreneur had found himself growing weary with the strain of his journey. So many visits with business people in various capitals had left him drained. The prospects for future success, which had seemed so bright but a few days ago, now began to pall, leaving him with an unaccountable sense of futility, and at times almost of foreboding.

He began to imagine that his fondest dreams might easily turn to dust, and this attitude he now saw reflected in the world around him. The day before sailing back home, when he had met with David Voorhies, the factor told him that the twenty thousand statuettes had undoubtedly been received by his New York office. The expression on Voorhies's face was one of amused condescension—or so, at least, Leland had interpreted it. And when that evening he had gone out to dine at Claridge's, he had suddenly felt a black wave of uncertainty engulf him. The waiter, an elegantly poised and deferential man with twenty years of service at the famous restaurant, remarked to his captain, after Leland had left the restaurant, "I declare, I've never seen a man so glum over so elegant a meal. And he downed a whole bottle of our best wine as if it were water. These Americans! They have no taste, at all—they have only money."

The black mood persisted as Leland took the boat train from London to the wharf at Southampton. He sent his luggage aboard, then went up the gangplank, his shoulders bent and his heart beating fast, as if the voyage were carrying him toward some unknown disaster. The purser greeted him on deck, checked off his name on the list, and showed him to his reserved cabin. Once inside, the entrepreneur flung himself down upon the bed, closed his eyes, pillowing his head in his arms, and gave himself up to the fit of melancholy that had so suddenly taken hold of him.

The fine air of confidence, the triumphant mood of all-conquering success against the worst adversities had vanished. In its place was dark self-searching. In this, Leland felt himself to be like a passive spectator at his own funeral fantasies, and it seemed to him now that all of his strivings had been in vain. He began to recall little incidents that suggested to him in the harsh light of hindsight that he had not been as successful as he had thought. Indeed, the recollection of his confident behavior, as he called upon the various foreign representatives, now caused him to wince in pain. How foolish he had been to think that he was making a good impression upon them, or winning their approval! It had all been a terrible charade, and obviously they must all have seen right through him! Why else, for example, would David Voorhies have smiled in that peculiar way, with his upper lip curling, an obvious flicker of amusement in his gray eyes? Obviously, he had thought Leland a fool, and that judgment had been well deserved! Leland was a failure, through and through; everyone had known it all along, and now—Leland sighed—he himself did, too. Twenty thousand statuettes—no doubt the bill for them had long since been sent. What ugly things they were, and now he'd have to unload them on the American market in whatever way he could. Oh, God, what a miserable shambles his life had become!

When the ship's steward knocked at the cabin door, he opened his eyes and turned his head, then replied in a listless monotone, "Come in; it's not locked."

"A good afternoon to you, sir. I was wondering what time

211

you'd like to dine this evening. We have two sittings, at six-thirty and again at eight o'clock.''

"Neither. If I want food, I'll order it here in the stateroom."

"As you like, sir. However, I thought you might like to know that we've assigned you to the first mate's table."

Leland pouted at the friendly steward, a short man, nearly bald, with an engaging smile. "First mate's?" he said. "I—I don't think I'll want to have company for dinner."

"Oh, but Mr. Kenniston, it's a great honor to be at the first mate's table. You'd even warrant being at the captain's table, but you purchased your accommodations only a few days ago, and the passenger list in the main had already been made up. Of course, I'll tell Captain McDonald you'd like to meet him—''

"No, no, please! I don't want to meet him, and I can't imagine that he'd want to meet me . . . why would anyone want to bother with me? I just want to be left alone." Leland sighed deeply. "Please go away now, and let me nap. I'm tired."

"Just as you say, sir."

The steward had a look of puzzlement on his face when he shook his head and closed the door behind him. As he went down the carpeted passageway, he encountered a pretty black-haired young Scottish chambermaid and murmured, "A word with you, Fiona. The passenger in 4-A seems to be in a bad way. When you make up his stateroom, you'd best be sure first that he's in a better mood. Any trouble and you report either to head of housekeeping or to me. Understood?"

"Yes, Mr. Brandon, and I'm grateful to you for telling me, sir." The chambermaid curtsied. "But then, I've been trained to deal with all kinds, if you know what I mean, sir. I'll take good care of him, never fear."

During the next two days, Leland Kenniston stayed in his stateroom. Only twice did he ring for the steward ordering food to be sent in: once at lunchtime the next day out and the following day at dinnertime. The steward tried to be cordial and solicitous, but the Irish entrepreneur brusquely waved such overtures aside and imperiously averred, "I'm not in the mood for conversation, if you don't mind, steward. Just bring what I ordered. Set it up on a table beside the bed and get out as quickly as you can."

212

When Fiona Laughlan knocked at the door shortly after lunchtime the next day and received no answer, she automatically used 'her passkey, presuming the cabin to be empty. Instead she found Leland in bed, lying fully dressed in sleep-rumpled clothes on top of the unused sheets and blankets. His hands were clasped behind his head as he lay just staring at the ceiling. "Oh! I—I didn't mean to disturb you, sir. . . . Perhaps I should clean the stateroom some other time today?" she stammered.

"Do what you have to do. But please . . . do it quickly," he sighed. He did not even bother to look at her. Fiona blushed, for she felt ill at ease and out of place, but she nonetheless tidied up the stateroom and then volunteered, as she was about to leave, "I've left you some extra towels in the washroom, sir. I trust you're all right?"

Leland only grunted, and Fiona, with a helpless shrug, let herself out and closed the door.

On the third day out, Leland contented himself with tea and toast for dinner. He ordered the steward to leave the tray outside the stateroom door and simply to knock to signify that it was there. "I don't feel like seeing anyone, so please, do as I ask," he pleaded.

As for the pretty chambermaid, Fiona, she encountered an even more distant response on the part of the Irish entrepreneur. When she knocked on his door about an hour before the noontime meal, to inquire whether he wished to have the room made up, she heard his faint voice from behind the closed door: "Leave me be for today. Come back tomorrow."

The next morning, Leland at last grudgingly allowed Fiona to enter. She was startled to see that he was wearing the suit of clothes he had been wearing the day before, and by now it was badly rumpled and stained. Moreover, he had not bothered to shave or even, she suspected, wash his hands or bathe. He sat on the edge of the bed until she at last gently remonstrated, "But, sir, I must change the sheets, and you can't sit there when I do that, you see, sir."

He nodded glumly, got up, and strode over to the porthole. He stood there silently all the while she finished her chores and did not even respond to her attempted cheerful, "I hope you're enjoying the voyage, sir."

Outside in the passageway, Fiona again met the steward

and anxiously told him how concerned she was about the appearance of this passenger.

"It might be an idea to have Dr. Murtrie just pay him a little visit—like a social call, as you might say, Fiona," he suggested. "He hasn't shown up for any of the meals; the first mate wanted to know if he was ill, and even the captain knows about him. Maybe he had some bad luck in Europe, or maybe he's going home to something—but, whatever it is, I'm distressed. Yes, I'll definitely have Dr. Murtrie call on him, today if possible."

Dr. Walter Murtrie was a fussy man with a bristly mustache and thick-lensed spectacles that made him look like a hirsute owl. His hands never were still, fluttering like moths before a flame. Nonetheless, he had received his degree from and had done work in a famous Vienna operating theater, and had conferred with some of the leading European physicians and therapists on the contingent mental problems arising out of various major illnesses. He was in his fifties, and he had decided four years previously to become affiliated with the Cunard Steamship Line because this position enabled him to fulfill a secret passion he had always had of traveling on the high seas.

As the doctor listened to the steward's report of Leland Kenniston's behavior, he frowned and adjusted his spectacles; then he took them off, breathed on the lenses, and polished them with a silk handkerchief. He replaced them while nodding his head ponderously as he attempted to make a prognosis from the steward's comments. Finally, he declared, "He apparently is in an extreme state of depression. This could be the result of a physical disorder—of perhaps the liver or colon, or it could be from acute indigestion—or he may have had some disastrous business or emotional reverses, perhaps rejection in love. All these things, steward, could have produced this outward effect. I don't want to pry, and if he's as morose and unsociable as you say, I'll have to be most circumspect. I may just call on him, if I can find a suitable pretext for my visit. . . ." The doctor seemed lost in thought for a moment, then his plump face brightened: "I have it! I write a column for the ship's news, you know, which is passed out on all our voyages. I will tell him that I'd like an interview with him because he's a prominent Irish-American

214

businessman, and we English are most interested in the success stories of our former subjects, as it were.''

"I don't think you'd better mention the English, Dr. Murtrie." The steward put his hand to his mouth to suppress a faint smile. "With all due respect, the Irish don't have much use for the English, sir."

"Quite right. Matter of fact, my great grandmother was Irish, and it didn't appear to do me any harm. But seriously, steward, I'll find a way of at least seeing him for a moment. Though that's not the best way of making any sort of diagnosis, at least I'll be able to see the outward manifestations, and if there's anything I think I can advise you on, you'll hear from me.''

"Much obliged, I'm sure, Dr. Murtrie." The steward gratefully inclined his head and hurried off to his other duties.

At about four in the afternoon, Dr. Murtrie gently knocked at Leland Kenniston's stateroom door.

"Who is it?" The voice within was faint.

"It's Dr. Murtrie. I write the ship's news, Mr. Kenniston, and I wonder if you'd grant me a moment of your valuable time.''

There was a long pause, and Dr. Murtrie could hear the shuffling of feet as the passenger within approached the door. Then the door opened slowly, and Dr. Murtrie beheld standing before him a tired-looking man, whose eyes were bloodshot from lack of proper sleep, his clothes badly disheveled, and his face terribly unkempt. The man had obviously not bathed since he came aboard the steamship.

"Why do you need to see me?" Leland's voice was dull and listless, as he opened the door a bit farther. Behind him, Dr. Murtrie could see the untidy stateroom, and on a table the remains of the day's lunch, which the occupant of the cabin had barely touched. He looked again at Leland, who was staring vacantly back at him.

"Why, it's well known what a successful businessman you are, Mr. Kenniston, and I thought the other passengers might be interested in your achievements. I'll only take a moment or two, if you can spare it.''

Leland vaguely passed his hand over his sweaty forehead and frowned. He waited a long moment, and then he sighed. "I don't give a damn about your passengers. I'm famous enough, but they'd never acknowledge the fact. Let them do

215

without an article! Besides, I'm not feeling too well; I don't want to see anybody.''

"As you say, sir. I'm sorry to have disturbed you." Walter Murtrie philosophically shrugged, shook his head as he turned away from the door and marched back down to the end of the passageway, where the steward was anxiously awaiting him. "No luck there," he reported. "Says he's not interested at all in publicity, and that he doesn't give a damn for the passengers. He doesn't look very well. I don't think he's intoxicated; I'd say—having had barely a sight of the man and no examination of him—that he's suffered some real shock or loss, and he's plunged into a very melancholy mood and is feeling sorry for himself. All I can say is, steward, you'd best have your helpful chambermaid try to look in on him whenever she can—if he'll let her—and report back to me, if she sees any alarming physical changes."

"Thank you, doctor. Incidentally, he really hasn't eaten very much—barely a meal a day. And he still hasn't shown up at the table to which he was assigned."

"I don't think he will, either, for that matter, steward. All the same, let me know if you learn anything more substantial. By the way, your concern for a passenger is certainly commendable. I shall point it out to the purser."

"That's very kind of you, Dr. Murtrie." The steward brightened, for a favorable report to the purser was often the catalyst that resulted in a raise in wages.

For the rest of the voyage, Leland Kenniston remained isolated in his stateroom, subsisting on toast and coffee in the morning, and only a slight meal at night. He did not again allow the chambermaid to enter his room until the final day of the voyage, the second of April, and then the steward entered behind her, urging, "Mr. Kenniston, we're going to dock in about four hours. Please allow me to pack your luggage. It'll save you a lot of trouble, sir."

Leland stared back at them, his eyes hollowed by fatigue. He hadn't shaved, and his heavy stubbly black beard made him appear even dirtier than he was. He had also lost several pounds because of his lack of food. The chambermaid was aghast at his appearance as he walked over to an armchair and flung himself down on it. He covered his face with his hands and ignored both her and the steward, who went about their tasks as swiftly and soundlessly as they could, so as not to disturb the singularly behaving passenger.

At last, when they had finished, the steward turned to Leland and suggested, "Perhaps you'd like something to eat and drink before we dock, sir? You really haven't eaten very much during the voyage—and Cunard wants all its passengers to be hale and hearty, you know." He permitted himself a tiny little laugh, which rang hollowly in the silent stateroom.

Leland at last looked up at him blankly, as if not recognizing him. Then he shrugged. "As you wish; whatever you want to bring. I suppose I'd best shave—" Abstractedly, he put a hand to his beard and grimaced. "Yes, I'll do that while you bring some food. And a stiff glass of brandy, if you will."

"At once, Mr. Kenniston. Come, Fiona!"

Leland went to the sink and shaved. He stared at himself in the mirror as if seeing a stranger's face. But the lather and the warm water seemed to revive him somewhat, and when he had finished, he patted his face with a thick towel and nodded, as if satisfied with his appearance.

Then, impulsively, he took out his wallet and examined the contents. Of his personal cash, he had spent all but seventy dollars, and he had used up his letter of credit, partly allocating it to purchases from a Viennese factor, Anton Gruber, and the rest of it to his newly appointed representative. Both men had urged him to make a down payment on the goods he had ordered, for as they did not know him, they did not wish to ship his large and unusual orders unless they had a substantial deposit.

In all, he had spent nearly forty thousand dollars on his trip and on purchases; that was apart from the poker debts to the three men he had met on the *Aurania*. And yet, now—strangely enough—the black mood began to pass as he stared out of the porthole and saw the familiar sight of the New York harbor. He recognized Bedloe's Island, and that brought back to him his conversation with Laure and the children when they had gone to see him off.

Of course! It was a good omen! He had concluded a trip during which he had impressed important people in the leading cities of Europe, and he had done a good deal of business. It would bring enormous profits, and what he had spent was nothing compared to the money that would be gleaned by his

217

acumen and foresight. In this sprightly mood, he ravenously ate the roast beef sandwich and salad and coffee the steward had thoughtfully brought to him, and he drank all of the brandy. He felt new life course through his veins. Once back in New York, once he had told everyone what he had done, he would be commended for his shrewd ability to drive good bargains, bringing advantages to himself and to his firm. Laure and the children would have everything they desired and more!

He went out to the deck to watch the steamship slowly begin its approach to its berth. There it was: the skyline of the city he loved best, the city where he was installed and ensconced like a pasha. Nothing could deter his successful future. Indeed, he had accomplished far more than he had set out to do—for he had also won the love and respect of Laure's oldest son, and he had approved of Lucien's choice of a future mate.

His eyes glistened with enthusiasm, and he breathed in the air. It was cold and windy, but the skies were blue, even if the sun was at the moment struggling to get through a solitary cloud to cast its weak early-spring rays over the scene. About him, the bustle of passengers ready to disembark served as a felicitous backdrop for his triumphant return home. Now he would take up where he had left off, with greater recognition and respect from his business colleagues than he had ever had before. Life was good, rich, and full; there were many joys he had yet to taste—and he would, before much longer.

Chapter Nineteen

Since Leland Kenniston had not cabled the day or time of his arrival, Kerry Dugan was not on hand at the dock to meet the steamship when it came into the port of New York at twilight on this Monday, April 2. As the passengers disembarked, they were met by a biting wind off the harbor that tugged at their hats and coats. The friendly steward who had been concerned about the Irish entrepreneur's strange behavior during the voyage had taken it upon himself to help carry Leland's trunk down the gangplank and now inquired, "Will you let me call you a carriage, sir?"

"Yes, indeed, steward, thank you very much." His face was bright now, his eyes glowing with the excitement of being home and with the belief that he had accomplished virtual miracles across the ocean. All the ennui, all the desolate and despondent recriminations had vanished, and in their place was a feeling of mild exultation. He glanced almost contemptuously at the passengers going their separate ways to find relatives and friends, to go on then to hansoms and carriages to take them to their various destinations. They meant nothing to the world, his look implied; he alone on this steamship was an important personage. He drew out his wallet, found a twenty-dollar bill, and handed it to the steward. "Just a little something for all your service."

"Why, that's most generous of you, sir. Hey there, this way, for Mr. Kenniston!" the steward hailed a passing coachman about fifty feet away who was looking for business. With a tip of his hat, the coachman acknowledged the call and halted his horse, and the steward wheeled the luggage over to the carriage. While the coachman lifted Leland's

219

trunk to the luggage rack, the steward carefully placed his suitcase to one side on the floor of the coach, then stepped back and held the door open for the entrepreneur. "I trust you're feeling better, now, Mr. Kenniston?" the steward asked, surprised but delighted at the rapid change in Leland's mood.

"Oh, yes, I'm fine. Thank you again." He nodded to dismiss the steward, then called up to the coachman the address of the house on Gramercy Park. He leaned back, folded his hands across his chest, and smiled triumphantly. Yes, it would have been good to have had a business associate or his family here to greet him, like a conquering hero who had returned victorious and carrying his shield. He recalled the fable of the Spartan mother, who instructed her son to return from battle either with his shield or on it. Well, he, Leland, was victorious. When he saw Jacob Cohen, the gemstone expert would applaud him for the many deals he had pulled off and the profits that would be made for the company. But first, to see Laure again, to have a bite of dinner with her and the children, and then to make love to Laure to show her how he had missed her all these long weeks away from her.

With a grandiose air and flourish of his hand, he told the coachman, "There'll be a fiver for you, if you make good time, coachman! I'm anxious to be home. I've just come back from a most successful European trip; practically tripled my business!"

"That so, mister? Good for you! I'll do the best I can. Streets are still slippery from the rain we had this morning. These damn cobblestones don't exactly mix well with horseshoes. But I'll do the best I can."

Leland smiled. Yes, he was back home for certain. The attitude of the New York carriage driver was characteristic and inimitable. He sighed contentedly. He knew that a comfortable, warm house awaited him, probably a good dinner and good wine, and then seclusion with his beloved honey-haired Laure. There could be no better culmination to his highly successful voyage!

"Here we are, mister; didn't do too bad, at that," the driver turned to him. "I'll give you a hand with your trunk, if you like."

"No, no, I'm still young and strong," Leland quipped as

he got out of the carriage, drew his suitcases and trunk onto the curb, fished out his wallet, and gave the driver his fare. "Plus there's the fiver I promised. A good night to you."

"And to you, too, mister," the driver grinned, pocketing the money, then slapped the reins and drove off.

Leland dragged the trunk up the front steps and went back for his suitcases. He decided it was too much trouble to fumble for his key, so he rang the bell. In a few moments, Clarabelle Hendry opened the door and gasped in surprise. "Why, Mr. Kenniston! We didn't know you were coming back this evening! I wish Mrs. Emmons had known; a special dinner could have been all ready for you, but as it is, we've just made something fairly basic for the children, you see—"

"Oh, that's all right, Clarabelle. Whatever they're having will be fine. Where's my darling Laure?"

Clarabelle's face fell. "Oh, Mr. Kenniston, she isn't here. . . . She's in Alabama."

"In Alabama?" he blankly echoed. "Why the devil should she go there? Why isn't she here to receive me and to welcome me back home, after my long arduous trip and all the business I did in all the important cities of Europe?"

There was a note of peevishness to his voice that Clarabelle found most unusual for him, and she looked askance at him for an instant. She then hastily tried to make amends by explaining, "Well, you see, Mr. Kenniston, she had a telegram from Alabama about three months ago. Some men set some fires and did other damage as well—and worst of all, poor Marius Thornton was shot. You'd just left for Europe, sir, so Laure asked me to look after the children while she went there to see what could be done. She said she was going to get Lopasuta to come from New Orleans and help her find out what was going on there."

"My word! What a dreadful state of affairs! Didn't anyone think to notify me?"

"Why, Mr. Kenniston," the governess declared forcefully, "no one knew how to reach you! You never did send word of your whereabouts, sir!"

"Oh, of course, that's right. . . . I completely changed my itinerary after I reached the Continent, to take advantage of some unusual business opportunities." He stood nonplussed, reflectively scratching his earlobe. "Well, at least my wife

221

has good help there, in Lopasuta. I suppose it couldn't be helped. But at the moment, now that I'm back, Clarabelle, I just want to relax a little and dine with the children."

"There's something else you ought to know, Mr. Kenniston."

"Oh?" he turned to eye her with a quizzical look.

"It's about Lucien. One Sunday afternoon in Dublin, when he and Mary Eileen were having an outing, there was some trouble between the Irish rebels and the English soldiers, and—oh, it's so tragic and it makes me want to cry just thinking about it—she . . . she was killed by a stray bullet. And he was so upset he decided to come home. Then, when he found out what had happened in Alabama and that his mother had gone there, he went there himself."

"My God—the poor boy! To think what he must have gone through." He shook his head, stunned by the unexpected turn of events. "Well, I don't suppose there's anything I can do this evening about the situation, is there? I may as well go and join the children, after I wash up a bit and take my luggage upstairs."

"Don't bother about that, sir," Clarabelle replied. "I'll ask Kerry to take it up for you. You need to rest after your journey. And I'll have another place laid for you at the table. I hope your crossing was a good one, by the way."

"Passable, thank you," Leland replied, as he distractedly picked up a sheaf of mail from the foyer table and began to scan the addresses, looking for letters he wanted to open.

Relieved that her employer seemed to have absorbed all her bad news with a certain degree of equanimity, Clarabelle's drawn features relaxed, and she excused herself to hurry back to the dining room.

As he climbed the stairs to his bedroom, Leland reflected that there was a great deal of irony in the news that he had just received from the conscientious widow. *Mary Eileen Brennert dead—my God, it's hardly possible to conceive of it! She was so lively, so lovely. And within so short a time after I met her, her life was snuffed out, her sweetness and beauty gone. . . . It is inconceivable indeed!* He remembered his own adolescence, and how he had thought himself madly in love with a red-haired girl named Susan Dunworthy, daughter of a rich landowner, and she had mocked and twitted him unmercifully at school. She had married an elderly man almost three times her age because he was enormously wealthy and certain to leave her and her parents all of his estate, which they coveted. Leland had gotten over her in time, and Lucien would get over Mary Eileen, too. Not yet eighteen, he had the whole world ahead of him and a long life and many women—for he was handsome, personable, and intelligent. Yes, there was no doubt that fate had arranged things for the better—discounting, of course, the fact that a sweet young girl's life had been ended for apparently no reason or purpose, simply through an accident—an act of God, as one might describe it in writing an obituary. At least she would not live to know the pangs of old age and disease, the dangers of childbirth, and all the multiple hazards with which life was filled. He crossed himself as he said a silent prayer for her soul, and then, brightening again, put away the contents of his luggage in the closet and bureau, made his ablutions, then went down to the dining room.

The children all greeted him with enthusiasm, and John gleefully cried out, "Did you bring me a present, Daddy?" This delighted Leland, and he beamed and patted John on the head as he took his place at the table. Then he said, "Oh, yes, but all the things were sent to the office. When I go down there tomorrow, I'll bring them to you. There's something for you too, Paul, and you, Celestine and Clarissa."

"Thank you, Father," eleven-year-old Celestine happily exclaimed. And Clarissa added her thanks by getting up from her chair, going around, and giving him a hug and a kiss. Leland chuckled, returned the hug and kiss, and gave her a pat as she scurried back to her chair, just as Mrs. Emmons came in with a tureen of steaming hot beef-and-barley soup. She proceeded to ladle out a generous bowlful for the just-returned traveler.

There was a beef stew, as well, for the weather was still chilly and Clarabelle Hendry believed that in such weather growing children should have plenty of solid food. Leland ate well, and drank two glasses of red Bordeaux. He allowed Paul to have half a glass and Clarissa and Celestine a quarter of a glass each. And when John protested that this was favoritism by saying in his most petulant manner, "I want some, too. I'm a big boy now," Leland obliged by offering John a swallow from his own glass.

After dinner, Leland briefly told them all about his trip. Then, when the clock in the hallway struck eight, he bade them all good night. He, too, went right up to his room; he was in a most pensive but good mood. The more he thought about what had happened in Alabama, the more he came to the conclusion that Laure and Lucien should be allowed plenty of time alone together in their reunion. Of course, if need be, he would eventually go there to do whatever he could to help, but he would not leave at once because his business affairs were foremost in importance. His entire future had been staked upon what he had bought and commissioned in Europe, and tomorrow he and Jacob Cohen would go over plans to expand the business.

He fell asleep with a happy smile on his face, and he dreamed of a lavishly furnished new suite of offices. Furs and jewelry for Laure, ponies for the girls, and yes, one for Paul, too. A handsome new watch for Lucien and some grand plaything for John. He would go to the Douglas Department Store and choose these things—except the ponies, of course. Yes, there would be idyllic months ahead, when he was at last reunited with his entire family!

He slept soundly, and it was nearly eight in the morning when he blinked his eyes and found himself in the wide, comfortable bed, with the shutters drawn and the bright sunshine outside filtering through the cracks at the very bottom of the window. With an exuberant laugh, Leland sprang to his feet, flexed his arms, and went through a series of exercises to tone his muscles and enhance his circulation. He had never felt so keenly alive. He had dined well and slept well; the business trip had been a huge success; and now, though it was a great pity that Laure and Lucien were not home, and that each had a personal crisis to overcome, his eventual reunion with his beautiful wife would be the fitting climax to all the weeks he had spent abroad. How he loved her! How he wished she were here so that he could draw her down beside him and kiss her in the way that she loved!

But first things first, and business was now the order of the day. When he glanced at the clock, he was grateful that he had not slept longer. Early though it was, Jacob would no doubt already be at the office poring over the books, a faithful, dedicated employee who could be depended upon to see things with a practical viewpoint. Let himself, Leland Kenniston, be the entrepreneur, the dreamer, and the fabricator of projects and schemes to make money; Jacob was the steady, faithful subordinate, without whom his business could not possibly be the success it was and would be!

He went down to the kitchen to find Mrs. Emmons preparing his breakfast. The children had already been fed and had just left for school. Just as he had supposed, the sky was blue, cloudless, and the sun bright. It was the augury of a very pleasant day ahead, one full of profitable business activities that would stimulate his mind.

"I was just about to bring up a tray, Mr. Kenniston." Clarabelle Hendry appeared from the hallway after overseeing the children's leavetaking.

"I'll eat down here; no need to go to any trouble for me. Well now, the children look fine and healthy, thanks to you. Are they doing well in school?"

"Oh, yes, Mr. Kenniston!" Clarabelle smiled almost with a proud satisfaction. "They're doing very, very well indeed. I'd say that Celestine and Clarissa are at least a year ahead, if not more, in their classes, and their teachers constantly praise them."

"That's very encouraging. And you're to be commended for their progress. As a matter of fact, I'll see that your wages are increased directly, Clarabelle," he jovially declared as he seated himself at the kitchen table. Clarabelle sat down as well, watching Mrs. Emmons set before Leland a plate of bacon and scrambled eggs.

Everything pleased him this morning. The sunshine, the breakfast, the report on the children's progress. . . . Decidedly, the Kenniston luck continued unchecked!

After he had finished his breakfast and a cigar—which he rarely smoked at the table, and never before in the kitchen, making Clarabelle Hendry cough though she politely tried not to show that it annoyed her—he went out the back door and through the courtyard to the stable, where he found Kerry Dugan polishing the carriage. "I'm home, as you see, Kerry," he genially greeted the young Irishman. "Can you drive me down to my office?"

"No sooner said than done, Mr. Kenniston, sir!"

"By the way, I want to stop at the telegraph office and send off a wire to my wife in Alabama. Just to let her know that I'm back from my European trip, you see," he airily explained.

"Of course, sir. I'm sure Mrs. Kenniston will be pleased to receive the news."

They stopped at the telegraph office, where the Irish entrepreneur wrote a lengthy dispatch to Laure, advising her of his return, and conveying his sympathies to Lucien for the youth's great loss. He added that whenever Laure needed him he would come, but barring emergencies, he would stay in New York for a week or two, to attend to business affairs.

This done, he climbed back into the carriage and was taken to his office. As he entered, he saw Jacob Cohen pacing the floor and talking to the middle-aged woman who served as receptionist. Seeing his employer enter, Jacob stopped short, lifted his right hand, which contained a sheaf of bills, and exhaled, "*Gottenyu*, Leland, you don't know how glad I am to see you!"

"Hello, Jacob. How are you?"

"Before I get to that, let me ask how *you* are? Did you receive the wire I sent about Lucien—?"

"No, but then I think that's because I changed my itinerary. I learned about Lucien's situation when I got home last night. To think that I dined with the poor girl—it couldn't have been more than a few weeks before she was killed."

"Yes, yes, a terrible thing. I hope the boy is doing well in Alabama." Jacob shrugged his shoulders and sighed. "But, Leland, I've something else on my mind—something you should know about the business. I hope you had a good rest during your crossing because you're going to need all the energy you have to help straighten out things. You were obviously very busy while abroad! My goodness—so much merchandise! I must say, I've been going crazy with these bills, and the shipments of things you bought in Europe have mostly arrived. But, Leland, I must ask you, what in the world are we going to do with some of the things?"

"Now, Jacob, you must have faith in me," Leland soothingly interposed. "Come into my office, and we'll talk things over. I've got big plans I want to tell you about."

As they walked down the hall together, Jacob declared, "I

want to have faith in you, but I just can't believe some of the things that have happened, Leland. You understand, I'm saying this because it's in your own best interest and that of the firm."

"I haven't the slightest doubt about your good intentions, Jacob." Leland jauntily waved his hand, dismissing the entire situation, as he turned and led the way into his private office. "Sit down and make yourself comfortable. Shall I have Mrs. Perkins make some coffee?"

"Oh, no, it would only unsettle my nerves, and they're bad enough already." With a groan, Jacob plunked himself down into the chair opposite his employer's desk, then laid the sheaf of bills and bills of lading on the desk in front of him. "Here are the bills; you'll be able to examine them and see that they're all in order. But before you do"—here Jacob paused—"there's something I must ask. I realize you're free to do as you wish, but I was startled by the gambling debts you ran up on the steamship going to Cobh. I went ahead and made payment, of course, because your signature was recognizable to me. I had no other choice."

"I understand that, Jacob, and there's no need for you to get excited." Leland leaned back and folded his arms across his chest, a complacent smile on his handsome face. "You did the right thing; you always do. I never have to worry about you, Jacob."

"Thank you for the compliment, but you know, I still don't feel right about this. That was a great sum of money you lost, and since you paid it out of business capital, you've left the company short. Not only that, I still don't understand how you're going to sell some of the things you bought. Like all those statuettes from London, for instance."

"I got a good deal on them, Jacob, and I believe we can sell them at a nice profit. Don't be so down in the mouth about things. I'm counting on you for enthusiastic cooperation."

"That's fine, Leland, but the fact remains that you have given me the burden of paying the bills. This is not exactly what you hired me for, if you'll remember. My chief interest is still precious gems."

"I know that." Again, Leland waved his hand and spoke in a soothing tone. "But you've become so valuable to me, I've increased your responsibilities. Granting you power of

227

attorney was a significant step. And don't worry, Jacob, there'll be a nice raise for you this coming Friday.''

"Thank you very much," Jacob somewhat stiffly retorted, "but at this point, I'm not sure you can afford to give me a raise, whether I deserve one or not."

"What do you mean by that, Jacob?" Leland bristled.

"Well, it's true that we haven't had the reports yet from San Francisco and Hong Kong, but I very much doubt, judging by last year's figures, that the profits from those two operations will offset the tremendous expenditures you've made in Europe on this trip."

"Look, Jacob—" Leland smiled in his most ingratiating manner. He leaned forward and retorted, "You haven't given my purchases a chance. You don't like the statuettes, but they're a big seller in Europe. And that false bottom makes it a useful as well as decorative item. They'll do very well here, I'm convinced of it, or I wouldn't have bought them."

"But the wicker baskets—*Gottenyu*, Leland, Indians all through the Southwest make baskets, and we can buy them more cheaply, if we want them, than the price you paid for them. And then, there's this business of the fabric inventor. . . . I've yet to see anything concrete from that man except his bill, which I paid. Now, really, Leland, all this worries me. I'm only trying to be practical, you see."

"I know, I know," Leland soothingly responded. "Just leave it to me. I'm going to make more contacts, get more factors, and I'll have a whole network throughout the country, as well as in Europe and across the Pacific. Why, we might even do business with China and Japan."

"That would be difficult. Don't forget, they have extraordinarily cheap labor, and we can't compete with them."

"I told you, you worry too much, Jacob."

"Leland, I'm a loyal employee, but when you put me in a position of having to pay out money to questionable suppliers, naturally I have to speak up. I wouldn't be of any use to you if I let all this go by the boards and didn't raise questions. For example, the goods you bought in Vienna—"

"I don't recall buying anything there," Leland interrupted. "All I did was find a factor."

"But, for God's sake, Leland, I already paid the bill on another eight thousand porcelain statuettes, these of a ragged urchin with a violin and a little dog looking up at him. I don't think they can sell, and I think you paid too much for them."

"Now wait a minute, Jacob." Leland sat upright in his chair, his eyes narrowing angrily. "I don't recall that at all. Look, maybe somebody made a dreadful mistake—maybe my factor overreached his bounds. Or else, maybe there are unscrupulous men who are plotting against me, trying to get money out of me by forging receipts."

"Leland, Leland, this isn't like you at all! How can you forget so quickly what you did in Vienna? I have the invoice with your signature, and I also have the note you sent to the Viennese representative here in New York, promising he would be receiving payment immediately."

"Just a minute—there's something very wrong here."

Jacob looked intently at his friend and then sighed. "Leland," he said, "I think we ought to discuss this further when we're both a bit calmer. I tell you what—since Laure and Lucien are in Alabama, why don't you and the other children come over to my place tonight for dinner? Then afterwards, we can talk about this at greater length."

"All right. That's a very good idea. I'm sure we can find a solution to this—but I still say I didn't buy anything like that in Vienna."

"Now, now, Leland, we'll save that for tonight. You need to relax. I know you're under a great strain from your long trip and all that has happened to your wife and your son. . . . Let's wait until we can be more congenial toward each other, shall we?"

"I'm willing. Now, if you'll excuse me, Jacob, I'll get to the things on my desk here. There's lots of correspondence to catch up on. I'll see you this evening—will six-thirty be satisfactory?"

"Fine, just fine, Leland. Thank you for understanding. Be patient with me—and remember, you hired me as an expert in diamonds and jewelry; I didn't know that I was going to be involved in bookkeeping and overseeing what you did on trips abroad. It puts me in a very delicate position, because if I say anything, you'll think that I'm criticizing you, and that isn't my point at all."

"That's all right, Jacob; everything is fine between us. I haven't lost the least respect for you, be sure of it. Well, I'll see you tonight, then."

Jacob Cohen could only nod helplessly as he rose from his chair and withdrew from the office without another word, then went back to his own office to telephone Miriam and tell her they would be having guests for dinner that evening.

Chapter Twenty

Kerry Dugan, much to his delight, had been given the evening off, since it was only a short distance from the Kenniston brownstone to the apartment building where the Cohens resided. A bright moon had begun to rise by the time Leland Kenniston, dressed in his very best suit, escorted Paul, Celestine, and Clarissa over to Sixteenth Street. John was still too young to be taken visiting, and Clarabelle promised the boy that, instead, she would play with him with his new set of tin soldiers, which Leland had brought him from England.

Paul Bouchard was in high spirits, for when he had come home from school this afternoon, he had found a letter from his friend and cousin in Galveston, Joy Hunter Parmenter, Arabella Hunter's precocious daughter. Joy was now fourteen, and she had ambitions of one day becoming a newspaper reporter—another Nellie Bly.

Joy had enclosed a clipping of her latest story, for which she had received five dollars and the editor's accolade for outstanding journalism. The lengthy letter went on to tell Paul how happy she was with her stepfather, Dr. Samuel Parmenter, who had now legally adopted her. She described how she and her mother and stepfather were able to participate in so many artistic and cultural things to make life really absorbing. "And what I hope to do one day, Paul," she wrote at the end of the letter, "is get a job on a New York newspaper—that's, of course, when I'm older, say around eighteen or nineteen. Then we could see each other often and read books together and talk about things we like and become much closer friends. Don't fail to tell me how you're getting along in school and about your friend, David Cohen, whom I want to see, too,

231

when I come to New York." She had signed it, "Your faithful and devoted friend and kindred spirit, Joy Hunter Parmenter."

When Miriam Cohen opened the door to greet Leland and the three children, Leland's eyes grew wide with pleasure. It struck him how little resemblance there was between the poor Russian immigrant whose husband he had employed nearly three years ago and the lovely woman standing before him now. Miriam was wearing a light woolen dress in a pale salmon shade. A cascade of lace made up the bodice of the high-necked, long-sleeved dress, and the drapery around the hips was pulled back into a bustle. Thanks to Laure's influence, Miriam wore her hair in an attractive pompadour, the overall effect of which was to make her look much younger than her thirty-four years.

Miriam's son, David, now also came forward. Dressed in a new suit, he looked somewhat uncomfortable, shifting from foot to foot because his father had also bought him a new pair of shoes, and they pinched a little at the toes. At his side was his younger sister, Rachel, who wore a pink dress with burgundy velvet bows around the skirt. She smiled fetchingly at Paul and bade him welcome.

Jacob Cohen, also dressed in a new suit, extended his hand to Leland Kenniston. "Be welcome to my house, my honored guest and friend and benefactor," he declared.

Miriam smiled at her husband, for he had struck exactly the right tone. The previous evening, she and Jacob had had a lengthy and worried discussion over Leland's singular commercial dealings in Europe, and Jacob had told his wife, "Frankly, Miriam, I'm very much concerned over this. If he goes on this way, he may bankrupt the firm—yes, it's as serious as that. I'm going to have to straighten him out, if I can, but with the utmost tact. I don't want to offend the man, and you know what he's meant to us and to our family."

On this evening, Miriam well understood her husband's show of deferential courtesy, and she now spoke up: "Everyone, dinner's almost ready. Go take your places at the table."

At this Jacob Cohen graciously escorted the guests into the dining room, while Miriam hurried back to put the finishing touches on the dishes she would serve.

While her husband pointed out the chairs where the children were to sit, Leland excused himself and went out into the kitchen. Miriam, startled, looked up from the kettle of chicken fricassee, which she had been preparing all afternoon. "Oh, Leland—"

"I just wanted to steal a moment to tell you how lovely you look tonight, dear Miriam. That dress is most flattering to your wonderful figure, and your new hairdo. . . . You're truly beautiful!"

"*Ach*, Leland, you mustn't try to turn an old woman's head. I've two nearly grown children! You're very kind, but I know my limitations."

"For me, you have none, dear Miriam." For a moment, he put his hand on her shoulder, and Miriam blushed, something she had not done in several years. It was an awkward moment, but fortunately for her, Leland then made her a courtly bow and said gently, "Jacob has a treasure in you." And with this, he went back to the dining room.

Jacob had told Miriam when he came home from work this evening that since Laure's children were coming, he would try to draw Leland aside after dinner. Then, while all the children were being amused and distracted by playing games together, he would undertake a serious discussion of the business. The conversation he had had that morning at the office not only puzzled him but also evoked a feeling of growing anxiety. In all the time he had known Leland Kenniston, he had never observed such inexplicable caprices and changes of mood, and he had always believed that his handsome, poised employer was the very epitome of grave judgment and conscientious integrity. Now, remembering the gambling debts and the incredibly ill-advised purchases that were coming at an alarming rate into the firm's warehouse, he did not know how to suggest that he felt his employer should consult with a doctor. Perhaps it was illness—whether of the body or of the mind, he did not know; but at any rate, it was beyond his own comprehension. He was also prejudiced in Leland's favor because of all the man had done to better the life of the Cohens; he could certainly not take a coldly impersonal stand regarding his employer.

Miriam had consoled him, understanding his quandary. "Look, darling, he respects you, and he knows that your advice is sound. When the time comes, you'll know what to say to him. I'm as worried as you, and I'm not so much concerned about ourselves as I am about Laure and the children.

233

If he does go bankrupt, they'll be the ones most affected. You, *Mensch*''—this with a goodnatured poke in the ribs and a tender smile—"are my life, and I trust you, and I know that no matter what happens, you will care for all of us. You did so on Hester Street, when you were in the midst of the worst poverty imaginable, and you did so in Kiev, when we lived with the terror of the Cossacks.''

Now, midway through the meal, Leland put down his fork and suddenly asked, "Jacob, I seem to forget—did we discuss my purchases in Europe?''

"Why, yes, Leland,'' Jacob answered, with a quick, mystified glance at his wife. "We had a very long discussion about it. You remember—the wicker baskets and the Viennese statuettes. . . .''

"Not the statuettes.'' Then he frowned and looked down at his plate. He picked up his fork but then let it clatter onto the bread plate beside his bowl. "I think that someone doesn't like me and wants to blacken my reputation purposely by sending merchandise I didn't order.''

"Your signature is on the invoices I received, Leland.''

"But I'm positive I didn't. Are you sure, Jacob?'' There was a wistful pathos in the Irish entrepreneur's voice as his eyes searched Jacob Cohen's homely, pleasant face.

"I can show you the bills again tomorrow, Leland. And we have some of the merchandise already in our warehouse. Of course, I'll have to await your orders for disposition to your various outlets.''

"Yes, but if it was merchandise I didn't order, it shouldn't have been paid for, and it should have gone back, Jacob. You'll have to see to that.''

The children were equally mystified by the groping, wandering conversation of their stepfather, and Paul left off eating to stare at Leland, his eyes as large as saucers.

Jacob made a helpless gesture with his hands, again glanced at Miriam as if for support, and then said soothingly, "Let's not talk business while we're enjoying the wonderful food my wife has cooked.''

At this, Leland seemed to come out of himself. "Absolutely true, Jacob! This is wonderful fricassee—rich and thick, and the sauce is absolutely marvelous, dear Miriam.'' Leland then lifted his glass of wine and toasted Jacob's wife. "Truly you are a pearl of inestimable value, and I only hope Jacob fully appreciates you.''

Again Miriam blushed, for there was an unmistakable ardor in his eyes as he stared openly at her. More than ever, she began to be deeply alarmed. She had never seen Leland Kenniston this way, and she knew how much he loved Laure; this absurd flirtatiousness—it was nothing else—was totally unlike him, and it was all the more pathetic for being carried out before the eyes of her husband.

"Father," Paul spoke up and chose what he believed to be the topic that would turn his stepfather's attention back to normal amenities, "I got a wonderful letter from Joy Parmenter. She wants to be a newspaper reporter when she grows up, and she's already had a few things published. She enclosed a clipping of her latest article—a very moving story about a deaf-mute and a dog. I'd like to read it, if it's all right with everyone—especially you, Mr. and Mrs. Cohen.''

"Of course, *boychik*.'' Jacob gave him a warm smile.

Paul hesitated, eyeing his stepfather, then took the letter out of his coat pocket and began to read it aloud. As he went on, his voice grew eager and excited, and he became oblivious to the reactions of those around him.

Leland frowned, put his hands over his eyes, and lowered his head. He appeared to be engrossed in thought.

Rachel, however, watched Paul carefully, observing his enthusiasm over the other girl's article. A look of jealousy began to creep across her face, but Paul was much too absorbed to notice. Rachel was certain that he did not know she had developed an almost unendurable crush on him, practically from their first meeting. The fact that Paul virtually ignored her only made her suffering all the worse, and his enthusiasm over the letter was a bitter blow.

The families said good night to each other shortly after eight-thirty. It had been obvious to Jacob that any further discussion about business matters would be futile, since Leland was apparently incapable of any more clarity this evening.

Leland and the children were home by nine o'clock, and Clarabelle Hendry and John were already in bed. Leland went around the house turning off the lights and mumbling to himself. He could not understand Jacob Cohen's insistence that he—an astute businessman—had supposedly purchased worthless items in Europe. Why on earth would he have bought wicker baskets? No, undoubtedly it was the work of someone who wanted to injure his professional standing as an internationally known tycoon. Well, tomorrow he would have it out with Jacob and look at those invoices. Someone had forged his signature. Things like that did happen, if one was not too careful.

At last, he went to his bedroom, still perturbed, the exhilaration of the day having completely worn off. He felt alone now, for the house was silent and dark. There was nothing better to do than sleep, and perhaps in the morning he would feel better. He would have to have his wits about him tomorrow when he looked at those invoices, that was for certain.

Slowly, he began to take off his jacket, and when he almost unconsciously put his hand into his pocket, he felt something hard. Puzzled, he drew it out and stared at it. It was a gold pendant of the Star of David. He realized that it must be Miriam Cohen's. How in the world did he happen to have that in his jacket pocket? He must have gone into her bedroom—though he didn't remember doing so. But, even so, even assuming he had gone to her bedroom—though he absolutely couldn't fathom why he would do such a thing— why would he have taken the necklace?

"My God," Leland whispered aloud. "What is happening to me? Could Jacob possibly be right? Did I really purchase worthless junk? Oh, God! What is happening? Am I now a thief on top of everything else?"

With a groan of despair, Leland Kenniston sank down on his bed and buried his head in his hands. He was terrified. He could not understand it or explain it. And now the black mood that had gripped him on the steamship returning home was once again in full command.

Chapter Twenty-one

Laure threw open the shutters in her bedroom and winced. The bright light made her eyes burn, for she had not slept a wink all night, despite having taken a sleeping draught to calm her nerves and help her rest. Disregarding Lopasuta's suggestion to lie down immediately, she had insisted on drawing a bath and scrubbing her body for what seemed like hours, in a desperate attempt to rid herself of the unclean feeling she was left with after the assault by Bevis Marley. Rather than relax and soothe her, the bath seemed to stimulate her, and the terrible recollections of that horrifying quarter hour kept leaping into her conscious mind, resulting in an entire night of tossing and turning, of quitting her bed and pacing the floor.

Now, early Thursday morning, she still could not rid herself of the sense that she was unclean and defiled, even though her assailant had not actually raped her. She began to walk up and down, as she had done for so many hours during the night, wondering how she could rid herself of the dreadful sense of foreboding that pervaded her every thought. She kept hearing the attacker's mocking words: "I'll just take me a reminder of what I almost had . . . and what *I will* have, right soon. . . ."

She shuddered and drew her robe more tightly around herself, feeling chilled even though the morning was already quite warm. She stopped her incessant pacing for a moment to stare out the window. Over by the dam she could just make out the figure of her son, Lucien, helping the workers shore up the levee against further flooding. She sighed, thinking that this was not at all what she had in mind for her oldest child; no, not at all. She had expected that he would continue his education right through college, perhaps even going on for a graduate degree. She had envisioned for Lucien the life of a lawyer or teacher—not a farmer.

She sighed again. She felt so sullied that she didn't even feel she could face her son as yet. That was one reason she had remained ensconced in her room and hadn't even gone to the kitchen for breakfast. "But I can't stay in here forever," she mused aloud. "I must do *something* to rid myself of this feeling."

Slowly, she walked over to the wardrobe, riffling through her dresses until she found one that was particularly chaste and demure looking. Laure took a long time dressing, and as she sat before her mirror, she kept searching her face for any outward sign that she had changed radically during the long night—as she felt she had.

When she had dressed, she left the bedroom and met Lopasuta coming down the hallway. He looked at her closely, solicitously asking, "How are you feeling, Laure? Can I get you anything?"

"I'm feeling as well as could be expected, under the circumstances," she replied, somewhat testily. Then, instantly contrite, she added, "Thank you for your concern, Lopasuta. Mostly, I want to be by myself today—no, I take that back. I've just decided that what I would most like to do is go into Lowndesboro and be with Mitzi. Would you be good enough to have a carriage readied for me?"

"Of course, Laure. And I think spending time with an old friend is the wisest thing you can do. I'll have the carriage brought around to the front as soon as it's harnessed," Lopasuta told her, putting a hand on her shoulder.

Laure jumped as though she had been touched with a hot poker. Mumbling a hasty apology, she scurried down the hallway, ashamed at her reaction to his touch. "Really," she whispered half-aloud, "I must get over this! What will happen when I see Leland again and he wants to kiss me and make love to me? Will I run from him, too? Oh, God! How long will I be so affected by men? I can't even imagine kissing my own son, now." She forced back the tears that threatened to spill over her eyelids, putting her mind squarely on the immediate tasks of finding her reticule and parasol for the short trip into Lowndesboro.

*   *   *

When she reached the main street of Lowndesboro, Laure hesitated momentarily, deciding whether she would be more likely to find Mitzi Sattersfield at home, at Dalbert's office, or at the general store. She decided to try their home first and guided the horse in that direction. The small two-wheeled phaeton bounced over the unpaved street, deeply rutted after the recent heavy rains.

Arriving in front of the Sattersfield house, Laure alighted gracefully and hitched the horse to the post. She glided up the pathway and knocked on the door. Receiving no answer, she knocked again, this time louder and longer. She sighed when she realized that no one was home, and turned on the doorstep, deciding where next to go to find Mitzi, choosing the general store as her destination.

She started to unhitch the carriage, then stopped and retied the reins. It was only a short walk around the corner and up the street to Dalbert's store, and suddenly Laure felt like getting some exercise. Opening her parasol against the hot sun, she set off for the main street of Lowndesboro.

As she walked along, she was only barely aware of the people she passed. Crossing in front of the barbershop, she didn't even notice the admiring glance of the barber as he stood looking out the large plate-glass window, waiting for a customer. Nor did she notice a young boy rolling a wooden hoop along the street, keeping it well away from the two young friends who were determined to take possession of it—although Laure was marginally cognizant of their peals of laughter. As she passed in front of the Lowndesboro Funeral Parlor, she was peripherally aware of the man lounging in the doorway. Turning her head slightly to look at him, she found that he was staring intently at her. For a moment, she sensed that she knew him from somewhere, but the feeling passed as she realized that she had never before seen his face, and she merely politely inclined her head to him and moved on. Continuing up the street for another fifty yards, she turned into Dalbert's store at the end of the block.

When he saw her, Bevis Marley felt first the shock of recognition at encountering his victim of the night before here in town. Indeed, he half expected her to start screaming when she looked into his face—until he realized that, of course, she couldn't possibly identify him because he had worn his hood throughout the assault. His momentary fear was quickly replaced by the thrilling knowledge that he was intimately familiar with her magnificent anatomy, now so completely swathed and hidden and yet—for him—easily recallable in his memory.

He felt himself becoming aroused again, and as he stared after her retreating body, licking his lips, he fingered the locket, hidden under his shirt, that he now wore around his neck almost as a fetish. His fingers glided over the polished metal; it was so silken to the touch—it was so much like her silken skin, which he had felt just the night before. He kept fondling the locket long after Laure disappeared from his view into Dalbert's store.

Soon, he told himself, *real soon*. . . .

Three days after the second attack on Windhaven Plantation, Elmer Gregory and his wife, Tess, as well as Doug Larson, were stricken with fever. Greatly alarmed, Laure sent Boyd Gregory to Montgomery on horseback to bring back Dr. Abel Kennery. Boyd was terrifed by the illness that had struck his parents; both to calm his fears and to put him to doing something useful, Laure sent the eighteen-year-old for the doctor. Eleven-year-old Lucille Gregory and seven-year-old Edward Larson then had complained of feeling sick and been promptly put to bed by Elinor Larson, who now had the responsibility of caring for two families.

When Dr. Kennery came, he went first to the Larson cottage to examine Edward. Since Elinor was tending her husband at the moment, Lopasuta accompanied the doctor to the child's room, as did Benjamin Brown. After a brief examination of the boy, Dr. Kennery scowled and turned to Lopasuta. "I can definitely state that it's typhoid fever."

"My God!" the lawyer ejaculated. "How do you know?"

"Mr. Bouchard, we've had many cases throughout the country, and most of them come from unsanitary conditions, like polluted drinking water, turned food, and the like. Most physicians who treat this fever recognize it by the fact that it causes diarrhea. Also, look at the child: Do you see the rose spots, the rash on the abdomen? That's a certain sign of typhoid. And I'm sure that the child's father is suffering from the same malady, as well as Mr. and Mrs. Gregory."

"The wells—" Lopasuta gasped, remembering.

240

"Exactly! If your dam broke and the Alabama River with its sewage from upriver and the city of Montgomery flooded and got into the wells, you'll have to take immediate precautions. You'll have to boil your water, for one thing. You'll have to check those wells that you think have not been affected, to make certain that no groundwater has seeped into them. It's most important, and Ben should give orders to have that done at once!"

"I'll do that, Dr. Kennery," the young assistant foreman solemnly promised.

The second well that supplied the chateau was directly in back of it, near Pintilalla Creek. Dr. Kennery examined it and was satisfied that it was still an unpolluted source. "If it furnishes enough water, I'd suggest that all your workers take their water from it. And even then, for the next week I'd suggest boiling, just as a precaution. It never hurts to be overly cautious when we face a disease like this."

"Is it fatal?"

Dr. Kennery paused a moment to reflect before answering. "I should say that one out of four patients dies, as a general rule. Fortunately, this doesn't mean that a young child would be necessarily weaker and succumb to the disease where the father would not. I shall do all I can for the Gregorys and for Mr. Larson and for little Edward. All we can do is give them clean water to drink—and sparingly—and to use cold compresses and perhaps a bit of quinine, which I can prescribe for you and that you can get in town. I don't believe in bleeding, not for fevers. That's the old practice, and though they use it in New Orleans, I'm against it, myself. In my book, you weaken a person by drawing blood, and you don't give him strength to combat the bacteria that cause a disease or fever."

"We'll get to work at once," Lopasuta promised.

"The other unfortunate consequence—an economic one," Dr. Kennery added after another moment's pause, "is that the produce that you've been growing on this land, where you know it to be flooded, is probably polluted, too. You certainly can't take it to market—the risk would be too great. You might cause an outbreak of typhoid wherever the produce is consumed."

"That would be deplorable," Lopasuta shook his head. "All of this couldn't have come at a worse time, what with Laure's husband away and she alone here to have to cope

241

with this disease, as well as the senseless attacks by people who have some grudge against Bouchards—well, it really is a crushing burden.''

"I wish I could have given you better news, but as a physician, I have to present the facts as they are, Mr. Bouchard," the doctor sympathetically declared. "Fortunately, I can devote a good deal of time for the next week or so to your patients here, so I'll come as often as I can."

"That's very good of you. You'll certainly be well paid—"

Dr. Kennery waved an impatient hand and shook his head. "I'm not even thinking of a fee, Mr. Bouchard. I'm thinking of stemming an outbreak of typhoid because I don't want it to spread, either to Lowndesboro or to Montgomery. Also, another dangerous thing about typhoid fever is its unpredictability: After a period of weeks a patient may seem to recover; then suddenly the disease returns with greater virulence than ever. In a situation like that, all we doctors can do is pray."

"I think you had best tell Laure what you've just told me, Dr. Kennery," Lopasuta soberly responded. He turned to the young assistant foreman. "Ben, do everything you can. Cheer the workers, tell them that we'll see that they'll be given the best possible care to overcome this."

"You can count on me, Mr. Bouchard." Ben Brown nodded and then followed them to the Gregory cottage. There they found Elmer Gregory and his wife, Tess, and their daughter, Lucille, in one room, each in separate beds; their two boys and their older daughter, Norene—none of whom had contracted the illness as yet—were in another room.

Dr. Kennery examined the Gregorys and found that Tess had the most serious case and was extremely weak. "It would be a good idea to move all the patients to one place," he said to Lopasuta, who nodded agreement. "It would be much easier to treat them if they were all together. Is there anywhere on this plantation that we could isolate them?"

"With the willing workers we have here, we could convert one of the empty cottages into an improvised ward," Lopasuta proposed. "Of course, Elmer is our best carpenter, but the others have been working under him long enough so that they've acquired some of his skills."

"Good. I would really like that done as soon as possible."

"I'll see to it, Dr. Kennery."

"Fine. And now I'd best go and speak with Mrs. Kenniston," the doctor suggested, and Lopasuta nodded.

Laure led them into the study and, seeing the serious look on the doctor's face, queried, "More bad news, Dr. Kennery?"

"I'm afraid so, Mrs. Kenniston." Dr. Kennery quickly outlined the situation for the anxious proprietor of Windhaven, describing the measures being taken to combat the disease. "I advise you to boil all drinking water," the doctor concluded.

"I'll tell Amelia," Laure promised.

"And I told Mr. Bouchard also that I'm afraid you don't dare sell the crops from those portions of land that the river flooded, Mrs. Kenniston," the doctor went on, explaining why.

"But that's our source of income. . . . Oh, dear! Everything happens at once, doesn't it?" Laure groaned helplessly and shook her head.

"I'm sorry to bring you such bad news, Mrs. Kenniston," Dr. Kennery sympathetically offered.

"Heavens, it's not your fault, Dr. Kennery. And I'm deeply obliged to you for coming so quickly to our call of need." She sighed and sat down on the sofa. "This is really terrible! Two attacks on the plantation, Marius dead, and now our water contaminated because they dynamited our dam—where will it all end?" She turned to the doctor. "If we can't sell our crops, can we sell the cattle?"

"No, you can't, because the meat would be infected for certain," Dr. Kennery told her.

"My God, Lopasuta," Laure moaned, "we're not going to have any revenue, perhaps for the rest of the entire year—and this is only March!"

"But you surely can fall back upon your bank accounts, Laure. In fact, I'd be glad to go to New Orleans to see to the transfer of funds—"

"No, Lopasuta," Laure said anxiously, "I need you here. Besides, most of the money I have is tied up in the casino—I authorized the manager, Jesse Jacklin, to make some major improvements in the building, and they cost many thousands of dollars."

"Then would you permit me to advance you some money out of what I have saved?" the Comanche lawyer earnestly inquired.

Laure looked at him, the anxiety of her expression softened

243

by affection. "Dear Lopasuta—always ready to help. But I couldn't ask you to do that. It wouldn't be right. If there are any transfers of moneys to be made, they must come from my husband's accounts. I've never asked him for money—beyond what we as a family require—but now I may have to."

Lopasuta was silent for a moment, then spoke solemnly. "I am sure he will assist with all the means at his disposal."

Laure rose from her seat and went to the window, beyond which could be seen the troubled waters of the Pintilalla Creek. "When I married my husband, I vowed to him that I would never, never ask him to underwrite a Windhaven enterprise—and that is what I consider La Maison de Bonne Chance to be. Lopasuta, I'm going to keep that vow. What Leland brings to this family, by way of financial support, should rightly be saved for the children. They are the heirs, and Leland's money should go to them intact."

"That is a very noble sentiment," Lopasuta rejoined. "But what about you, and the plantation, in the meantime?"

Laure turned again to the window and stared for a long moment at the landscape beyond before turning to reply. "Lopasuta, I have reached a decision that may startle you, but I think it's the best—maybe even the only—way. I shall sell La Maison de Bonne Chance. No"—she raised a hand— "don't object. Even if we did not have the present troubles and financial setbacks, I think it would be wise. Jesse Jacklin has reported to me that while we have been doing quite well, we have not been expanding our business in the past year or two at the same rate that we enjoyed five or six years ago. The improvements we made last year were intended to increase our business—but concrete results have yet to materialize in a thoroughly gratifying way. I'm beginning to feel that I should sell now, before the business shows any signs of leveling off or even declining."

"Perhaps, but have you consulted your bankers?"

"No," Laure replied, "and I don't need to. Though they'll help me with the particulars, I'm sure, the decision is mine alone to make."

"And you seem to have made it, Laure," Lopasuta said, with a smile, as he came to her side. "Leland would be proud to know that you, too, can make difficult business decisions."

"Thank you, Lopasuta," Laure smiled. "At any rate, the casino is mine free and clear, and I feel clear in my conscience about doing with it as I see fit. I shall send a wire up to Leland, asking him to oversee the sale as soon as he returns. I want you here with me, until we can get over all these problems—now that we have this new and terrible one added to our burden.''

"He should be able to sell it. He knows New Orleans, and of course he has many business contacts there,'' Lopasuta nodded confirmation.

"That's what I was thinking. So, tomorrow morning, I'll send a wire off to our house—I hope he'll be back by now.''

"It's a drastic step, since you'll lose some long-term income, but it's the right one, I'm sure,'' Lopasuta agreed. "I'm going to go into Montgomery tomorrow to buy some more weapons for our private guards, as well as for the tenant-owners, and I can take your wire with me. And''—he added with a encouraging smile—''let no one say that Laure Kenniston does not know how to deal with a crisis!''

"Dear Lopasuta, you are always so reassuring,'' Laure said, with a sigh. "I never dreamed that all of this would happen when I first got that telegram from Ben Brown.''

"Nor I, Laure. And I promise to give you and Lucien all the help I can to find out who was responsible for those two attacks. When I do, we can take legal action to bring those men to account for their damnable handiwork,'' the tall Comanche vehemently declared.

Chapter Twenty-two

When Laure's telegram to her husband in New York—prevailing upon him to go to New Orleans and oversee the sale of the casino that she owned—had been delivered to their house in Gramercy Square, Leland Kenniston had not yet returned from his European trip. Clarabelle Hendry signed for the telegram and put it away in the top drawer of her employer's desk in his private study. But when Leland returned so unexpectedly, Clarabelle, conscientious though she was, completely forgot about the vital message.

Indeed, it was not until the morning after Leland and the children had dined at the Cohens' that, shortly after sending the older children off to school, she suddenly uttered a cry, clapped her hand to her forehead, and said aloud, "Oh, my Lord, I completely forgot about that telegram from Laure! How could I have been so stupid and forgetful? Oh, I've got to find it and give it to him at once."

When Leland came down for his breakfast a few minutes later, he was still in his dressing gown and unshaven. He wore a dazed look on his face, and he was singularly silent.

Though Clarabelle, wringing her hands, was obviously upset, he scarcely noticed her distracted attitude, for he was still preoccupied by his terrifying discovery that he had somehow taken home with him a piece of Miriam Cohen's jewelry.

Finally, after Mrs. Emmons served Leland his bacon and eggs and poured his coffee, Clarabelle found the courage to speak up: "Mr. Kenniston, I—I've done something just dreadful. I don't know how I can possibly apologize enough . . . it was absolutely stupid of me to forget this telegram. But please do read it—I'm sure it's important, sir, and it came over a week ago, while you were still traveling."

"All right, Clarabelle. Don't be upset." He uttered a long sigh and looked up at her. "Let me see it."

"Here—here it is, Mr. Kenniston. I'm terribly sorry. . . ."

"Never mind. All of us make mistakes." Again he sighed, thinking of the pendant that he apparently had taken. Then, opening the telegram, he read Laure's message, slowly laid it down on the table beside him, and frowned.

"I do hope it's not more bad news," Clarabelle anxiously faltered.

"Well, yes, it is." Leland sounded utterly despondent. "There was another attack—they dynamited the rebuilt dam, and the river overflowed and ruined some of the well water. There's sickness down there . . . and they won't be able to sell their crops or livestock at all. Laure wants me to go to New Orleans to sell her casino. I suppose I'd better get off a telegram to her right away to let her know that I've received her message and that I'll go there immediately after I finish with my affairs here in New York."

"I'm so sorry—believe me, sir." Again, she tried to apologize.

"Never mind, it doesn't matter now." He looked up, his eyes weary. "I couldn't have done much about it anyway, since I couldn't have gone even if you'd given me the telegram the day I got back. My business concerns had to be settled first, of course. I'll have Kerry Dugan take my reply to Laure down to the telegraph office and get it off at once."

"Thank you for understanding, Mr. Kenniston. I've never done such a stupid thing before in all my life—"

"That's enough," he said, raising his hand in a vague gesture. "Let me eat my breakfast now."

Clarabelle Hendry left the room and went upstairs to the children's playroom, ostensibly to prepare for John's lessons. However, once there, she cried silently for a few moments until she regained her self-control. She didn't understand Mr. Kenniston at all; he was usually so buoyant and good humored, but he had actually looked at her with anger in his eyes—not that she could blame him, after what she had done.

Downstairs, Leland finished his breakfast, had a cigar, and then went into his study to think. Perhaps the trip to New Orleans would be an excellent idea, at this point. He was tired, so very tired. This latest news from Windhaven Plantation was but the last in a string of troubling occurrences.

What was he to make of his own behavior—whether last night at the Cohens', or in the preceding weeks in Europe? Those statuettes of the dog—he had been sure they would be an appealing and highly salable commodity in America. . . . Was he wrong? Was Jacob right? Leland trembled in terror: If Jacob was right, they could lose thousands of dollars. But there was more—those statuettes of the urchin Jacob said he had bought, for example. From Jacob's description, they, too, sounded unsalable. Try as he might, he still could not remember even placing the order.

Beginning to perspire, Leland pulled out a handkerchief and wiped his brow. He tried again to recall the face of the man from whom he might have purchased the statuettes, but nothing came to him. A terrified thought recurred to him: Could he be losing his grip, mentally? Wearily, he sank back in his chair and closed his eyes.

He slept, and when he woke with a start, he saw by the clock on his desk that nearly two hours had elapsed. Thinking of the tasks he must complete this day—the telegram to Laure, a visit to his office—he jumped up, left the study, and ascended to his dressing room, where he shaved and put on a clean shirt and his best suit. The short nap, so unusual for him under ordinary circumstances, had refreshed him, and as he knotted his cravat, he began to feel—for reasons he could not entirely fathom—that all was not as dark as he had supposed. No, there was some reasonable explanation for that shipment from Vienna—some reason for its having been sent without authorization. It had to have been done by someone trying to cheat him. Yes, he was sure of it. As irksome as that idea was, it seemed more reasonable than to imagine that he could not remember placing the order. Clearly Jacob would have to write a strongly worded letter to the exporter in question, challenging the shipment. And as for the pendant— well, he would just hand it back to Jacob and hope that a simple apology would suffice between friends. Then he could go to New Orleans with a clear conscience.

New Orleans would be diverting, and it would certainly be warmer than New York in early spring, with the raw winds and the cold drizzle and the dreary, dull skies. It was a pity he had missed Mardi Gras—how well he remembered courting his beloved Laure there! But there would be other adventures, and he looked forward to selling the gambling casino. Yes, he had forgotten that Laure owned one. Well, if she wanted to sell, he would try to get her the very best price. While he was there, it would be foolish not to have a turn at the wheel and at the cards. He was an excellent poker player, for one thing, and he could play vingt-et-un with the best of them, he was certain.

His good humor was totally restored. All that mattered now was having a last session with Jacob Cohen, getting the European business straightened out, and going on down to New Orleans. When he finished there, he could at last have a wonderful reunion with his beautiful wife!

Dr. Abel Kennery had paid many visits to Windhaven Plantation, and he was exhausted, for he was handling this epidemic—any news of which he was trying valiantly to suppress so that the citizens of the area would not be alarmed—along with his regular duties and practice. His beautiful wife, who was also his nurse, assisted him, and she, too, was weary.

Little Edward Larson succumbed to the fever, lingering just three days with it. Only the fact that her husband needed her care kept Elinor from breaking down completely under the weight of her grief. Fortunately, Doug Larson was fighting off the fever and was on the road to recovery, though still very weak. Tess and Lucille Gregory recovered; however, both had little strength. Tess had lost considerable weight. Her husband, Elmer, contrarily, made a quick recovery. But three workers in their late twenties, who had been hired by Benjamin Brown earlier this year and who worked in the stables and at the cotton gin, also succumbed to the malady. This had caused a great deal of alarm on Laure's estate, and one week after she had sent the telegram to Leland to urge him to sell the casino in New Orleans, two other workers came to her, hired early the previous spring, and announced their intention of going elsewhere for work.

"It's too dangerous, ma'am," Fred Laird, a tall, towheaded young man of twenty-six told her as he twisted his hat in his hands. "I'm scared of this fever thing—scared I could come down with it any day. You see, ma'am, I've got me a fiancée in Mobile, and I told her when I saved up three hundred dollars, I'd go down there and marry her. Well, ma'am, you treat us real good, and the wages are fine, but I

249

might just die before I could save up the hundred dollars more I need to marry my Peggy.''

"I understand, Mr. Laird. Mr. Brown has told me you've worked faithfully here, and I appreciate what you've done. What I'm going to do is give you a month's pay and a bonus of fifty dollars. As a matter of fact, it'll come to one hundred dollars.''

The towheaded young man brightened, his eyes widening incredulously. "You mean that, ma'am, for certain?''

Laure nodded and smiled.

"Gee whiz, ma'am, that's right decent of you! My God, I can go right down to Mobile now and get myself hitched and then find a job—maybe there'll be a good one down there!''

"Of course there will. Try the docks down there, or some of the clearing houses. There's always work for a good hand like you, Mr. Laird.''

By the end of the week, five more workers from Windhaven Plantation had decided to seek employment in a less dangerous place, and had left the area. On the evening when the last man left, Laure turned to her son and sorrowfully said, "Lucien, all the hope we have now is that Leland will be able to sell the casino. I haven't heard from him in response to my wire, so I can only conclude that he's still in Europe, or at least on the way back. I pray God he'll be able to get there in time to bring us in some much-needed revenue.''

"I know. It's very serious, Mother,'' the young man agreed. "And what also concerns me is that we have a lot of repairs to make—and it's going to take a considerable amount of time and labor and money to permanently rebuild that dam.''

"I'm reminded of the Bible story of Job; undoubtedly you heard it in sermons at St. Timothy's,'' Laure told him as she mopped her brow with a cotton kerchief. "You know—the story of how Satan taunted God and said that he would corrupt Job, whom the Lord upheld as a faithful and loyal servant. And Job sustained all manner of tribulations and agonies, but he denied the power of Satan—and, in the end, he emerged happier and wealthier and more in God's favor than ever before. I only hope that parable holds true for us.''

After he had mulled over the telegram from Laure, urging him to sell the New Orleans gambling casino, Leland Kenniston

250

went to his office late in the afternoon. Jacob Cohen greeted him warmly, but there was a trace of nervous anxiety on the man's face, which Leland at once interpreted as a sign of gloom. "Come now, Jacob, your face is as long as the list of grievances against your people," he quipped.

"That was unkind, Leland," Jacob quietly responded. "For centuries, the Jews have been persecuted, and we've survived. You and I will survive all of our problems, too. I just urge you to be a little less forgetful about what you did in Europe. Even though you tell me that some of those purchases are not yours, I'm afraid your signature on the bills is so authentic that I have no recourse except to pay them. I've been going over the books again this morning, by the way—and they're in very bad shape. Our revenues from San Francisco and Hong Kong are being held up, and we've already had letters from your factors out there indicating that they're likely to be much less than expected. With that in mind, and with the European expenditures—I won't even mention the gambling debts—we may be facing a financial crisis of considerable magnitude."

"Now, calm yourself, Jacob, and don't give me any sidelong remarks about gambling. It's a gentleman's pastime and prerogative. Besides, I'm here to tell you that your worries are all over. See this telegram?" Leland took it out of his coat lapel pocket, unfolded it, and put it on the desk before his faithful aide. "Laure wants me to go to New Orleans to sell her gambling casino. From what I know of gambling and New Orleans, that should bring a pretty penny, more than enough to clear up all our debts, even those I don't think we rightly should be expected to pay. Certainly we'll have enough to give us a handsome profit."

Jacob Cohen looked askance at the tall, handsome Irish entrepreneur. This indeed was a new Leland Kenniston, who could speak so callously of taking over his wife's assets and using them to pay off his own debts—debts with which Laure had absolutely nothing to do. However, he had the feeling that to argue would not only be futile but would also strain the bonds of their friendship to the breaking point. So, calmly he replied, "I do hope you're right, Leland. When do you plan to leave?"

"In three or four days. I want to spend the rest of this week going over the books again, because I can't quite agree with

251

your gloomy prognostication. If I have any questions, I'll call you and Johnson in, Jacob. By the way, I'll need some money for my New Orleans trip."

"I—I suppose you will." Jacob scowled, then scratched his head and went through his ledger book. "We've got about five hundred dollars in petty cash, and I guess that'll do till you can realize the sale of the casino. What do you think it'll bring?"

"Property like that ought to be worth at least a hundred thousand dollars. There's big money in New Orleans these days, and the casino is in a fine location. It's a beautiful place, and the manager, Jesse Jacklin, has been extremely adroit ever since we put him in charge—that is, since Laure put him in charge. I didn't know her at that time, of course, but now that we're married, the casino is communal property."

Jacob took a deep breath. At least Leland was acknowledging, by his reference to communal property, that the casino had once belonged to Laure alone. The laws of Louisiana might put such property into her husband's hands; if so, the questions of what Leland now did with it was more a moral than a legal one—and Jacob could not presume to answer it for his employer. "If," he replied, "Laure is agreeable to letting the money derived from the sale of the casino figure in the ledger of your business enterprise, Leland, then I should say that we can pull out of this mess."

"That's a little better, but you're still very gloomy. Don't you worry, Jacob. I'll bring back enough money to see us sailing absolutely smoothly again, and have plenty left over to make some new acquisitions. And now, if we've nothing further to discuss, I'll go off to my office and look at the ledger."

Suddenly Leland remembered what he had discovered in the pocket of his jacket when he had returned home with the children from the Cohens'. "By the way . . . I—I—er—" He fished into his coat pocket and drew out the pendant. "Jacob, I know this sounds odd, but last night when I was over at your place, I picked up something I found—I actually don't recall when. Because I had my mind on business and all the troubles that poor Laure has had, as well as Lucien, I must have put it in my pocket without thinking about it. Would you please give it back to Miriam and express my profound apologies? I certainly hope she didn't think that I stole it."

252

"Good heavens, why would anyone think that of you, Leland? I'm sure Miriam will be glad you found it for her. Well then, I'll see you when you finish with the ledger."

Leland nodded, tucked the ledger under his arm, and walked out of the office. Jacob stared after him, a look of utter bewilderment on his face. Then he shook his head and uttered a long, baffled sigh, wondering once again whether his friend would agree to consult with a doctor about his peculiar behavior.

Chapter Twenty-three

It was noon of April 10 when Leland Kenniston arrived at the New Orleans railroad station. The weather was warm and humid, the sun blazing down, and Leland was in a wonderful mood. Everything about New Orleans was associated with his past successes, and remembrance of all this gave him the feeling that the trivial problems that Jacob Cohen had insisted on reiterating all during his stay in New York would be blown away as by a gust of wind now that he was here in a city so lucky for him. And the very name of Laure's casino, La Maison de Bonne Chance, The House of Good Luck, was in itself auspicious, and as a further talisman of good fortune, he would stay at the same hotel where he had last stayed.

Taking up the single suitcase he had with him for the journey, Leland strode along the levee and hailed a fiacre driven by an elegantly groomed Creole driver who wore a becoming silk top hat.

He checked into the St. Charles Hotel and ordered the largest suite available. The tall, bespectacled manager, who was himself manning the desk at this hour, assured Leland of the finest accommodations and also offered him the services of the hotel safe, in order to keep whatever valuables he had brought with him. Expansive under the manager's obsequious attentions and wishing also to appear obliging, Leland placed in the hotel safe all but one hundred dollars of the five hundred in cash that he had brought with him. He smiled wryly as he thought how pleased Jacob Cohen would be at this prudent step, unnecessary though Leland felt it to be. Pocketing the receipt that the hotel manager gave him in exchange for the cash, he followed the bell clerk up to his room, where he unpacked his suitcase and changed into a fine new suit that he had purchased in London. Then he descended to the street once more, where he found another carriage that would take him to the gambling casino.

It was about three in the afternoon when he entered the casino and asked the doorman to let Jesse Jacklin know that he, Leland Kenniston, wished to see him. The wiry Tennesseean, now fifty-five, was ensconced in his office, going over the books, for it was almost time for his monthly report to Laure Bouchard Kenniston as well as to the Brunton & Alliance Bank.

The doorman ushered Leland into Jesse's office, and the rangy, gray-haired Southerner sprang up from his desk with the alacrity of a man half his age. "Welcome to New Orleans, Mr. Kenniston," he said as he came forward to shake Leland's hand. "It's a pleasure to see you. Is Mrs. Kenniston with you in town, by any chance?"

"No, but I've come here to take care of her business," the Irish entrepreneur began. "I've been in Europe and just came back to find that my wife went to Alabama to deal with a very bad situation. Some night raiders attacked the plantation, burned some buildings, and shot the foreman, Marius Thornton, who died as a result of his wounds."

"That's terrible! I'm sorry to hear of this. Mrs. Kenniston told me what a fine man Mr. Thornton was—she really depended on him. Will you be going on to Windhaven yourself?"

"In due time, Mr. Jacklin. My immediate reason for being in New Orleans is that my wife sent me a telegram asking me to come here on her behalf. You see, Mr. Jacklin, there has been a second attack, which destroyed the dam on the Windhaven property, polluting both the drinking water and the land set aside for this year's planting. I'm afraid that the revenue my wife could ordinarily have expected from the crops simply won't be coming in. As a result, she finds herself forced to put the casino up for sale. After we chat, I'm going on to the bank to see if they can give me a hand in finding a buyer. But please don't be alarmed—I know that you've done very well for her; I'm grateful for that, and I'll certainly give you the highest recommendation when I find a buyer. Very likely the new owner will want to keep you on. If not, then—well, casinos are big business in this city, as

255

you know, and experienced and astute managers are in demand."

Jesse Jacklin sighed deeply and was quiet for a moment. Then he leaned forward on his desk. "Well, Mr. Kenniston, you surely take me by surprise with your news. But I know how to roll with the punches. Naturally, I hope I'll be able to continue, because I've enjoyed managing the casino—I don't mind telling you. I've always insisted that we run an honest place. There are no prostitutes attached to it; Mrs. Kenniston would never stand for it, nor would I. Actually, I've accumulated some money of my own, and my wife, Edith, has some savings from past years. So, if worse came to worst, I'd have enough to tide me over. You needn't be concerned, and if you have to sell this place to help your wife out, then I'm all for it."

"Thank you, Mr. Jacklin, for being so understanding. Now, if you will excuse me, I'll go right now to the bank before they close, and tomorrow I'll let you know what they propose to do. We'll be in close touch until this sale can be accomplished. I bid you a very cordial afternoon." Leland genially nodded, rose from his chair, and again shook hands with the casino manager.

About ten minutes later, he descended from the carriage he had hailed and entered the Brunton & Alliance Bank. Drawing out his card and handing it to the guard, he asked to see the president. The guard, observing how elegantly Leland Kenniston was dressed, hurried to the office of Henry Kessling. Seconds later, he reemerged. "Come this way, Mr. Kenniston. He'll see you directly," the guard courteously averred.

Henry Kessling was a bluff, candid man, with thick sideburns, a bushy mustache, and cold, gray eyes. He was stocky of build, and in his fifty-fourth year. Thanks to his shrewd investments and his hiring of outstanding employees from his former bank, the New Orleans Alliance, he had doubled the reorganized bank's capital in the short time since he had bought it from Laure's old friend, Jason Barntry.

"Glad to see you, Mr. Kenniston. How may I help you? Take a seat, please. Have one of my Havana cigars." Henry Kessling proffered a teakwood box, and Leland helped himself to a cigar, took the clipper that the bank president handed him, and accepted a light with a grateful nod.

"Excellent! It draws very well; good mellow tobacco. Well

256

then, Mr. Kessling, I'm here on behalf of my wife, Laure Bouchard Kenniston. If you'll allow me, I have this telegram from her." He unfolded it and set it before the bank president, who scanned it and then eyed him quizzically. "I should be very grateful if you could help me find a buyer for the casino as quickly as possible. I'm sure you've heard of it, La Maison de Bonne Chance?"

"Indeed, sir, and who has not?" Henry Kessling chuckled, drawing on his own cigar and blowing a wreath that slowly wafted to the ceiling. "It's a very salable piece of property, I can tell you that. I'll have no trouble finding any number of interested clients for you; the trick will be selecting just the right one—someone who is extremely solvent. I assume that your wife will want as much of a cash down payment as possible and wouldn't particularly care for a long-term note?"

"My feeling is that she would indeed prefer cash, Mr. Kessling. With all the trouble at the plantation, there is a good deal of repair and restoration work to be done. And in view of the fact that we won't have a crop this year, we'll need as much cash on the barrelhead as possible, to meet routine expenditures later on."

"Well, you leave everything to me. Where are you staying?"

"At the St. Charles."

"You've good taste. It's the best in town. I'll be getting a message over to you there in a few days. Meanwhile enjoy yourself at the fine restaurants and the theater. I promise I'll do everything in my power to get you a quick sale, without sacrificing the real potential of that excellent property."

"I'm grateful. By the way, I remember that my wife used to deal with a lawyer here named Hollis Minton. As I recall from what she told me, he presided over the original purchase of the casino, about six years ago."

"That's true, Mr. Kenniston." The bank president rose from his desk. "He would be an excellent choice to represent you again. The only trouble with that is, he's retired and moved to San Francisco. So, I suggest you find another lawyer—if you need help in that regard, I can recommend one, for the bank does business with several attorneys who have excellent standing in this city."

"That won't be necessary. I just thought I'd use Minton again if he were around because of his familiarity with the property. However, since he isn't available, I'll use my firm's lawyer—Lopasuta Bouchard. He's also my wife's adopted son, by a former marriage.''

''Yes, I was going to mention him. He's one of the best. Quite an interesting fellow. I understand he's of Indian and Mexican birth, and raised himself up by his bootstraps. He's looked upon as one of the leading lights among our practicing attorneys.''

''Yes, that's all true. He's been of great help to me, certainly. I'll try to have him handle the legal aspects of the sale, Mr. Kessling.'' Leland thrust out his hand, a jovial smile on his face. ''I'm indebted to you, and I'll await hearing from you at your convenience.''

With this, he left the bank and, hailing a carriage, ordered the driver to take him to his New Orleans office. Upon arriving, he was greeted by Judith Marquard, who informed him that Lopasuta had not yet returned from Windhaven Plantation, where he was assisting Laure; but, she said, Eugene DuBois was expected back within the hour, and he was a capable lawyer in his own right—as he had repeatedly proven to the firm. Leland laughed his agreement, saying that, indeed, he was delighted that he would again see the young Creole. Meanwhile, he was quite content to wait, for he was captivated by the lovely Judith Marquard. He engaged her in conversation and was so gallantly complimentary to her that she blushed deeply and was obliged to direct all her attention to some legal correspondence that she was transcribing.

Eugene DuBois came back within twenty minutes, and Leland sprang to his feet. ''Eugene, how are you? It's been quite some time since I was here, hasn't it? This is rather abrupt, but I need some legal help at once, and I understand Lopasuta is still in Alabama—''

''Mr. Kenniston, how nice to see you again! Indeed, it has been some time, and, yes, Lopasuta is still away. But I'll certainly give you whatever help I can.''

''Thank you. Now then, I daresay that you are familiar with my wife's holdings, particularly the casino, La Maison de Bonne Chance?'' the Irish entrepreneur inquired.

Eugene nodded. ''Yes, indeed. Jesse Jacklin has done an excellent job of managing it.''

''I'm glad to hear you say that, Eugene. It heartens me a little, for I'm afraid I'm going to have to tell you that we're going to try to sell it immediately.''

"I don't understand."

"Let me explain. You must know that there was an attack on Windhaven Plantation, since Lopasuta went to Alabama to assist my wife in the aftermath of the crisis—"

"I do know that."

"Then let me explain the rest." Quickly Leland reviewed for Eugene's benefit the events that had necessitated the sale of Laure's casino.

"I understand." Eugene replied, when Leland had finished. "And may I assume you want me to represent you and draw up the papers of the sale when you find a buyer, is that it, Mr. Kenniston?"

"That's it exactly. I've just come from the Brunton & Alliance Bank, and Mr. Kessling, the president there, assures me that he will have no trouble finding a buyer within a short time. I'm sure that you'll do very handsomely for us all."

"You're very kind to say so, Mr. Kenniston. Since you're looking for a quick sale, I take it you're going to stay here in New Orleans until the sale is made final."

"Yes. Then I'll go to Alabama to be of what service I can to Laure, to help her through these trying times."

"Well, I hope that your stay will not have to be too long, for I know how eager you must be to rejoin your wife, Mr. Kenniston." Eugene smiled as an idea came to him. "In the meantime, you must come for dinner. In fact, why not tonight? Mei Luong would be so thrilled to see you again. She's spoken of you so often to me—as, of course, has Lopasuta—of the circumstances under which you met. Do say yes!"

"Why, that's uncommonly kind of you, Eugene. I shall accept your invitation before you change your mind," Leland replied.

"She'll be so delighted. Now, then, perhaps you ought to tell me what you think is a fair asking price for the property—and also, what would be the lowest that you would accept? That's important, because in selling property, it's wise not to panic and take the first offer. A hasty decision could cheat you out of many thousands of dollars."

"As to prices, I don't know—I've been tossing figures around in my head ever since I saw Mr. Jacklin earlier this morning. With the volume he does, I should say that a hundred thousand dollars would be certainly a minimum price, don't you think?"

"By all means. To be sure, since Mr. Jacklin has seen to it that there is no prostitution at the casino, he may have been losing some business now and again, especially to first-time visitors to our city who are eager for the excitement of the wheel and the cards and then the gratification of their carnal desires. There are, of course, other houses here that cater to both types of pleasure. On the other hand, I'm sure a look at the books will reveal a reasonably attractive profits picture." He rose and went to the door, and called out, "Judith, would you mind going over to La Maison de Bonne Chance to ask Mr. Jacklin to give us some recent financial statements? We'll need them for potential buyers."

"At once, Eugene!"

When Judith had returned a short time later, Leland took the statements from her and then, much to her embarrassment, seized her hand and kissed it, with a flowery little speech. "You are beyond a doubt the loveliest creature I've seen since I came to New Orleans."

"You—you're much too kind, Mr.—Mr. Kenniston," Judith faltered, unable to hold back her blushes and glancing desperately at the Creole in the hope that somehow he would divert the forceful man's attention. She was, so to speak, a captive audience to him, since she did not dare show any hint of coldness or hostility. She was well aware that Leland Kenniston was her ultimate employer: Although Lopasuta Bouchard had hired her, it was Kenniston & Co. that paid her salary. All the same, if she could have turned herself invisible and vanished, she would have been extremely grateful!

Eugene DuBois was sensitive enough to appreciate what was going on and quickly interposed, "Why don't you use Lopasuta's office, Mr. Kenniston, since he's not here? You can have complete privacy and devote all your attention to the financial reports. Then, when you're ready, we'll go over them. I think you've done very well so far to have gotten Mr. Kessling to make a commitment that he would certainly find a buyer for you in a short time. That alone should convince you how desirable a property it is—and that's why I'm saying to you, don't take the very first price offered."

"I'll take it under advisement, as you lawyers would say," Leland quipped. He took the file under his arm and walked to the vacant office, turning to eye Judith once again. She swiftly turned her face away and made a pretense at being extremely busy. Leland chuckled softly to himself, nodded to Eugene, and closed the door.

Dr. Abel Kennery had just come from the house of Hughie Mendicott. That sturdy black worker, who had been associated with Windhaven Plantation for many loyal years, had just succumbed to the virulent typhoid fever. His sons, Louis and Davey, now twenty-eight and thirty, came outside with Dr. Kennery and unashamedly wept. "He was such a good man," Davey muttered, taking out a red bandanna and loudly blowing his nose. "Pa loved this place so, but I think it hurt him a lot when Ma died, and he wasn't quite the same after that. He didn't suffer much, did he, Dr. Kennery?"

"No, Davey," the handsome young doctor compassionately murmured, "he didn't have any pain, and he died in his sleep. Pray God all of us have as easy a death."

"Amen to that," Louis solemnly said. "Damn those night raiders anyhow!" He scowled and clenched his fist. "If they hadn't dynamited the dam, Pa'd still be alive today, you know what I'm saying? If ever I catch up with them, they're gonna pay me back for taking Pa away from Davey 'n me. I'll get me a gun, and I'll notch a few marks on the stock before I'm done with them, just see if I don't!"

"Louis," Dr. Kennery interposed, "you know what is written in the Bible: 'Vengeance is mine, saith the Lord.' The wicked will be punished, Louis, don't you worry. Their misdeeds will catch up with them, and your father will be avenged."

But the two brothers were inconsolable, and Davey turned to Louis and muttered, "I'll be right up next to you with a rifle in my hand if I hear them bastards comin' on this land again!"

Chapter Twenty-four

Leland Kenniston uttered a cry of delight at the sight of Mei Luong DuBois as, opening the door to his house, Eugene exclaimed to his wife, "Mr. Kenniston will be our guest for dinner this evening—and forgive me, my love, for not telling you in advance and thus causing you so much work!"

"Mei Luong, what a pleasure to see you again! You're as lovely as ever, my dear!" the Irish entrepreneur loudly exclaimed. Moving ahead of his host, he went up to the attractive young Chinese woman, took her hand, and kissed it. "You don't look a day older than you were when we first met four years ago. I've never forgotten our trip from Hong Kong to San Francisco by steamer, when you and Lopasuta were returning to America with his son."

"I have often thought of that trip, Mr. Kenniston—I think of how fate has brought us to where we are, and I am so happy." Then, shyly withdrawing her hand, she turned to her husband and said, "I am so happy you have brought your employer. You know, it is no trouble, my dear husband; and it is my privilege and honor to welcome you, Mr. Kenniston," she added, turning back to their guest.

"Will you not make yourself at home in the living room? The large chair toward the left is the most comfortable, and since you are our guest, you must take it. And may I bring you a drink before dinner?"

"Thank you; a glass of wine, perhaps, if you have it."

"I do. And as it happens by great good luck, I am preparing mandarin duck this evening. I hope you like it. There is plenty for the three of us. Now please be comfortable, and I will bring you the wine directly."

Leland smiled and nodded and sank down into the chair. Then he exhaled a sigh of utter contentment.

In a few moments, the young Chinese woman brought him a glass of white wine and a dish of salted almonds to nibble at while dinner was being prepared.

"Did you know that my wife has given me a son?" Eugene suddenly asked Leland, as he seated himself on the couch and sipped the wine that his wife had brought to him, after having first served their guest. "Jean-Pierre is just three months old, yet already it is clear that he has his mother's beautiful eyes and her sweet mouth. He is sturdy and healthy, and we have a nurse who thinks the world of him. We named him after my grandfather; he was a wonderful man who lived to be ninety and who loved books and music. He ardently believed that man would one day overcome all his hatred and prejudice and make the world a place of peace and happiness."

"I am happy for you. You know the saying that a man who has a wife and children has given hostages to fortune," Leland replied, as he lifted his glass to toast Eugene and Mei Luong.

"So many things have happened," Leland continued, "since I first chanced to meet Lopasuta and your own lovely wife on board that steamship. Perhaps as Mei Luong says, fate has had a hand in all of this. You see, I've just come back from Europe, and I have made myself wealthy and famous by going to many great cities and establishing representatives there, who will carry on my commerce throughout Europe. If you and Lopasuta continue to handle my affairs, there's no limit to the profits you'll make and the reputation you will garner by being associated with me."

Eugene politely nodded. Inwardly, he was somewhat surprised that his employer should be boasting in such a manner, but he ascribed this to the man's dynamic enthusiasm and his enterprising nature.

Presently, Mei Luong came in to announce that dinner was ready, and they adjourned to the dining room, where Leland was loud in his praise for every course. The mandarin duck was delicious. It had been cooked with wild rice and toasted almonds, served with asparagus as well as a dish of kumquats in Mei Luong's own delicately flavored sauce. After dinner, instead of a liqueur, there was plum wine.

Abruptly, Leland rose from the table and, to Eugene's

surprise, went into the kitchen, where Mei Luong was brewing some tea. As she bent to put more coal in the stove, the slit in the side of her cheongsam revealed her shapely leg almost halfway up her thigh. She suddenly sensed his presence behind her, and quickly turned, her eyes very wide and searching. "Mr. Kenniston! You mustn't come out here; you're our guest and cannot offer your help in the kitchen. Now please go back to the dining room, and presently I will have some tea for you."

"Thank you. But I must say, Eugene is very lucky. You're really very beautiful, Mei Luong. Every time I travel to Hong Kong, I realize how exquisite Oriental girls can be." He chuckled and shrugged. "Perhaps I should have brought back a Chinese wife myself—but, there again, fate crept in."

Mei Luong was again embarrassed by his sensual interest in her, for she observed that he was staring at her body, which was enticingly displayed by her dress to a degree that no western fashions did. Fortunately, a pot began to boil at this moment, and she gasped, "Oh, now the tea's ready, Mr. Kenniston. I'll bring it out to you. Please, I don't want to spill any on you, and this is a small kitchen—"

"Of course, of course," he soothingly placated her. "I'll return to my place at the table. But I just had to come in here and tell you how wonderful dinner was . . . and how beautiful you are."

"Thank you. I am happy that you enjoyed my poor efforts."

He laughed loudly and then went back to his chair. Eugene had been about to rise, a little concerned over the length of time his guest had spent in the kitchen with his wife, but settled back in his chair when he saw Leland return and seat himself. "I told her what a wonderful supper it was," Leland said. "Yes, Eugene, decidedly, you're a most fortunate young man."

"Thank you, Mr. Kenniston."

As they sipped their cups of tea, the Creole lawyer tried to turn the subject away from his wife to business. "You say you had a most profitable trip in Europe, Mr. Kenniston?"

"Oh, yes, decidedly I did! London, Paris, Berlin, Vienna— and all these cities now know the name of Kenniston. Of course, you understand that international trade takes longer than what we do here in the United States, Eugene. If Laure could only have waited a little, the profits that I have guaranteed through my efforts on my trip would have taken her out of all her financial difficulties. But then," he shrugged and smiled, "this is the way women are, Eugene. And that's why I came to New Orleans, to prove to her what a loyal and loving husband I am by selling the casino quickly for her so that she won't have to worry about money."

"You're most thoughtful. Well, now, may I take you to the nursery to show you Jean-Pierre?"

Leland Kenniston sprang to his feet with an alacrity that startled the Creole lawyer. "I'd very much like to see him. What a fortunate man you are—but I've already said that, haven't I? Well, then, let's go see the son and heir!"

On the following Friday, the thirteenth of April, Henry Kessling sent a messenger over to the St. Charles Hotel to inform Leland Kenniston that he had found a reputable buyer for Laure's casino.

During that waiting period, Eugene DuBois had acted as a guide to the Irish entrepreneur. They spent one afternoon sightseeing out along Lake Pontchartrain. In all his visits to New Orleans, Leland had never seen the first railroad ever completed in the South, the first one west of the Alleghenies: It was a line of only four and a half miles, and very likely the only one equipped with sails for auxiliary power. As Eugene humorously explained, "Sometimes the steam engine fails, so the engineers put up the sails, and the gusts of wind from the Gulf send the locomotive hurrying along the tracks. It was built in eighteen twenty-eight and has become something of a landmark here."

The next evening, Eugene had insisted on taking Leland and Mei Luong to the French Opera House, a plastered brick structure of Italian design that rose four stories and had space for some two thousand music lovers.

Leland and Eugene and Mei Luong were in luck that evening, for Adelina Patti was singing Violetta in *La Traviata*, a role that had made her Giuseppe Verdi's favorite prima donna. She had sung at this very opera house many times— the first being at the start of the house's second season in 1860, when she was not quite eighteen. Her golden voice and its volume, emerging from the slim, dark-haired woman, dazzled the patrons.

The Creole found Leland in exceptionally high spirits during these outings, except it sometimes exasperated him to have his employer pay such flowery compliments and unctuous attention to Mei Luong. The lovely young matron took it in stride, trying to placate her husband, lest he have the slightest feeling of jealousy, by telling him one evening after Leland had returned to his hotel, "My dearest, it is really you whom he is complimenting all this time. You see, I think that he is a little envious, and also very lonely. You must not forget, Eugene, that his wife is away from him. A married man who thus becomes a widower, so to speak, can be pardoned for noticing someone else's wife who is happy with her husband—as I assuredly am with you, and you need never doubt that."

At last, the long-awaited summons to the bank came, and Leland, enormously enthusiastic, brought Eugene along with him to call on Henry Kessling. The prospective buyer was already on hand in the bank president's office, a suave, black-bearded and mustachioed man in his mid-forties, who was introduced to Leland Kenniston as Hector Galvez. He had been a *hacendado* in Mexico and had sold his estate about a decade before and come to New Orleans—for he was an inveterate gambler—and there he had prospered.

"Well, now, Señor Kenniston," the affable Mexican began, "you are eager to sell, and I am eager to buy. Señor Kessling has shown me the prospectus, and I find the property in excellent shape—indeed, I visited it just last night, and I may say that I won a thousand dollars playing vingt-et-un."

"A very auspicious beginning, Señor Galvez," Leland chuckled.

"I think I know what it is currently worth and what its potential is. On the other hand, Señor Kenniston, since you require a very large cash outlay, I hope you will be content with what I offer: I can put up seventy-five thousand dollars now against a total purchase price of one hundred twenty-five thousand dollars; the remaining money can be paid to you in four installments over the next two years."

Leland frowned and was silent for a moment, considering the offer. A portion of the seventy-five thousand dollars would surely tide Laure over by restoring Windhaven Plantation to solvency until the disastrous ruination of the crops could be offset by next year's planting and harvesting; the rest would allow him a reserve that ought to satisfy Jacob Cohen's

266

grumblings about excessive bills. He barely considered the fact that the casino was, from the moral standpoint at least, entirely Laure's. Indeed, he had already begun to think that the entire proceeds of the casino were actually his and that, as a generous and sympathetic husband, he would disperse a sufficient sum to take Laure out of her present difficulties.

So, at last, with a nod, he said to the Mexican, "Very well, I will accept. How soon can the transaction be effected?"

"At once, Señor Kenniston, if you are willing," Hector Galvez chuckled, drawing a wallet out of his coat pocket and opening it. "I propose giving you a draft for thirty-eight thousand dollars on my personal account. It can be converted into cash at once, if you desire. Señor Kessling, meanwhile, will take the other thirty-seven thousand from a business account that I still have in Mexico—Señor Kessling, I will write out a withdrawal order for you."

"I should like the cash, so I shall certainly convert the first draft; the second draft I can send to my wife in Alabama—yes, that would be sensible." Leland ignored the slightly raised eyebrows of Eugene DuBois, who was startled to find that Leland wanted or needed such a sum in cash.

"Very well, Señor Kenniston. We shall conclude the transaction. Señor DuBois, you are the *abogado* of Señor Kenniston; do you agree to this proposal? Does it meet with your legal approval?" the Mexican politely inquired.

"I see no obstacles to it, and you will have clear title. Mr. Kessling, if you'll provide me with one of your clerks, I shall proceed to draw up the bill of sale. We shall need copies for the bank, for Mr. Kenniston, for Señor Galvez, and one for our own office," the Creole lawyer averred.

Two hours later, the transaction was concluded, and Hector Galvez turned over the two drafts for thirty-eight thousand and thirty-seven thousand dollars to Leland Kenniston. Leland, for his part, had taken the extraordinary step of converting the note for the larger amount into thirty-five one-thousand-dollar bills and thirty one-hundred-dollar bills. This was accomplished by a visit to Señor Galvez's bank, with Eugene along to witness the transaction. When they had returned to Kessling's office, Señor Galvez shook Leland's hand. "Now then, Mr. Kenniston," he asked, "do you wish me to send the four remaining installments to your *abogado* here, or to you?"

"Mr. Kessling," the Irish entrepreneur turned to the bank

president, "I assume that these four notes are virtually as sound as legal tender."

"Oh, yes, Señor Galvez has a letter of credit and many properties in New Orleans already. By your question, I take it to mean that you might wish to draw upon them before they mature, is that correct?"

"It's possible," Leland airily responded, at which Eugene's eyebrows again rose in surprise. Why, he asked himself, was this highly successful businessman wanting to draw on fifty thousand dollars that would not actually be his until the end of two years? To do so would mean that Leland was in effect asking for a loan against these notes, a situation of needless indebtedness, in Eugene's view. What possible expenditures could he foresee that would require more than the thirty-eight thousand dollars in cash that he already had in hand and the draft, which he had said he would send on to his wife?

But Leland now interposed, "I was thinking only hypothetically, you understand, Señor Galvez, Mr. Kessling. Let us say that I were to do some gambling and would need collateral."

"Well, those I.O.U.'s could be used as stakes, I'm sure—that is, if your opponents would agree to that. Then they, in turn, would be able to collect the money—should you lose it, which I trust you are not contemplating"—this, with a dry chuckle—"and it would be paid to them, instead of to you," the bank president explained.

"Very good. Well, then, I'm indebted to you, Mr. Kessling, for finding me this very gracious gentleman. And now, there's one final point, Señor Galvez. The present manager, Jesse Jacklin, has been exemplary in every respect during the six years he has been charge of the casino. My wife and I hope that every consideration can be given to his staying on."

"Indeed, señor, I had an opportunity to observe him when I visited the casino. Since Señor Jacklin has done so well in bringing the establishment to the attention of the finest citizens of this fair city, I shall not seek to replace him. Doing so would, perhaps, change the luck. If you will be so good as to communicate that to him, I am sure it will put his mind considerably at ease. Indeed, I plan to meet with him in a day or so and introduce myself formally—and I shall tell him that we shall draw up a new contract for his services. If I prosper, so will he."

"That's most generous of you," Leland replied. "Thank you, and I wish you every success with La Maison de Bonne Chance."

"I do not intend to change the name of it either, Señor Kenniston," the Mexican buyer declared. "It has already been lucky for you, and for me as well. Since I have found it to be an extremely honest operation, I shall maintain that tradition, you may be certain. Now, then, señores, I wish you all a pleasant evening. I shall immediately go home and tell my wife that I am now the owner of the finest casino in all of New Orleans!"

After taking leave of Eugene DuBois, thanking him for having effected the sale so smoothly and swiftly, Leland Kenniston hailed a carriage and had himself taken to one of the elegant private baths near Rampart Street. There, he luxuriated in a warm tub and let a burly masseur give him a massage. The feeling of oil being rubbed into his body and the pummeling and expert kneading of his muscles served thoroughly to relax the Irish entrepreneur, and he was in an ebullient mood when he left the bath house. He spent the hour before twilight slowly walking the streets and pausing to look into the shop windows, trying to select a gift for Laure.

Hugely satisfied with his accomplishments of the day, Leland went to Antoine's for dinner, taking with him the bulky packet of thirty-eight thousand dollars in cash. He treated himself to a lavish meal, insisting that the maître d' bring out the chef, to whom Leland gave a long, rambling dissertation on the way he wished his entrée prepared and the special dessert he wanted, called a *bombe surprise*. To begin his meal, he ordered crawfish cooked in wine and herbs, to be followed by a bowl of superb gumbo; pompano with an endive salad comprised the main course, along with side dishes of assorted vegetables, including okra, sweet yams, and snap beans. To accompany the pompano, he bade the waiter bring him the finest Chablis in stock, and with the dessert a bottle of Chateau Climens, one of the great sauternes of France. There followed the strong, dark chicory-based coffee so dear to the Creoles, a snifter of twenty-five-year-old cognac, and an excellent Havana cigar.

He took two hours to sup, luxuriating over each mouthful and each glass of wine, exactly as he had done during the bath and massage. The euphoria and physical well-being that swept him made him feel thirty again, at the very peak of his mental and physical powers. Briefly, he remembered Jacob Cohen's scoldings about expenditures, and scowled—the thought was absolutely abhorrent to him in his present mood, and he asked himself whether Jacob was not overstepping his authority and becoming a kind of gloom monger, perhaps purposely because he was jealous of what his employer was accomplishing. But Leland dismissed the thought as quickly as it had come and, after drinking another cup of coffee, paid the check, bestowed a generous tip upon both the maître d' and the waiter, and told the latter to hand the chef a ten-dollar bill to express his appreciation for an incomparable repast. This done, and amid the bowing of the staff in tribute to so generous and flamboyant a customer, Leland Kenniston stepped onto the street, hailed a carriage, and glowingly directed, "To La Maison de Bonne Chance!"

Chapter Twenty-five

As Leland Kenniston entered the casino, he amiably saluted Jesse Jacklin, who had come forward to greet him.

"Mr. Jacklin, I've the best of news for you," the Irish entrepreneur smiled and told him. "This afternoon, I transferred title to this casino to a certain Hector Galvez, who you may know is a wealthy Mexican now residing in New Orleans. He indicates that he is quite satisfied with your management, so he wants you to know that you don't have to retire or seek another situation, and indeed Señor Galvez intends in the next day or two to visit here and draw up the contract that will give you every incentive to keep your position."

"That's very welcome news, Mr. Kenniston. I look forward to meeting this Mr. Galvez. And now, Mr. Kenniston, what can I do for you?"

"Despite how others may feel about Friday, the thirteenth, I feel in a lucky mood tonight, Jacklin," Leland airily declared. He eyed one hostess, a woman of about twenty-five, coppery-haired with enormous blue eyes, wearing a spangled red gown. "Perhaps this charming lady could accompany me to one of the tables and be a mascot to me tonight. By the way, Jacklin, don't think that I'm going to play on credit. I have here"—he delved into his coat pocket and produced the greenback-stuffed envelope—"ample sufficiency to meet losses—which I don't intend to have."

"Well, Mr. Kenniston, if you've sold the casino in so short a time—I personally thought it might take a good deal longer—then, indeed, you may be riding on the crest of the waves. Let us see if this carries over onto the tables. Margot, would you escort Mr. Kenniston?"

"It will be my pleasure, sir." The attractive young woman

271

gave Leland an engaging smile and inclined her head in respect. "What is your pleasure this evening?" she asked, as she stared boldly at his handsome face.

Leland's eyes fixed on the voluptuous bosom that was displayed above her bodice, and with a soft chuckle, he almost unconsciously responded, "You, my fair charmer. I've a feeling you're going to bring me luck tonight. I'd like to play poker."

"I shall take you to the table of Henri Duraldier. He arrived from Paris only six months ago, Mr. Kenniston, and he has already brought in a good deal of business because he is so pleasant and so expert."

"I should welcome playing at his table," Leland said.

Henri Duraldier was tall, with sleek black hair and exaggerated sideburns. He had already mastered the Creole patois, and he was effusively gracious to the fair sex when their representatives were seated at his table or, as often occurred, when the women stood behind their male escorts, encouraging them in their play. Margot made the introductions, and Henri courteously bowed. "Welcome to La Maison de Bonne Chance, M'sieu Kenniston. And these others at the table with you are M'sieu Charles Aventour and Philippe Mercier."

"A pleasure to know you, gentlemen." Leland politely nodded to the two middle-aged, affluently dressed patrons already seated at the table as he took his own chair.

"Some refreshment, perhaps, Mr. Kenniston?" Margot proffered.

"Yes, I think so. I had a superb Chablis at Antoine's, and if you can match it, you will make the evening a memorable one indeed, *ma jolie*."

"I will do the best I can, Mr. Kenniston," the hostess told him. Leland watched her go to the end of the room toward the sideboard on which were placed carafes of red and white wines, as well as decanters of brandy and cordials. Once again, a warm sensuality pervaded him. The excellent supper and the considerable amount of wine he had already consumed had put him in a triumphant and happy frame of mind. Did he not have some reward coming for his perspicacity in finding a buyer at such an excellent price? Best of all, the fellow had paid a substantial amount in cash, which was not ordinarily expected in such matters. And to prove how considerate a husband he was, he had thought first of Laure in sending her off that draft for thirty-seven thousand dollars; that should be enough to rebuild several dams and repair what damages those men had done to the houses, the chateau, and the fields, and leave a substantial amount left over to pay the workers and tenant farmers for the year. So now, it was time to enjoy with zestful pleasure the diversions that awaited him tonight!

The hostess returned with a goblet of white wine, which she set down before him. Leland was perusing his cards; since it was draw poker, he intended to take three new cards. He had a pair of jacks, sufficient to open, but the rest of the hand was worthless. As the dealer eyed him, he tapped the discards with his right forefinger and indicated, by holding up three fingers, what number he wanted. Once they were handed to him, he tucked them into his hand very cautiously, warily glancing at his two rivals at the table. He could tell very little from their faces, but when he casually glanced at his hand, he almost gasped with surprise. He had picked up two more jacks, and that was just about unbeatable. Indeed, the evening was beginning just as he had known it would! Why, if this luck continued—and why should it not?—he would double his half of the cash down payment on Laure's casino in one evening's play!

He sipped his wine while he matched the two other customers' bets, and then, when the dealer called for a show of cards, he calmly laid down his four jacks and the worthless ace of clubs.

"I congratulate you, M'sieu Kenniston," Henri Duraldier said as, with his croupier's rake, he shoved the chips over to Leland's side of the table. "It is a very fortunate beginning."

"I note that you say 'beginning,' M'sieu Duraldier, and that is very good, for indeed I have only just begun. I shall have many more chips before the night is over, this I promise you. Perhaps you'd best ask M'sieu Jacklin to furnish you with a reserve supply, for I mean to break the bank here."

The dealer had heard such boasting before, not only in Paris but also in a roadside inn not far from Trenton, New Jersey, where he had spent a month while waiting for the connection that would bring him to New Orleans. He merely smiled politely, nodded, and handed the deck to Leland, whose deal it now was. After having had the cards cut for him by one of the two others at the table, Leland began to

273

deal with a flourish. There was a broad smile on his face, and when he had finished dealing the cards, he drank the last swallow of his wine and turned to Margot. "You've brought me great luck, *ma chérie*. I tell you what—" He brought out his wallet and extracted a bill at random, handing it to her. "This is for you, if you'll stay with me and bring me luck, as you just did."

"But, Mr. Kenniston, this is a hundred-dollar bill!" Margot incredulously gasped.

"I'm well aware of that, *ma poupée très chère!*"

The second hand he won also, with three tens, and this game required some bluffing in order to convince his two rivals at the table that it was simply not their night.

But these small triumphs served to be cumulative in their effect. Buoyed by his victories at the very start of the evening, Leland beckoned to Margot and, reaching into his wallet again, took out another hundred-dollar bill, and this time he tucked it into her low-cut bodice. "You mustn't leave me, not for a moment," he warned. "You are the goddess of luck itself, and I shall reward you each time I win."

But the third and fourth hands went against Leland, and he lost half of what he had won in the first two. The other two customers had each won a hand, and Henri Duraldier now took the deal again. As he was about to distribute the cards, Leland spoke up, "Let us play for higher stakes. I see that you're opening here with ten dollars. Let us make it a hundred dollars."

"If you wish, M'sieu Kenniston. And you, messieurs, have you any objections?" the handsome dealer addressed the two other patrons. Each of them, after a moment's hesitation, shook his head. "So be it, a hundred dollars to open, jacks or better," the dealer announced in his richly accented voice.

Picking up his cards, Leland saw that he had three queens. He glanced over to smile at Margot and then, seeing that she had smiled back, called out, "Please bring me champagne. By the bye, is there any caviar to be had?"

"The kitchen has some tins of it, yes, M'sieu Kenniston."

"Well then, I tell you what, Margot, sweet princess of fortune: Bring several bottles of champagne—enough for everyone at this table—yes, including our dealer—and a tin of caviar to each, as well."

"Directly, M'sieu Kenniston."

"You needn't keep any tab, for I'll pay cash each time," he called after her.

He won that hand, recouping about a third of what he had lost in the previous two, and for the next ten hands, he broke about even. But now, having drunk most of one bottle of champagne and eaten nearly all of a tin of caviar, he grew even more seignorial. "More champagne and caviar for my friends here—and you, Margot, champagne and caviar for your own delectation. Let us increase the stakes to two hundred dollars for openers."

One of the two men who had been sitting with him all evening, and who had been content with modest winnings, now rose and shook his head: "M'sieu, it has been a most enjoyable evening, but I must go home. You will please forgive me—I hope you will understand."

"But, of course, of course!" Leland made a grandiose gesture with his hand, as if nothing in the world could daunt him now. "I am sure there will be others who wish to try their skill against me."

As he spoke, a portly, gray-bearded man, sporting a large diamond stickpin and an ornamental gold watch fob, approached and took the place quitted by the Creole. "My name is Sebastian Lorrimar, at your service, M'sieu Kenniston—I know your name because I have been listening to it all through the evening. And since I have done very well at the roulette wheel, I wish to invest some of my winnings against the skill you profess to have. Two hundred dollars for openers, you said? I accept."

"You are a gentleman of parts, of substance, and of intelligence," the Irish entrepreneur quipped. "I have ordered champagne and caviar for everyone—and it would please me greatly if you would partake of these delicacies by way of celebrating our new acquaintanceship."

"With the greatest of pleasure, Mr. Kenniston, thank you." Lorrimar settled himself, belched softly—putting his hand over his mouth—then he nodded to the dealer, who recognized him as a frequent customer. "Whose deal is it?"

"It turns out to be yours, M'sieu Lorrimar," the dealer declared.

"That's a good start! Let's see if my luck carries over," Lorrimar chuckled.

Margot approached with a tray heavily laden with more

bottles of champagne and tins of caviar. She set these down at the table, but not before Leland had gallantly risen and assisted her. "It's much too heavy for one so beautiful as you, *ma jolie*. Let me take it. There we are. Now you may serve."

The game was won by the newcomer, and Leland lost two thousand dollars on the hand. He shrugged philosophically. "I'm still ahead, and the evening is still young. Margot, you moved away from me, and that is why I lost that hand. Come closer. Besides, you're so lovely, I want to fill my eyes with the sight of you."

The dealer glanced at Margot and arched his eyebrows, the faint trace of a smile on his handsome face as he resumed the play. Leland now urged, "Let's make it three hundred for openers."

"That's too rich for my blood." The other Creole who had been there at the outset shook his head, abruptly rose, and took his chips over to the counting desk at the other end of the room, where one of Jesse Jacklin's attendants exchanged chips for money.

"Well, then, it's just between the two of us and Henri here," Sebastian Lorrimar jovially boomed. Lifting his glass of champagne, he declared, "A toast to you, sir. And let us see whom Lady Luck smiles upon before we've finished."

She did not smile on Leland Kenniston. It was true that he won the next two hands, after each of which he stuffed a hundred-dollar bill into Margot's bodice. His hand lingered caressingly, and the hostess, who had made thus far in this evening more money than she usually earned in months, arched and preened herself, a cloying smile on her face as her eyes met his. "You're ever so generous, M'sieu Kenniston," she purred.

At the end of two further hours of play, he had managed to go through every penny of the thirty-eight thousand dollars in cash he had brought with him to La Maison de Bonne Chance. Henri Duraldier eyed him and said, "If you wish to continue, m'sieu, you should arrange for credit. Shall I call M'sieu Jacklin over? I see him over at the baccarat table."

"Of course, do so at once," Leland commanded with a lordly gesture. "My luck will change, and I have all the credit necessary."

Jesse Jacklin, having seen his dealer signal to him, hurried

276

over to the table, and Henri whispered into his ear. Straightening, the casino manager politely said to Leland, "Well, Mr. Kenniston, I'm certainly willing to extend you credit. If you can show me some collateral, however, the amount of that credit can, you understand, be greatly increased."

"Of course I've collateral. Here now—" Leland took out of his pocket the copy of the bill of sale for the casino. "Look here—Señor Galvez owes me fifty thousand dollars in two more years, in four payments. And my banker tells me that I can use this for my stake."

"Well, I guess you can. Mr. Lorrimar, is this agreeable to you?"

"I think we can trust M'sieu Kenniston. I'm not so greedy for cash that I have to have it this evening," the portly man smiled and replied.

"In that case, I am willing to extend to you twenty-five thousand dollars of credit," Jesse said as he turned to regard Leland. "Beyond that, I do not think you yourself would wish to continue. Of course, I shall need to hold the bill of sale, as you know."

"I understand you, Jacklin," Leland impatiently countered. "And just to show you that I am confident of my luck, and also a man of probity, I have no objection to your holding my note for the entire fifty thousand against your advance to me of twenty-five thousand. I'm sure I'll be retrieving the note before the night is over. Now then, let's get on with the play, shall we? Margot, *chérie*, come stand closer to me. I need your help now, for I plan to recoup my losses. They're small, anyway, and I'm sure that I'm on the threshold of a great victory here at this house of fortune."

Jesse gave Leland pen and paper, and the entrepreneur signed a statement making over the balance of the casino payments back to the new owner. The casino manager then nodded to the handsome dealer, who promptly shoved with his croupier's rake the requisite amount in chips to match the credit that had just been granted.

"Now, that's much better," Leland said. He took one of the chips off his pile and tossed it to Margot. "Stick that where I stuck the bills, my beautiful one. And don't desert me now!"

Jesse Jacklin walked away from the table shaking his head. All this time he had been under the impression that Leland

Kenniston was a man of honor and integrity—a perfect husband for someone as wonderful as Laure. Now, however, after seeing this blatant display of what was to all intents and purposes infidelity as well as behavior of the most intemperate nature, Jesse suddenly felt that Laure had perhaps chosen most unwisely. But, he reasoned, such things were none of his business . . . even though he was sympathetic. With another shake of his head, he went back to his office.

Two other gentlemen had come over to join Sebastian Lorrimar and Leland Kenniston at the table. Spectators, too, struck by the Irishman's loud, boisterous comments and having heard how he had leaped the table stakes from ten dollars to three hundred, came over to watch, whispering among themselves.

By three in the morning, the cards had gone completely against Laure's husband, and he lost the entire twenty-five thousand dollars he had received in credit against his collateral. "Well, I'm afraid I shall have to arrange for more credit before I can continue, it appears," he said with a wan smile. "Oh, well, there's always tomorrow."

"It is getting late, M'sieu Kenniston," the dealer tactfully suggested, "and you look a little tired. Perhaps you should get some fresh air to revive you. We shall be happy to see you again whenever it suits your fancy."

"M'sieu Kenniston," Margot bent to whisper into his ear, "we're going to close in about half an hour. If you like, I'll see you home safely."

"Why, my beautiful one, that's the best luck I've had tonight!" Leland chuckled as he rose, somewhat unsteadily, from the table. Margot clung to Leland's arm as if she were a limpet. Even though this distinguished-looking man did not seem to have more money on him at the moment, there was always the possibility that he might find more hidden away, once they were alone together. If not, no matter. With the money she had accumulated this evening, she could persuade her fiancé to marry her soon, and not wait until he had found a profitable venture. Yes, this money would help him open a shop, and then she would have her darling Jacques, who made love so divinely.

"Come along, dear Mr. Kenniston," she purred in an insinuating whisper, as he still stood there uncertainly, glancing at the men at the table, and then at the dealer. The spectators had drifted away, discussing among themselves the wildly erratic gambling of this man who had done so well at the start and then had lost a considerable fortune, now that it was all over.

Jesse Jacklin, off to one side of the room near the counting desk, was talking to the young attendant in a low voice. "Well, Hector Galvez, who will be our new owner, got La Maison de Bonne Chance for a song. Do you know what Mr. Kenniston just did? He managed to lose or spend not only thirty-eight thousand dollars in cash, he also signed over— and promptly lost—a bill of sale worth fifty thousand dollars that Galvez promised to pay him within two years. And all I could allow Kenniston was twenty-five thousand dollars in chips, and he also lost those. By rights, the note now belongs to the house—Mr. Galvez will in a sense be paying himself the fifty thousand. Naturally, I'll suggest to him that we should send twenty-five thousand of it to Kenniston—after all, we did give him only half the value of the note in credit, and even if he was foolish enough to sign away the whole amount, I doubt that we should hold to the letter of that arrangement. Mr. Galvez is a fair man, I am sure, and I think he'll see it the same way. He'll still be getting the casino for a mere fraction of what he originally offered for it." He sighed and smiled at his assistant. "Well, Harold, let's get ready to close."

With Margot clinging to his arm, Leland walked slowly down the stairs and out to the entrance. "I won't leave you, dear M'sieu Kenniston," the hostess promised. "I know how low you must be feeling, after losing all that money. But you were so nice to me, I want to be nice to you, too. My place isn't far from here—but maybe you'd rather go back to your hotel?"

"Oh, yes, of course I would. It's the St. Charles."

"Do you know, M'sieu Kenniston, I've lived here nearly all my life, and I've only once been inside the lobby of that hotel. I hear tell it's simply scrumptious—I'd love to see it with you. Can we?" she wheedled.

Leland Kenniston looked at her and then chuckled. She was very close to him, and he could feel the pressure of her full round breasts against his arm. "By all means, you shall see it to your heart's content, *ma jolie*," he answered.

* * *

With the coppery-haired young hostess clinging to his arm—covertly rubbing her hip against his, intimating that now that she had left her place of employment, the rule of propriety no longer prevailed—Leland had a feeling of great euphoria, and it seemed to him that he was almost floating on air. The cheap perfume of the hostess, the pressure of her resilient hip against his, the sly squeezings of his arm, and the fluttering eyelashes that accompanied her coy glances at him seemed to stimulate him almost violently. He felt himself a pasha about to enter his seraglio, and the favorite of all his concubines had been summoned to gratify his most inordinate desires.

"Is it really true, Margot, that you've never been farther inside the St. Charles than the lobby before?" he asked her, as they alighted from the carriage.

She shook her head. "Never, Mr. Kenniston—"

"You may call me Leland, *ma belle*. It was kind of you to accompany me, by the way."

"I wouldn't have missed it for the world, dear Leland," she cooed, giving his arm another squeeze, as the doorman, bowing, opened the portals of the elegant hotel to this eccentric but wealthy patron and his companion of the evening. It was not really evening anymore, seeing as how it was close to four in the morning, yet Leland Kenniston felt not the slightest fatigue. He was aware that he had lost a great deal of money, but he still persistently believed that it was a mere bagatelle, and that he would recover it by some strategic coup—one as yet not conceived in his fertile brain, but one certain to be evolved within the next day or two.

"I would have taken you to my place, but it's a very dreary little apartment for which the rent is far too dear. But, thanks to your generosity tonight, dear Leland," she whispered, "now I can move to a much better place. And I want to show you my appreciation for being so sweet to me tonight. My gracious, you must have given me over five hundred dollars!"

"You are worth every penny and then some," he gallantly responded. Taking out his key, and not without some difficulty, he managed to fit it into the lock and to turn the knob and enter. "Perhaps some light—" he mumbled.

"Oh, no! It's much more thrilling in the dark, dear Leland. I'll show you. Now you just go lie on the bed and get real comfy, and Margot will take good care of her darling Leland," the red-haired hostess whispered. As if to show him that she meant precisely what she said, she turned to him, put her hands on his shoulders, and gave him a stinging kiss on the mouth. Then she released him, and he breathed heavily, his face flushed with the incipient carnal desire that swelled within him. This was a fitting conclusion to an incredible day and a gala night, one during which he had transacted a great deal of business and sent off money that would save Laure from her desperate financial predicament at Windhaven Plantation. He was entitled to this moment of surcease, after all the tumultuous and arduous work he had done: going to Europe and establishing so many connections for his business—vital and powerful and profitable connections, too; seeing that his family was happy. . . . He had done these things and many more. What was a small hour of passion stolen away with no one's being the wiser?

He made his way toward the huge, comfortable bed, removed his jacket, and started fumbling with his cravat. But Margot was quickly by his side to help him. By the dim light from the window, he could see that she had drawn off her gown and camisole and was standing now in her corset, pantalettes, and high-buttoned shoes, whose soft leather flaps ended just above the anklebone. The corset was laced tightly, giving her a wasp waist under her sumptuous bosom, and the pantalettes were provocatively sheer over her lushly rounded thighs and buttocks.

"Lie down on the bed, Leland darling; let me take care of you. You're such a sweet man, such a dear man—you don't know how grateful I am for all the money you gave me. I did try to bring you luck, I truly did!" she was whispering as she gently pushed him down into a seated position, and then, taking hold of his shoulders, eased him back onto the bed, then lifted his legs and stretched them out. Swiftly, she removed his shoes and then began to unfasten his trousers, and then his shirt. Leland felt himself grow virile, as her heavy round breasts were thrust brazenly in front of him as she undressed him.

"You're very beautiful," he said hoarsely, surrendering himself to his unconscionable lust.

"You understand that we're not supposed to—well, you know—with the customers. Only, it was quitting time, and you were a gentleman, and if you wanted to take me home safely—because New Orleans is such a dangerous place at night, as any girl in her right mind knows—why, Mr. Jacklin couldn't really object, could he?" she prattled away, all the while stroking his thighs and loins with the tips of her fingers. Then she giggled, "Oh, gracious, I only hope I can make you happy . . . you're so wonderfully big . . . are you going to stay long in New Orleans, Leland darling? I'd be glad to see you again. . . ."

"Hush . . . just love me . . ." he panted, arching and writhing in the throes of his burning sexual urgency.

Margot, tantalizingly, prolonged the descent of her pantalettes, wriggling and undulating for him as a belly dancer might do at the court of an emir. Then she joined him on the bed, placed herself over him, and silenced his gasp with a passionate kiss.

He gave himself up totally to what was happening. Her clever manipulations and erotic skills, her lush warmth, her satiny skin, the smell of her perfume, her kisses, and her sly words of lascivious praise of his manhood, whetted him to ungovernable lust.

He had fallen asleep and, when he wakened, he groped for his watch on the night table beside the bed. It was nearly noon. He put a hand to his forehead, for he felt drained and surfeited. The champagne had left a sour taste in his mouth, and he could almost taste the caviar-flavored bile when he regurgitated. He grimaced with nausea, tried to sit up, and then sank back. Now he remembered. He did not know when she had left him, for he had fallen into a deep, dreamless sleep. But he could clearly see the results of what had happened before she had gone, for the bed was violently rumpled, and the corset he had ripped in their amorous gymnastics was left in a heap on the floor.

He groaned, and then he finally managed to sit up. His head was throbbing. My God—what had he done? Not only had he taken a slut home from the gambling casino after stuffing hundred-dollar bills down her bodice, he had lost all that cash . . . and he had sold the promissory note as well!

What a fool he had been! For a night of transient pleasure—ephemeral as the money that had been exchanged for chips on the gambling table—he had been unfaithful to his wife, and he had used almost all the money derived from the sale of the casino, Laure's money and certainly not his, in his wild gambling.

He groaned aloud as lucidity returned to him. He did not know what was happening to him. Was he going mad? He had no other explanation for his behavior, certainly. The only thing he knew for sure was that he must somehow go to Laure as quickly as possible to lend a helping hand. Only in doing that could he make amends—but he was not certain that it was wise to tell her right off how foolishly he had behaved.

He suddenly burst into tears and covered his face with his hands as it all became too much to endure. The zestful joy with which he had entered the casino last night had evaporated; in its place was nausea and disgust and feverish impatience with his own stupidity. And if Laure were to declare the marriage voided by his errant, obstinate behavior, she would be within her right.

He sat sobbing on the edge of the bed for some time. Then he slowly rose up and got into his clothes. He would go to the bath house and steam the poison out of him. After that, he would get a good night's sleep and take the train for Alabama in the morning.

Chapter Twenty-six

"Lopasuta, Leland has sent a draft from New Orleans! It's more than enough, I'm sure, to take care of the rebuilding of the dam and the other repairs from the damages of those two attacks," Laure exclaimed with delight as the lawyer entered the study to find her seated at the *escritoire*. She had been reading her husband's letter, in which he told her of having negotiated the sale of the casino, saying further that he looked forward to their reunion at Windhaven in the very near future.

"Oh, yes, that's more than enough money, Laure," Lopasuta gently smiled as he glanced at the draft Laure handed him, folded it, and placed it in his waistcoat pocket. "It will help us meet our operating expenses for the year—and it will ensure that repairs we make are in fact improvements. I have been looking over what is needed, and I think today I'll go into Montgomery to interview a contractor recommended by Benjamin Brown. Ben says that he's heard the man is quite capable and has good references. He's a black man who evidently has pulled himself up by his own bootstraps, and he's done a lot of rebuilding. He just recently moved to Montgomery from upstate, but Ben has seen work he did at the Tuskeegee Institute, and apparently it's excellent. I'm feeling very confident about the man, I must say."

"That sounds wonderful. Well, if you're going to Montgomery, will you do me a favor? I wrote this note to Leland"—she reached into the desk drawer and extracted an envelope—"and I'd appreciate your mailing it for me." She sealed the letter and handed it to Lopasuta.

"I'll see that it goes out as quickly as possible, Laure," he said. "I'm very glad for you. Then you think Leland will be coming here soon?"

"Yes, I hope within the week."

"I'm looking forward to seeing him. I always welcome his advice—he's so competent and levelheaded. Goodness knows we need the help. At the moment, I'm concerned about the fact that, since a number of the workers were frightened by epidemic and decided to leave, we're shorthanded. We'll probably have to hire others, and I should look into it while I'm in Montgomery."

"Do whatever you think best. I have perfect confidence in you, Lopasuta dear."

"I'm only glad that I can be on hand. The other day, incidentally, I sent a letter off to Eugene DuBois in New Orleans telling him that I probably would stay on here through the end of April and maybe into May. He's quite capable, and I'm sure he can handle what affairs we have in the courts."

"You'll never know how deeply I appreciate your rearranging your schedule to come here to aid me, Lopasuta," Laure told him. "I just regret the added burden it places on Geraldine. I'm sure she misses you."

"Perhaps one day soon, when this trouble is over, you can invite her to come up and visit you. I'm sure she'd like that."

"Oh, yes, Lopasuta, certainly—and the children, too, of course."

"In the meantime, being here is the least I can do for you. Incidentally, I think it would be a good idea to involve Lucien more with the plantation—it seems to be what he wishes. I really admired the way he handled himself the night of the raid. He dispatched those two poor horses without flinching, and then fought the fire alongside the other men. Mean work it was, and he made a man's job of it. I'm going to take him with me to Montgomery, to meet the contractor. Perhaps he'll have his own opinion of the fellow."

Deeply touched, Laure smiled at him, her eyes filling with tears. "Lopasuta, how dear of you to think of my son this way. Being a father yourself has apparently given you even greater wisdom than you had before."

They stood a moment looking at each other, and then, himself moved, Lopasuta brusquely declared, "I'd best get going now if Lucien and I are to get these things straightened out."

* * *

Lucien had told Lopasuta that he would enjoy riding horseback, as he had done in his childhood, and so the two men went to the stable and selected sturdy geldings for their ride into Montgomery. Lucien's eyes brightened, and his face seemed to lose its look of drawn constraint as he mounted into the saddle. The gelding pricked up its ears, whinnied once, and responded immediately to Lucien's gentle kicking of his heels against its belly. The two men called to each other and laughed in the brisk, warm wind that blew against them from the south, ruffling their hair and giving them a zest for the outdoor way of life.

They did not talk much during their ride, but as they reached the outskirts of town, Lopasuta turned to his companion. "I'll be glad to know what you think of the man we're going to see." Then he turned his mount and led the way down a side street until the two riders had reached a small red-brick house, where they dismounted. "This is where we're supposed to find Mr. Washburn, Lucien," Lopasuta said, hitching his horse to a post. "Benjamin Brown gave me his address; I only hope that he's not out on a job."

"Well, if he is, we can ask around and go where he's working. From the way Ben spoke, this man sounds like he'd be a good person to have on our side."

They walked up the gravel path toward the house, and as they were about to knock, it opened and a bushy-bearded, tall black man of about forty-five emerged. He had thick eyebrows under hair receding high above the temples, and he wore dungarees and a worn blue denim shirt. He greeted the two men, saying, "Well, gentlemen, what can I do for you?"

"You're Enoch Washburn?" Lopasuta inquired.

The black man nodded. "I am—and since I don't know your names, you have an advantage over me, gentlemen."

"My name is Lopasuta Bouchard. This is Lucien Bouchard. Benjamin Brown, who is assistant foreman out at Windhaven Plantation near Lowndesboro, suggested that we come see you about a job. I'm told that you're quite a capable contractor, and that you don't mind working with your own hands to make sure everything goes right, even though you have a crew to do things for you."

"I guess you've got me dead to rights, Mr. Bouchard. Come right in. Tell me, what sort of job do you have?"

"The fact is, Mr. Washburn, we've had a couple of raids

by night riders on Windhaven Plantation. Twice they've blown up the dam, and this last time a few weeks back the river water polluted some of our wells. We had a real siege of sickness for a time there, and we lost a lot of workers—some by dying of the fever, others because they were scared and decided to look elsewhere for a living. I'm just telling you all this to let you know the difficulties.''

"And I appreciate your bein' frank with me, Mr. Bouchard. Buildin' a dam, is that it? Well, I've never done anything like that, but I'm sure I could figure how to do it.''

"If you're free and willing, I'd be glad to hire you on. It will be on a trial basis, at first, but that's just a formality. From what I've heard, I'm sure you'll acquit yourself very well. And we can pay you good wages.''

"I suppose you'd like me to start yesterday, that it?'' the bearded black said sarcastically and chuckled. "Well, I could start in a couple of days. Just let me finish up a job I'm workin' on, and I'm your man. I get sixty-five dollars a week for myself and my crew, plus the cost of materials. How does that sound?''

"Great,'' Lucien spoke up. "Lopasuta, here, he's a lawyer. He can draw up a contract, so it'll be all legal and proper.''

"That's the way I like it. A lawyer, huh? I haven't had to deal with a lawyer since I did work for Tuskeegee. But 'cause the Institute is run for and by blacks, the lawyer they had was a black man, too. I knew *he* wouldn't try and get the better of me. Well, all right, then, you draw up an agreement, and I'll hire the extra men I'll be needin'—probably eight more oughta be enough, if they work hard. And men who work for Enoch Washburn work their butts off. 'Course they get paid for it—but they don't always like my guts. That reminds me of somethin'. . . .''

"And what's that, Mr. Washburn?'' Lucien questioned.

Enoch Washburn nursed his chin with his strong, big-fingered hand a moment. "I don't think you should let out to folks 'round here that you've hired yourself a black man to do any contractin' work for you. That's my honest opinion. If you've been the target of some Klan-type raiders, it ain't gonna make it easier for you if these folks know you've hired a black and not a white man, that's for sure. They'll be madder 'n hornets that you didn't hire one of my white competitors.''

"I know what you're saying," Lopasuta at once replied. "God knows, I look for the day when things are different—when a black man can stand up and show that he's proud to be a professional man, supervising the work of others. But for the present, we'll keep it quiet. If anyone comes around, any strangers, you'll just be a worker there—which is true, of course, since you work right along with your crew."

"Yes, sir, and I dress that way, too—I like to be real comfortable when I'm on the job—so no one will take me for an uppity supervisor," Washburn chuckled. "Oh, by the way, I've got references if you want to take a look at them."

"If you have them handy, I would very much like that," Lopasuta rejoined.

"Be right with you, gentlemen." Washburn rose with surprising agility for a man of his bulk and height, and strode over to a desk at the very back of the spacious living room. He opened the drawer and took out a wooden box, thick with folded papers. This he brought back and handed to Lopasuta, who quickly perused the letters of recommendation, then glanced up and nodded. "I'm satisfied. I can see you've been working mostly up in Tuscaloosa and Birmingham, so none of these names are familiar to me. But all of your clients obviously are pleased with your work. These are good enough for me. How do you feel, Lucien?" He handed the box to the youth, who quickly scanned the letters.

"Well, it certainly seems that Mr. Washburn has a lot of satisfied customers. I'd say that we'll probably be giving out the *next* letter of recommendation, if the job is done as well as these others appear to have been." Lucien smiled at the man and handed back the box.

"I just want to warn you again, gentlemen," Washburn said, not without a trace of bitterness and a scowl on his face. "Even though the law says they've got no right, folks're ridin' around in their white robes again. I've been feeling it comin' the last couple of years. What we got from old Abe Lincoln and then the courts—well, it 'pears that people don't like the fact that we who were born with black skin have such rights. That's another reason I don't want it to be talked around that I'm doin' a job for you."

"You need have no worry on that score, Mr. Washburn," Lopasuta assured him as he rose from the couch, gesturing to Lucien that it was time to go. "By the way, I'll bring back the contract this afternoon. We're going into town now and have a bite of lunch and pick up some supplies, and then I'll go over to a notary's office and draw up the papers. You'll be here, say around four o'clock?''

"Sure will. Just have to get over to the place I'm finishin' up at for about an hour. As I said, the job is nearly done, so I could start at your place in a few days.''

"We're grateful, and we'll talk further about salary details when I bring back the contract.''

"Suits me fine,'' Enoch declared. "You've got yourself a contractor. I'm lookin' forward to it. I'll see you this afternoon, then. Thanks for comin'.''

Outside, as Lopasuta and Lucien mounted their horses, the youth turned to the Comanche lawyer and said, "I like the way he talks. He knows the score, and he's right about keeping it quiet that he's going to work for us. If those same fellows are still on the prowl who hit us twice, and they find out about him, they might try it again. In fact, when we come back this afternoon, Lopasuta, perhaps we should ask him to hire men who happen to be handy with guns, as well as with tools. It won't do any harm to have some extra protection.''

Chapter Twenty-seven

In the weeks since his arrival at Windhaven Plantation, Lucien Bouchard had determined to put his memories behind him. He knew that he would always think of Mary Eileen Brennert, and that most likely he would never entirely be able to rid himself of the feeling that if he had not taken her to the park that day, she might well still be alive—despite the fact that by all the tenets of the faith in which he had been brought up, he understood that it was within only God's power to decree who should live and who should die.

Thus, the excruciatingly sharp hurt of that tragedy had gradually dwindled to a dull, nagging pang, in which contrition and sorrow were mingled. At the same time, because he was healthy and energetic in mind as well as body, young Lucien Bouchard was determined to be as helpful as he could here on Windhaven Plantation, rather than lean on his mother for consolation. He would try to be a bulwark of steadfast aid and affection for her. Only in this way, he told himself, could he alleviate the pain of Mary Eileen's death.

As for Eleanor Martinson, she seemed now to be almost like a fleeting dream, an unreal interlude that had served for a time nearly to banish his distress. True, she had awakened him as a man, but then she had cut herself off from him in that abrupt parting note, as if to say that he should put out of his mind any notion that there could be a follow-up to their amorous exchange. And in the weeks that had followed, the impact of Eleanor's sensuality had receded, yielding to the grief for Mary Eileen that swept in on him once more with the force of a riptide. There were several nights during which he woke in a sweat from a dream wherein he saw himself standing beside her gravesite, casting a handful of moist soil upon the coffin, and bidding farewell to all his adolescent yearnings and his first true love.

He decided to dedicate himself to hard work, eventually acquiring the self-discipline needed for pursuing a livelihood, one that would summon up all his potential skills and talents. If he had learned a lesson from the Irish school, it was to think for himself and make his own decisions, and that in essence was what his tutor, Sean Flannery, had secretly hoped he would carry away from all his tragic experiences.

Perhaps it was for this reason that Lucien found himself drawn at once to Lopasuta. In one sense, it might have seemed incongruous to the youth to find himself with an adopted brother nearly twice his age. But the Comanche easily bridged the difference in their ages, winning young Lucien's admiration by showing him the same respect that he would a peer.

Lucien had often heard his stepfather extol the lawyer's virtues, not only in conversation between the two of them but also in letters that Leland had written to his stepson in Dublin. Since Lucien had studied enough American history to learn how the Indians—native Americans—were driven off their land by both legal and illegal measures, he had all the more admiration for Lopasuta. Although the tall, well-spoken man might be regarded by bigoted strangers as an outsider and a half-breed, he had mastered the foundation of the white man's law, been admitted to the bar in both Alabama and Louisiana, and now handled his employer's complex legal and corporate affairs. There could be no better proof that merit and intelligence could overcome prejudice and ignorance—and that, too, was one of the lessons that Sean Flannery had attempted to instill in young Lucien Bouchard at St. Timothy's Academy.

Because of his determination to overcome his loss, and because of his love for his mother and his admiration for Lopasuta, there was no task, however humble, that young Lucien hesitated to perform. Somewhat to his mother's consternation, he had insisted upon helping boil the polluted water. He spent several days out in the fields with the workers, watching them construct a kiln to make bricks for reconstruction of the dam; he himself learned how to make bricks and apply mortar. He was pleased with himself when Lopasuta stopped by one afternoon and surveyed his work, then said with a warm smile, "You have a good many intellectual

291

skills, Lucien, but it never hurts to acquire a skill with one's hands. I'd say you could earn an excellent living as a mason, if the need arose. Your attitude toward hard work is all in your favor for the future.''

Lucien had grinned broadly and worked all the harder, not so much to impress Lopasuta as to maintain the friendly respect that had already grown between the two of them. Two afternoons later, after work was done for the day, Lopasuta invited him to ride to Lowndesboro to buy more quinine, which Dr. Kennery had prescribed as an antidote against various types of fever.

It was a bright sunny day, and halfway to town Lopasuta challenged Lucien to a race over the rest of the distance. Lucien urged his black gelding forward, and Lopasuta watched the youth forge ahead before calling gently to his own roan, which at once pricked up its ears and began to gallop after.

Lucien was exhilarated; the color was high in his cheeks, and his eyes were sparkling as they rode into Lowndesboro practically in a dead heat. "You handle a horse well, my brother," Lopasuta reached over to pat Lucien on the back. "It was a fair race, and we will call it a draw."

"I know you were holding back, Lopasuta, but I enjoyed it a lot anyway!" Lucien grinned.

"I only held back at the very first. No, Lucien, you rode very well, and you seemed to understand how much energy your gelding had for the last stretch when we were racing together." Lopasuta's eyes twinkled. "I daresay Lucien Edmond would be proud to see you ride this way—he might even hire you as a vaquero at Windhaven Range."

"I doubt that," Lucien responded. "From what his son Hugo wrote me once—he's a doctor in Wyoming now, you know—his father can be a demanding taskmaster."

"Maybe so, Lucien, but I still say you're good. The way you held the reins told your mount exactly what you wanted of him, and so he responded. And I think this may be a lesson that can be used with men, as well as with horses. It's wise sometimes to give a man his head, to show him what the obstacles are ahead of him and then let him take the swiftest course to overcoming them."

"That sounds like philosophy. You remind me a little of my teacher in Dublin, Sean Flannery—who was a very good friend as well as a mentor," Lucien responded.

"You know, speaking of teachers, I'd like to tell you something. As I've said, I admire the way you've been learning to work with your hands; all the same, I think you should consider continuing your education. You can go very far, Lucien; you've the mind for it."

"That's what Sean Flannery thought, too, Lopasuta." Lucien stopped on the porch of the store, turned to the tall Comanche lawyer, and held out his hand. "I'm very glad you're my adoptive brother, Lopasuta. I also think you're a wonderful friend."

"Thank you; I feel the same about you. And now, let's get the quinine and hurry back. Perhaps tomorrow, if you like, we could go for a walk to the east, beyond the Bouchard land, and see who the neighbors are and what they are growing."

"I'd like that."

"Then, perhaps, we should climb to the top of the bluff to your father's grave. I will tell his spirit that I'm grateful to Laure for having brought me here, so that I could become the friend of the son of his blood. I will tell him also that in this friend who is my brother, I see the seeds of the same greatness and warmth and truthfulness that I found in Luke."

Lucien colored and modestly lowered his eyes. He hoped to prove himself worthy of the compliment from the Comanche, to prove to himself and others that he was changing and maturing. He felt that he had at last overcome the restless impatience that had very nearly gotten him expelled from St. Timothy's. He had learned to deal with crises and, most of all, with himself; to hold himself in check and let his mind work, rather than his emotions and the first furious impulses of his young heart.

On the following afternoon, Lucien sought out Lopasuta, and together they climbed the gentle slope of the tall bluff by the river till they were at the summit and standing beside the graves of the founder of Windhaven Plantation, his beloved woman, and Luke.

"Do you know, Lucien, that when I first came here from the stronghold thirteen years ago," Lopasuta turned to the youth and fixed him with an earnest gaze, "I blessed this man, your father, who brought me here and gave me a chance

293

at the life I now lead. Without him, I should have been still a half-breed, a *mestizo*, despised by whites, and not quite accepted even by my own Comanche people—for although my true father was a proud, pure-blooded war chief, my mother was a Mexican, from a wealthy family and well educated. It was she who instilled in me the eagerness to learn, to read and write, and to express myself. I became a lawyer because your father received a letter from Lucien Edmond, describing what he had learned about me from Sangrodo, our tribal chief. It was Sangrodo who first observed my eagerness to learn all I could to be worthy and helpful to those with whom I would live."

"And then my father adopted you."

"Yes," the lawyer gravely nodded. "He did me the great honor of giving me his name. When I was in Montgomery studying law, there were many who looked down upon me because they knew that I was not white. Then I met Geraldine, who defied her parents—who then disowned her—because she cared for me. I have been most fortunate, in spite of the fact that I have had tragedy in my life. . . . You've probably heard your mother speak of how six years ago I was sent for by a man in New Orleans, who wished to rob your mother of her casino. When I arrived at his house, I was drugged and put on a ship, and then I found myself in Hong Kong. There I worked like a slave for a greedy, selfish man who destroyed the letter and cable I sent to poor Geraldine. She then thought that I had deserted her."

He paused and smiled to himself. "And then, through great good luck, I was able to get away. I met your stepfather on the return voyage, and one day, when the sea was rough, I was able to prevent him from being pitched overboard. And after all these vicissitudes, I have prevailed—I have my wife and a family, and I have built up a good practice and can defend people who have a just cause. Do you see what education means, Lucien—particularly when it's combined with fortitude? I told you in the fields that it is good to have skill with one's hands. But I think it is even better to have a keen, receptive mind, one that will enable you to reject temptations because you know that they are evil. You gave up your school in Ireland because of the death of your sweetheart, but you must not put an end to your education because of

294

it—and she would not want you to, either. Do you know, yet, what you wish to do in later life? Have you given much thought to it?''

"No—not really, Lopasuta,'' Lucien faltered, looking down at the graves. He sank down on his knees before his father's grave; he touched the earth, and his eyes were filled with tears.

Lopasuta smiled knowingly and then knelt down beside the youth. "We shall pray, the two of us here alone, to make a pact as brothers—for we are brothers, in the best sense, since your father gave me the honor of the Bouchard name.''

Lucien Bouchard nodded and extended his hand to Lopasuta, who warmly held it. And as the two knelt before Luke Bouchard's grave, they bowed their heads and prayed silently.

They rose and turned to descend the slope. As they approached the bottom, Lucien put a hand on Lopasuta's arm. "I'd like to visit Marius's grave, too,'' he said.

The Comanche obligingly led the youth along a narrow path at the foot of the bluff, to the spot where Marius had been buried beside his Clemmie several weeks earlier. Together they prayed again, and Lucien said his farewell to the man who had been his friend for as long as he could remember.

As they returned to the main path, Lopasuta turned to Lucien. "Let me ask you again; have you thought of what you want to do, more than anything else in the world? What has happened to you has tempered your mind and steeled you, as tragedy and adversity always do. I am sure now that you would not do some of the things you did last year. . . .''

"No—certainly I wouldn't go into Dublin and try to take on all the British soldiers I could find.'' Lucien uttered a little laugh, as if to break away now from the solemnity of the moment that he and Lopasuta had shared on the bluff.

"Exactly. But what *will* you do?''

"I—I don't really know. Right now, I want to stay at Windhaven and help Mother. I want to see everything repaired and all the people working and happy, and no more trouble.''

"Of course you do, as do I, and we're doing all we can to make certain that this will come true. But, after that, once the trouble is all over, what then? You can go back to New York, I suppose; your stepfather lives there now, and I am sure that your mother will rejoin him when all the trouble is over. Will you eventually go back to school in Ireland?"

Lucien shook his head. "No, there's nothing there for me now, and that's not only because of Mary Eileen, Lopasuta. It's a whole lot of things. When she died, I suddenly felt that I was a stranger at school, not a part of it. Even though I had some friends there, I felt—well, different from the other boys, somehow. No, I won't go back. Besides, there are lots of fine schools here in America where I could go to continue my education."

"You're right, there are many, particularly in the East. Being educated, of course, wouldn't preclude your being a farmer and landowner, as your father's will has provided for you."

"I'm aware of that, Lopasuta."

"Do politics interest you?"

"In theory, yes. But I know that politics can be an awfully dirty profession—people are frequently trying to buy your votes and do things that benefit a few, but leave most people poorer."

"I hear in your words the voice of a born reformer." Lopasuta chuckled. "And I can't help feeling that Andy Haskins or Dalbert Sattersfield might have some wise comments on this point. They'll tell you that reformers don't always succeed. Those who oppose them have power and wealth on their sides—or they resort to violence, such as has already happened twice on Windhaven. Still, reformers are needed, and certainly Andy was one, in his time, even if he did understand harsh realities. But if politics isn't very appealing, perhaps you could become a public speaker, or even a writer who can point out wrongs, educating others to follow the right path."

Lucien Bouchard suddenly stopped on the trail and put his hand on Lopasuta's shoulder. His eyes were wide as he said, "Or else, perhaps I could even become a teacher, Lopasuta— like Sean Flannery."

"Now there is a fine profession, and in some ways even better than the law," the tall Comanche concurred. "It is something for you to think about when it is time for you to return to school and finish your education."

"I do want to think about that, Lopasuta. I'm grateful to

you for this talk we've had. And for taking me up to Father's grave. I hope that one day, I too will be remembered the way he was.''

"You no doubt will be, my brother," Lopasuta Bouchard murmured. Then, in comradely fashion, an arm around the youth's shoulders, Lopasuta led him back toward the house.

Chapter Twenty-eight

As Leland Kenniston stepped down from the carriage that had taken him from the train station in Montgomery to Windhaven Plantation on the afternoon of April 15, his mind was a jumble of conflicting emotions. As much as he was thrilled by the idea of seeing his beloved Laure once again after being separated from her for so long, he was terrified at the same time, shuddering to think of how much she would loathe him when he told her that he had gambled away the entire sum of money—other than the thirty-seven thousand he had wired her—from the sale of La Maison de Bonne Chance. "It certainly wasn't *my* house of good luck," he muttered to himself as he pulled his valise out of the carriage.

"Beg your pardon, sir?" the driver politely asked.

"Nothing, nothing," Leland scowled. He turned and looked at the chateau. As always when he visited the plantation, he was impressed by its imposing yet graceful contours, which seemed to suggest the integrity and power of the Bouchards . . . an integrity and power that now seemed to mock him, throw back into his face his own failings and weaknesses and moral turpitude.

Looking at the house through lusterless eyes, he almost winced as he remembered the feeling of hope and joy that had prevailed on the day of his nuptials. *How could I have been so wrong?* he thought. *Laure is bound to hate me and wonder why she ever married me, and Lucien will resent me, I'm sure. I wouldn't be surprised if they both told me to leave immediately.*

Picking up the valise he had let drop at his feet, he slowly made his way up the steps to the front door of the chateau. Each step he took was a torment, bringing him much closer to the inevitable. As he walked, he thought with revulsion of the lavish way in which he had ordered champagne and caviar, how he had stuffed hundred-dollar bills down Margot's bodice, then taken her to his room at the St. Charles Hotel and there indulged himself in what he now saw was a wanton act of betrayal that yielded only transitory pleasure. He suddenly decided that he would withhold this part of his confession to Laure. He could not tell her about the abhorrent culmination of that detestable night—no, he could not bring himself to do that; she would surely draw away from him in disgust and contempt. The money could be recouped somehow—he would do everything within his meager power to earn it back—but the other, the inexplicable lust he had felt for a whore . . . he could never tell her about that.

He felt a sudden sharp pain in his stomach, a reminder that he had eaten no breakfast and scarcely any lunch today, for his mind was too much on his vagaries. He could not explain why he had done what he had done, except that he knew how wrong it was, and how in more than one sense he had betrayed his beautiful Laure. His mind was so much upon that treachery that he quite forgot the affable driver who carried over his other suitcase to the steps and waited to be paid.

It was fortunate for Leland that when he had been gambling at La Maison de Bonne Chance, he had utterly forgotten about the four hundred dollars he had placed in the safe of the St. Charles Hotel, at the manager's suggestion. Accordingly, as he left the city, he had been able to pay not only for his room, but for his fare to Montgomery. And he was able now to reach into his pocket and pull out some bills, which he handed to the driver, grunting, "Thanks."

The driver held out Leland's change, but when there was no response, he merrily thanked his taciturn passenger for his generosity and scurried back onto his carriage, humming to himself over the five-dollar tip.

Leland Kenniston observed nothing. His eyes were fixed on the door with its great brass knocker, and he knew that, once he struck it and Laure admitted him, there would be no turning away from the consequences. He remained motionless for some time, a suitcase in each hand, stiffening his back and trying to ready himself for the unpleasant moment of truth that awaited him.

At last, he set down the luggage and lifted his right hand

toward the knocker. But his hand was immobilized in midair. He did not know which was worse, the memories of that fateful night that ceaselessly swirled through his mind, or the anticipation of having to reveal to Laure how he had squandered away a fortune, tossed away her money as if he were a drunken sailor in some foreign port whose only concern was to impress the ladies of the night.

At last, taking a deep breath, he put his hand to the knocker and struck twice.

Amelia Coleman answered his summons, and her eyes widened as she saw Leland's haggard face, the hollowed eyes, the rumpled suit—for he had slept in it, or at least, tried to sleep during the hours aboard the train. "Oh, my, Mr. Kenniston! Come in. I'll go get Miz Laure directly!" she exclaimed. "She'll be so glad to see you. Mr. Lopasuta, too, only he's gone to Montgomery for the day—won't be back till late. Now let me take your luggage!"

Her cheerful welcome and bustling manner served only to plunge him further into the morass of abject despair and remorse. He did not know what he could do to divert the oncoming scene with his wife. All he could think of was that he would promise restitution—yes, of course! He would be able to pay her back from his business profits, for certainly in all the traveling he had done, all the contacts he had made and the things he had ordered in Europe, there would shortly be tremendous profits. There *had* to be!

A few moments later, Laure hurried down the stairs and rushed to him, flinging her arms around him and kissing him ardently. "Oh, Leland, you don't know how glad I am to see you, darling!"

"I'm sorry I came back a little later from Europe than I thought—but then I went to New Orleans as soon as I could after I got your wire."

"Yes, I know you did! And that draft you sent was a godsend; you don't know how much we needed it here! But oh, how tired you look—you do, Leland—you poor darling, working there for me and probably going without sleep and rushing around trying to find a buyer—but you did at last, and I'm so grateful to you—"

"Please, please don't. . . . Laure, I—I'd like to sit down . . . and—talk to you. Talk to you privately—please!" he faltered hoarsely.

"Of course, of course, my darling! You come along to the study. There's a comfortable couch there, and you can lie down and rest. I'll have Amelia bring you some tea and a sandwich—you look starved. You haven't even shaved—my goodness, have I made you work so hard as that?"

"No! No—please, Laure, let's go there so we can talk. I—I don't want anything to eat, only to talk to you!"

"As you like, dearest. You don't know how wonderful I feel now that you're back with me, my beloved husband!"

Brightly, smiling tenderly, her eyes misting with tears, the honey-haired matron grasped his arm and gently led him toward the study. Opening the door, she gestured to the couch. "Take off your suitcoat, dear; just relax and make yourself comfortable. You look as if you haven't slept—"

"I didn't, last night. And I haven't too well the last few nights, either, Laure." Despondently, his head bowed, his arms dangling at his sides, the absolute picture of dejection, he moved over to the couch, then halted and turned to her with an almost pathetically helpless look.

She caught her breath, commiserating over his anguish, not understanding it, believing it due entirely to fatigue. "I'll help you with your coat, sweetheart," she volunteered. Gently, she worked it off and then urged, "Now you lie down. I'll take off your shoes, too."

Lovingly, Laure knelt down and removed his shoes as Leland lay back on the couch, a hand over his face, his eyes closed. Needing her to help him in this way seemed to be the very nadir of his follies. He did not know how to begin, for his mind was a black purgatory of self-loathing and disgust, and obscuring all else was the almost subconscious terror of not knowing exactly why he had behaved as he had done. But now he forced himself to examine and demand an answer to these questions. He was still the same man, still Leland Kenniston, still the entrepreneur who had built a business out of his own hard work and shrewdness and imagination. . . . But how had he come to such a pass, ashamed to face his own loving and beloved wife?

"What is it, my darling?" her voice was full of concern as she rose, reached for a padded ottoman, and drew it up close to the couch, then seated herself on it. Clasping her hands, leaning forward, she stared at him, her eyes misty with tears, wanting to share with him the unknown burden that seemed to

301

plague him so and to hold him back from communicating with her. "Are you ill, dearest?"

"No—it's nothing like that, Laure." His voice was hollow and lifeless, and he kept his hand over his eyes. He did not move as he lay on the couch. "It's something much worse. Much, much worse."

"It will ease your mind to tell me about it. We're husband and wife, and there shouldn't be secrets one from the other. Try me, dearest—I'm strong, and I've learned to be even stronger after what's happened here." She gave him a nervous little laugh. "If something's bothering you, share it with me—and with two of us to fight against it, it won't be so bad after all, I'm sure!"

"I don't deserve you. What I've done . . . I still can't believe it. And yet I thought it was going to make us a great deal of money—"

"But what are you trying to tell me, sweetheart?" she anxiously pursued.

He uttered a long, desolate sigh and, turning his face to the back of the couch and away from her, began in a faltering voice: "I was a fool . . . I don't know why . . . I went to New Orleans, you know that—"

"Of course, my darling!" she cheerfully interrupted. "And you sent that draft for thirty-seven thousand dollars, which came just when we needed it. We've started making all the repairs—"

"But that's only a part of it. The rest of the money—" He paused and swallowed before blurting out, "I lost all of it at the casino. Not only thirty-eight thousand dollars in cash, but the promissory note for the balance of fifty thousand that would have been paid in four installments over the next two years. I put that up as a stake and got half of its value . . . and I lost it all—"

"I don't understand, dear," she replied, a questioning note entering her voice. "What do you mean, you lost it? How?"

"Laure, I gambled it away! I can't remember exactly what happened, except that I kept betting larger and larger sums. And I lost."

She was silent for a moment, stunned, as she sought to comprehend what Leland was telling her. When she spoke, it was with a quavering voice: "M-my God, Leland . . . how could you? How . . . how could you have done such a thing?"

"I—I was so sure I'd win . . . I wanted to—I wanted to double the money, and then you and I could have every luxury. I won at first—I was certain that I was lucky because I was doing it for you . . . but then I went and lost it all. Oh, my dear—I can't understand why I behaved this way. . . ."

"*You* can't understand why you behaved in such a manner?" Her voice began to rise in a crescendo of fear and anger. "Oh, my dear God, Leland, what can I say? If you can't understand it, how in the world am *I* supposed to understand it? Oh, Leland . . ." She turned pale and stood up, pacing for a few moments. Then she sat down on the chair at Luke's *escritoire*. "Why, Leland? Why have you done this? I can't believe you don't have an explanation—a good, rational explanation, not that poor excuse you gave me a moment ago. Gambling away a fortune! *My* fortune! If it had been your money it would have been bad enough—but to throw away money that isn't yours . . . Oh, this is simply too much. . . ."

"Oh, Laure, if you send me from you—"

"Could you blame me?" she shouted. "What in the world has come over you? Lucien confessed reluctantly that you had embarrassed him terribly when you visited with him in Ireland, but that I excused as your excitement over your forthcoming business plans . . . but this! Oh, Leland, I'm absolutely sickened by this."

"Laure, my darling—"

"Hush, Leland! At this moment I am definitely *not* your darling! In fact, at this moment I am so furious that I simply cannot even stand to look at you. If you will excuse me, I need to be alone. . . ."

"But Laure—"

"I said I need to be left alone, Leland. Please do me the courtesy of granting this small wish. I need to have time to think, and I cannot do it with you lying there." Her eyes blazed with anger, and her breasts rose and fell with her heavy breathing.

Leland sat up on the couch, his handsome face lined with pain. "I hope you can find it in your heart to forgive me—" he began.

She turned away, determined that Leland not see how close her resolve was to breaking, how easily her anger could change to compassion. She was determined not to falter. This man in whom she had placed so much trust, for whom she had had so much respect and admiration, the man she loved so dearly, had in one rash act nearly destroyed all of these things. Her mind swam in confusion. No, she *did* need time to think and to decide just what course of action she should take.

"Please excuse me, Leland," she repeated, not turning around. "I will see you at dinner."

He sighed heavily and picked himself up off the couch. Shuffling to the door like an old man, he stopped as his fingers closed on the doorknob. He was about to open his mouth and say her name one more time but decided against it. Instead, his trembling hand turned the knob, and he opened the door and walked out, closing it softly behind him.

Leland slowly made his way along the bank of the swollen river, his head throbbing so painfully that even the soft rushing sound of the water was an assault on him. He suddenly sank to his knees and began to weep—deep, wrenching sobs that completely engulfed him, body and spirit. He sat for a long time rocking back and forth, his cries mingling with and muffled by the water. Then the melancholia seemed to abate, and drying his eyes on his sleeve, he stood up, brushed the leaves and twigs off his clothes, and turned back along the river path that led back to the chateau.

As he picked his way along the path, he thought to himself how glad he was that no one had seen him, for he certainly didn't want anyone's pity—least of all Laure's. He put his fingers to his temples; the headache was less severe now, and perhaps if he had a glass of wine it would disappear entirely. Yes, that was the answer. A few glasses of wine would calm his nerves and help him relax. He was just pushing himself too hard these last months—what with the European trip, all his business responsibilities, his familial responsibilities . . . why, anyone, no matter how strong he might be, would suffer this type of emotional stress under these circumstances.

In the distance, he heard the sad and yet somehow consoling cry of a swallow on the wing, no doubt calling to its mate as the birds dipped and swooped over the distant meadow. Almost at the same time, he heard one of the Windhaven workers shouting to others in the fields. He took out his pocket watch: six o'clock, time for the world to rest from its labors and recoup strength for the morrow. He himself should return to get ready for dinner. Breathing in the fragrant air of the balmy evening, he resolved that he would go in and have a nice glass of wine, then join Laure and Lucien for a lovely meal. . . . It was strange that he hadn't yet seen the lad—but then, he was probably out in the fields somewhere. He wondered how the boy was doing, whether he was coping with Mary Eileen's death. Perhaps he should buy him something special, something that would distract him from his unhappiness. . . .

Money. Suddenly he was back to square one. "How am I going to make this up to Laure?" he asked himself aloud. "Jacob said we were low on our cash reserves, of course, but surely by now he's found many enthusiastic buyers for those wonderful goods I purchased in Europe. Why, of course he has! I can just draw upon those new payments! I'll write my banker tonight, asking him to transfer money into the Brunton & Alliance Bank in New Orleans—the exact amount that I was so silly as to have lost." He sighed, a look of contentment on his face. His steps brisk, he ascended the front steps of the chateau.

Dinner was at seven-thirty, and as Laure approached the dining room, she could see through the open door that Leland and Lucien were already seated at the table. Though they appeared to be engaged in light, amiable conversation, she had no doubt that her husband was awaiting her further response to the afternoon's revelations, and his anxious glance at her, as she stood in the doorway, confirmed that fact.

Laure had done a great deal of thinking the past hours, and she had concluded that while she would never be able to understand Leland's outrageous behavior, still she would be able to forgive him. The compassionate impulse that she had at first pushed from her returned again and again, forcing her to recall her own foolishness on past occasions—as when she had allowed William Brickley to dupe her and nearly ruin her when he was managing her casino. These memories made her wince with remorse, and she began to see Leland's mistakes in a new light. Granted that he had lost an enormous sum of money; nevertheless, he had never given her any indication that he was reckless and unconcerned for her and her children's welfare. No, surely it was the result of driving himself too hard for her and for the children; he was so determined that

305

they should have every conceivable comfort that he was just beyond the point of exhaustion, and his aberrant behavior was the result. Watching the slightly bent and somehow aged figure of her husband, his lined face creased in a soft smile as he shared some private joke with Lucien, she knew she loved him and could never leave him. He had all the most important qualities one could want in a husband, in spite of his peccadilloes, and the essential decency of his character was evident in the gentleness and affection he manifested toward her children.

She came into the room and smiled at Leland and Lucien, bending over and kissing each in turn.

"Laure—" Leland began, rising slightly in his chair.

"Please don't get up, my dear," she said lightly, hoping that her tone would indicate to him her decision. She gently squeezed his shoulder and then took her seat. "Well, what have you two been discussing?" Laure asked.

Lucien smiled and said, "I've been telling Father about my new brick-laying skills, and he told me that with all the building going on in New York City, if I wanted to be a mason up there, I'd probably be able to write my own ticket." He grinned impishly and declared, "I must confess that it would be tempting for about two hours at a time—but then I'd get awfully tired! I think I'd best stick to less exhausting skills."

His parents laughed with him, and Leland caught Laure's eye and winked at her. The Irishman then heartily declared, "Actually, I think what Lucien is enjoying best about being at Windhaven is the fact that there are no rivals for his parents' attention. Isn't that so, my lad?"

Lucien tried on a mock-indignant expression, but it quickly gave way to a giggle. "I confess that I do miss Paul a great deal—but Celestine has gotten to an awfully moony stage. Clarissa's easy to put up with—like most ten year olds she's happy just playing with her dolls, but—" He sighed, and shook his head. "John, on the other hand—oh, Mother, that little one is an absolute tyrant! No, don't laugh, it's true. He's always ordering poor Clarabelle around, and she spoils him terribly by giving in to him."

Laure wiped her eyes with the corner of her napkin, finally controlling her laughter. "I know, dear. And I, of course, am the person most guilty for his being spoiled. But . . ." Suddenly her face became serious, and she looked down at her lap. "I suppose that when your father was killed—well, John was like a last gift from Luke, and perhaps I have treasured him a bit too much above all of you others because of this." She sighed wistfully, thinking of her six-year-old son. Then, with a mischievous grin, told Lucien, "You're absolutely right! I shall tell Clarabelle that if he misbehaves, he will have to forego his cocoa. *That* should keep him in line."

The three of them laughed to think of the look of indignation on John's face at such a turn of events, and by the time Amelia Coleman came in with the first course, it was as if there were nothing at all troubling the diners—as if no raid had ever taken place, as if no stray bullet had ever found its way to a lovely young girl, and as if no money had been foolishly gambled away. It was as if these three people were determined to get on with their lives and put the tragedies of yesterday completely behind them.

After dinner, when Lucien had gone up to his room, leaving Laure and Leland alone, Leland took his wife's hand and gazed into her eyes. "My dearest Laure, I have missed you so very much."

"And I have missed you, Leland." She paused for a moment before continuing, "I want you to know that I will be perplexed for some time over what you have done—but I will try not to be angry about it. I'm sure you meant nothing harmful or heedless—it was just poor judgment brought on and exaggerated by being so overworked and weary. I think you should consider taking a vacation, Leland—a complete break from work for perhaps a month or so."

"No, I couldn't do that—not yet, anyway," he replied. "For one thing, I have to get back and make sure that we find qualified buyers for the goods I purchased so that there will be ample money going into the business's bank account to leave a substantial balance after I make over a transfer of funds to you." He smiled and brought the wine glass to his lips and sipped it.

"I don't understand. . . ."

"It's very simple, my dear," Leland said. "This very evening I will write to my New York bank and request that they transfer to *your* bank the balance of the casino transaction—eighty-eight thousand dollars. It was your money that I foolishly lost, so therefore it is only fair that I repay you."

"But Leland, I thought . . ."

"Never mind what you thought, Laure. In a few days' time, I shall have everything put to right. Trust me."

Laure rose from her chair and came up behind Leland. "I do trust you, my darling," she whispered in his ear, her voice becoming husky. "And right now I want to *show* you how much I trust you . . . and love you . . . and want you. . . ."

Chapter Twenty-nine

Almost from the first moment the contractor had begun work at Windhaven Plantation, young Lucien Bouchard had been greatly puzzled by Enoch Washburn's behavior toward him. On the very first day that the middle-aged black had appeared at the plantation with his chosen crew, Lucien had volunteered to show him the location of the tool sheds and that section of the dam that had suffered the second, more damaging dynamiting. Following the tour, Lucien had stayed with Enoch, for the young man was eager to watch the skilled contractor in his work. For some reason unfathomable to Lucien, his presence seemed to irritate Enoch, who finally turned to him and said, "If you don't mind, sonny, we can get on with our work now. Don't you have somethin' better to do than to tag along after us?"

"Why—yes, of course, Mr. Washburn; if you'd prefer, I—I'll just be on my way," Lucien had faltered, hotly coloring. And as he had turned away, he thought that he had seen a sort of contemptuous sneer curve the black man's lips.

He had reported this to Lopasuta about an hour later, when the two were having lunch, adding that he was beginning to question his initial favorable impression of the man.

"I'm sorry to hear that, Lucien," the tall Comanche lawyer said. "All I can think of is that maybe he thinks you're still a lad and not an employer who has the right to oversee his work. You'll just have to bear with him, for he does seem to be a very competent man. I looked over the members of the crew he brought along today, and I'm quite satisfied that they're good hard workers. Heaven knows we need them if we're to get this dam rebuilt and the other repairs taken care of."

"Well, I'll just keep on doing my work, and hope that I don't make Mr. Washburn too unhappy," Lucien declared.

Later that afternoon, Lucien went walking with Lopasuta, and they encountered Enoch Washburn at work supervising the rebuilding of the dam. In the light of the man's behavior that morning, Lucien was startled by Washburn's deference to Lopasuta.

"My men are gettin' hold of the work right off, as you can see, Mr. Bouchard," Enoch said. "I hope it's to your likin'."

"I'm sure it will be. But we may be working against time. I want it so solid that it will be very difficult for anyone to blow it up again," Lopasuta averred.

"Do you really think they'll try it again, Mr. Bouchard?" the contractor asked.

"Anything is possible when you're dealing with lunatics, Mr. Washburn. Well, I'll leave you to your work. Incidentally, do you have everything you need?"

"We've plenty of supplies, except I might have to send Ed here"—he gestured to a tall, lanky black man in his late thirties, who stood near him—"for some more shovels and pickaxes."

"Get whatever you need. Dalbert Sattersfield has two stores, and both of them carry equipment like that," Lopasuta told him. "Just charge it to the Windhaven account."

"I'll do just that, Mr. Bouchard. Thanks for your help." He gave Lopasuta a friendly nod and touched his finger to his forehead. When Lucien looked at him, however, he felt Enoch's expression change to one of insolent contempt, just before the man abruptly turned away to confer with Ed.

Lopasuta and Lucien walked down the fields to the south, and Lucien finally spoke up, "You noticed that, didn't you, Lopasuta? I mean, he just about ignored me completely, but then, just as we were leaving, he gave me a look that told me he doesn't care for me one little bit. Well, I sure wish I knew what I've done to offend him."

Lopasuta looked at the youth curiously. Cocking his head slightly, he asked, "What makes you think you've offended him? I must say, Lucien, I didn't find his behavior peculiar or nasty at all—nor did I notice him looking oddly at you." He put his arm around the young man. "Come, we've got much more to do today than stand here and worry about . . . slights. When you're older and you've dealt with more people—and

310

more diverse types of people—you'll come to recognize it when someone is *really* being offensive toward you."

"You don't believe me!" Lucien almost shouted. "You think I'm making this up."

"No, no, not at all," Lopasuta soothed him. "I'm sure you *believe* that Enoch Washburn behaved in an unwarranted manner. I'm simply saying that perhaps it wasn't quite the way it appeared. Perhaps he had something else on his mind that he was thinking of and was upset about, and it just so happened that he was looking your way at that moment. Come, my boy, don't let such an insignificant matter disturb you." He clapped Lucien on the back and led him toward the chateau. Diverting the youth by changing the subject, Lopasuta declared, "I'm going to ask Enoch what his men would want in the way of additional pay to act as guards for as long as they're working here. They can live in some of the cottages of those workers who've quit recently."

"Do you think there'll be another attack?" Lucien asked.

"Who can say?" Lopasuta replied. "But as long as we've got the manpower available, I'd like to be ready for those bastards—just in case."

Doggedly, young Lucien determined to make a friend of Enoch Washburn. He earnestly wanted to learn all he could about the physical chores that went with the running of the plantation, including repairs and the construction of buildings and dams. The thought had come to him—though it was simply a passing fancy at the moment, to be sure—that perhaps for the next few years, until Windhaven Plantation could once again run smoothly and make steady profits for his mother, he would do well to devote all his energy and intellect to the task of becoming an agricultural expert. The land was fertile and productive, and although Windhaven Plantation's acreage had been polluted temporarily, Lucien was sure that soon it would be once again ready to produce wholesome food for the Bouchards, their workers, and for the community at large.

To that end, he took it upon himself to risk following Washburn around again, silent at first and merely observing the contractor and his crew at their various duties. To his relief, Washburn appeared not to object to his presence, so after two days, he took a chance and asked the man a question about the strength of the walls of the dam.

The black contractor turned and shot him a hateful look. "Look, I've told you to stop followin' me around like a puppy dog, sonny! You're holdin' up my work. I'm not gonna let you do anythin', so there's no point in askin'. If you want to learn somethin', just watch how my men do their jobs. Understand?"

"Yes—yes, Mr. Washburn. I didn't mean any harm. . . ."

"Maybe not—but you're a damn pesky kid," Washburn snapped, turning his back on the astonished and mortified young man as he went to confer with one of his workers who was rebuilding a shed.

Perhaps it was obstinacy, or perhaps simply Lucien's desire to win over someone whose enmity he could not fathom that made him wish to break down the strange barrier between them. When Lopasuta had come out to confer with Washburn, Lucien had observed that the contractor was deferential and polite, almost even fawning. What, then, had he himself done to offend the man, Lucien asked himself. And because he had no answer, and because he was a pragmatist by nature—or, at least, so his former mentor, Sean Flannery, would have described him—he persisted in following the contractor about and continuing to ask questions.

Almost every time, he was rebuffed, and while Washburn did not come out with any specific utterance that addressed their differences, nonetheless Lucien could feel the dull anger and irascibility of the man whenever the two met and looked at each other. Occasionally, the contractor would give him curt explanations to his questions. And then, about a week after Leland Kenniston had come to Windhaven Plantation, late one afternoon that had turned out to be extremely warm after an early morning rain, Lucien asked another question about tools. Washburn put his hands on his hips and scowled, his eyes narrowing. He harshly retorted, "Now look here, sonny, I've had just about enough of these questions. They tell me you went to Europe to get some schoolin', but in my book you've still a lot to learn. I told you once before, just watch what my crew is doin', and you'll learn fast enough. I'm not your teacher, and I don't have to look after you. Now let me be—do you *mind*?"

Lucien mumbled something and walked away. Tears were

stinging his eyes, for the rebuff was harsh, indeed. And in his sensitive and vulnerable mood, trying desperately to forget the tragedy of Mary Eileen, and the rebuff by Eleanor, Enoch Washburn's rejection of him took on a monumental force, wounding him more than it ordinarily would have done.

A few days before the end of April, Dalbert Sattersfield came over to breakfast with Laure, Leland, Lucien, and Lopasuta. Dalbert turned to Laure's oldest son and proposed, "I've got something that ought to interest you a great deal more than working in the fields. How'd you like to pay a visit to the capital this afternoon and meet the present senior state senator from our district?"

"I'd like that."

"I've made an appointment with him—wrote a letter last week, in fact, and just got the answer yesterday. His name is Martin Haynes, and he was elected last year to his third term. Thanks to Andy Haskins, who introduced us, I knew him slightly when he was a state representative, but then he dropped out of politics for years after marrying a woman a lot younger than himself. She died a couple of years ago. He has a daughter—must be in her late teens by now. I haven't seen her since she was a little girl."

Lucien gave no response, but merely lowered his eyes to his plate.

"My main reason for calling on Senator Haynes," Dalbert continued, "is to sound him out about ways to counteract what I see as a backlash we've been experiencing the last year or so in this state. I'd like Alabama to go on record as being for civil rights and against civil violence. I'm not happy with the way things are in this state—or in this country, for that matter. I'd like Senator Haynes to make some sort of statement, if he's willing. I understand that a case may go to the Supreme Court next fall that challenges everything Lincoln and the Fourteenth and Fifteenth Amendments accomplished."

"I'd very much like to meet the senator," Lucien repeated.

"All right, then, since you like to ride horseback so much, we can ride into town about eleven o'clock this morning, stable our horses, have a bite of lunch, and then go over to the capitol building and see Senator Haynes. Even though he's very learned, he's a friendly and easygoing man, and he knows a lot more law than practically all the lawyers in

313

Montgomery put together. That doesn't include you, Lopasuta, because, strictly speaking, you're not a Montgomery lawyer any more."

"That much is true," Lopasuta said, grinning.

It took Dalbert and Lucien a little under two hours to make the ride to Montgomery, where they had lunch in a restaurant run by a friend of Lopasuta's. It was a favorite spot of both the Comanche lawyer and Andy Haskins in the days when they lived in Montgomery. The owner personally waited on Dalbert and Lucien when he heard who they were. Expressing his pleasure at meeting Lucien, he declared, "Your father won't be forgotten around here, believe me, young man."

Following lunch, they strode over to the capitol. As they ascended the steps of the building and walked down the long hallway, Lucien was impressed by the imposing structure, with its high-vaulted ceilings and statues of Alabama patriots. Dalbert was a frequent visitor to the capitol, for as a mayor, he had a more than passing acquaintance with many of the elected state officials. Indeed, several representatives had tried to convince him that he should seek higher office—but Dalbert was content.

As the two men walked down the long colonnaded hallway, Dalbert spotted a familiar face and called, "Matthew! I wonder if you can help us. We're here to see Senator Haynes."

A grizzled man in his sixties, hobbling about with a cane, declared, "Well, good to see you, Dalbert. The senator's in chamber, there. The page'll take you."

Then Dalbert and Lucien walked on toward the private chamber of the senate, and a young page, hearing the request, bade them wait outside the door for a moment and said that he would announce the two of them to the senator. A moment later, the page opened the door and said, "Come in. Senator Haynes is anxious to see you, Mr. Sattersfield, sir, and you, too, Mr. Bouchard."

Before them stood a distinguished-looking man in his early sixties, with a leonine head of white hair. Tall, powerfully built, he radiated energy and geniality. He was clutching a sheaf of papers and standing in the center of the room, in a formal pose, from which Lucien deduced that he had been interrupted while practicing a speech. But, having observed this, Lucien found his gaze drawn almost at once to the other

314

person in the room, a breathtakingly beautiful young woman who could not have been much older than himself. She was tall, almost as tall as he, with large hazel eyes and auburn hair drawn back from her temples and formed into a chignon at the back of her neck. She wore a blue silk frock and carried a parasol.

"Good to see you, Dalbert. So this is young Lucien Bouchard, is it?" Senator Martin Haynes boomed, as he came forward to offer his hand first to Dalbert, and then to Lucien. "Gentlemen, may I introduce my daughter, Samantha. Samantha, my dear, this is Dalbert Sattersfield—the eminent mayor of Lowndesboro."

"It's a pleasure to meet you, Mr. Sattersfield." She curtsied to him.

"And this is Lucien Bouchard. The name is a great one, young sir," Senator Haynes said to Laure's oldest son. "It carries a wonderful heritage to be proud of."

"And I am, Senator Haynes," Lucien said with simple directness.

"Well, I'd guess that you and my daughter must be about the same age—seventeen," the senator added.

"Yes, we are, Senator. How—how do you do, Miss Haynes?"

"Very well, thank you, Mr. Bouchard. Father has often told me about the Bouchards and Windhaven Plantation. It's a privilege to meet you." And with this, she dropped him as graceful a curtsy as young Lucien had ever seen.

"You know, Senator"—Dalbert saw how rapt Lucien was in his contemplation of his friend's exquisite daughter and attempted to divert attention from the lad by taking the center of the stage—"I came here today to talk to you about a problem that is of concern to me and my neighbors along the Alabama. We've had some trouble down that way, and I'm here hoping that something can be done about it. I'd like to see stiffer penalties for those who resort to mob violence against decent folks' property."

"I'm at your service, Dalbert, you know that. I'm here to serve my constituents in any way I can. What is more, I have a particularly high regard for you—I've followed the way you've run your lovely town; I like the way you've kept radical elements from taking over. You and I are very much alike in our beliefs."

"It's kind of you to say that, Senator Haynes. Are you going to be busy this afternoon, or do you have a little time to chat?"

"Today's session is fairly routine—all I have to do is answer a roll call. There's the gong now, as a matter of fact; that means we senators have to go in and be counted. When that's done, you and I can spend a little time in my private office down at the other end of this hall."

"I'd like nothing better, Senator," Dalbert declared.

Turning to Lucien, the senator then prompted, "How about you, my boy? Which is your preference—a political brainstorming session with Dalbert and me . . . or a guided tour of this lovely building by my even lovelier daughter?"

"Well, sir . . ." Lucien began, floundering somewhat.

"Oh, come, come, my boy." Senator Haynes winked at the youth. "Don't hesitate to speak freely. If I were in your place, I know which answer I'd give."

"Well, I *am* certainly interested in hearing what you have to say, sir, truly I am."

"Of course you are—and I promise you that Dalbert will tell you all about it when we're done," the senator chuckled.

"Indeed I will, Lucien," Dalbert assured him. "Why don't you two young folks meet us back here in, say, one hour? Lucien, I'm sure Miss Haynes would like to hear about your studies in Dublin."

"Why, indeed I should," Samantha Haynes spoke up. She had a rich contralto voice, and her presence had, it must be confessed, made Lucien momentarily forget both Mary Eileen Brennert and Eleanor Martinson.

"I'll be back then, Dalbert, after the roll call," Senator Haynes promised. He extended his hand to Lucien. "Mighty glad to meet you, young Mr. Bouchard. I'll see you again after your tour. And Samantha, our young friend looks like a trusting soul, so don't go making up any fanciful tales to lead him astray!" And, with a wink at Dalbert, the senator strode from the room.

As Lucien Bouchard walked beside Samantha Haynes, he was, for a while, completely speechless. He finally vouchsafed, "I—I recently got back from Dublin, as you may have gathered, Miss Haynes."

"I'd like to hear about it, if you'd like to tell me," she

316

sweetly said. "Perhaps you'd prefer to sit down for a while. Come, there's a bench over there by the farthest wall, near the statue of Jefferson Davis."

He was almost absurdly grateful to her for taking charge, for he was beginning to feel extremely self-conscious, left alone to his own resources with this dazzlingly beautiful young woman. "That's a fine idea, Miss Haynes," he said, his voice still a little unsteady.

"Oh, do call me Samantha, and I'll call you Lucien. It'll be ever so much easier. Formality can be so awfully tedious, don't you agree?" She turned to smile at him coyly.

"Oh, yes—I think that's true. It's a lovely name—Samantha. I like it very much," he blurted.

"How sweet. Here we are, now. This is comfortable—though Daddy might not like us sitting so close to Jefferson Davis!" She giggled, then said, "He's always going on about that silly old war. Well, I don't like to talk about it." She pouted slightly, then turned to him and smiled. "Let's talk about interesting things—like your school. Would you say it differed much from an American school? What were your friends like? What did you do for fun?"

She plied him with questions, and he soon forgot his initial self-consciousness as he told her about Father O'Mara and Sean Flannery, about his chums Edward Cordovan and Ned Riordan. She interrupted him then to ask him what Irish boys were like, and when he could not reply, she teased him and bade him continue. After a little hesitation, he went so far as to describe his squabbles with English soldiers, taking pains to make it clear that he now realized he'd been foolish in what he'd done.

"My goodness, that was very rash of you! Do you always take such chances? They could have hurt you dreadfully!"

"I wish that it could have been me who was hurt—" he began, then stopped and looked down at his feet.

"Oh?" she softly prompted. "Was anyone else hurt? I mean—one of your chums?" But then, seeing him hesitate, she added, whining slightly, "Of course, if it's something you'd rather not tell me, Lucien—"

He took her wavering to be delicacy of feeling, so he hastened to assure her that she was not being too inquisitive. "I—I want to tell you, Samantha—" he stammered, looking down at his feet.

317

She looked at him intently, her face bright with interest. "Well?" she said, softly insistent.

He raised his eyes and caught her expression of expectant curiosity, so he took a deep breath and told her all about Mary Eileen, finally reaching the tragic events of that never-to-be-forgotten Sunday.

"How dreadful!" she exclaimed. "How horrible for you! Oh, Lucien, I'm sure you must pine for her! You've lost your one true love. It's the way people live in books. I mean, it's so romantic, wouldn't you say? You've done something that no one else that I know has done."

"I don't know, Samantha, it's all still pretty confusing. I've experienced such grief and guilt over what happened. . . ."

"But you weren't responsible! It was those terrible soldiers that did it. You—you were a hero, Lucien, having Mary Eileen dying in your arms and all!"

Lucien didn't feel like a romantic hero at all—indeed, he felt nothing but a sense of loss and a terrible awareness of his own inadequacy. It would take time for him to sort it all out.

"Well, here I am, silly old me, asking you a lot of questions, and I haven't even started to show you the capitol," Samantha said brightly. "You must think me terribly stupid and dull—"

"No—no, Samantha, not at all," Lucien countered. "I—I'm glad you asked about these things. Thank you for being so sympathetic."

She smiled at him. "Well, *I'd* like to think that you and I will be good friends—and that's what good friends are for."

"Now then, Dalbert, what's on your mind?" Senator Haynes asked, as he waved the mayor to a comfortable chair opposite his polished mahogany desk, seating himself with a grunt of comfort. "You know, Dalbert, thanks to my good wife, God rest her soul, I had a chance to acquire a little polish, but scratch the surface, and you'll see I'm basically just a big, hulking farmer lad, born in the Alabama back country and right proud of it. Maybe I've come up in the world some, but I still have a lot of respect for a man who knows what to do with a shovel, rake, or hoe, and has respect for the land he's working on, the land that gives him his daily bread."

"I know that, know it well, Senator. That's why I think you're the very man to sponsor this idea I've got and to make it law. You never were a believer in slavery, even though you were born in Alabama.''

"That's true enough. I'll admit my views were none too popular before secession, and they probably still aren't. I always believed that the blacks should be free and have every chance that whites have had. But tell me, what's this idea of yours? What sort of bill would you have me sponsor?''

"Well, you know the South has always stood by the principle of state's rights, even against federal law. In fact, that was one reason for the secession. Therefore, it seems to me that every state has its own responsibility to legislate a tough law that'll punish people who decide to take matters into their own hands and go looking for trouble—or who just want to terrorize the blacks as well as white folks who don't seem to conform to their own bigoted way of thinking.''

"I think I can see what you're after, Dalbert. Let me draft something and then get back to you with it. Of course, that would mean using either militia or state troops, not federal troops.''

"That's the way it should be. If the state is going to do its own policing, it's got to be with its own civil authorities, and not with any help from the federal government,'' Dalbert earnestly declared.

"I'm certainly on your side, Dalbert. If I had my way, I'd put all the Klan members in jail for a long time. They're outlaws, hoodlums, criminals. It's a shameful blot on the escutcheon of the South; I'm emphatic about that!''

"I leave it to you as to how to phrase this bill, Senator. I presume, though, that it wouldn't be aimed just at the Klan, but at lawlessness in general.''

"Agreed. Well, then—we've had a useful discussion, I'd say.'' He rose from his chair. "Let's go back out and collect Samantha and Lucien. I like that boy, Dalbert.''

"He's got good stuff in him, and he's a Bouchard. You couldn't ask for a better recommendation than that,'' the one-armed mayor averred.

The two men walked out into the huge hall, and Dalbert smiled to himself to see Samantha Haynes and Lucien Bouchard sitting side by side on the bench, completely absorbed in their conversation. He was delighted that Lucien had responded to the young woman, thinking to himself that her charms were exceedingly obvious.

"Well now, Samantha, have you enjoyed getting acquainted with Mr. Bouchard?" her father boomed.

"Yes, Daddy." Samantha rose, and Lucien hastened to his feet, flushing self-consciously, as her father's eyes, twinkling with amusement, considered him.

"I'm glad, because since Dalbert and I have a project in mind, and you probably would like to be able to hear more from young Mr. Bouchard about his travels, I've a capital idea. Mr. Bouchard, I'd like to have you and Dalbert be my guests for dinner this evening at my house."

"That's very kind of you, Senator Haynes!" Lucien enthusiastically exclaimed.

Dalbert agreed. "Fine, Senator. I'd like to explore this idea some more with you. Maybe after dinner I can help you sketch the wording of the bill. In my book, the faster it gets written into law, the faster we'll have protection to forestall any more dangerous nonsense."

"That's exactly what I was thinking. And if we can get it worked out tonight, I might even be able to introduce it from the floor of the Senate in a week or so," the white-haired senator proffered. "Well, then, gentlemen, I'll expect you for dinner, say about sevenish. You know where my house is, Dalbert."

"I do, indeed."

"I'll see you both to the door. Gentlemen, the only way to save the South is by moderate men of good judgment joining in the cause to fight hooliganism. I'm certainly heartily glad, Dalbert, that you thought to call on me—heartily glad, indeed!"

Lucien, surreptitiously peering at Samantha Haynes, was thinking exactly the same thing. And he felt an unbounded gratitude toward Dalbert for having brought him along to Montgomery today.

Chapter Thirty

At the end of the first week in May, Lopasuta Bouchard received a letter from Eugene DuBois in New Orleans, asking if he could return by the middle of the month so as to appear in court on a case that was on the court's docket for the twenty-first. The Creole lawyer explained he had prepared the brief in the case, which involved a defaulted contract by one of Leland Kenniston's shippers. "I, of course, could handle it, Lopasuta," Eugene wrote, "but your courtroom acumen will ensure that Mr. Kenniston wins, whereas my own inexperience before the bench might very well lose it. I do hope you can conveniently return, and either way I'd appreciate it if you'd wire me. Mei Luong sends her very best wishes, and we both hope that you have managed to straighten everything out at Windhaven Plantation."

Lopasuta wired back that he would stay another week and arrive in New Orleans about the middle of the month; also, that he was familiar with the case, and that two or three days would be all that he required to prepare his strategy for the courtroom appearance. He thanked the Creole for attending to the case so punctiliously and conveyed his best greetings to Eugene DuBois's lovely Chinese wife.

This week also brought Leland Kenniston a letter postmarked from New York, and he recognized the logotype of the bank to which he had earlier written. He excitedly tore it open, unfolded the letter, then stood there stunned and speechless. It read as follows:

> Dear Mr. Kenniston:
>   We have received your letter requesting a transfer from your business account to the Brunton & Alliance Bank of New Orleans in the amount of $88,000.

We must inform you that the present standing of your account, as of this date, is $2,497.86. It will, therefore, be impossible to comply with your wish, and you will have to make other arrangements if you desire a capital investment of the size you mentioned.

When you return to New York, we should like very much to discuss with you the future handling of your account. There have been a few discrepancies—minor, I assure you—and it would be in your best interests to work out with us a plan of investment and transfer of funds, so that a situation like the above mentioned will not recur.

I have the pleasure to be,

Yours faithfully,
J.R. Dartwell
Vice-Persident

"I don't believe it . . . I can't believe it . . . it's impossible!" Leland Kenniston muttered. His eyes were glassy as he stared out the window. His mind's eye did not take in the trees, grass, flowers, or stream; instead, he saw only, like a wraith, the worried and reproachful face of Jacob Cohen.

He turned away from the window, the letter dropping from his trembling hand. "I don't understand it. I just don't," he muttered to himself. "Now I won't be able to give Laure the money right away. But what other arrangements can I make?"

Almost simultaneously, a letter from Jacob arrived for Leland, and it was a short but startling one, which stunned the Irish entrepreneur. Jacob had not divulged all that he had on his mind, but what he did say was enough to make Leland report to Laure, "I'll have to go back to New York at once, my darling. Things seem to be in a very muddled state, and I have to straighten them out. Besides, since your repairs are coming along smoothly enough, I'll only be a hindrance here, worrying about my business. I'm sure everything's going to be all right, once I get there."

At the news that both Lopasuta and her husband were about to leave, Laure had the feeling that she was being left entirely alone to cope with the problems of rehabilitation and restoration. And with the death of Marius Thornton, she felt all the more isolated. It was true that Benjamin Brown was just as capable

322

and certainly as willing; what was more, he was younger and more energetic. Nevertheless, he was a relative newcomer to Windhaven, and the loss of Marius Thornton, not so much as an employee but as a loyal and devoted friend, left her feeling irretrievably alone.

Lopasuta sensed her discomfiture as the time for his departure drew near, and one morning he had an inspiration. "Laure, perhaps you could send for Lucien Edmond in Texas. I realize that he has work of his own to tend to, but I'm sure he'd want to do everything he could to help," the lawyer suggested.

"I hesitate to do that," Laure replied thoughtfully, "because when I heard from Mara a while back, things at Windhaven Range were not good. Evidently their cattle business is suffering from competition with ranches farther north, and I'm sure Lucien Edmond has a lot on his mind."

"At the same time, though," Lopasuta urged, "he is Luke's eldest son, and is, in a sense, the head of the Bouchard family. I think he would insist on being here, if he knew his presence could make a difference. In fact, if I may say so, you almost owe it to yourself and your children to avail yourself of his help. Though Lucien will one day be able to take charge, he's too young for that now."

Laure looked at the Comanche for a long moment, then slowly nodded her head. "I suppose you're right, Lopasuta. Yes, as long as you put it that way, I'll do it. I'll send off a wire immediately. After all, Lucien Edmond came to my rescue once before. . . ." She was thinking back to the time six years before, when, after Luke's death, she had hired an unscrupulous manager and almost lost Windhaven Plantation to his nefarious partner, William Brickley. Lucien Edmond had come to her rescue, and it had been he who had brought William Brickley to account for his attempt to cause the financial ruin of Windhaven and the Bouchards. And though Brickley had never admitted complicity in the deed, Lucien had proved to his own satisfaction that the malefactor had been involved in the kidnapping of Lopasuta.

The next day, Elmer Gregory, who had by now completely recovered from the typhoid fever he had contracted after the flood, rode into Montgomery for supplies and took Laure's wire to the telegraph office. Two days later, Lucien Edmond's reply was received, announcing that he would leave at once for Windhaven to assist his stepmother.

This relieved Laure greatly, as did Lopasuta's final arrangement before he left: He called upon the three guards he had hired and sternly reminded them that, although nothing had happened in the past few weeks, they should be continually vigilant. He urged them to keep their presence secret, and not to discuss anything with others if they went into town.

Laure, for her part, resolved to continue her practice with both the derringer and the rifle that she had acquired after the last raid. Lopasuta, who had taught her the rudiments of loading, firing, and cleaning the weapons, heartily praised her growing skill and encouraged her to keep up her efforts and to take further lessons from Lucien Edmond.

With that, the Comanche lawyer packed his bags for the journey back to New Orleans. Laure and Lucien rode with him to the Montgomery station, and as he was about to board the train, he reassured the beautiful matron, "If you need me again, you've only to send for me. But I think with Lucien Edmond here, and with Dalbert and Lucien and the guards looking over the place, you should be well protected."

Dalbert, who had ridden over from Lowndesboro to join in the farewell to Lopasuta, shook the Comanche lawyer's hand. "Take care of yourself, Lopasuta, and don't worry. If the raiders try anything else, they'll answer for it. The bill that Senator Haynes is going to introduce will see to it that such miscreants receive long prison sentences."

"I hope so, Dalbert. In the meantime, I'm relieved that you'll be here to help Lucien and Laure." Then, turning to Lucien, he put a hand to the youth's shoulder. "Be well, my brother. I know the plantation will be in good hands with you here to assist your mother." And with a final kiss for Laure, the Comanche lawyer ascended the steps into the train and was gone.

When Leland Kenniston arrived back in New York on the thirteenth of May, he went at once by cab to the house on Gramercy Park. As he arrived in the front hall, his coat dripping from a spring shower, Paul and young John bounded down the front stairs with joy, and Celestine and Clarissa emerged from the parlor to welcome him home. But all four children instinctively squelched their enthusiasm when they perceived the expression of profound gloom on their stepfather's face. Celestine, who had wanted to give him a welcoming kiss, silently took his coat and took it down to the laundry room to be dried and pressed, while the other children stood around in confusion.

Leland likewise had few words for Clarabelle Hendry, who came up from the downstairs, after hearing from Celestine that her stepfather had returned. Replying to Clarabelle's inquiry about Laure with a dejected sigh, he said, "Everything is going as well as can be expected, Clarabelle. And now, if you don't mind, I'll lie down a bit before dinner. By the way, please ask Mrs. Emmons to bring it to me in my room."

"Of course, sir, just as you wish," the pleasant widow agreed.

As Leland ascended the stairs, Clarabelle returned to the kitchen, where she confided to Anna Emmons, "I'm worried about Mr. Kenniston, I really am. When he came back from Europe, he was in a black fit and nothing went right. And now he still looks the same way. I don't know what happened over there, or at Windhaven Plantation, but he's surely not himself."

Kerry Dugan greeted his employer cheerfully the next morning when Leland entered the carriage house, where the Irish coachman was busy polishing the brass trim of the carriage. "Faith, 'n it's good to see you again, sir!" he exclaimed. "I'll have the carriage ready in a jiffy, Mr. Kenniston, and take you right to your office. I suppose that's where you're bound this morning?"

But Leland only glumly nodded without a word, his face drawn and aloof as if he scarcely heard the greeting. Thus rebuffed, Kerry said no more but hurried to harness the horse and then opened the door of the carriage for his employer to climb inside. Taking up the reins on the coachman's seat, he drove uptown and stopped at the building that housed Leland's suite of offices. "Want me to wait for you, Mr. Kenniston, sir?" he asked as he doffed his hat.

But Leland did not even glance at the man and only shook his head. With a terse "No," he strode into the building, leaving Kerry to look after him, not certain what to make of his employer's dour mien.

As he entered the office, Leland saw Jacob Cohen leaning over a desk at which was seated a skinny, middle-aged man with thinning hair and thick-lensed spectacles. The man was poring over a pile of invoices, and Jacob was shaking his head in consternation. When the door opened, Jacob looked up. His eyes widened, and he cried out, "Leland, thank God you're back! We're just about going crazy trying to clear up things here!" He nodded at the other man and said, "By the way, this is Joshua Landers, who's a very skillful accountant. Mr. Johnson said that matters had gone far beyond his skills as a bookkeeper, and he suggested that we hire Mr. Landers so we can clear up the mess."

"Mess?" Leland blankly echoed. "Your letter to me sounded gloomy, and that's why I hurried back. But are you sure you're not exaggerating, Jacob?"

"I wish to God I were, Leland, I wish to God I were!" Jacob groaned, pressing his palms against his cheeks. "Let's go into your office, Leland; I want to tell you something."

"All right, Jacob. Good morning to you, Mr. Landers. If you're a good accountant, I'm sure you'll be able to straighten everything out to our satisfaction." When they entered Leland's office, Jacob at once went to a chair and sat down heavily. He was practically in tears.

Closing the door behind them, Leland turned to his associate and demanded in a flat voice, "Now, Jacob, what is all this? What was the sense of sending a letter down to Alabama where Laure might have seen it? Don't you think she has worries enough? You certainly frightened me—that's why I came back. But if worse comes to worst, we'll just send back what I didn't order, and the profits from our foreign sales—the receipts from Hong Kong and San Francisco—should be enough to tide us over."

"I just wish and pray it was that simple, Leland," Jacob fervently answered. "Mr. Landers has been here for a week, and he's shown me everything. Do you know that unless we take urgent steps, we'll face bankruptcy?"

"You can't mean that!" Leland shouted, and stared at his associate. "That's impossible! Bankrupt? How can I be? What about the sales from our foreign offices?"

"Hong Kong and San Francisco are down by at least sixty percent for this last three-month period. We've had to pay a lot of taxes at the various ports where we have ships bearing

Kenniston cargo. Facts are facts, and we have to face them, Leland. We've spent at least five or six times as much money as we've taken in—maybe even more than that; we'll know exactly how much after Mr. Landers gets through compiling everything. All that merchandise in our warehouse now—we've paid for most of it, but I couldn't meet all the bills with what we have. We'll have to pay the other bills out of future sales. But even if it were merchandise that was desirable, we couldn't afford the costs involved in shipping and distributing. I tried to countermand your order of the Viennese statuettes, since you couldn't recall placing it, but the foreign dealer sent back the original copy of the order with your signature, saying that we had no choice but to reimburse him. Warehousing adds to our overhead. And don't forget, you have a payroll here as well as abroad—our jewelry staff, the clerical staff—and they expect to be paid. . . ."

"Now, now, Jacob, you're getting me unduly alarmed. Surely you are jesting with me," Leland declared to his friend, who had begun to perspire and, taking out a large handkerchief, mopped his face, breathing heavily.

"If I could tell jokes, I'd be in a music hall, Leland. This is no joke; this is deadly serious. We're broke—that's the long and the short of it.

"I'll have Mr. Landers in here directly with the ledger, and he'll go over things with you. It'll just be a repetition of what I've told you, except it'll be specific. We have debts—debts amounting overall to at least forty-eight thousand dollars."

"That much?" Leland gasped.

Jacob nodded his head; his face was bleak. "Yes, sir—and our creditors all want payment now. Leland, we've got to decide today what we're going to do. If you have to dispose of this business, you must consider your family. That's an important step, and you're the one who's going to have to make it."

Leland Kenniston sat immobile, staring at Jacob Cohen, his eyes unwavering. He was in a state of shock, and the morbid shadows that had crept into his mind at unpredictable times now leaped back in all their full fury. He could not believe what he heard, and he frowned at Jacob as if hoping against hope that at any moment the man would smile and say that it was all a joke, and that he merely wanted to scare him and that everything was all right. But Jacob returned his gaze unwaveringly, his face serious and lined with worry.

"It is—it is true, then? We are really so badly off, Jacob?" Leland at last breathed.

"It's as bad as that and worse. My God, I don't know what's come over you. I kept telling you that you'd purchased things we didn't need and couldn't sell. Oh, yes, while you were in Alabama, I tried to dispose of some of these things— everybody laughed at me. Who wants statuettes? Who wants imported wicker baskets? People are not going to spend their money on—I hate to use the word, but it expresses it perfectly— just plain *drek*! And to order in such huge quantities, to say nothing of the European tariffs we have to pay to get them into this port and then to ship them on to our other supply posts. . . . Why, my God, Leland, we've gotten so far in debt I don't see how we could ever bail out. And neither does Mr. Landers."

"And the debts are legitimate?" Leland whispered, as he stared entreatingly at his associate.

"The debts are legitimate."

"Oh, my God!" Leland ejaculated. "What am I going to do?"

"As your friend, Leland, I want to give you the best advice I can. You've got to liquidate. In order to pay the bills, we'll have to discharge everybody—yes, that includes even me."

"Oh, no—not you, Jacob!"

"Yes, me. *Gottenyu*, it has to be done! You'll probably even have to sell your house to meet these debts. I'm sorry I have to give you such dreadful news, after all you've been through."

"If—if it has to be done, it has to be done. Oh, my God!" Leland bowed his head and covered his face with his hands. His shoulders shook with muffled sobbing.

Jacob took a step toward him, his face twisted in anguished helplessness. This man had done so much for him: He had taken him and his family away from the slums and brought them to a life of dignity and material comfort; he had provided the means for educating the children . . . but now he saw his benefactor in a position of complete desperation. He swallowed hard, and then he said in a shaking voice, "Leland, Leland, listen to me—one day everything will again be fine for you. I'm sure it will."

328

"I *have* to succeed. Oh, my God . . . I can't believe this has happened. This will break poor Laure's heart . . . and the children's. Oh, God. Oh, my God!" Leland hoarsely repeated.

"Leland, something else I want to say to you—as your friend. We've broken bread together; we respect each other; our sons are great friends, and our wives work together. We're bound by many ties, Leland, so what I'm going to say to you is advice I hope you will take. Please listen to me, Leland. It's for your own good."

Slowly, Leland dropped his hands from his face and looked up at Jacob. "Say what you must, Jacob. I don't know why this has happened—but I guess I deserve whatever you say to me. I can't believe it's happened, though. I started off so well—all the factors I signed up in Europe—all the merchandise I bought . . . everyone knows me now in Europe—"

"I know, I know, Leland." Jacob nodded and tried to adopt a soothing tone, as if speaking to a troubled child. "Leland, I think you ought to see your doctor. Dr. Wilkinson, he's a good man. I've been thinking of this for some time, but I've been reluctant to say anything to you."

"You—you think I should see my doctor?" Leland echoed. He was like a child repeating words said to him by an elder, wondering about their explanation and their meaning. He stared fixedly at Jacob, in whose eyes tears clearly shone.

"Yes, you should. I've talked this over with Miriam, and she agrees with me. I think you have some kind of medical problem, Leland. It's the only way to explain your . . . odd behavior. Will you please make an appointment, Leland? It'll relieve my mind—and maybe the doctor will be able to explain to you why you don't remember some things. Please go to him, Leland."

"Well, if you insist. I ought to take a friend's advice. All right, Jacob. If it'll make you happier, I'll go see Dr. Wilkinson."

Chapter Thirty-one

On a bright mid-May morning, tall, blond Lucien Edmond Bouchard, now almost forty-five years old but still in superb health, bent down his weatherbeaten face and took off the worn Stetson that shielded his face from the hot south Texas sun. He bade farewell to his wife, Maxine, taking her in his arms, and as he kissed her upturned face, he thought to himself that she still retained the fresh loveliness that had struck him so when he had first met her in Alabama, all those years ago. He then embraced his sister, Mara, and finally he kissed his four daughters: Edwina, now almost fifteen and bidding fair to inherit a great deal of her mother's unaffected loveliness; Diane, twelve and Gloria, ten, both sassy tomboys; and five-year-old Ruth, who promised to be a carbon copy of Maxine.

His two oldest children, Hugo and Carla, had had birthdays this May. Hugo, a physician, had turned twenty-two, and several of his patients in Wyoming had helped his wife, Cecily, organize a party at the home of their neighbors. And Carla had just celebrated her twenty-third birthday in Paris by attending the opening of another exhibition of her paintings, in a gallery patronized by wealthy admirers of the modern school to which she subscribed. Her most recent letter home had included a column by the art critic of *Paris Monde*—a critic amusingly described by Carla as an *enfant terrible* who made it his personal mission to destroy budding careers, but who had been forced to admit the merits of Carla's latest showing. Though she displayed the unmistakable influence of Manet and Cezanne, he wrote, "There is a pleasing candor to Mlle Bouchard's work, which indicates that she is well aware of the influences she has absorbed and is seeking to finalize her own individual style. We predict a fine future for this talented and lovely American painter.''

Although Lucien Edmond and Maxine had not yet completely forgiven their daughter for entering upon a liaison with young James Turner, they had become reconciled to the arrangement—especially since in her last letter, Carla had said that she and James were toying with the notion that if both their one-man shows were successful in the fall, they would get married and—assuming they could get backing from some influential art dealers—open their own gallery. Moreover, Carla had frequently mentioned in her letters to her mother that James was a sensitive, hardworking, and decent young man—not at all a sort of Bohemian transplant like so many other American expatriates who used painting merely as an excuse to be in Paris and enjoy its pleasures.

Maxine had just the previous week said to Lucien Edmond, ''We'll just have to say prayers that it's going to be a lasting and happy union. She's proved that she has real talent, and she is beginning to earn a living from it. That's what she wanted, Lucien Edmond—and parents have no right to deny children their own fulfillment, even if the choice the children make goes against the grain of the parents. You know perfectly well that if Hugo had tried to please us—you especially—by staying here on the ranch, he would have been desperately unhappy. Instead he has found himself—and of course he's aided by the fact that he married an absolutely wonderful young woman who is as dedicated as he is to the medical profession. We must give Carla the same choice. We've been pretty darn fortunate thus far with our children—God willing, it'll be that way when all of them grow up.''

Lucien Edmond had ridden the dusty trail to Corpus Christi—following the very path his father, Luke, had taken in bringing his family out to Texas after the Civil War, and in returning again the following year to marry Laure and take her to Windhaven. There, he had stabled the sturdy gelding and boarded the train that would take him—after a change or two—to Montgomery.

As he watched the countryside roll past his window, he thought to himself that it had been six years since he had last gone to help his stepmother. He would be happy to see Laure again, but he was sorry that this second visit in six years was, like the last, occasioned by extremely unpleasant circumstances. At least since then Laure had remarried and, in so doing, had chosen a fine, upstanding, mature man. Although she had not mentioned it in her wire, Leland Kenniston was undoubtedly there in Alabama, helping her—and that was a husband's duty, Lucien Edmond thought.

He smiled as he thought of his own partners. Though things were not going as well at the ranch this year as in times past, they could get along without him for a short time. He was glad that Joe Duvray, Lucas Forsden, and Eddie Gentry were all so capable. He was especially glad that his brother-in-law, Ramón Hernandez, had once again plunged into his work, trying to make up for the time he had lost during his long absence in Mexico searching for his kidnapped daughter. They would all work together to meet the challenges ahead.

Lucien Edmond sighed. If the cattle market had remained strong, he could have looked forward to spending more time away from the cares of business. He had wanted to take a trip to the East Coast with Maxine, perhaps to visit Baltimore and look up her living relatives there. He had even thought of taking her to Europe—the ocean liners made the journey so easy and luxurious. Alas, that was not to be—not in the near future, at least—for Windhaven Range was feeling the full effects of both the overabundance of cattle raisers and the north Texas syndicates.

He thought that it would be a good idea, when he returned to Carrizo Springs, to sit down with Ramón, Joe, Eddie, and Lucas to make definitive plans for the future. The fact that the cattle market had fallen off so drastically for them had made him consider plans for devoting more of the most fertile land to marketable produce. Refrigeration was now available on the railroad, and there was no reason why he could not furnish San Antonio, Houston—or even New Orleans, St. Louis, and Chicago—with citrus fruit, melons, and the like. Some of the vaqueros might grumble and say that they were being reduced to the status of dirt farmers; a few, inevitably, would drift off—heading north to the bigger ranches, or south into Mexico, where most of them had come from. But the majority would remain: They were commited to Windhaven Range—the school that Catayuna and the nuns had started for their many children had seen to that.

There was still another way to diversify Windhaven Range.

Last week, Eddie Gentry and Ramón had come to him after dinner, while he was in his study, and they had both earnestly recommended that they expand their efforts in the raising and training of horses. They had always raised their own cow ponies, of course, for the remuda that they took along on the cattle drives; but now so many ranchers were in the cattle market that there was an increased demand for really good mounts. One or two of the north Texas ranchers had already sent word via their agents in San Antonio that they would gladly purchase strings of horses for their operations. The sale of well-trained quarterhorses and Morgans would help to make up for the diminution of the cattle trade.

The silver mine, of course, was mined out and had been disposed of. When he thought in retrospect how close he had been to building a house up in Leadville and moving Maxine and the children there, he shuddered. It would have been sheer disaster. They had been very fortunate in their dealings with the old prospector, Frank Scolby, and their involvement with mining ended just in time. The amount of money they had taken out of the mine, though considerable, would probably be diminished in the years ahead—for there was still talk in the East about an economic depression. Some said, however, that the Presidential election next year might turn the tide. Well, the Bouchards would have to be prepared to adapt themselves. They always had in the past—he had learned this from his father, who he knew had learned it in turn from his beloved grandfather. These brighter thoughts occupied his mind during the journey and put him in a more optimistic frame of mind, as he prepared to cope with his stepmother's difficulties.

When the train pulled into the Montgomery station the next day, Lucien Edmond descended from the platform and greeted a waiting Dalbert Sattersfield, whose face was wreathed in a smile at seeing the handsome Texan once again.

"Glad you could come, Lucien Edmond! It's too bad Lopasuta couldn't have been here, but he had to go back to New Orleans to handle a case in court. Come—here's my carriage. My, Laure will be very happy to see you. You look fit—did you have a good trip?"

"The best," Lucien Edmond declared as he clapped Dalbert on the back and strode to the carriage. "This journey brought back many memories."

The two men talked nonstop during the ride to the plantation, with Dalbert filling Lucien Edmond in on all the details of the attacks and how they were coping with the repairs and plans for defending Windhaven against any further incidents.

When they reached the chateau, Amelia Coleman opened the door, and she warmly welcomed Luke's oldest son. Laure came down the stairs, having heard the sound of voices, and hurried to greet him. "It was wonderful of you to come, Lucien Edmond! I'll never be able to thank you enough!"

"It's my duty, Laure," Lucien Edmond said as he embraced her. "I'm sorry I didn't get here any sooner."

"So am I, Lucien Edmond, dear. You missed Lopasuta by a day, and Leland went back to New York a few days ago."

"That's a shame, I was hoping to meet him, after all the letters you've written to us at the ranch saying how happy you are."

"Yes." She paused momentarily, and a shadow drifted over her lovely face, but she did not pursue the topic. There would be time later on to tell him of her concern for Leland, how distressed she had been over his inexplicable behavior and his strangely altered physical condition. "But you'll meet him soon, I'm sure of that. Now, let's get you settled. I'll put you in Luke's old room in the south wing."

"I'd like that very much, Laure."

He followed her up the staircase and along the hallway, carrying his valise easily in one hand. As Laure pushed open the door to Luke's old room, Lucien Edmond's face suddenly became wistful. Going over to the window, he drew the curtains back and stared out over the rolling lawn, letting his eyes rest on the now-placid waters of the Alabama River. "I've forgotten how beautiful it is here, Laure. Thank you for giving me my father's room, with this magnificent view."

"Thank _you_, Lucien Edmond, for coming to my assistance," she rejoined with a smile. "Incidentally, how is everyone in Texas? I trust Maxine and the girls are well."

"Oh, yes, everyone is just fine, and they all send their love—"

"Hallo!" a voice suddenly called out.

Turning around, Laure and Lucien Edmond found themselves staring into the dirty, sweaty face of Lucien, a broad grin splitting his face. He had seen his half brother's carriage arrive while he was toiling in the fields, and had dropped his

334

hoe to go running inside. He was delighted to see Lucien Edmond again after so many years, for although he had been only eleven at their last meeting, Lucien had formed a great liking for the older man and looked upon him almost as a character out of a novel because of what Lucien perceived as Lucien Edmond's exciting and adventuresome life in the West.

The three of them chatted animatedly for a few minutes, and then Lucien Edmond declared, "If it's all right with you, I'd like to unpack, then freshen up a bit. After that, I'd like to go out into the fields and talk to the workers—see what most needs to be done, whether they have any complaints or suggestions. I'm sure you'll be able to offer some, too, Lucien. You obviously have become quite a worker yourself, judging by the amount of good Windhaven soil that you're wearing."

The youth grinned broadly at the compliment and looked over at his mother as if to say, "See? I'm no longer a useless child—I'm a working man, now."

It was midafternoon by the time Lucien accompanied his older half brother out into the fields. He was especially anxious for Lucien Edmond to meet Enoch Washburn, because the youth was still smarting from what he saw as the black man's rejection of him, and Lucien very much wanted to get Lucien Edmond's opinion of the man.

As it happened, the contractor had ridden into Lowndesboro to buy some extra tools for his crew, so Lucien Edmond had no chance of meeting him. Lucien, for his part, didn't want to allude to Washburn's almost contemptuous treatment of himself, not wishing to influence his half brother's verdict. To this end, he pointed out the new dam, which was still about two weeks away from completion, showing how it had been fortified as a precaution against any further vandalism. Then he showed Lucien Edmond the new sheds and the stables. "There's been a lot of work done here, Lucien," his half brother observed. "And I understand from Dalbert Sattersfield there's no guarantee that those raiders won't come back. I take it the authorities have apprehended no one?"

"That's correct, Lucien Edmond. And although we're not completely sure, it seems as though the only reason we've been attacked is because of the black tenant-workers here."

"Racial trouble again! What a tragedy it is—it plunged us

335

into civil war and now, years after, there are repercussions because the blacks won their freedom." He sighed and shook his head. "I wonder if people will ever learn that it's all so useless to go on living with hate."

It was already warm, and the hazy sun promised high humidity as well, as Lucien and Lucien Edmond started out to the fields together early the next morning. As they walked through the high grass, they saw Enoch Washburn talking to two of his men. Seeing them, the black contractor broke off his conversation and approached them, with an obsequious smile toward Lucien Edmond.

"Good mornin' there, sir. I take it you are Lucien Edmond Bouchard. I am Enoch Washburn."

"Good morning to you, Mr. Washburn," Lucien Edmond politely replied. "Please, go on with what you were doing. I don't want to take you away from your work. Lucien and I are just going around and ₋eeing how things are coming along."

"Oh, it's no trouble at all, sir. But—well, you see, sir, we had a problem last night. I don't know how it could have happened." Washburn's face fell. "Somebody must have got here late last night when everybody was asleep and nobody was on guard. Look there, do you see? The top of the dam? Some of the brick is smashed right in the middle. Over here, Mr. Bouchard, sir."

They followed him over to the dam, and Lucien Edmond scowled upon seeing the gaping hole at the very top of the rebuilt structure. A great many bricks had been dislodged and lay in desultory piles here and there on the ground. The sledgehammer that had been used for the vandalism was close by.

"I thought there were guards here working shifts through the night," Lucien Edmond declared. "I was given to understand that Lopasuta Bouchard hired three men in Tuscaloosa and brought them out here."

"Oh, yes, Mr. Bouchard, sir, I know who you mean. Those fellows Hornung, Connery, and Berndorf. Yes, sure, Mr. Bouchard, sir; I asked them about it this mornin'. They didn't see a thing. I don't understand it myself. Well, I'll have my men fix it again. . . ."

Lucien Edmond scowled again and shook his head. "The

336

noise a sledgehammer makes smashing bricks should have been heard all through the fields, it seems to me. . . . Well, there's no use talking about it now; it's done. Let's go on and look at some of the other things. I understand you rebuilt one of the barns.''

"Oh, yes, we finished that a couple of days back, Mr. Bouchard, sir,'' Washburn said.

"Well, let's take look at it, shall we?'' Lucien Edmond pleasantly proposed.

"Of course, of course, Mr. Bouchard. This way, sir!'' Enoch Washburn seemed to fawn on the tall, blond man.

Lucien gave the black contractor a covert, wondering glance as he walked slightly behind the other two while Washburn led the way to the barn.

This particular barn was used mainly for cows, but it also housed a few Clydesdales, large draft horses that were used to pull the heavy plows. Also, in a front section of the building, the breeding boar and the sows were kept in separate, well-made pens.

"Here we are, Mr. Bouchard, sir,'' Washburn gestured with his right hand, a satisfied smile on his bearded face.

"I see,'' Lucien Edmond slowly remarked, as he stared at the barn. "It's built rather differently from the ones I've seen down in Texas. The roof is pitched rather extremely, isn't it?''

Instantly, Washburn bristled and took offense at this casual remark. "Mr. Bouchard,'' he heatedly responded, "I know my trade. So do the members of my crew. That structural design was done at Lopasuta Bouchard's request, as a matter of fact, sir.''

"Now, wait a minute.'' Lucien Edmond turned to him, his eyebrows arching. "I'm not at all accusing you of poor workmanship or design—I'm just saying that the roof looks unusual to me. You see, I've become used to almost flat roofs. Please don't take offense and don't think anything personal was meant.''

The contractor seemed to relax, and the angry lines of his face eased. Once again, he was his unctuous self. "I'm awfully sorry, Mr. Bouchard, sir. I didn't mean to fly off the handle. It's just that—well, you can understand, my men and I are workin' around the clock gettin' all this work done, and there's a pile of it, let me tell you. And, of course, I pride

337

myself on wantin' to do a good, honest job for the money I'm gettin'. Don't forget, Mr. Bouchard, sir, when I finish this job, I'll be goin' on to others, and if Miz Kenniston puts in a good word for me, then I'll do all right. So, naturally, I'm not goin' to lay down on the job. But let me explain to you, because you see, there's a reason for a pitched roof here. We have heavy rains in this part of the country, heavier than you're probably used to. From what I've heard tell, you're a lot drier out there in Texas.''

"Well, that's certainly true enough," Lucien Edmond admitted. "If it does the job and sheds the water better, I'm sure it's a sensible design.''

"It is, believe me, sir. I've built lots of stables and barns and cottages and, of course, houses with roofs like this, Mr. Bouchard, sir, and I haven't had any complaints so far. All I'm worried about—and this is the God's honest truth, Mr. Bouchard, sir—is that those damned raiders might come ridin' back.''

"I thank you for your concern, Mr. Washburn, and thank you for being so candid with me.''

Lucien Edmond watched the man walk quickly back to his crew. Then, with an affable smile, he turned to his half brother. "How would you like to take a horseback ride along the river, just as a breather? Then we can have lunch, and go on with the inspection tour this afternoon?''

"I'd like that fine, Lucien Edmond," the youth promptly responded.

As the two of them walked over to the stable on the other side of the red-brick chateau, Lucien Bouchard found himself more and more baffled by the peculiar behavior and the shifting attitudes Enoch Washburn demonstrated, attitudes that he had observed on many an occasion and for which he could not quite accept any logical explanation.

338

Chapter Thirty-two

The third Saturday in May was an unbearably hot and humid day in Montgomery, Alabama. All morning, the faint rumble of thunder could be heard to the west, and Montgomery's sweltering citizens hoped that relief from the week-long heat wave would shortly arrive.

But by midafternoon, the few clouds had disappeared, and the sun shone down unrelentingly from a hazy blue sky. There were four men lolling in chairs on the porch of a small hotel across the street from the capitol building. They all waved straw fans as they did their best to disregard the heat. The street was almost deserted, for aside from the weather, it was a day when few people came to this part of town, anyway. Moreover, both the House of Representatives and the Senate were having a brief recess, and the next session wouldn't take place until the following Thursday. It was expected that after about another week of work, both houses would declare an adjournment for the summer and reconvene sometime in mid-September.

Fat, porcine-featured Magnus Borden grunted and looked over toward the lawn of the capitol building, where two black gardeners were toiling in the sun. "See them niggers there? They're better off than they ever were, and they still aren't grateful, black sons of bitches. I tell you, boys, the time's comin' when they're gonna learn their true place. Why, hell, everybody knows a nigger's got no brains. He's poor and shiftless, lazy as a coon in his burrow, sleepin' it off after pokin' his missus, havin' a passel of brats he cain't even fend for, gettin' drunk 'n uppity. . . . Next thing you know, they'll be walkin' down this street 'n passin' nasty remarks about our white women. I tell you, boys, I don't wanna live to see that day—and no nigger is gonna, either, mark my words!''

Next to him sat the gaunt-faced barber, Cyrus Williams. He was again letting his assistant do what haircuts and shaves would be required today. He preferred to take his ease next to his cronies and to comment on the deplorable state of affairs in his native state. ''We got an invite, Magnus,'' he now added, ''over to Durfry's store in Lowndesboro this afternoon. Me, I'm goin'—what about you?''

''Sure, I'll be there,'' Borden grunted. ''Hell, when I see what's going on around here, it fair makes me puke. And them Bouchards don't seem to have got the message, yet, do they?''

Towheaded, lanky Bodine Evans, who had the day off from the hotel in front of which this quartet sat, shook his head and scowled. ''No, they sure as hell ain't. But, you know, it's a funny thing. I heard yesterday that somebody took a sledgehammer to that dam they wuz rebuildin' out there, and knocked down a passel of bricks. And I hear tell also that that uppity nigger Ben Brown, who took over as foreman when that Marius Thornton kicked the bucket, he blamed it on the folks that hit them twice—meanin' us. Ain't that a laugh!''

Tobias Hennicott, a short little man with an unmistakable wart on the tip of his bulbous nose, cackled. ''Yeah, sure funny to be blamed for sumpin' that this time we ain't had nothin' to do with, that's for certain. Too bad we don't know who really did it. Why, if we did, we might like to team up with him or them, or whatever, huh?''

All four of them laughed and nodded.

''You said it,'' Evans chuckled. ''Well, I'll meet you all out there at that store 'round about four o'clock this afternoon, that right?''

''That's it. And each of us is goin' in separately, so nobody'll figger out that we have anything workin' for us,'' Williams directed. ''Well, I've had enough of this heat. I'm goin' back to my barbershop and see if I can cool off somewhat inside. Damn if I wouldn't like to take off and go somewheres for a coupla months. Mebbe even up north where it ain't so hot.''

Magnus Borden spoke with more forcefulness than was his

wont. "You cain't do that, yet, Cyrus—not until we do what
hasta be done, and don't you forget it."

They all met in the back room of the ramshackle store in
the poorest section of Lowndesboro, over at the southeastern
end of town. The store carried only a few staples, some
questionable produce, and even more questionable meat.
Ostensibly, the owner, Jed Durfry, ran it to make a few
dollars to supplement what his sharecropping tenant, Bud
Corley, eked out of the rundown plot of farmland he owned.
But principally, this store was the headquarters for those men
of the Montgomery and Lowndesboro communities who had
determined to take matters into their own hands and to rele-
gate blacks to the position they had occupied in the days
before the Civil War.
The men who assembled were assured of privacy, for the
store owner had put up a sign saying that he would be closed
today. There was not much trade anyway, for most folks went
to Dalbert Sattersfield's two stores, where they got quality
merchandise at fair prices and courteous treatment on all
occasions.
Jed Durfry himself was seated on a broken-down chair by
the stove, which at this season was not lit, while nearby his
cronies, Bevis Marley, Jake Elmore, and Sam Arlen, either
slouched on old crates or lounged against dusty barrels of
merchandise. They were passing around a jug of whiskey
from the new still that Tobias Hennicott had built on his farm
outside of town, while Hennicott himself was locked in earnest conversation with the three others present—Cyrus Williams,
Bodine Evans, and Magnus Borden.
Sam Arlen took the jug from Hennicott's hand, took a
swig, and passed it on to Jake Elmore. "We gotta wet our
whistles now," Arlen said, " 'cause we're gonna talk a while
here, and we'll get mighty dry. It chokes me in the throat
when I think of all them niggers struttin' around, makin' like
they wuz equal to us!"
A low murmur of angry affirmation greeted this sally.
Presently, the door from the main part of the store opened,
and Bud Corley entered. He had helped himself to one of the
packets of chewing tobacco that Jed Durfry sold out front,
and he was working a plug around in his jaw.
"Dammit all, Jed, your chewing tobacco ain't worth

341

nothin'," he loudly complained. "Cain't you get a better grade?"

"Just you shut up about my merchandise," the store owner retorted. "It's good enough for the likes of you. And you better be damn sure you left money on the counter for what you took or I'll add it to your next month's rent."

Smarting under the reminder that he was Durfry's tenant and a sharecropper, Corley slumped down next to Jake Elmore and proceeded to wrest from his hands the jug of whiskey. "You've had more 'n enough, Jake," he sneered, "leastways, more 'n is good for a runt like you."

Elmore, who stood no more than five feet four inches, sprang to his feet and was about to retaliate for this insult when Magnus Borden smoothly intervened. "All right, boys, time to call this meetin' to order and figger out how we're going to do in the Bouchards."

Sam Arlen spoke up. "Bud here tells me, Magnus, that we're gonna talk about a scheme you have where we'll be able to have all the fun we want with the nice-lookin' wenches they've got at Windhaven Plantation—includin' that sweet piece of an octoroon who married that nigger-lover, Burt Coleman. Plus which we'll teach 'em once and fer all not to put niggers onto the same footin' as us whites!"

"That's right, Sam. We're all of the same mind. Now then, I see that the Bouchards have got a black buck in charge of repairs. Well, it's as if they want to ram it down our throats that they think they're right, and that they're gonna put niggers above white folks. They don't seem to understand that it's white folks that made the South great, and it's only white folks that'll make it great again. The Bouchards have to learn that they shoulda hired whites, and not niggers—besides, niggers oughtn't to be taught white men's work in the first place. Everybody knows they're animals; they've got no brains, and they're good for nothing, except being slaves."

"You can say that again, Magnus!" Bodine Evans, caught up in the fiercely hostile spirit of the meeting, shouted out.

"That's the ticket, boys," Borden exulted. "Now, listen carefully. As you know, we've got the sheriff on our side—hell, Tom Brennaman used to be an overseer in this state before the war, so he had niggers of his own and knows how shiftless they are and also how dangerous they can be, if you give 'em too much freedom.

"But what you boys may not know is that Tom's not the only one who's gonna look the other way when we strike again. 'Member that second attack? Well, we made that German guard the Bouchards hired so scared he practically wet his britches. He won't dare warn anybody because he was told if he blabbed, we'd take good care of him. And we've got others on our side, too. Somebody took a sledgehammer to the top of the rebuilt dam. Now, whoever did that—and it wasn't any of us—feels the way we do. I don't know who he is, but we'll find out in good time."

Cyrus Williams drawled, "I'm ready for action whenever you say."

"You just wait till I give the word, then, Cyrus. In the meantime, boys, pass that whiskey around. We'll all drink a toast: To white supremacy—as it was and as it's gonna be!"

Chapter Thirty-three

Leland Kenniston had taken Jacob Cohen's advice and made an appointment with his personal physician, Dr. George Wilkinson. That physician had been recommended to Leland the previous year by Dr. Cummins, the kindly, conscientious gynecologist who had attended Laure when she had suffered her miscarriage. At the time, Dr. Cummins had gently implied to Leland that it behooved him to take as good care of himself as he did of his wife—a bit of advice that Leland had heeded, visiting Dr. Wilkinson for a general physical examination. Nothing had turned up, and Leland was pronounced in excellent physical condition. Somewhere within the last months, he reflected with bitterness, his condition had evidently taken a dramatic turn for the worse.

Nevertheless, Leland kept his new appointment with Dr. Wilkinson with some measure of hope. He knew the doctor to be an erudite and imaginative practitioner, a firm believer in sound diet and exercise and the ability of the human body to cure itself. He believed that the mind and the body were intertwined inextricably, so that many ills could well be caused psychosomatically rather than by some organic malfunction. Perhaps, Leland thought ruefully, he could offer some remedy for the malady that had afflicted him.

It was about four o'clock on a Wednesday afternoon at the end of May when Leland opened the door of the doctor's office and seated himself in the small reception room. A pleasant, middle-aged woman in a starched white nurse's uniform told him brightly that the doctor would be with him shortly. Leland then sat down in a large chair, leaned back, and closed his eyes. In his mind, there passed in review, though in a desultory kaleidoscopic pattern, all the events that had taken place since his embarkation on the European trip. He wanted desperately to retain all his impressions, all his recollections; he wished to provide Dr. Wilkinson with as thorough a case history as was possible, so that the physician could properly and accurately diagnose whatever malady it was that had caused these peculiar behavioral aberrations.

A few minutes later, the nurse ushered him into the examining room, where a tall, bearded and bespectacled doctor stood waiting.

"Well, Mr. Kenniston, how may I help you?" The doctor asked in a frank, solicitous tone calculated to put the patient at ease. "What seems to be the problem?" He motioned the Irishman to a stool by the examination table.

Already, gloom assailed the Irish entrepreneur. The wait in the reception room had allowed him the time to ponder all the things that had happened, and he had seen only the desperate side: his infidelity to Laure, the squandering of her money, his excessive purchases, and Jacob Cohen's vehement remonstrations. . . .

"I—I don't know how to start, Dr. Wilkinson. I've been acting—well, my associates say very strangely. I don't understand the reason for it. I seem to be compelled to do things that I later forget and have no awareness of having done, and I have long spells of utter melancholy, during which I consider myself defeated and useless. Then again, at other times, I feel confident—perhaps too confident, for others don't seem to share it, and they tell me it's getting me into trouble."

"I see, Mr. Kenniston. I think this certainly merits attention. I'm going to ask you to disrobe; I want first to give you a complete physical examination."

"Of course."

After Leland had undressed, the wiry, white-haired doctor began by examining Leland's pulse and heartbeat, and followed that with an exhaustive battery of other tests. After an hour, he concluded the examination. "You can dress now, Mr. Kenniston. When you are ready, please come into my office."

Leland quickly put his clothes back on and joined Dr. Wilkinson in the wood-paneled office.

The doctor looked at him from across the oak desk and said, "Your blood pressure is somewhat higher than the last time I took it, and your heartbeat is slightly erratic. That in

345

itself would cause me little concern. But you seem listless, which is out of character for you, according to your records. And your description of these alternating fits of melancholy and exaltation—for I will call them that—suggests a curious pattern that does alarm me. Can you tell me exactly when you began to notice this change in yourself, Mr. Kenniston?''

With a piteous ring to his voice, trying to formalize his thoughts, Leland began to detail all of his exploits since he had first boarded the *Aurania*.

When he had finished some twenty minutes later, Dr. Wilkinson asked, ''Have you had any headaches or nausea?''

''Yes, and they've been more frequent of late,'' Leland admitted.

''I see.'' The doctor pursed his lips as he wrote into Leland's chart. ''And you say you've had these symptoms since about January, so far as you can recall, and never before then?''

The Irish entrepreneur shook his head. ''No, I'm certain of that. Never before.''

''Your parents,'' the doctor went on, ''do you recall if either your mother or father had similar behavior patterns, so far as you can remember?''

''Not in the least. They were sane, normal—oh, God, to use the word sane . . .'' Leland groaned aloud, bowed his head, and cupped his face in his hands.

The white-haired doctor rose, went to the window, and looked out into the street below. Then he turned and said gently, ''We have a great deal of progress yet to make so far as diagnosing causes, where the human mind is concerned, Mr. Kenniston. Symptoms such as you describe could have a number of causes, some of which have been researched in recent years. It might be that you are suffering from a subtle emotional disorder of unknown origin, but given the relative suddenness of the onset of your symptoms, I am strongly inclined toward a different diagnosis—some physical cause, such as a tumor on your brain. If this is the case, the pressure from the growth on the lobes could be causing your erratic behavior.''

''Oh, God! That sounds hopeless!'' Leland moaned. He rose from his chair and, his fists clenched, stared poignantly at the physician. ''If, as you suggest, it is a tumor, is there any operation or cure for it? Or am I to be condemned for the

346

rest of my life to have to experience these terrible periods of insane behavior when I act totally out of character and destroy all that I have always worked so hard to achieve?''

"I can't answer that truthfully because, as I told you, our science is still terribly limited when it comes to the human brain. I have read in medical journals of experimental operations to remove growths from the brain—but it is an extremely delicate and difficult form of surgery and the chances of success are very, very small. On the other hand, you may go on for quite some time—there may even be a remission of the growth at some point—and so to seek a solution as drastic as surgery may not be warranted. If I were you, I would seek the opinion of a specialist. If he confirms my diagnosis, he'll also be able to recommend the best course of action. Here is the name of the man I have in mind. He is downtown at Beekman Hospital. Go see him and talk to him. This would be my earnest recommendation, Mr. Kenniston.''

"I—I almost wish I *were* insane!" Leland declared in a hoarse whisper. Slowly, almost painfully, he rose from his chair and, absently shaking hands with Dr. Wilkinson, left the doctor's office and descended the stairs into the busy street.

His mind was in a whirl of anxiety and fear, and he was not certain what he should do. He didn't know which he dreaded more—insane behavior or death. For a moment he almost welcomed the latter, but then his mind screamed out, *No, not yet! Oh, God, not yet!* There was so much to be done, his business to be put back into order, the debt to be paid to Laure, the recouping of his financial losses so that the children would want for nothing—no, it would not be just or fair for him to die now!

Dazedly, he stood in the street, hardly conscious of the bustle of traffic beyond him—the clatter of horses' hooves and the rolling wheels of the carriages—and still less of the passersby, who sometimes jostled him and gave him angry glances for standing in the way. Until this moment he had never thought of death. But now, in his forties, he was well aware that man was all too mortal, and that what he had within him branded him as a candidate for the termination of all that he held dear—taken from his beloved Laure, his business, the children, all the pleasant things and comforts he had learned to love.

Remission—what did Dr. Wilkinson mean by that? Was there hope that this thing would pass and not visit him again? He would rest. He would go home and have a light dinner and rest. Tomorrow, perhaps, there would be a better verdict. Also, some revenue might come in from Hong Kong and San Francisco, after all. Things were not necessarily so black.

Perhaps some of the bad news was contrived by Jacob Cohen—yes, it was definitely a possibility. To make him doubt himself even more, Jacob could invent things that had not happened. All the things Jacob had reported could not, must not have happened. Jacob was simply being overly dramatic, overly protective—yes, that's what it was.

He would have to go to the bank, also, to straighten out that mistake in the letter they had written to him. Something was very wrong. He could not be so low in his accounts. He had saved a great deal of money over the years; he was affluent and could buy anything he chose whenever he chose. Surely, all of this was exaggerated.

So for now he would go home, eat something light, and sleep well. And then, in the morning, everything would be brighter. Dr. Wilkinson had said there was a good chance of remission. Perhaps it had already begun. Perhaps he would never be visited by those gloomy ghosts of conscience and despair ever again. Indeed, he was now sure this was possible.

Leland slept until eight the following morning, awakening with a dreadful headache and a feeling a terrible depression. He pulled himself off the bed and stumbled over to the dresser. Looking in the mirror, he saw a haggard, bleary-eyed face staring back at him, and he shuddered. Once he had been terribly handsome; now his face was dissolute, lined with care, the eyes suspicious and narrowed without the usual bright luster. Hastily, he washed and shaved and then, dressing with particular care, he went down to the kitchen to ask Anna Emmons for a bite of breakfast.

He ate in a moody silence that made Mrs. Emmons and Clarabelle Hendry exchange worried looks. Finally he rose from the table and said to them, "I'm going for a walk now. I don't know when I'll be back. You needn't worry about my dinner. Just take care of the children."

"Of course, Mr. Kenniston," Clarabelle said, then volun-

348

teered, "It's so lovely out. I can understand your wanting to take a long walk."

"Well, I'll see you when I see you," he said, and abruptly left the kitchen.

Mrs. Emmons muttered to her colleague, "It does beat all what's happened to that man ever since he came back from Europe. It's a wonder Mrs. Kenniston puts up with him. But then, maybe she didn't, which is perhaps the real reason he came back from Alabama so soon."

"I know what you mean, Mrs. Emmons," Clarabelle concurred. "It's getting harder and harder to be patient with him." With a sigh, she picked up her coffee cup and turned her attention back to the lessons she was preparing for John.

Leland walked aimlessly, scarcely conscious of where he was going and caring still less. There were people all about, coming out of houses and office buildings, going into stores; there was the noise from horse-drawn carriages and omnibuses and the clatter of the elevated railway. But he was impervious to all this. He found himself walking downtown, maintaining a slow pace. Even at that, the physical exertion made him perspire, for indeed the weather was warm.

The muscles of his legs had tightened, for he was not used to walking so far. Yet another sign of the deterioration of his body, Leland reflected somberly. Well, what difference did it make now? How long did he have to live? If Dr. Wilkinson was right, there was nothing that could help him, short of drastic surgery, and that so risky as to seem not worthwhile. Oh, he could watch his diet, and perhaps he would drink less wine and brandy. Dr. Wilkinson had suggested this as he was leaving the office, but he had hastened to add that mere abstinence was no guarantee of a cure; nothing was guaranteed. The study of the mind was not yet a science—the doctor had said as much—and Leland decided that if it would not become so until it was—for himself—too late.

By the time he walked to the very end of Manhattan Island, it was twelve o'clock. Before he even knew where he was, he caught the smell of the salt water off the bay. Unknowingly, he had walked so far downtown that he was at the approach to the newly opened Brooklyn Bridge. The wharves were filled with sailing ships and steamers, and overhead loomed the massive bridge with its great spans and seemingly delicate

349

tracery of steel cables. He decided to walk the bridge promenade at his leisure.

Because it was noontime and so much of the city halted then for lunch, there were not many passersby—either walking or in conveyances—upon the mighty bridge. He was glad, for it suited his mood to be alone now, to breathe in the salt air, and to hear the cries of the gulls. To him, they were desolate cries, those of lost souls in pain. He walked on, his right hand on the rail, scowling and thinking. When he had reached the halfway point, he paused again and turned to look disconsolately out into the eddying current of the East River.

Suppose he were to climb over to the edge and jump? If he did, if he died, surely Laure and the children wouldn't be saddled with his debts. Most important of all, he wouldn't be a burden to his beloved wife, forcing her to watch him deteriorate more and more. Because even if Dr. Wilkinson was right and there could be a remission, there could also be the reverse—there could be gradual weakening, loss of mind and will. . . . *Oh, no! Dear God please, no!*

He took hold of the railing with both hands, and he stared out into the water as the wind ruffled it a little. He thought of how the *Aurania* had cleaved the water on its way to Ireland, and how in the short time since he had boarded that steamship, his life had tumbled topsy-turvy. What could he do? One answer awaited him below.

350

Chapter Thirty-four

At virtually the same time as Leland Kenniston was deciding his future, a thousand miles away, Senator Martin Haynes rose from his seat in the Alabama State Senate chamber, requesting permission of the president of that body to address the legislators.

The visitors' gallery was crowded, for the *Advertiser* had printed a column that very morning previewing the speech the distinguished senator was slated to deliver. In the front row sat Dalbert Sattersfield, Lucien Bouchard, and the senator's daughter, Samantha.

For Dalbert, the senator's remarks would be tangible proof that his political associate agreed with him and had determined to introduce a strong bill aimed at curbing lawless violence throughout the state. For Lucien, the occasion was an opportunity not only to see the democratic process in operation, but also to hear the public statement of a man he had come to admire.

Lucien turned toward Samantha with a smile, wanting to share with her this moment of anticipation. He was startled to see her not watching her father, but instead looking to the opposite balcony, intently watching a handsome young man who was talking to a fashionably dressed woman. Before he had a chance to reflect on her behavior, the president of the Senate spoke, giving Senator Haynes leave to make his address, and the hall fell silent in anticipation of his words.

Senator Haynes appeared even taller than his six feet as he stood at his desk; his white hair bespoke his long years of experience, while his shoulders—broad and unbent—showed that he still possessed the vigor of middle years. Before beginning his remarks, he looked around the room, fixing his gaze upon each and every one of his colleagues, then permitting himself a fleeting glance at the gallery and the faint suggestion of an affectionate smile in the direction of his daughter.

"Mr. President, my fellow senators, and distinguished visitors," the white-haired speaker began, "I am gratified that the public has shown, by its presence, its interest in today's proceedings, for the bill that I propose to introduce for the consideration of my worthy colleagues concerns the safety and well-being of every man, woman, and child in the great state of Alabama."

The senator paused and, with another glance up at the gallery, went on, "I need not tell you of the bitterness and hatred that has plagued our region for these past thirty years or more—before, during, and after the great conflict between the North and the South that brought tragedy and sorrow to nearly every Alabama family—except to point out that the lessons growing out of this period of strife and misery are twofold:

"First, that the Union cannot survive if it is divided. I do not shrink—even in this august chamber, where once the cause of the Confederacy was so earnestly championed—from invoking the memory of the martyred Lincoln, who knew that the Union must be saved, and who to the last held out to his brothers in the South the olive branch of peace. He had no desire to take any retribution whatsoever against those men who wore the gray uniforms of the Confederacy. It can only be lamented that his death altered the course of events that he had set in motion. It gave to men like Thaddeus Stevens the opportunity to force the South to its knees—to crush it and keep it in a bondage every bit as harsh as that impugned to the Southern landholders who once owned slaves."

Again the senator paused and looked round the chamber, his sharp eyes now espying one or two colleagues in the back benches who were whispering to each other in low tones, as if in dissent from the speaker's words in praise of Lincoln. Ignoring these murmurings, he continued:

"Fortunately, we have survived the scalawags and carpetbaggers that the North sent to us as a part of their plan to render us forever a defeated and dispirited people. Nevertheless, shadows of the past linger with us, ghoulish shadows, like those of vultures that prey upon the weak and the ill. I do not

352

refer alone to the Ku Klux Klan, for which we have federal legislation declaring it to be outlawed—though to be sure the riders of that clandestine and criminal organization still go about their dreadful errands under the cover of night. No, I refer to less well organized but equally sinister outbreaks of violence against the helpless—violence carried out by small-minded men who have no right to call themselves part of humanity, who strike out at all those whom they consider to be inferior, who believe that the black man must be terrorized and kept forever in fear of his life and without hope of justice or a decent livelihood. These vicious men—the more dangerous and sinister, I believe, for their being numerous and without central organization—wreak havoc throughout our fair state, and threaten to ruin us all.

"We come then to the second great lesson we have learned from the tragic conflict of our generation: Violence begets violence, and hatred can breed only more hatred. Now, in the year of our Lord eighteen hundred and eighty-three, eighteen years after the war's end, we have found some measure of recovery at long last from the moral, political, and economic devastation of war and its aftermath. We are rebuilding, and we seek again our independence as a sovereign state that owes no debt of servitude to any other state in this great Union. But what will defeat us in our noble endeavors, and bring harm to our children, and our children's children, is the legacy of hate and bigotry that—mark my words—exists scurrilously and in many hidden places. I myself know of two drastic instances, involving the noted Windhaven Plantation, founded by Lucien Bouchard when the growth of this region was in its infancy. It is well known to most of you; in every generation since old Lucien first came here, the name of Bouchard has stood for honesty, complete racial tolerance, and a belief that a man must be judged on what he does, not by what color he is or what his religion or personal creed might be."

Again there was a murmur in the Senate, as some of the older state senators agreed, whispering among themselves of their own personal knowledge of the Bouchards and confirming what Senator Haynes had just said. He nodded solemnly. "At the outset of this year, gentlemen, Windhaven Plantation was twice struck by men who covered their faces, much like the Ku Klux Klan. And why? Because these men resented the

353

Bouchards' way of offering opportunity and purposeful work to blacks who are legally free, and wished to punish the Bouchards for letting black men walk the same earth as do whites with their heads held high and the knowledge that they earn an honest livelihood for their own families.

"And this is why I ask you today for your support for Senate bill number four hundred ninety. I will not take your time by reading it, for you all have copies on your desks. In essence, it seeks to supplement the federal law that outlaws the Klan. It also establishes uniform and mandatory punishments for any and all acts of violence or vandalism upon the person or property of any man, black or white. The bill further stipulates that if anyone should be killed as a result of such attacks, those liable for that person's death shall be guilty of murder in the first degree. The worthy foreman of Windhaven Plantation, one Marius Thornton, was shot in the first of the attacks on Windhaven. He lingered but eventually died a cruel and needless death. My bill proposes that when his murderer is at last uncovered, he shall stand trial in a state court with the death penalty to be carried out against him, if he is found guilty.

"This bill proposes, finally, that subversive meetings for the sole purpose of advocating racial discrimination and racial attacks shall be outlawed. For such meetings, gentlemen, are the noxious breeding ground of riots, which all of us must abhor."

He paused to sip from a glass of water and then again stared at his audience, both on the floor of the senate and in the balcony. He spoke quietly now, as if to reason with his auditors, without employing the strident tones of the politician:

"There are those among you, I know, who would declare that no uniform state code is necessary or even desirable; that local law officers must be permitted free rein to enforce the laws in their own ways. But I say that a state statute can only strengthen and enhance the efforts of honest enforcement officers; it will insure that we never again return to the old ways of administering so-called 'justice'—by the whip and the chain.

"There are those, too, who may fear that a statute outlawing meetings of a certain kind is an unconstitutional interference with the right to free assembly. But I ask you, gentlemen, in all candor: Can an assembly rightly be called 'free' if its object is to degrade and enslave others?''

With a long look now up at his daughter, Senator Haynes moved to conclude his remarks.

"Let me close with an appeal to all of you—to you up there in the balcony, and to my colleagues here before me. There is a need for men of good will and moderation to come forward and to speak out against the pattern of hatred toward the black that has once again emerged and that threatens to destroy all we have gained since Appomattox. How can we, as Southerners, prove to the rest of the nation that we who love the South and were born here are able to manage our own affairs, without help, hindrance, or intervention by the federal government, *unless* we abjure all violence? My bill will strengthen our hand in so doing. With God's help, and with the loyalty of every citizen of Alabama, we will put an end to bigotry, prejudice, and violence. I pray God this bill will be a legacy to our children and grandchildren, and I thank you for your consideration as I humbly await your verdict on the merits of the measure now before you.''

The floor of the Senate rang with thunderous applause, and many of the members rose up to give Martin Haynes a standing ovation.

In the balcony, Lucien's eyes glowed with enthusiasm, and deeply moved by what he had heard, he turned again to Samantha. This time her eyes were fixed on her father and shining with pride—though whether because of what he had said or because of the applause now being accorded him, Lucien could not say.

Chapter Thirty-five

On a Thursday afternoon late in May, about an hour before dinner, Laure entered the study and seated herself at Luke Bouchard's old desk. She picked up a pen and toyed with it, thinking about what she would write to Leland. She had not heard from him since he returned to New York, and she was greatly concerned. Not just because he had promised her that he would immediately straighten out the enormous debt he had run up in New Orleans—for she steadfastly believed that he would, since throughout their marriage, short-lived though it had been thus far, he had never yet failed her. Her primary concern was for his emotional state, which had seemed so unstable. Because she truly loved him, she was determined to write him in a way that would hearten and inspire him, brush aside the feelings of remorse that she knew he felt, and give him an impetus to go forward.

She rose and went to the window, drawing momentary solace and peace from the gentle flow of the winding, narrow estuary of Pintilalla Creek. Then she thought of the attacks against the plantation and became dispirited. She wondered how Luke would have retaliated against the skulking cowards who had come at night to work their evil. Marius Thornton had done what he could to defend the plantation, and he had given his life in that cause. . . . And now she was alone—no, not alone, for there was Leland. With a sigh, Laure caught herself wondering if Leland would be equal to the task of aiding her to meet the challenges that lay ahead and the possibility of new attacks. He was so dear; he loved her so, and for all his recent failings, so mystifying at times, he was her husband. . . . No, she mustn't even *think* thoughts that might be disloyal. In spite of the gambling and the consequent debts, he deserved her unfeigned love.

She returned to take her seat at the writing desk and, closing her eyes, allowed memories to float back to her. There were so many vivid recollections of happy occasions with Leland. She recalled how, before their marriage, he had asked her to join him at the Mardi Gras in New Orleans, and she had accepted—thereby sealing her future with his. She remembered how she had drafted her wire to him, setting their wedding date. She had been seated at this very desk.

Sighing, she took up her pen and started her letter. After a few minutes, she paused and reread the lines.

Dear Leland:

Words aren't enough to tell you how much I miss you, how much I need you. Beloved, I was so concerned when I last saw you, for you looked so tired and hurt. Leland, please believe me when I say how much I love you. In fact, I think I love you more than ever, because now at last I feel that you need me. Until now, my darling, our marriage was one in which I relied upon you to be my pillar of strength. Now I am happy that I feel I can be of help to you, to give you strength and new courage and new hope, just as you gave me. Forget what has happened; go forward as you can. We shall work this out. We shall

Suddenly she put down her pen, and laying her head on her arm, she began to weep. Somehow she instinctively knew that the words would mean nothing to Leland, that his peculiar morbidity would be untouched by whatever she might say to him.

Laure's tears spilled upon the letter, blurring the words. Raising her head, she looked at the unfinished missive and thought to herself that despite the comforting presence at Windhaven Plantation of her oldest son, despite the help and support of Lucien Edmond and of all the loyal workers and tenants on Windhaven Plantation, not in many years had she felt so alone and so vulnerable.

At almost the same moment that Laure was pondering her future, Leland Kenniston was still standing on the Brooklyn

Bridge, still staring out to the water far below, conjecturing how easy it would be to lose himself in the total oblivion of death. How easy it would be to let himself drop, letting the water close over his broken body and draw the last breaths from his lungs. Then everything would be over. He would have no more problems, and the terror of the deterioration of his mind would be gone forever.

His knuckles were white as he gripped the rail with both hands and looked out over the steel beams that formed a cage over the roadway below—a minor obstacle to one who was determined to put an end to his pain. It was now the start of the evening rush hour, and traffic was beginning to get heavier. As horse-drawn carriages and omnibuses went by, and as dozens of other pedestrians crossed the walkway, gawking at the new marvel of engineering science, only vaguely did Leland hear the sounds and see the people.

He was waging a fierce inner struggle, and his mind was completely caught up in weighing the alternatives of life and death. As he stood mumbling to himself, passersby looked at him curiously—although no one was overly interested, for odd people speaking to themselves were a common occurrence in New York.

He stood still in the middle of the walkway, paralyzed by the inner struggle between an easy death and the far more uncertain and painful prospect of life. It was a life marred by illness and tainted with failure—yet, to throw it all away? Was there nothing, no other way out?

For long moments he stood motionless, while beneath his feet the mammoth form of a three-masted ship, powered by huge side wheels, floated under the bridge on its course down the East River to the crowded harbor beyond. Gulls wheeled over and under the bridge's roadway, while the wind moaned in the cables above his head.

Suddenly, his entire body seemed to relax. He almost visibly shook himself. He turned and started to walk, slowly at first, then faster and more purposefully as he strode in the direction he had come, driven by the will to self-preservation that had at last seized him. For out of some corner of his soul, he knew not how, had come a flicker of hope that had brightened into a flame of resolve and even defiance. All his life he had looked on the positive side of things, and he was determined to continue to do so now. He would force himself to believe that he would beat the odds—he would either defeat the disease or come through experimental surgery successfully.

He must have hope. It would take all his courage and strength to keep his mind out of the morass of despair into which he had so often fallen these last few months. He would face reality; he would do his best to cope with it. Only in this way would there be any hope for his future—and for Laure's.

His footsteps were brisk as he traced his way back across the bridge. Now, for the first time, he was aware of the beauty of the incredible structure—the combined impressions of delicacy and strength imparted by the builder's design. He now recalled that the builder—John Roebling, a Prussian immigrant—had encountered innumerable problems erecting the bridge and, indeed, had died as the result of contracting tetanus after his foot had been accidentally crushed. It had been Roebling's son, Washington, who finally completed the awesome structure. The Brooklyn Bridge was a monument to. man's determination—and Leland suddenly felt that it was fitting and appropriate for him to have found his way here, to this triumphant span, as the site on which he recovered his own sense of determination.

Squaring his shoulders, he increased his pace for the long walk home, and the rigorous exercise felt good. It heightened his sense of being alive, and every ache in his calf and thigh muscles was a reminder of how very close he had come to giving up that life.

When he reached Gramercy Park, it was almost eight-thirty. Hearing the sound of the door slam, Clarabelle Hendry came out of the parlor and greeted him. "Why, Mr. Kenniston! You've put in a long day at the office, haven't you? When you didn't return at your usual time, Mrs. Emmons and I presumed that you were going to be working late, and so we've all eaten. I hope I was correct in my assumption that you'd dined out," she somewhat tentatively said.

He smiled warmly at her, not wishing to tell her where he had really been all day. Such matters were better kept to oneself, he knew. So he simply said, "Actually, I didn't have the chance to eat, but I'll just put together something for myself—that is, if Mrs. Emmons isn't in the kitchen. She never lets me fend for myself—but I rather suspect that's because she doesn't want me intruding upon her domain, rather than from a desire to fuss over me," Leland told Clarabelle, smiling again.

Clarabelle smiled back, delighted that her employer's sense of humor seemed to have returned. Then, excusing herself, she turned to go put John to bed.

"Clarabelle . . ."

"Yes, Mr. Kenniston?"

"I wonder if you would be good enough to ask the children—except John, of course—to join me in my study in a little while. Say, in about half an hour. And I'd like you and Mrs. Emmons to come, as well. I—I want to talk to all of you."

"Why, certainly, Mr. Kenniston. Is there anything wrong?" she asked, her face showing concern.

He hesitated before saying, "Well, let me just say for the moment that we will have to make some changes. I'll be more specific later. But please . . . I didn't wish to hold you up from what you were doing. Go and put John to bed, and I'll have a bite to eat; then we'll all meet."

"Certainly, Mr. Kenniston." Once more, Clarabelle turned and this time mounted the stairs to the second floor.

Leland went down the hall to the kitchen and there found some stew and biscuits left over from his family's dinner. He filled a large bowl with the stew—for he had worked up a hearty appetite from all his exercise—and took two of the biscuits and put the food on a tray. He carried it to his study, balancing the tray carefully while he cleared a place on his desk.

As he slowly ate, he set his mind to the task that lay before him. He knew he must tell Paul, Celestine, and Clarissa, as well as Clarabelle and Anna Emmons, the truth without dissembling. He must convey to them all the reality of their current situation. He had plunged them all into poverty, and he had a physical affliction that boded poorly for any future he might have left.

Clarissa and Celestine entered the study, and Paul self-consciously followed his sisters in. Clarabelle Hendry came after, somewhat breathless in anticipation of what Leland would have to say. She seated herself in an armchair by the window, smoothing her skirt meticulously. Mrs. Emmons took a seat next to Clarabelle in a matching chair.

Clarissa and Celestine glanced at each other, then seated themselves on straight-backed chairs, while Paul placed himself on an ottoman that faced his stepfather's desk. Everyone sensed that this was far from an ordinary conclave, and they all exchanged wondering glances.

Leland Kenniston cleared his throat and began, "I'm sure you all know how much I care for you and am concerned about your well-being. But even the best intentions sometimes miscarry in this world. As you all are aware, I have been traveling a good deal this year—first Europe, then New Orleans, then joining Laure—your mother in Alabama. . . ." He paused, not quite sure of how to couch his words, which would be so very startling to them all. "I'm afraid I am digressing because the news I have to tell you is difficult, to say the least.

"You all may have been aware—as I'm sure you must— that I have been acting somewhat peculiarly of late. Oh"—he held up a propitiatory hand and smiled at their protests—"I know I have, despite your saying otherwise. The fact of the matter is, my behavior has caused some major financial reversals. The fact of the matter is . . . I'm afraid I am bankrupt."

Everyone gasped. Paul declared, "No, Father! I can't believe it." Celestine and Clarissa started to cry softly, and Clarabelle did her best to console the girls, although she felt like crying herself. Only Anna Emmons said nothing, remaining stonily silent as she stared at her employer.

"It is true, Paul. You see—" He paused again, for the next piece of information he had to impart was even more painful to him than the first. "You see, I am very likely suffering from what is called a tumor on the brain—a dangerous growth that is pressing on the brain, causing erratic behavior. Dr. Wilkinson has told me that it can in fact remain in remission for some time, so I am quite hopeful that this will be the case for me. If not, they have been developing some wonderful new surgical techniques, and if the time comes that it is medically indicated, I will undergo such surgery." He tried to maintain a hopeful tone to his voice, although it was becoming increasingly difficult. "So you see, one way or the other, I will survive this . . . predicament. However, because of my financial reverses—owing to the bad investments I made while in Europe, among other things—I'm afraid I shall have

361

to sell our house to cover some debts, and we will have to move down to Windhaven Plantation.''

There was an audible intake of breath from everyone sitting in the room, and the two girls continued to cry softly.

"Oh, Father," Celestine whimpered, "how terrible for you! A brain tumor . . .''

Both Clarabelle Hendry and Anna Emmons dabbed at their eyes with their handkerchiefs, trying hard to maintain their composure in front of the children. They realized that if they gave in to their feelings, the effect would be like a dam bursting, and the children would then become quite inconsolable.

Suddenly, with an instinctive wisdom that belied her twelve years, Celestine knew that the kindest thing to do for her stepfather was to lessen his burden of guilt and also to distract him from the terrible medical diagnosis. Accordingly, she broke the tense silence in the room, and declared, "It will be wonderful to go back to Windhaven, actually. That means we'll see Mother and Lucien again; that means we'll all be together.''

Paul immediately joined her in expressing his approval of the prospect—as well as saying how much he looked forward to swimming in the Pintilalla Creek in the summer and running barefoot in the cool grass of the sweeping lawns that surrounded the chateau.

Clarissa, however, was quiet, and she sat looking pensively down at her hands folded in her lap.

"How do *you* feel about the situation?" Leland gently asked her.

She frowned thoughtfully, then said, "I'll miss my friends in school, Father. I'll also miss my teachers. . . .'' She brightened. "But perhaps someday we'll be able to move back.''

"That's possible, dear. But then, you'll make new friends in the place where you're going; I'm sure.''

As he heard these last words, Paul Bouchard considered his situation again and suddenly realized that he and his best friend, David Cohen, would be separated by many hundreds of miles. Of course, they could write to each other, but it would not be the same. He knew that it was very likely they'd never see each other again.

At this moment, his stepfather looked at him and asked, "What is on your mind, Paul?"

"I—I was just thinking that David and I won't see each other anymore," he truthfully answered.

"I'm sorry, my boy," Leland responded, anguish clearly in his voice. "I'm so very sorry."

Again there was silence as the three children pondered how this major change would affect their lives. Mrs. Emmons exchanged a worried look with Clarabelle Hendry, and Leland intercepted it. He said as apologetically as he could, "I'm going to do everything I can to keep you both on. You know how much the children and I rely on you two ladies. . . ."

"That—that's very kind of you," Clarabelle said. "I'll admit though, Mr. Kenniston, I—I'll miss New York."

"No more than I will, Clarabelle," he said somewhat gruffly, and a shadow of irritation crossed his handsome face.

Mrs. Emmons suddenly spoke up. "Mr. Kenniston, I want you to know that I very much appreciate your wanting to keep me in your employ, but—truth to tell, sir, I'd be like a fish out of water down there in Alabama." She still held her handkerchief and was surreptitiously twisting it in her hands as she began to contemplate her immediate future.

"I realize," he said to her, "that this has come without any warning at all, and I'm deeply sorry for it."

"I'm not blaming you, sir," Mrs. Emmons assured him. "However, I know how hard it'll be for you to try and make ends meet, now. I want you to know that you don't have to struggle to do so on my account, because—truly, sir—I'd much rather stay in New York. I'm sure I'll find another position easily enough—good cooks are hard to find," she said in her forthright manner.

Leland smiled at her self-assurance and said, "Of course I'll give you a letter of recommendation, Mrs. Emmons, and I hope you'll continue here until such time as we actually leave the house. I'm going to put it up for sale just as soon as I can; I'll probably go to see a real estate broker tomorrow."

"I—I'll be happy to stay just as long as you need me here, Mr. Kenniston," Mrs. Emmons replied, suddenly allowing her emotions to surface.

"I appreciate it; I really do. Well, then, Clarabelle, you and I will take charge of the packing and the like. I'll have to sell most of the furniture, I'm afraid, except for some small

363

odds and ends. Well," he sighed, "I'm glad I have this all out in the open. Again, to you, Mrs. Emmons, and you, Clarabelle, my sincerest thanks for all you've done. God bless you both!"

He went to the children and hugged them and then swiftly left the parlor and climbed the stairs to his room.

The children quietly filed out of the parlor and went to their rooms. The two women remained behind.

Mrs. Emmons dabbed at her eyes with the handkerchief and shook her head. "I was afraid something was really wrong, Mrs. Hendry, ever since he came back from Europe. He's been acting so strange, poor man. . . . So I guess he lost a great deal of money—I feel sorry for him . . . and those poor children. First uprooted from Alabama, and then just when they're finally settled in school here and have friends and all, they have to be uprooted again and go back. I do hope it will work out for them. They're such lovely children."

"Yes, they are. But I'm worried about Mr. Kenniston even more. And poor Mrs. Kenniston . . . I wonder if she knows the truth of the situation."

"I wonder, too, Mrs. Hendry." Mrs. Emmons shook her head and sighed philosophically. "Well, it's as they say: The Lord giveth, and the Lord taketh away."

On the first Sunday in June, Leland Kenniston and his family prepared to go to the apartment of Jacob Cohen for a farewell dinner.

In little more than a week, Leland had manfully done what had to be done—though inwardly he grieved over the ruin of his business and, though he tried hard not to believe it, his life. He had gone to his New York lawyer, a pragmatic realist named Michael Lutz, and after discussing Leland's situation, they had together gone to Leland's bank. There the Irish entrepreneur told the bank president unabashedly of his mistakes abroad and his intention to sell his house, garner what assets he could to pay off debts, and leave for Alabama as soon as all this had been done.

Both his lawyer and the bank president had been sympathetic, for they knew his former reputation and financial standing, and they admired his forthrightness in coping with the drastic reversal of his fortunes. The brownstone had been sold only three days after he had listed it with a realtor, for it was in a highly desirable location. A prominent young architect and his wife of four months purchased it for eighteen thousand five hundred dollars, and Leland, on the advice of his lawyer, kept only four thousand of that amount to wind up his affairs, arrange transportation for the children, himself, and Mrs. Hendry back to Alabama, and give him a small nest egg to pay immediate household bills, until such time as he could again take up the thread of his interrupted life.

The young architect had decided to buy most of the furniture that Leland had offered for sale, and as a consequence, there were very few loose ends to be tied up. Clarabelle Hendry and Mrs. Emmons exchanged sad glances as they saw how many of what they had considered family treasures would remain with the new owner.

And so it was done. The family was going back to Windhaven—just as, years before, Luke and Laure had returned there, back to the place where old Lucien had begun the monumental saga of the Bouchards.

As Leland walked with Paul, Celestine, and Clarissa to the Cohen apartment, he thought to himself how glad he was that Jacob had been offered an excellent position with a noted jewelry merchant on Twenty-second Street near Fifth Avenue. Leland had written a glowing recommendation, and as a result, his former employee had been engaged at an excellent salary. Also, most of the elderly Jewish jewelers, diamond cutters, and watchmakers whom Jacob had supervised had been offered work by the same merchant.

The previous day, Jacob had gone into Leland's office and said, "I won't ever forgive you if you and your children leave New York without having a farewell dinner with us, Leland."

"I accept, Jacob. I don't want to say good-bye to you like this; I'd like to do it by breaking bread with all of you," the Irish entrepreneur had sadly declared.

Miriam Cohen, wanting to make the meal a special one, had purchased a rack of lamb. Rachel helped her in the kitchen, and Miriam noted how wistful her daughter was, for after the farewell dinner, Paul Bouchard, on whom her daughter had a crush, would leave New York—perhaps forever.

For her part, Rachel wanted desperately to be alone with Paul for a few minutes and to urge him to write her and to

365

keep up their friendship. She knew that she was still a child, but her mother had once told her that European-born girls mature well before American ones do, and that already she was becoming a young woman. If that were true, within a few years it was not beyond the realm of possibility that she and Paul might marry—except for one enormous obstacle: He was Catholic, and she was Jewish. But at the moment, this fact was not on her mind; all she could think of was that he was going away for a very long time, and she would miss him terribly.

Miriam Cohen, wearing her best dress, received her guests at the door. She hugged John, kissed Celestine and Clarissa, and warmly shook hands with Paul. Then she faced Leland, held out her arms, and said softly, "My dear Leland, I'm so glad you could come tonight. We want to honor you and the children and try to express how much we love you."

"You're very kind, dear Miriam. I shall treasure our friendship always." Leland's reply was dignified and heartfelt, with none of the flirtatiousness that had marred his last visit to the Cohens.

"I want to tell you that I am sure God will bless you, and your health and your business will be restored swiftly. Then you'll be back here. We don't want to lose our friendship with you, Leland."

He was greatly moved by her words, and his eyes glistened with tears, which he tried to ignore as he took her hand and kissed it.

At that moment Jacob Cohen came into the room and greeted the Irish entrepreneur. "Let's make tonight one that will carry our friendship through until we see each other again. We've so many good memories to share, Leland; I'll never forget them."

"Nor I, Jacob. You like your new job?"

Jacob clasped his hands and smiled broadly. "Does a duck like water? It's marvelous—Samuel Lawrence even speaks a little Yiddish, and we get along famously. He's a kindly man, and of course he wants to make money as everybody does, but he looks upon me as a fellow human being. That's very important. Thank you, Leland."

Leland brightened as David came out of his room. With

366

hands outstretched and a warm smile on his handsome face, Leland declared, "It's been a long time since I've seen you, David. Why, it seems like only yesterday that I attended your *bar mitzvah*."

"Yes, sir," David responded, "and I was so glad you could be there."

At this moment, David's younger sister entered from the kitchen. "Well, *I'm* about to be thirteen, and I wish I could have a celebration like David's!" she said firmly.

Jacob smiled benignly at his daughter. "Perhaps someday there will be a ceremony especially for young girls," he said, "and I for one would have no objection, even though it is not traditional."

Celestine, who had stood by her stepfather throughout the conversation, looked up at Leland and wonderingly asked, "What's a *b-bar mitzvah*, Father?"

It was Jacob who replied. "Well, it means 'son of the commandments.' When a boy reaches the age of thirteen, he is considered on the threshold of manhood. And a *bar mitzvah* is a celebration of the fact that this young man is now entitled to read the Torah—our bible—the holy words of God." Jacob paused for a moment, allowing his words to have the proper degree of solemnity, then he clapped his hands once and heartily declared, "Well now, come in to the dinner table and be comfortable. We'll have a glass of wine and drink a toast to the future!"

Leland responded with a smile, but inwardly he was sad. He remembered past evenings with the Cohens, when they all looked forward to many more shared times together—and now those times were reaching an end. His mind drifted to thoughts of Laure—what her reaction must have been when she received his telegram saying that he and the children would be returning to Windhaven Plantation. He had told her nothing about his financial ruin nor about his terrible illness; such things were best relayed in person. Instead, he merely alluded to needing a rest and a complete change of climate— and he wanted to be united with his beloved wife again.

Still, Leland could not but feel strengthened by the knowledge that he had come face to face with ruin and poverty and bankruptcy, met them, and adapted himself to them. Of course, when he went back to Alabama, he would be living off Laure's generosity—and that was an onerous thought. But thanks to his banker, he had set aside a few thousand dollars, out of the reach of his creditors; on this he could at least subsist for a year or two. Perhaps by then, he would have found a cure for his illness, if it persisted; then there might be hope of a normal and happy life again.

After dinner, Jacob took Leland aside while Miriam ushered all the children into the living room.

"I've purchased a bottle of the finest Irish whiskey money can buy," Jacob began. "Each of us is going to have a glass of it, and we are going to toast each other. I am going to toast the recovery of your health, your business, all the happiness you knew, and the resumption—no, the continuation, rather!—of our friendship. And the friendship of our children for each other. . . ."

Suddenly Jacob Cohen could no longer control his tears. They coursed down his cheeks as he unsteadily handed Leland the glass he had just filled. Then he clinked glasses with the Irish entrepreneur and said, "*L'chayim* and *mazeltov*! I wish you peace and good luck from the bottom of my heart, Leland. My good friend, may God give you back all that you've lost, and more."

Leland bowed his head. It was a solemn benediction, and it touched him. He said softly, "Thank you, Jacob. Thank you for your understanding—although I don't think I deserve it."

"You mustn't think that you've done evil, please!" Jacob earnestly protested. "You are terribly ill! I am only amazed at the strength and perseverence you are displaying in the face of such disheartening news. I think you are being very brave, Leland—and I am very proud to call you my friend."

Jacob paused and sipped his whiskey. "Look how charitable and kind you were to us—our lives are so much better because of your kindness and generosity. You mustn't blame yourself or accuse yourself of anything. Come now, drink your whiskey; then let's get back to the others. By the way, we'll all go to see you off at the station on Monday—I've already arranged it with Mr. Lawrence."

Leland slowly finished his drink, then set the glass down.

He held out his hand, but then, giving in to his true feelings, he flung his arms around Jacob Cohen and hugged him. Now it was his turn to shed tears for what had been and what, if God were willing, might one day be again.

Chapter Thirty-six

Wednesday, June 6, was sunny and dry, a relief from the recent humidity. For Laure, it was an augury that better days were indeed ahead for all of them, and she smiled to herself as she, Lucien Edmond, and young Lucien drove to the Montgomery railroad station in two carriages to meet Leland, the children, and their governess, Clarabelle Hendry. They took the two vehicles so that there would be room for everyone and the luggage without needing to hire a carriage at the train station. Lucien Edmond drove one of the carriages, while young Boyd Gregory eagerly volunteered to drive the second.

The train was on time, and as the chugging engine pulled to a stop, steam blowing out along the rails, Laure excitedly turned to her son. "Won't it be wonderful to have everyone back?"

"Yes, Mother. I can't wait to see Paul again. I've missed him a lot—and Father, too, of course."

Lucien watched the porters swing down from the cars and place wooden steps up to the platforms so that the passengers might alight easily. He tried to mask his concern over his father; he felt instinctively that for him to have made so drastic a decision as to give everything up in New York to come back to Windhaven Plantation was something that didn't bode well. His stepfather was too much a cosmopolitan man to opt so readily for the bucolic, unexciting life of rural Alabama.

Clarabelle Hendry was first down, and then Paul, who helped Clarissa and Celestine descend. Leland Kenniston appeared next, holding John by the hand. Laure uttered a cry of joy at this sight, but the sound was choked in her throat as she saw Leland's lined face, the hollow, lusterless eyes, and the tense mouth. He tried to force a smile, but it was readily apparent that it was affected.

A porter lifted John to the ground, then helped Leland down, taking him by the elbow to steady him. Laure hurried up to him. "Oh, my darling, it's so good to have you back! Clarissa, Celestine, Paul, darling John—now I have my family with me! It's a happy day for all of us!"

But Lucien Edmond, though he smiled and cheerfully introduced himself to Laure's new husband, did not quite share her happy receptive spirit. He did not at all like the way Leland looked—like someone very ill who is trying desperately hard to hide it. The man's legs were shaking, there was perspiration on his temples and down his sideburns, and his skin was ashen.

"Let me take care of John for you, Father," Lucien genially called as he now came forward. John welcomed his eldest brother with a cry of delight, and Lucien smiled. "Come, John. Take my hand and we'll go see the carriage we'll be riding home in. . . ."

Leland turned to Laure and put his arms around her. Her tears flowed down her cheeks as she kissed him and clung to him. But even as she did so, she felt him sag, buckling at the knees. "Leland," she cried. "Oh, my God! What's the matter, darling? Lucien Edmond, Lucien—what's happened to him?"

He had fallen forward, then rolled over onto his side. His eyes were wide and staring, his mouth agape, and he was breathing stertorously.

Lucien Edmond was instantly at his side, and Lucien let go of John's hand and also came to his stepfather's aid. "We'd best get him to a doctor right away, if he can be moved," Lucien declared, as he and his half brother kneeled down to assist the entrepreneur.

"No—no, that—that's not necessary. . . ." Leland suddenly said in a hoarse, shaking voice. He managed to pull himself to a seated position, and then he declared, "No, I—I'm just exhausted. If we get right home, I can lie down and rest—honestly, that's all it is. Just take me home, please!"

"What do you think, Lucien Edmond?" Laure tearfully asked, as she took hold of little John's hand.

Lucien Edmond knew he was being asked to take charge of

371

the situation. "We'll take him right home if that's what he wants. But what I'm going to do, with your consent, is send young Boyd here over to Dr. Kennery's office with a message asking him to meet us at Windhaven. Lucien can drive the second carriage home. Is that all right with you, Leland?"

"Yes—that'd be fine. I told you, I'm just tired out . . . all I need is rest . . . do what pleases you. Help me up, would you please?" Leland spoke in an unsteady voice, with jerky pauses between his words.

Lucien Edmond and Lucien helped Leland to his feet; then, their arms around his shoulders, they guided him toward the first carriage. "Just take it easy. You'll be fine," Lucien Edmond Bouchard soothingly told the Irishman. "Lean back, close your eyes, and rest. We'll be home soon enough, and then we'll put you to bed, and you can recover from the long train trip. I know I myself wouldn't want to take one that long," Lucien Edmond tried to put Leland at his ease.

Paul, Celestine and Clarissa had been so startled by their stepfather's sudden collapse that they had stood mutely by. Seeing now that Leland was recovering to some extent, Paul turned to Laure. "You know, Mother, before we left New York, Father told us—"

Clarabelle's firm hand on his shoulder stopped him. "Paul, why don't you help your sisters with the luggage and get into one of the carriages. I'll be along presently." Paul started to protest, but Clarabelle silenced him again. "Just do as I say," she expostulated.

Reluctantly, Paul led Clarabelle and Celestine away, the three of them whispering among themselves.

They made good time going back to the red-brick chateau. There would be about two hours before dinner, and Laure told Lucien Edmond, "Leland can rest, then dine. I'm sure he'll feel better after that and a good night's sleep. He really has been on the go so much—first Europe, and then New Orleans, and then here, and then back to New York, and then here again—why, I suppose even a strong man would be weakened by all that traveling and business and everything."

Leland had been taken to the largest guest room in the south wing of the chateau, and Lucien Edmond and young Lucien helped him remove his shoes and outer garments. Meanwhile, Laure went to confer with Amelia Coleman about

372

dinner, and Clarabelle—hoping to wait for a more propitious moment to tell Laure the truth about Leland's condition—made a point of keeping the children occupied.

Outside the guest room, Lucien Edmond turned to his half brother, declaring, "I don't like the way Leland looks. When you saw him in Ireland, did he look this way?"

"No, not really," Lucien answered. "He *looked* all right—but he acted a bit strangely."

"Hmm. I suppose it could be tension, overwork—but . . ."

"Well, Boyd Gregory should be back with Dr. Kennery any time now," Lucien interjected. "Surely the doctor will be able to diagnose Father's condition. At least," he added somewhat wistfully, "I hope so."

Boyd Gregory escorted Dr. Kennery up the front steps of the chateau and knocked on the door. Amelia Coleman answered the summons and immediately took the doctor in to where Laure was sitting with her children, enjoying their long-awaited reunion.

"Thank you for coming so quickly, Dr. Kennery. My husband has just arrived from New York, and I'm very worried about him. He—he collapsed at the railroad station; he says it's from exhaustion, but I'd like your opinion. When he was here before, he didn't look too well, and now he looks worse. He's been taking a nap; please come in, and I'll go see if he's awake."

"Of course, Mrs. Kenniston. I'll wait here until he's ready to receive me."

Leland had just wakened and was trying to sit up, pushing the pillows behind him and leaning back with a sigh, when Laure opened the door and, seeing that he was awake, came hurriedly to him and bent to kiss him. "Darling, Dr. Kennery's here. Do you feel up to seeing him now?"

"I—I'm much more rested, Laure. Let him come in. I know you set great stock by him—"

"Yes, I do. I'll bring him right in. Now, you just rest there," she urged.

A moment later, Dr. Kennery walked into the guest room. Laure preceded him, brightly announcing, "Here's Dr. Kennery, dear. I'll go out and leave you alone now."

She closed the door behind her, and Dr. Kennery, a kindly smile on his handsome face, came forward. "It's a pleasure

373

to meet you, Mr. Kenniston. Let me take your pulse, if I may.''

"Go right ahead, Dr. Kennery.''

Dr. Kennery put right thumb and forefinger against Leland's left wrist and waited, measuring the pulse. "It's a little flurried and fast, but nothing to be alarmed about. I understand you've been traveling a good deal, Mr. Kenniston.''

"Yes, I have.'' Leland detailed his travels since the beginning of the year, concluding, "I arrived here just today.''

"Obviously a very strenuous schedule. I'm told that you had a fainting spell at the railroad station,'' Dr. Kennery said.

"It—it was really nothing. I—I guess I was just overtired, Dr. Kennery.''

"Mr. Kenniston,'' the doctor was suddenly serious as he leaned forward, "I want you to tell me the truth. Have you seen any doctors in New York about this? Be honest with me; it's to your advantage.''

Leland suddenly turned his face to one side and closed his eyes. A shiver ran through him. Finally, in a low, trembling voice, he admitted, "Yes—yes, I did consult my own personal physician. Dr. Wilkinson.''

"And what did he tell you?'' Dr. Kennery relentlessly pursued.

"I—I'd rather not say. You see, I don't want my wife to worry. She has troubles enough.''

"Tell me. Everything should be out in the open. Your wife is a very strong woman, and I think you should keep that in mind. Surely if it's as serious as you make it sound, she would want to share this with you, comfort you. . . .''

Leland sighed and nodded his head. "I—I'll tell you. Give me a minute. I—I have to compose my thoughts.''

"Of course,'' the doctor gently said. "Do it at your own pace; don't force yourself.''

Slowly, laboriously, Leland described his visit to Dr. Wilkinson's office and the diagnosis.

"Did the doctor have any recommendations?'' Dr. Kennery inquired when Leland had finished.

"He—he gave me the name of a specialist . . . at a hospital downtown—the Beekman Hospital, I believe.''

"And did you consult him?''

"No.''

Dr. Kennery was silent for a moment. "That's a pity, for

374

he might have been able to provide some additional insight into your condition. As it is, I would have to say, from what you describe, that I concur in Dr. Wilkinson's diagnosis. I'd recommend that in due course you see a specialist—I know of one or two in Atlanta; in the meantime, I'm concerned about the mood swings you describe. You believe they have been the cause of your bankruptcy, and they're the reason you had to return to Alabama?''

Leland Kenniston could only nod wordlessly and, with a choking sob, buried his face in the pillows and turned his back on the doctor.

"You know, Mr. Kenniston," the doctor said after another pause, "I'd be inclined to recommend a sanatorium as a place where you can get complete rest until we see what we're dealing with here. Would a place such as Andy Haskins now manages be acceptable to you?''

"Y-yes, if you really feel that's necessary, Dr. Kennery,'' Leland almost pathetically replied.

"Decidedly. These changes of mood, these black periods of despair replaced by moments when you feel yourself unsurpassable—you could become increasingly dangerous to your family. Your behavior may become more and more erratic if the tumor increases in size. I won't lie to you, Mr. Kenniston. You could do no better than go to seek Mr. Haskins's help.''

"My God . . . I never dreamed my life would end like this.'' Leland groaned, then covered his face with his hands.

"May I have a word with you, Mrs. Kenniston?'' Dr. Kennery asked Laure, as he stepped out into the hall. She had been standing there, wringing her hands, deeply concerned over her husband's condition.

"Why—why, yes, Dr. Kennery, of course.''

"I don't want to alarm you, Mrs. Kenniston, but your husband's a very sick man.'' The physician told the lovely matron all that he knew, holding nothing back.

"A brain tumor? Oh, my God! No wonder Leland has been acting so oddly. Oh, my poor Leland, my poor darling. What will this mean for him, Dr. Kennery?''

"Prepare yourself, Mrs. Kenniston. If he does indeed suffer from a tumor, it means that his mind may continue to give way. And unless your husband is very lucky and the tumor

375

goes into remission, I'm afraid that without surgery, it's probable that your husband will die.''

"Oh, my God—please, don't say that—''

"But I must say it, Mrs. Kenniston. He's a very sick man. My recommendation is that he go to Andy Haskins's sanatorium. He can receive proper attention there. Then, of course, he should see a specialist to confirm the diagnosis.''

Laure put a hand to her forehead, closed her eyes, and swayed. The doctor hurried forward, but with a visible effort the honey-haired matron steadied herself and regained her composure, as she said, "If that's what is needed, by all means do it. If it'll prolong his life, by all means send him off to Tuscaloosa. Tell me this, honestly, Dr. Kennery—what is your prognosis? Does my husband have a chance to live—to have a normal life?''

"I can't answer that; no doctor can, Mrs. Kenniston,'' Dr. Kennery earnestly told her.

Chapter Thirty-seven

When Andy Haskins received Laure Bouchard Kenniston's telegram requesting his help for her ailing husband, the former Alabama state senator made immediate plans to go to Windhaven Plantation and take charge of the Irish entrepreneur. Before leaving the Tuscaloosa sanatorium, Andy—in his position as director of the institution—arranged for the finest room in the facility to be put at Leland's disposal. The private room was large and sunny, and the view from the south-facing windows was of the beautifully maintained lawns and the forested area beyond.

Andy took the train to Montgomery the day after receiving the wire. He had also received word from Dr. Kennery asking him to stop by the doctor's office on his way through Montgomery, to review Leland Kenniston's case. Accordingly, after hiring a carriage at the station, Andy proceeded to Dr. Kennery's downtown consulting room, where he spent more than an hour conferring with the physician. In the course of this discussion, the possibility of consulting a specialist in Atlanta was raised, and Andy soberly concurred that such an action might be advisable. He promised the physician that the staff doctors at the sanatorium would keep both Dr. Kennery and the family apprised of Leland's progress.

By the time Andy rode out along the river road from Montgomery to Lowndesboro and headed toward Windhaven Plantation, it was early afternoon. In the drowsy heat of the day, nothing stirred, except for the cicadas, whose long, high cries from the thickets along the roadways made Andy nostalgic for the life he had once led as a farm owner—downriver from Windhaven—having no greater concerns than the care of his own plot of land and his family. But duty had called him away—first to the state legislature and then to his present post as hospital administrator, with scores of people dependent on him for their well-being. He hoped that in Leland's case—an especially difficult set of circumstances—he would be equal to the challenge.

He arrived at the chateau shortly before two o'clock and was greeted at the front door by Laure and Lucien Edmond, who both expressed their delight at seeing their old friend once again after so long.

"It is so good to see you Andy," Laure declared. "I only wish the occasion were a happier one." She sighed and shook her head.

Andy put his arm around her shoulders. "I'm so sorry for you, Laure. I never expected that when I finally got to meet your husband, it would be as a new patient. But"—he smiled and hugged her—"if there is any place where Leland will be assured of the finest care, it is at the sanatorium. I've made all the arrangements for his stay; you don't have to worry about a thing."

"Thank you, Andy," Lucien Edmond broke in. "You've greatly relieved our minds. Without you, I don't know what we would have done."

Andy was silent for a moment; then he gently suggested, "Perhaps I should go in and talk with Leland now, Laure. That is, if he's awake."

"Oh, I'm sure he is. Dr. Kennery has given him a sleeping draught to take at night, but Leland has been staying awake most of the day. Come, I'll take you to his room."

Laure led Andy to the guest room, where they found the handsome Irishman lying languidly in bed. After making the introductions, Laure discreetly withdrew from the room, leaving Andy and Leland alone.

"Well, I'm honored finally to meet you, and I hope I may call you Leland," Andy began, smiling kindly at the ailing man. "Of course, you must call me Andy, since we'll be spending some time together. I trust that Laure has told you of the arrangements we've made—that you'll be staying at the sanatorium until you're well rested."

Leland smiled wanly at the one-armed Southerner and said, "You don't have to speak in euphemisms, Andy. I assure you I know what the prognosis is, and I have no illusions about my chances of recovery. I'm putting myself in your hands because I don't want to do anything more that might hurt my wife and children—and there is the distinct possibility that I would do just that were I not under some medical care at all times. I—I . . .'' Leland suddenly began to weep, and he turned his head away from Andy.

Andy was silent for a long moment, but finally he said, ''I think you're being remarkably brave, Leland—and I hope you realize that in no way does Laure think any less of you because of your behavior. She completely understands that your actions were the result of your illness.''

''Thank you for reassuring me,'' Leland hoarsely whispered. ''I know that Laure is a wonderfully sympathetic woman, but I find it hard to believe that she can completely forgive me—even if I *wasn't* fully responsible. I don't know how much Laure has told you,'' the Irishman went on. He then briefly sketched some of the more lurid episodes he had involved himself in of late, including losing much of the money from the sale of the casino. ''Right now—well, I suppose part of the reason I seem so sane, so logical, is the medication Dr. Kennery has me taking. But if I were left to my own devices . . .'' He gave Andy an eloquent shrug.

''Don't worry, Leland,'' Andy told him. ''I have the finest physicians on my staff, and they'll keep an eagle eye on you for as long as you're with us. And besides, according to what your Dr. Wilkinson has said—and incidentally, I've wired him for a copy of your medical records—it may very well be that your condition will spontaneously go into remission and cause you no further difficulties. But,'' he smiled, ''we'll leave that in God's hands. Right now, why don't we start packing your toiletries so we can catch the five o'clock train back to Tuscaloosa? I don't want to have to make a last-minute dash for the station—it wouldn't do for your condition.''

''I understand,'' Leland said with a heavy sigh. ''I'll cooperate fully with you because I want to stay well. *I must*!'' His voice rose quickly almost to an agonized shout.

''Relax, Leland. Don't excite yourself. Just try to tell yourself constantly that you will improve, you will get better, and that we'll all help you in every way we can.''

''I know you will, Andy. And I'm very thankful that Laure has such a good friend as you.''

''I'm your friend, too, Leland,'' Andy assured the distraught man. ''Besides, you've made Laure's life meaningful

379

again—and I want to make sure that you go on doing so. If for no other reason than that, I will do everything I can for you."

Laure held onto Leland's arm as they stood saying their good-byes on the front steps of the red-brick chateau. She had wanted to accompany her husband to the train station in Montgomery, but he preferred a more private leave-taking. Laure had readily acceded to his wishes, wanting to make their parting as comfortable as possible.

He had already said good-bye to the children, but while Lucien and Paul readily accepted what was going on, Clarissa and Celestine were terribly upset. After all, their stepfather was leaving them, and they had just been reunited as a family again after months of being separated. And John, upon learning of his stepfather's imminent departure, had burst into tears. He was, at the moment, being consoled in his bedroom by Clarabelle Hendry.

Now, as Leland climbed into the hired carriage, Laure held his hand and looked into his eyes. In a husky voice, she promised, "I'll come to see you as often as I can."

But Leland shook his head. "No, my darling. I want you to remember me as I used to be—not as I am now or may become. If my ailment goes into remission, if I am able to leave the sanatorium, then I will come back here to be with you and the children—but if my condition deteriorates, I simply wouldn't want you to see me that way. Please. Do as I request if you still love me."

"Of course I still love you, Leland! How can you say such a foolish thing," Laure said, her voice breaking with emotion. She put her arms around him and drew him down to her. They exchanged a long and tender kiss. Tears fell down Laure's cheeks, and then, disengaging herself, she bravely declared, "This isn't forever. Please remember that, dear Leland. Under Andy's care, you'll soon be well and strong—I just know it. I'll write you all the time. I promise that."

"That won't be a substitute for you, darling, but I'll learn to make do with letters until I feel we can be together again." Leland philosophically shrugged his shoulders.

Andy Haskins, standing some distance away to give them a bit of privacy, was satisfied that they had said their farewells. He now walked over to the carriage and kissed Laure on the cheek, then climbed into the driver's seat and took up the reins.

As the carriage pulled away, Lucien put his arm around his mother's shoulders. "You're not to worry about anything, dear Mother. I'm the man of the family while Father's away, and I'll take care of the responsibilities."

"No, Lucien." She firmly shook her head. "We will *all* learn to shoulder responsibilities—none of us any more or less than the others. It's the only way our family will pull through this crisis and stay together," the honey-haired matron told her son. "We'll manage very nicely. You watch and see."

Inwardly, though, she began to wonder if she would ever reach a point in life where she would once again be happy. Was there, indeed, hope for the future? Was Leland's illness capable of being permanently cured, and would he return to take his place at her side, where she could inspire and encourage him?

The carriage had disappeared from view, and now once again she felt herself alone. Melancholy assailed her, and she put her hands to her face and wept softly, as Lucien, his arms still around her shoulders, tried his best to comfort her.

A week later, Laure received a letter from Leland enthusiastically declaring that the sanatorium was an extremely pleasant place, the attendants, nurses, and doctors most gracious, and that he felt no uneasiness about staying there for therapeutic treatment. He closed by expressing his unending love for her and the children.

Laure was greatly heartened by the letter. He expressed himself clearly, and there was optimism in his every phrase. Even though she knew that her husband was being assailed by one of the most terrible physical maladies the human body could endure, under Andy Haskins's supervision Leland would make progress—she was convinced of that.

During the period that Leland was away, Lucien Bouchard found himself drawn closer to his older half brother, perceiving the Texan as an affectionate uncle. In his turn, Lucien Edmond was reminded by Lucien of his own son, Hugo, who had shown a precocity at about this same age. Knowing to what purposeful end Hugo had shaped his life, Lucien Edmond faithfully believed that young Lucien would turn out quite as creditably.

While Lucien Edmond was expressing his thoughts to Laure one evening at dinner, Lucien himself was in Montgomery, dining at the home of Senator Haynes. A courier had brought the invitation that very morning, and Lucien had been overjoyed at the prospect of seeing the beautiful Samantha again.

Late that afternoon, Lucien had thoroughly bathed and carefully dressed in what he felt were his most elegant clothes. He had spent almost a quarter of an hour tying and then retying his cravat before he was satisfied with the way it lay against his ruffled shirtfront. Laure had thought he looked terribly grown up when he hurriedly left the chateau just past five o'clock and leaped into the carriage that the stableboy had harnessed for him. The two-hour ride into Montgomery had seemed interminable; however, the sight of Samantha standing at the door, waiting to welcome him, completely dispelled his impatience.

Over coffee and dessert, Samantha turned to him and said airily, "You know, this fall, Daddy is sending me to William and Mary College in Virginia. But I'll be leaving here in August because I have a second cousin there, and we're going to spend some of the summer together before school starts."

"Oh! I—that means I won't see you, once you're gone," Lucien lamely faltered, blushing and cursing himself inwardly for being such a naive fool as to show his feelings so openly.

"But, I'll write," Samantha earnestly promised, and the look she gave him suggested that her airy manner of announcing her departure was not completely indicative of her sentiments for him.

His heart began to pound a little faster, and he stammered, "I'll write you, too—every day, Samantha."

"Well now, young man," Senator Martin Haynes boomed from the head of the table, having overheard the dialogue between the two young people, "I like to see such determination in a young man. Naturally you don't want to make promises you can't keep." He gave a sly wink in Lucien's direction. "Of course, I recall I said the same thing to Samantha's mother back when I was courting her—and you can see the results for yourself."

"Daddy!" Samantha gasped, and then it was her turn to blush violently, which, in Lucien's eyes, made her all the

382

lovelier. "You mustn't say such a thing, or else Lucien here will think that . . . you know what he'll think."

"He wouldn't be much of a man, if he didn't think that you're a very desirable filly, Samantha dear," her father chuckled.

"But Lucien and I are just friends! We barely know each other," Samantha protested.

Young Lucien's hopes were dashed by her emphatic statement. He had secretly believed that by now Samantha would consider their relationship to have progressed beyond this point.

"All the same," her father rejoined with another chuckle, "I think he's a splendid young man, and certainly were he to ask for your hand in marriage, I would consider him a very eligible candidate. But, as you say, you're both just friends."

"Yes, s-sir," Lucien stammered, quite ill at ease at the turn the discussion had taken. The young man's mind was whirling: Although he wasn't sure that he loved Samantha, he certainly was quite smitten with her—especially with her beauty, so different from that of the unsophisticated Mary Eileen. At the thought of his martyred first love, Lucien felt a twinge of guilt at even being in the current situation, assessing his feelings for another. Then he remembered his all-too-fleeting shipboard encounter with Eleanor Martinson, and for a moment he felt his pulse racing. Lucien suddenly sensed Samantha staring at him, and he glanced at her and reddened. Thinking about Eleanor made him realize how much he longed to kiss Samantha—a desire that he hoped would be fulfilled before much longer.

It was on this note that dinner came to a close, and Senator Haynes, Samantha, and Lucien then rose and went into the drawing room. Senator Haynes beseeched his daughter to play a lively tune on the upright piano, a request she quickly honored. Indeed, Lucien had the distinct impression that Samantha was using this opportunity to show off her talents to him, for all through the lilting tune the young woman sent Lucien unmistakably come-hither glances.

Finally, when it was time for the youth to leave for his two-hour ride home, Lucien had the chance to be alone with Samantha. To his surprise, when he reached for her hand, she promptly drew away, scornfully remarking, "I declare, Lucien

Bouchard, I thought you had more respect for a lady than that."

"Forgive me, Samantha," Lucien exclaimed in bewilderment. "I guess I misunderstood your feelings for me." He looked at her for a long moment, then continued, "If I've annoyed you, I'm sorry. But I thought that you were interested in having more than a friendship with me. Apparently I was wrong. I won't bother you again." He started to go out the door when his sleeve was caught by her hand.

"Wait! You—you weren't wrong, Lucien. I *do* want to know you better." Samantha released his sleeve and coyly looked down at her feet. "Will I see you again before I leave for Virginia?" she finally asked.

"If that's what you want."

"Oh, I do, Lucien! And I promise I'll write to you all the time when I'm away. I hope you'll write back to me." She looked up at him; her eyes were large and alluring, and her tongue ran across her lips, moistening them seductively.

Lucien had the irresistible impulse to take Samantha in his arms and kiss her passionately—but he quelled the impulse, for Martin Haynes had, a moment before, come into the hallway to bid him good night. Sighing softly, Lucien told himself that perhaps when he next saw her, just before she left for Virginia, he would have the opportunity to express his feelings in the manner he wished.

Turning to glance at Samantha one last time before opening the door to leave, he was more than a little disconcerted by the expression on her face. Rather than affection and longing, he thought for a fleeting instant that he saw an unmistakable look of scorn. However, looking again, he realized that it must have been a trick of the flickering lamplight, because just before the door closed, Samantha winked and blew him a kiss.

Chapter Thirty-eight

On Monday afternoon, the second of July, the raiders who had taken part in the two attacks on Windhaven Plantation met once again in the back room of Jed Durfry's store on the edge of Lowndesboro. The shutters drawn, the men lounged at their ease, passing from hand to hand another jug of moonshine that Tobias Hennicott had brought from his still.

"I cain't wait for another chance at the fancy Kenniston lady," Bevis Marley said. "That's the sweetest bit of tail I ever did see. Almost had it, too, only Magnus here had to go and interfere!"

"I told you not to mess with the womenfolk, Marley," Borden hotly retorted, "but you had to do it anyway. If I hadn't come along, you could have got us all in trouble. There'll be plenty of time in our next raid to see that everybody gets a good poke at the gals—including the high and mighty Kenniston bitch. I heard tell she was a whore once, down New Orleans way, back durin' the war, so she oughta be ready for all of us." Borden rose to his feet. "Now listen good, all of you. We've let the Bouchards off for a couple of months, and nobody suspects anything. They don't know who we are, to start with, and they probably figure that we've given up the notion of raiding. Oh, sure, I read in the *Advertiser* where that mealymouthed old bastard of a senator— what's his name? Oh, yeah, Martin Haynes. Anyhow, he's gettin' a bill passed that's supposed to make it a crime for us to do what we're doin', but anybody in his right mind knows we're just rightin' the wrongs that have been done to us by the niggers."

"So when we gonna do somethin' real good to even the score, Magnus?" Bodine Evans eagerly wanted to know.

385

"Yeah, I'm ripe for some more fun," Cyrus Williams added.

"Tomorrow night, after midnight. You see, boys, that'll be the Fourth of July. And what could be a better time, when everybody's plannin' to celebrate that great day of independence with fireworks and such. We'll start off a few of our own to show that we want to be free of the niggers who are tryin' to run this whole damned country—and will, if people like them Bouchards are allowed to get their way."

"That's a great idea, Magnus!" Bud Corley chuckled. "I like it a lot."

"I thought you would, Bud. Tom Brennaman likes it, too."

"Do we got enough men for this?" Arlen wanted to know.

"Hell, I reckon," Durfry replied.

"Don't worry, boys," Bordon interjected. "We'll have darkness on our side, as always, so we oughta be all right. Beside which, Tom told me he's goin' out to see those two hog butchers outside of town—Dan and Herb Weinbold. Hell, with all the slaughterin' they do, they oughta be handy with knives, in case there's trouble."

"We won't have no trouble," Durfry brashly declared. "There's no one here in Lowndesboro who can stop us. Exceptin' our uppity mayor."

"You mean Dalbert Sattersfield? He's got no authority, and he's got no sheriff or anything. What the hell could he do, 'cept maybe protest? By the time the sun comes up on the Fourth of July, we'll be long gone—but they'll find our callin' card. Before we go, I promise you, we'll have our fun with them wenches there—that goes for you, too, Bevis—and maybe we can steal ourselves some horses and guns and, who knows, maybe even a little cash if there's any lyin' around. Might as well make a clean sweep of it. Maybe this time they'll get the point, once and for all!"

Arlen rubbed his hands together in gleeful anticipation. "I remember there's a neat colored gal over in one of them houses by the southern boundary of the Bouchards' place. What I wouldn't give to poke her!"

"Maybe you'll be able to do it tomorrow night, Sam—so I wouldn't drink too much if I was you. Too much drink before pokin' makes a man all talk and no performance," Bevis

Marley salaciously countered, amid a roar of bawdy laughter from his eager listeners.

"A little likker never stopped me, Bevis!" Arlen retorted, taking another swig from his jug. "An' you ain't got nothin' to talk about, what with the way you go at it. Maybe if you stayed away from the jug, you'd have a few more of your teeth left, 'stead of losin' most of 'em in brawls. Don't hardly think the Kenniston broad is gonna take to you, the way you look!"

Marley started to voice an angry reply, but Magnus Borden raised a conciliatory hand. "Don't get all riled up, boys. Save it for the Bouchards."

"Yeah," Hennicott joined in. "My likker cain't hurt your looks, Marley. Nothin' could make you look worse!"

The others guffawed loudly at the joke, but Bevis Marley angrily stood up.

Jake Elmore, sitting beside the undertaker, rose too and put an arm on the angry man's shoulder. "Aw, Bevis," he said, "we don't mean no harm. Here, take a swig of this, an' you'll feel better." He handed the jug to Marley, who took a long drink from it, and then both men sat down.

"Now," Borden continued, "are we all set on what we're gonna do?"

"Sure are!" was the answering chorus.

"We'll meet over at my funeral parlor, so's to throw off any suspicion, in case anyone's watching this place. Be there on time—we'll want to go over the final details so everybody's clear as to what he's got to do. Then we'll hit them. Now, let's have a drink and toast our Fourth of July celebration!"

On this same afternoon, Sheriff Tom Brennaman left his office on the main street of Montgomery, then leisurely ambled around the back of the building to the small stable where two horses and a buggy were kept for official county work, intended for himself and his newly hired young deputy, John Blake. It had been a sweltering day, so the threat of a rainstorm didn't in the least perturb the corpulent law officer. He was wearing neither the star of his office nor his holster and two pistols. Today, he was going on a private mission.

He chose the dappled gelding because it seemed to have better wind on a long ride than the mare. He saddled it, mounted, and rode at a slow pace through the outskirts of the

387

town, heading southwest. In so doing, he took the trail that curved beyond the Alabama River and the easternmost boundaries of the Bouchard plantation, and headed for the outskirts of Lowndesboro.

It was a good twenty-four miles, and he estimated, having made the journey several times before, that it would take him about two hours. This would be at the gelding's natural pace, without any danger of foundering the animal, which he particularly prized. One of his constituents had made him a present of it two years ago, for helping him out of a paternity scrape with an underage girl. Tom Brennaman had put the fear of God into the girl's heart, threatening her with telling her stepfather to give her a thrashing, so that she would not aim quite so high when she was in heat. He grinned to himself, remembering the episode as he neared his destination. The secret of being a successful law officer was minding one's own business and scratching an influential fellow's back every now and again, when there was something to be gained from doing it. It was a policy that Brennaman had followed most of his life and one he saw no reason to discard at this juncture.

The trail narrowed now and wound through dense undergrowths of bushes and brambles. Brennaman cursed under his breath as the gelding whinnied, but it still was the safest way to avoid being seen. He had no wish to be recognized.

He drew in his reins at last as he approached a dilapidated farmhouse, some three hundred feet away. He grimaced with disgust. The Weinbold brothers were, in his private opinion, the lowest of white trash—yet they were white, which was what mattered most. They were only, in his estimation, one step above the niggers whom he despised—but still, they were that one step ahead.

A strong odor had assailed his nostrils as he rode up, and now he saw why. Dan Weinbold, the older brother, was in the process of butchering a hog. The front yard was muddy, and there was a flock of chickens pecking for what they could pick up, while three goats bleated as the chickens got too close to them for comfort. The smell was overpowering, and again Brennaman grimaced, drew a kerchief from his hip pocket, and lustily blew his nose. Unpalatable as this journey was, it was important: The Weinbold brothers had to be told of the secret meeting of the raiders.

Brennaman's excuse for not going to the assistance of the Bouchards was for him a plausible and logical one. As sheriff of Montgomery County, he was responsible only for that which occurred within the boundaries of his own established community. What happened in Lowndesboro was no concern of his—and that was exactly why he meant to make things happen that would redound to his own advantage and to others like him who felt that the black man had lorded it over the whites far too long since that Northern bastard, Abe Lincoln, had set them free.

He dismounted and tied the reins of his gelding to a wobbly hitching post leaning rakishly to one side, grimacing again as he came toward Dan Weinbold. Just then, a large mongrel dog began to bark furiously and rushed up at him, baring its fangs as if to nip at his ankles.

"Get away from me, you lousy cur!" Brennaman swore, as he kicked at the dog but missed. It lunged to one side, drew back, and sitting on its haunches, barked furiously at him.

"Shut up, Mack! I mean it, you ornery son of a bitch!" Dan Weinbold cursed. Then, slashing at the carcass of the hog, he cut off a scrap of bloody meat and tossed it. The mongrel yowled with pleasure and raced toward it, grabbed it, and curled up with it some fifty feet away.

"Dammit all, Weinbold, I don't know which is more disgusting, the way you butcher your hogs, or the way you keep your property looking like a pig sty. God help me if I ever have to live in a hovel like this!"

With this, grimacing again, he took his kerchief and wiped some indeterminate slime from his riding boots, a brand-new pair of fine black leather boots that he had just received from a mail-order house up north and of which he was inordinately proud. *Dammit all*, he said to himself, *I should have changed them before I rode out here*.

"Damn your own eyes, Sheriff. Look, if you worked for a livin' like honest folks, 'stead of prancin' around with your shiny tin badge and your fancy-pants boots, maybe you'd be a little more understandin'. So say what you have to say and get the hell off our property, if you think it's such a pig sty!" was Weinbold's answer.

Brennaman glared at him, tucked away the kerchief, and

then said, "Tomorrow night at midnight, you're wanted, you and your brother, Herb. Everyone's meeting over at Borden's funeral home. There's gonna be another raid—same place as the first two times. You get my meaning?"

"I sure do, Brennaman. Right as rain." Weinbold grinned, exposing tobacco-stained, stubby teeth. "Them Bouchards again. Does my heart good to ride out against uppity folks like them. Think cuz they got money, they're better 'n we are. Okay. I got your message, Brennaman. Now be off my property."

Brennaman nodded, strode to his gelding, mounted, and rode off without looking behind him. Dan Weinbold hawked and spat. "Fancy son of a bitch. He thinks he's better 'n me, 'n Herb, too. I wish he wuz this hog. I'd cut him up real fine!" So saying, he again attacked the carcass with his butcher knife.

Tom Brennaman arrived back at his office and immediately called to his deputy. Four months earlier, so as to give himself more leisure time for some of his own personal pursuits—one of them being visiting his favorite bordello—Sheriff Brennaman had hired John Blake. Blake was twenty-six, blond, sturdy of build, soft-spoken and genial, and well liked around town. He had worked at a number of odd jobs in Montgomery—for the blacksmith for a year, for a feed and farm equipment store for another two, and, for a little more than a year, for the Montgomery Grammar School as a janitor.

Tom Brennaman had taken a liking to young Blake because the young man was extremely respectful. Knowing that the school board paid very little for such a menial job and that there would never be any advancement, the sheriff had visited John in his tiny house and made him an offer. The post of deputy sheriff paid the munificent sum of sixty-five dollars a month and such other benefits and privileges as the sheriff himself was able to glean from his enthusiastic constituents. For Brennaman—by dint of adopting the policy of seeing, hearing, and speaking no evil—was the recipient of bottles of whiskey and good wine, whole hams and slabs of bacon, stewing hens, and the like, as well as a few dollars now and again, when he had rendered a citizen an especially helpful service.

Brennaman now eyed his deputy sheriff and then casually remarked, "Well, John, you've done pretty good work for me, gotta give you credit. You like your job?"

"Yes, thanks, Sheriff Brennaman. I'm mighty obliged to you for it."

"My pleasure." Pausing a moment, Brennaman looked at John and declared, "I'm gonna give myself some time off starting tomorrow. I'm going out of town for a few days over the Fourth—got some business to attend to, and I need a little rest besides. You understand."

"Yes, Sheriff."

"You're a smart boy, John. Now, you know, I like your work so much there might be a few dollars more a month for you, if you do what I tell you to."

"I've always tried to observe the law, Sheriff. I respect it a lot."

"Sure you do, John." Brennaman put his arm around the tall man's shoulders. "Sure you do. I do, too, 'cause I'm sworn to uphold it. But there are times when the law doesn't cover certain things. There are times when the law has to stand aside and let folks work things out the way they want to. The way I see it, that's what democracy's all about. If a majority of folks wants to take a little 'corrective action,' as the lawyers say, well, as I see it, that's their business and their right. You'll find that out with experience. Now, for instance, there's a lot of folks around here don't like niggers. You know that as well as I do."

"Sure, Sheriff Brennaman." The young deputy nervously fidgeted but looked attentively at his superior.

"And you know, too, John boy, we've got some folks around here with some mighty strange ideas about what a nigger's place is. Now you take them Bouchards in that big brick house over near Lowndesboro—know who I mean?"

"Yes, I do, Sheriff."

"Well, they put niggers equal to whites—hell, they even approve of them intermarrying. They've got a white fellow there, name of Burt Coleman, and he up and married an octoroon gal named Amelia. Now did you ever hear tell of such disgusting foolishness? Why, if that was to spread throughout the South, there wouldn't be any pure whites left."

"I—I don't think that would happen, Sheriff," John uneasily replied.

Brennaman tightened his hold around the young man's shoulders and uttered a genial chuckle. "Well, maybe I'm stretching things a mite, just so you get the point. Anyhow, I want to tell you something real confidential. Now, the Bouchards have had a little trouble—"

"I heard about it. But I'm sure nobody'd try it again, knowing we'd do something about it," the deputy hesitantly proffered.

"You think not, boy?" Sheriff Brennaman scowled. "Then you're missing the whole point of what I've just been telling you. All right, I'll spell it out for you. I hear tell there might be a little holiday celebration out at the Bouchard place, just a few fireworks to usher in the Fourth, if you see what I mean. But the Bouchards are down near Lowndesboro, and whatever happens, so far as I'm concerned, we don't have jurisdiction there. So while I'm away, if anybody comes to you to get some help out there, all you have to do is tell them that the sheriff's office in Montgomery doesn't handle what goes on in Lowndesboro. Oh, you can take down the facts in a report, if you like, but then you just put it on my desk, you get me? That's all you have to do, John boy."

"I—I think I understand, Sheriff Brennaman."

"Good boy! I knew I could count on you. Well, I'll see you, mebbe Friday or Saturday—all depends how long it takes me to finish up my affairs where I'm going." He gave John a lewd grin and a wink. "Have a good holiday, John boy!"

"Thank you, Sheriff. I'll try my best."

"That's the ticket! You've got the key, so you can be here bright and early tomorrow. Wednesday, too, if you've a mind to. Might be a good idea: Seeing as how that's the holiday, it'll make the voters figure they've elected conscientious officials. Always want to give the public a good impression, John. That's the first lesson you've gotta learn if you want to run for office. Maybe when I feel like quitting you can run for mine—but that won't be for quite a while yet. Well, see you around!"

The sheriff walked slowly out of the office, chuckling to himself. John Blake stood staring after his superior. He didn't like what had been said to him, and he wasn't sure that what the sheriff meant for him to do was covered by the oath he had taken to uphold the law, when Sheriff Brennaman had first sworn him in as deputy sheriff. He had to think about it. All he'd heard about the Bouchards was that they were fair, decent people. They deserved as much protection as anybody else, so far as he was concerned. Yes, he was going to do some serious thinking.

Chapter Thirty-nine

The third day of July dawned sunny and hazy, and a steamy day for the area around Montgomery, Alabama, was forecast. Laure Kenniston relaxed in the relative cool of the dining room, where she sat with Lucien Edmond, drinking her first cup of coffee while the children happily wolfed down a substantial breakfast of hotcakes and sausage.

Lucien Edmond was making suggestions for the Independence Day celebration that would take place the next day on Windhaven Plantation for everyone who lived and worked on the land there. "I don't know that I'd go in for fireworks," he now said with a grin. "They're a bit too incendiary—and a bit too much of a reminder of some of the unexpected and unwanted fireworks that have gone off around here of late."

"Amen to that!" Laure agreed.

Lucien Edmond took a sip of his coffee before continuing, "Perhaps we can have a picnic as an early dinner, and then, around sundown, we can have music and dancing. I think that would be a good morale booster for everyone here, and it would show them that we're still very much a united family."

"I think that's a splendid idea, Lucien Edmond!" Laure animatedly agreed. "We might even give prizes to the best dancers—or something like that."

Celestine hurriedly swallowed a bite of sausage to voice her opinion. "I like that idea very much. Could I join in, Mother? You know that I'd been taking dancing lessons with Madame Jonteau back in New York, but you had to leave for the plantation before our first recital, so you've never seen me perform. I know this isn't the same kind of dancing—but I'm sure I can use some of my new skills and do very nicely."

She suddenly made a rueful face. "Oh, dear! I hope I'm not being too bold or immodest about myself."

Laure laughed and patted her daughter's hand. "Not at all, my dear. One is allowed a certain amount of self-assurance, I should think. And I look forward to seeing you dance."

"Then may I be excused? I want to look through my clothes and find something special to wear tomorrow," Celestine declared.

"Me, too, Mother," Clarissa piped up.

"Go along, then," Laure told them. "But do be good darlings and take John up to Clarabelle. She's waiting for him in the nursery.

"Aw," John protested, "she wants me to do lessons—and nobody else has schoolwork to do."

Laure stood up and walked around the table to her youngest child. Kneeling down to his level, she looked at him earnestly and said softly, "I know, John. It probably seems unfair to you—but you don't have to do any chores, do you? Everybody else does. So you see, Lucien and Paul are probably jealous of *you*. And later today, Celestine and Clarissa will have to help with the picnic—and you'll be able to watch while they work."

John's face brightened, and he ran off happily to the combined nursery and schoolroom. Watching him go, Laure laughed merrily as she confessed, "Of course, I don't dare tell him that if he were to help us with the chores, we'd probably end up having to work twice as hard to fix what he'd mess up."

"That's for sure, Mother," Lucien agreed.

"Boys," Lucien Edmond spoke up, "what do you say to going with me and conferring with Ben Brown about the celebration? He'll probably have some good ideas to contribute."

"Sure," Lucien replied.

"I'd like that," Paul agreed, eager to show as much enthusiasm as his older brother.

"We'll probably be back in an hour or two, Laure," Lucien Edmond told the honey-haired matron. "Then we'll go into town and get what we'll need for the picnic."

Laure looked up and said, "Amelia and I will prepare a shopping list for you. I don't think there's enough cured meat down in the cold cellar, so you may have to purchase a side of beef or a hog from Dalbert's store as well."

"I'll take a look down there before we leave," Lucien Edmond assured her. "Don't worry. We'll have plenty of food on hand for everyone. Nothing will get in the way of our celebration. I promise. You've been having some especially hard times lately, and I want to make up for that. You deserve a wonderful fete—as do all the hardworking people on Windhaven—and by God, we're going to have one!"

An hour later, Laure was chatting merrily with Amelia Coleman as they sat at a massive rectangular wooden table placed in the large kitchen at the back of the chateau. They had gone over their supply of stores and were almost finished with the list of what was needed for the Fourth of July celebration that would take place tomorrow. Amelia was pleased to see that her employer—really more a friend at this point—had recovered her spirit after the misfortunes she had experienced of late.

"Do you think we should get some extra flour? I know there's enough for the amount of biscuits we plan to make, but perhaps we should make half again as many, just in case some neighbors come by," Laure now said. She made a slight face, then continued, "Of course, nobody's stopped by at all since we've been back, so I suppose it isn't likely. Tell me honestly, Amelia, do you think it's because no one remembers us—or is it because they don't like the way we run the plantation?"

"I presume by that you mean treating us blacks the way you treat whites," Amelia said, somewhat wryly. "And I'm afraid the answer to that is yes, I think that's exactly why people haven't come to call. Except, of course, your old friends."

Laure sighed. "I wonder how Luke would have dealt with this situation." She shooed a fly away from her face, then brushed back a wisp of blond hair that hung lankly over her left eye. "My, I've forgotten how debilitating this humid weather can be. I think as soon as we've finished this list, I'm going to change into my bathing costume and take a dip in the creek. Would you like to join me?"

Before Amelia could answer, Boyd Gregory appeared in the kitchen doorway. He cleared his throat, saying, " 'Scuse me, ma'am. I don't mean to interrupt, but this here telegram just arrived for you, and Mr. Bouchard, he asked me if I'd take it in here to you."

"Oh, thank you, Boyd," Laure responded, holding out her hand for the yellow envelope.

She tore it open, and her face immediately changed. Crestfallen, she looked up at Amelia. There were tears in Laure's eyes as she said, "This is terrible! It's from Andy Haskins, and he tells me that his doctors are now certain that Leland has a tumor, and they feel his condition has deteriorated to the extent that he should have immediate brain surgery! Oh, my God! Amelia, I suddenly feel faint. . . ." The telegram fluttered from her fingers to the floor.

The beautiful octoroon rushed to Laure's side and put her hands on the older woman's shoulders. "There, there, Miz Laure. You just try and relax. Can you sit up by yourself? I'm going to get you a cup of cool water."

Amelia crossed the room to the sink in two quick strides and hurriedly tugged on the handle of the water pump. In a few moments, the cool, clear spring water gushed out, and Amelia filled a white porcelain cup.

Giving it to Laure, she stood hovering over her protectively. She sat down again only when the color returned to Laure's cheeks and she was sure her friend wouldn't swoon.

"Th-thank you, Amelia. I'm all right now. Oh, dear . . ." Laure put her head down on her arm and began to weep.

Amelia picked up the fallen telegram and read the rest of it to herself:

. . . I am making arrangements to have Leland taken to a hospital in Atlanta where they have been doing pioneering work in the surgical field. If all goes according to schedule, his surgery will take place in a week's time.

I know this comes as a shock, since Leland's condition had seemed to be in remission, and I am thankful that you have all your children with you for support and comfort.

I will wire you again as soon as we reach Atlanta.

Andy Haskins

Laure lifted her tearstained face, looking at Amelia, and said softly, "I'm sorry, but I just can't continue with the plans any longer. But I don't want the celebration canceled because of this. I insist that everything go through. This party is for all of you, not for me. It's merely a token of my appreciation at the way you have all stood by us despite the turmoil and the danger. Please, Amelia, promise me that you'll complete whatever tasks have yet to be done."

"I promise, Miz Laure," Amelia gently replied. "Why don't you go lie down now. I'll call you when dinner's ready."

"No, I think I'll go find the children. I want to tell them that I have to leave them again for a little while—I want to be by Leland's side when he goes in for the operation. I want him to know that I love him with all my heart, and that nothing he has done because of his brain tumor has made me love him any less. He will need all his strength if he is to have any chance of survival—I know that. So I want to do everything I can to bolster that strength."

John Blake had come to a decision. He was well aware that he was subordinate to Sheriff Tom Brennaman, but even during his leanest, hardest times, he'd never been tempted to break the law or look the other way from it. The sheriff was within his rights to turn his back on another attack on Windhaven Plantation, but he, John Blake, was going to warn the owners. That was the very least he could do. He personally couldn't stop a raid, not one man with a gun, but if he gave the Bouchards a warning, they could organize the people on the plantation to defend it.

Since the raid was going to take place near Lowndesboro, John had decided that first thing in the morning he would ride out to see the town's mayor, Dalbert Sattersfield. He presumed Sattersfield knew the Bouchards and might himself take some measures, which his office perhaps empowered him to use, against the would-be attackers.

He now rode down the river trail past the Bouchard place until he came to Lowndesboro. Dalbert's main store was just about to open when the young deputy dismounted and tethered the bay mare to the hitching post outside and hurried up the steps.

Dalbert's manager, Buford Phelps, and Buford's wife, Dulcie, were standing by the front door, and the manager said with a smile on his face, "Hang on a minute, mister, and I'll have this here door unlocked for you."

"That's all right; I was actually looking for Mayor Sattersfield. Do you know where I could find him right now? It's really important."

"Well, I can take you to his house; it's only about a mile from here."

"I'd appreciate that a lot. Thanks."

Buford turned to his pretty wife. "Dulcie honey, I don't think we'll be too busy for a while yet. I'll be back within half an hour, at most."

"That'll be fine, Buford. I can handle any customers by myself. I've done it often enough, goodness knows," Dulcie assured her husband.

Buford's horse was tethered in back of the store, placidly eating from a bag of oats that the black store manager had given him. He gently removed the bag, patted the gelding on the head, and said, "Sorry to interrupt your meal, Abednego, but we've got work to do." So saying, he vaulted into the saddle and, gesturing for John Blake to follow him, rode off toward the Sattersfield house.

Ten minutes later, they reached the Sattersfields' attractive brick and frame house. Buford, with a pleasant smile, turned back toward town, leaving John Blake to dismount, tether his horse, and knock at the door. Mitzi, who had been preparing the family breakfast, answered the summons, and when John explained his errand, she quickly led him into the dining room, where the children were arrayed in their chairs while Dalbert amused them with one of Aesop's fables until breakfast was ready.

John introduced himself, then said, "I'm awfully sorry to bother you at home, Mr. Mayor, but I think you ought to know what I've got to tell you."

"By all means," Dalbert responded. "Please be seated. Would you like a cup of coffee?"

"Yes, thank you. It's a tiring ride from Montgomery, and I could use a cup."

"You rode quite a spell. It must really be important. Mitzi honey, pour this nice gentleman a cup of your good coffee."

John leaned forward, his handsome young face earnest and grave with anxiety. "I don't want you to think that I'm going behind my boss's back, Mayor Sattersfield, but just before he left for a short holiday, he said something that I couldn't quite take. He said that there might be some trouble at the Bouchard

399

place, but since it is in Lowndesboro, he claims we don't have any jurisdiction there. He said that if I was to be told that help was needed there, I should just write it down in a report, but that there was nothing I could really do about it.''

"An attack on the Bouchard place?" Dalbert echoed, turning to Mitzi. "So, they're going to try it again, are they? Have you heard anything about when this attack might take place, young man?"

"That's the funny part about it. From the way the sheriff spoke, I was pretty sure he knew something specific—maybe even tonight.''

"I see,'' the mayor grimly remarked. "So these cowards want to have their own celebration of the Fourth, do they? Young man, you've done a real service. I tell you what. We'll both ride over to the Bouchard place and give them the warning. They'll have plenty of time to get ready and give those raiders a warm reception.''

"I wouldn't want to see anyone hurt, but I don't think it was right for Sheriff Brennaman to tell me what he did. I guess I'll have to look for another job if he ever finds out I took matters into my own hands,'' John ruefully said.

"Don't you worry about that. You can go to sleep nights with a clear conscience. If people were harmed there because you didn't spread the news, you'd feel a lot worse, believe me. As to a job, it just so happens I'll be needing a sheriff in my own bailiwick. Mr. Brennaman has proven to my satisfaction that he has no interest in what goes on outside of Montgomery, so I think the Alabama courts will grant me the right to appoint a new sheriff for Lowndes County. And frankly, I'd be likely to consider you for the job, seeing that you're a man of conscience.''

After having been visited by Deputy John Blake, Dalbert Sattersfield had taken the lawman to Windhaven Plantation, where Lucien Edmond, Lucien, and Benjamin Brown had conferred with him at once. The new foreman called all of the workers into the study of the red-brick chateau, to explain to them what was planned and how they could best repel it.

John Blake said to Lucien Edmond, "I'd like to be here, Mr. Bouchard, because then you'll have a representative of the law to see what's going on, in case you need a witness.''

"That's damned brave of you, Blake,'' the tall Texan

400

gravely responded. "We can use every man we can get here. I don't know how many attackers will be mustered, but I have a feeling this is going to be an all-out battle."

"I can probably get some of my old friends from Civil War days," Dalbert emphatically offered. "There are as many as half a dozen who live right in Lowndesboro. I'll ride back right now and talk to them. They've all got Whitworths, and while those may be old guns, they're still accurate up to five hundred yards."

"I can't believe all this is happening," Laure exclaimed. "First the news about Leland, and now this. Thank goodness you're here. You're all so determined and so brave; I'm only praying there won't be any bloodshed. But God bless all of you for helping. I'll stay right here till this is over. I'm ready to bear arms myself. I've been practicing with both a rifle and my derringer for weeks."

"Now then, Laure," Lucien Edmond spoke up, "I hope you won't get involved in gunplay. I know you can shoot well, but you should be out of harm's way. As a matter of fact, I'd feel a lot better if you'd take the children into Lowndesboro, to stay with the Sattersfields—"

"I'll send the children with Dalbert—if that's all right with him—but I won't hear of leaving myself!" Laure emphatically declared. "My place is here at Windhaven, just as Luke's was. And I can shoot well enough now to do my part. Mitzi will look after the children, won't she, Dalbert?"

"Of course, Laure," the mayor replied. "I'll take them back to town right away."

"Good, thank you, Dalbert, and thank Mitzi, too. I'll get the children ready—all except Lucien, who I expect will want to stay, much though I'd prefer he didn't. He's nearly a man now and will insist on the right to make up his own mind."

As she withdrew, Dalbert turned to Lucien Edmond. "I'll bring back Buford Phelps," he declared. "He has a few scores of his own to settle with the likes of these blackguards."

"Thanks, Dalbert, I appreciate all that you're doing."

Dalbert held out his hand to Lucien Edmond, who shook it, and murmured, "What a friend you've been over the years. God bless you!"

Then Dalbert turned and, with a nod to everyone, strode out to the back of the house, where Laure was already putting the children into a buggy for the journey back to Lowndesboro.

Young John Blake stood in the doorway, not certain what role he was to play. Laure walked over to him and held out her hand. "Thank you, Mr. Blake, for bringing us the warning and for offering to help us. I pray you won't get into trouble or be hurt."

"I can look after myself, don't you worry none. I don't like people who come disguised in the dead of night, wanting to do mischief." With this, politely nodding to Laure, he hurried out to join Lucien Edmond and Lucien.

Seeing the three men come out into the fields, the black contractor, Enoch Washburn, called out, "Can I be of service to you, Mr. Bouchard?"

"It's all right, Mr. Washburn," Lucien Edmond replied. "We're not here to discuss your work—which is commendable. I actually need to speak with the guards, but I guess it concerns you as well."

The three men, followed by the contractor, made their way toward the cottage being occupied by the three guards. John Hornung was outside, shouldering a rifle, for it was his shift. Lucien Edmond told him, "I need to talk to all of you men. Are your two friends inside?"

"Yes, sir. They're sleeping."

"Wake them up." Lucien Edmond's tone was brusque. "Mr. Washburn," he turned to the contractor, "why don't you ask all your men to join us? I want everybody to know exactly what to do."

"But what's this all about, Mr. Bouchard?" Washburn looked puzzled.

"This man here, John Blake, is a sheriff's deputy. He's come to warn us that we can expect an attack from that same group of raiders who hit us earlier—it could come as soon as tonight. Needless to say, I want everybody to be ready for it."

"I didn't think they'd have the guts to try it again," Washburn said, almost to himself. Seeing Lucien Edmond's eyes narrow, he amended, "I mean, nobody's bothered you for a long time now, so I thought it was all over with. Anyway, I'll go get my men, just as you say, Mr. Bouchard, sir."

Washburn's crew, along with Ben Brown, gathered around, and Lucien Edmond, while he waited for the guards, explained what was going to take place. "I know you men just hired on to do restoration work, not to fight our battles, but if you opt to help us, I can assure you that you'll be amply compensated.

"We'll have all of the womenfolk gather inside the chateau by sundown," Lucien Edmond continued, "so we won't have to worry about protecting the individual cottages from attackers. And, of course, all of you men will be armed, as well. Ben, here"—Lucien Edmond nodded to the young black foreman at his left—"will be passing out the weapons and ammunition. If you choose to fight, you'll be fighting not just for the Bouchards, or for the land, but for yourselves and your right to live and work as you choose. These people hate blacks, and that's why they're attacking us. Now, if there's anyone here who doesn't want to fight, I won't call him a coward, and I won't say a word against him, and he's at liberty to go into the chateau with the women. I'm not asking any man to shed his own blood, or to risk the danger of laying down his life to these skulking cowards. But I appeal to all of you, as free men, as men who undoubtedly know the Bouchards and what they stand for, to band together with us to defeat the hateful, cowardly, bigoted fools who want to damage this place and hurt people like you, just because they don't like the color of your skin."

There was a simultaneous cheer from those who listened to him. "We're with you, Mr. Bouchard, we're with you!" "We'll fight, we'll show them!" "They'll be sorry they thought of a thing like this, yes, they will, Mr. Bouchard, sir!"

"Are you really sure they're going to attack us, Mr. Bouchard?" Enoch Washburn suddenly asked. "There's been no trouble so far, not since the time somebody took that sledgehammer and busted the top of the dam."

"All I know is what Mr. Blake here told us—and I believe he's correct," Lucien Edmond replied. Then, seeing the three guards appear in the doorway of the cottage, he excused himself to the contractor and walked over to the trio.

John Hornung had wakened Frank Connery and Sidney Berndorf, and the three of them stood whispering together. Lucien Edmond Bouchard asked them, "Would you tell me your names again?"

"I'm Connery," the second guard said.

Lucien Edmond nodded and turned to the German. "You're Berndorf, then? Someone told me that you really don't like to fight. You're not much good as a guard, if that's the case."

403

"I—I'm not, I'm afraid. I needed a job, Mr. Bouchard, but, *Gott,* I don't want to do any killing," Berndorf quavered.

A sneer curled Lucien Edmond's upper lip. "Then you won't have to. At sunset, you can go into the house with the women. And you'll get no gun, so you won't have to use one. Just keep out of trouble, *out of sight,* that's all I'm asking of you. What about you, Connery, Hornung? Are you willing to do the duty for which you were hired by Lopasuta Bouchard?"

"I sure am, Mr. Bouchard," Hornung fervently declared.

"I feel the same way," Connery agreed.

"Good. All right, Ben, let's distribute the weapons and the ammunition. Then we'll have a little rehearsal, so to speak. Everybody is going to know what to do tonight. Those raiders'll get one hell of a reception if they try anything!"

Chapter Forty

Magnus Borden's funeral parlor in Lowndesboro was at the opposite end of town from Jed Durfry's ramshackle store. It was much smaller than Borden's establishment in Montgomery, and since Lowndesboro's population was not more than three thousand, it was not worthy of so spacious and well-equipped an establishment as that which the undertaker operated in the capital city of Alabama.

A dozen men, garbed in the white cloaks made familiar by the Ku Klux Klan and carrying hoods with cutouts for eyes and mouth, crowded into the small workroom at the back of the parlor. The hour of midnight, combined with the locale of this meeting, terrified most of them; only Bevis Marley, the man who worked in the parlor for Borden, and the Weinbold brothers, who slaughtered animals for a living, had no feeling one way or the other for where they were. The others—among them Bodine Evans, Jed Durfry, Cyrus Williams, Tobias Hennicott, Sam Arlen, and Jake Elmore—could not help glancing around fearfully at the jars of embalming fluid and the tools used for the dissection of the cadavers, as if they felt themselves in a cursed, unhallowed place. Bud Corley, who was also present and the most superstitious of the lot, was particularly fearful, and he took great care to keep his distance from the long, rectangular table in the center of the room, which was used both for the preparation of the dead for burial and for the conducting of any autopsies that were required in Lowndes County.

Magnus Borden stood up, and clearing his throat, he addressed the gathering. "Well, this is it, boys. We're gonna go over the details one more time so nobody makes any mistakes. We're gonna get those Bouchards and get 'em good!"

A chorus of, "You said it, Magnus boy!" and "That's the ticket for those nigger-lovers!" broke out from the hooded men.

Bodine Evans chortled, slapping his thigh. "Say, maybe this time we can finally grab ourselves some of those goodlookin' gals for pokemeat. I'm just itchin' to get a shot at that octoroon gal who works in the kitchen."

"So am I," Sam Arlen spoke up, his lips curled in an appreciative leer.

"You'll get your chances, don't worry," Borden promised. "But I've got first dibs on the octoroon filly, seein' as how I'm leading this foray."

"That's the way to talk, Magnus!" Tobias Hennicott sniggered.

Borden scowlingly interrupted, "But don't worry, there's plenty of gals to go around. And money and other stuff. This time, we'll make a real job of it. We'll drive those Bouchards out forever. They won't ever want to come back to Alabama. Why, it might be that all of you folks'll get a chance to live in that fancy red-brick palace. You'll be the ruling class!"

As Hennicott passed around a few jugs of his whiskey, Jake Elmore noticed a dissecting knife gleaming under the single candle that provided the only illumination in this somber room. Smiling to himself, Elmore surreptitiously palmed the knife when no one was looking, and thrust it into his jacket pocket.

A few minutes later the meeting broke up, and the hooded men left the funeral parlor, filing slowly out one by one into the street. The little town was virtually deserted at this hour, so there were no witnesses as the men headed off in the direction of Windhaven. Now that they had made their final plans, they exulted with anticipation over the success of their intended venture.

It was one o'clock in the morning on the Fourth of July, 1883. The night was still, as it had been all day; the hot, fetid, humid air was oppressive. Even the night birds seemed silenced by the sultry atmosphere.

Inside the red-brick chateau, all the children and the women were quartered, as was the German guard, Sidney Berndorf. But in the cottages dotting the fields of Windhaven Plantation, the men were armed and waiting. Young Lucien was preparing to fight alongside his older half brother, although both Lucien Edmond and Laure had tried to talk him out of it. Laure had pleaded, "You're too young to risk your life!" But Lucien had been as adamant as Laure had expected he would be, reminding his mother that at seventeen he was a man, and he was doing no less than his father would have done.

Lucien Edmond had intervened, saying, "I don't like the idea at all, but I know how you feel. There comes a time when we have to expose ourselves to situations that can be dangerous or risky, and we can't let others fight our battles for us. But promise me that you'll stick close to me at all times."

Young Lucien had nodded, eager to be in the fray. He thought to himself that the cowardly attacks on this good land were born of malice and hatred, envy and bigotry, and that these were the same qualities that had given rise in Dublin to conflict between the English soldiers and the Irish citizens. In a sense, he told himself, he was fighting to avenge Mary Eileen's death, as well as the affronts given his mother.

Lucien Edmond and Lucien had gone to confer with Ben Brown at midnight, and the foreman had then gone around to all the cottages, telling the men to have their firearms loaded and at the ready. "Blow out all the candles and lamps. I want us to have the advantage when they come in," he instructed them. "And take your time shooting. Make every shot count. If we take them by surprise the way we've planned, they won't try it again, and we'll beat them off on the first rush. Keep low, keep out of sight, and get those lights out now!"

Davey Mendicott, his rifle raised, said under his breath, "Don't worry. Louis and me'll get these yellow cowards. And we'll do it for Pa."

"You're damn right," answered his brother, Louis.

Lucien Edmond and Lucien moved out to the southwestern edge of the fields and crouched behind a row of corn. The corn was ripe, golden, and the tassels and the tall stalks made a perfect camouflage and hiding place for the two half brothers. The two men were armed, although Lucien Edmond still felt uneasy about Lucien's involvement in gunplay. Suddenly he realized that part of the reason was that he hadn't seen the youth in so many years and he still thought of Lucien as a young boy. Trying to make amends for any blundering behavior, Lucien Edmond almost contritely exclaimed, "I understand you see very well in the dark; watch from every direction to see where the attackers come from. It's about time for them now, I'd say.''

There were twenty men now, all hooded, for the contingent from Lowndesboro had been joined by another from the town downriver, whose members Sheriff Brennaman had notified about the coming fracas. Still maintaining his authority over the group, Borden led them along a back path that cut through some disused fields some three hundred yards from the river. The area was deserted, so there was no danger of detection as the score of men reached the southwest boundary of Windhaven Plantation, where Borden signaled to them to halt. They pulled their mounts up, circling round him.

"I'm going to pick seven men to get right into the house and take over," Borden declared. "That way, we'll be sure of havin' women, since some of the women are bound to be in the house, like that octoroon beauty who married Burt Coleman. And there'll undoubtedly be money there, too, and probably weapons. Now, listen—Bodine, Cyrus, and you, Tobias, you three will go in through the kitchen. Two of you others—Bud Corley and Dan Weinbold—you'll go in from the northeast, breaking in through one of the side windows. Bevis, you and Jake will gain entry by way of one of the front rooms. That way, you men will have the house completely surrounded. The rest of us will approach from the other direction and go directly into the fields and the houses of these black bastards."

"It'll be a night to remember," Sam Arlen lewdly chuckled. "Some of those nigger gals are definitely worth havin' fun with."

"You can have all the fun you want, Sam," Borden tartly retorted, "after the job is done. This time, we're going to set fire to the tenants' houses, and we're going to take over the big house once our seven friends have gotten in there. Now remember, our plan will come out right if you do what you're told. Let's ride!"

As they rode, Jake Elmore fingered the pocket of his jacket, where he felt the reassuring bulge of the dissecting knife he had stolen earlier in the evening. If all went well, murder would follow rape this evening.

*　　*　　*

Inside the chateau, Dalbert Sattersfield, along with Buford Phelps and three of the six Confederate veterans whom Dalbert had recruited in Lowndesboro, were guarding the house. The one-armed mayor had sent Buford and the three veterans to the kitchen, saying, "If they try to get in from the back, they're certain to break in here." He had stationed the other three men away from the house, over by the bluff, hidden in a clump of bushes. "We're prepared for just about every way they can strike us," he had told Laure.

The young deputy, John Blake, had gone outside, crouching low as he ran across the spreading acreage of Windhaven Plantation. As planned, he joined Lucien Edmond and Lucien in their hiding spot behind the corn, murmuring, "If my hunch is correct, the attack will come any time now."

"We're ready. Let's say a prayer that none of our side gets killed or seriously hurt. I'm not intending to kill the raiders, unless they try to kill us—but I *am* aiming to teach them a lesson that they'll never forget," Lucien Edmond vowed.

Upstairs in the bedrooms were the workers' children and wives, brought for their protection into the house; but Laure had insisted on remaining downstairs, where she would be better able to defend her home, if necessary. She had sequestered herself in the dining room, where, holding her loaded rifle across her lap, she sat talking with an equally determined Clarabelle Hendry.

A few minutes earlier, Laure had returned from the small chapel in the north wing of the chateau, where she had knelt to pray that the night would pass without danger to any of her family or those of the loyal workers who had rallied to the cause of the Bouchards. At the same time she had offered a prayer for her dear Leland, now so far away and beset by adversity of a different kind. Though these few minutes in the chapel had comforted her to some extent, she was still fearful, most particularly for young Lucien, who had in her view been rash in his insistence upon joining the men in the field.

"I tried to stop him, Clarabelle," she explained as, still grasping her rifle, she anxiously rose to stare out through the dining room window into the gloom of the night beyond. "There was simply no holding him back. After all he's been through, I guess he felt he had to be doing something."

"I've known Lucien ever since he was a child, Laure, and I think he'll be fine," Clarabelle comforted her. "He's a man

409

now, doing a man's job, and you've every right to be proud of him. Lucien Edmond will see that he takes no unnecessary risks."

Laure turned away from the window to smile at her friend. "I'm grateful to you, Clarabelle, for trying to ease my mind. To think you came all the way down here from New York—to this. It breaks my heart to see you endangered so. Sometimes I wonder if I was right to come back. . . ."

"Hush, Laure," Clarabelle gently remonstrated. "This is no time to worry about might-have-beens. You were right to come, and in your heart you know it."

In the parlor, Dalbert Sattersfield eyed the middle-aged German guard, who was huddled in an armchair. He approached Sidney Berndorf and said, "You know, fellow, you were hired as a guard. But from what I've gathered, you haven't been worth your keep. If you don't want to get out into action and use a gun, as you were paid to do, why the hell did you take the job?"

"I—I can't help it—honest, I can't! Please don't blame me!" Berndorf babbled.

"What the hell are you talking about?" the one-armed Confederate veteran coldly demanded.

"The last time . . . Mr. M-Mayor—" the German stammered, "one of them came up at me when I wasn't looking, put a knife to my back, and said that if I said anything at all, they'd come back and kill me. I've been scared to death. . . . I didn't dare tell anybody. . . . I only hoped they wouldn't come again! Honest—I'm not on their side, Mr. Mayor. You gotta believe that—"

"You make me sick!" Dalbert tersely countered. "But we might need you as a material witness, in case this thing ever comes to trial. Maybe you can identify the voice of the fellow that threatened you. Stay there out of mischief, and don't you dare move."

"Why, yes, sir, I—I swear—I swear by all that's holy—"

"Save your swearing for a jury and a judge. All right, I'm going to the other side of the house and up the stairs to the tower. Maybe I can see things from there that'll help you fellows down here get a better idea of where we might be attacked!" Dalbert declared.

At Dalbert's order, all the lights in the house were extinguished; however, the bright half-moon cast light stream-

410

ing through the large windows, providing ample illumination. Amelia Coleman came in from the kitchen and stayed huddled next to Laure and Clarabelle. The tension in the air was almost palpable now, and the sound of heavy breathing filled the room. But nothing more was said, and they all silently waited.

Magnus Borden held up his hand, and the twelve men with him halted their horses. "As soon as they break in the house, boys," he said in a low voice, "they'll give us a signal. Somebody will fire three quick shots in a row. But in the meantime, we've got work to do in the fields and those cottages. Shoot down any niggers you see. And it don't matter if some of the bullets hit white folks, either—they're just as low as the niggers, 'cause they're lettin' them live with them! Now, let's go. All of you know what to do!"

From their hiding place in the tall corn, young Deputy Blake, Lucien, and Lucien Edmond Bouchard heard the muffled sound of horses' hooves approaching from the southwest along the river trail, and Lucien Edmond whispered, "They'll be coming around the base of the bluff now, so hold your fire. I've told Ben Brown to do the same thing. We'd best not waste ammunition. When they're right on top of you, then let them have it."

From the top of the bluff, there was the faint cry of a screech owl. Borden gestured to his men, then spurred his horse forward. The other men spread out on either side, in a wide swathe, riding into the fields past the dam.

By this time, Bodine Evans and his six companions had ridden from the other direction, preparing to break into the red-brick chateau. They rode at a walk to the far edge of the courtyard, being as quiet as possible; there they dismounted and dispersed immediately to their assigned positions. There was no one in sight. Evans chuckled to himself, put a finger to his lips, and dismounted, carrying his rifle. Holding the rifle at waist level, he edged forward toward the kitchen door. Then he looked back to nod to the two comrades assigned to break into the kitchen with him, whispering, "This'll be easy. They're all asleep in there!"

He cautiously tried the knob and found it open. "Hey, we're in luck, fellas! The stupid bastids went and left the door

411

unlocked! Come on in—but I got first crack at the fillies here.''

He opened the door and moved in, his two friends behind him, all with their rifles and pistols ready. But, as the door opened, the light from the moon backlit their figures in the doorway, and the Confederate veterans waiting inside for them at once opened fire. Bodine Evans uttered a gurgling shriek, spun around, and pitched forward on his face, his arms spread out, a bullet through his forehead. The two men behind him, Cyrus Williams and Tobias Hennicott, were wounded in the shoulder and hip, respectively.

"Put on the light, Purdy," one of Dalbert Sattersfield's men muttered. "Let's see what we've got here."

As a lamp was lit, the two raiders on the floor groaned and writhed. Hennicott moaned, "You busted a bone there! I'm gonna die!''

"No great loss if you do; no loss at all!" the man who had shot him sarcastically countered. The Confederate veterans unmasked the two wounded raiders, who babbled for mercy.

"Gimme sumpin' or I'll bleed to death,'' Williams pleaded.

"Git your hands behind you, mister.'' Jesse Purdy prodded him with the muzzle of his rifle. "Frank, tie him up good. Then I'll see what I can do about stopping his blood—though it'll be a waste of taxpayer's money to have him stand trial and then feed him meals till they hang him!''

At the sound of the gunfire, Laure had jumped from her chair in the dining room with her rifle in hand and rushed from the room before Clarabelle could stop her. Her heart beating fast and her face flushed with anger, Laure started making her way toward the kitchen, when a noise from the supposedly empty study made her halt in her tracks.

She stood outside the room, listening intently. A scuffling sound reached her ears, and—drawing in a sharp breath, holding her rifle at the ready—she grabbed the knob and turned it, flinging open the study door.

Her heart raced when she found herself facing two robed and hooded men, one fairly large and stocky but the other seeming to be even smaller than she. It was this smaller man who seemed to be the more fearless of the two, and he came at her, menacing her with a knife, totally disregarding the rifle she held in her hands.

"Don't take another step or I'll shoot!" she shouted.

412

But the man continued to ignore her and came on.

Sucking in her breath to steady herself, Laure fired the rifle, momentarily closing her eyes as she did so. As she reopened her eyes, she saw the small man crumple to the floor, a gaping hole in the middle of the hood where his mouth had been. She felt sickened and faint. Her knees started to buckle under her, but then she remembered the presence of the other man.

Laure struggled to regain her fortitude, but the raider had been quick to realize that he had the upper hand. In two short strides he was at her side, grabbing the rifle easily from her hands and tossing it aside and, at the same time, kicking the door shut with his foot. Wrapping one burly arm around her waist, he pulled her to him. With his free hand, he pulled off the hood he wore, revealing his toothless smirk. Carelessly dropping the hood to the floor, he then reached inside the collar of his robe and pulled out a shiny metal object.

Laure blanched when she recognized the pendant: It was the locket that Luke had given her so many years ago, the one her would-be rapist had taken from her neck.

Watching her face, Bevis Marley savored her reaction. Satisfied that she now knew who he was, he whispered into her ear, "That's right, my fine lady. It's me, back to finish up what I started. And this time there ain't no one around to stop me. I've been waiting a long time for this moment—and I'm gonna make it worth the wait."

He pulled her hard against him and pressed his mouth over hers. But she retched at the smell of his rancid breath, and this infuriated Marley. "You're gonna be sorry you did that, missy. You surely are. You're gonna be beggin' me for mercy long before I'm through with you—but I ain't gonna listen. I'm gonna have you but good."

He dragged Laure over to the settee, tugging at the bodice of her dress. The fabric wouldn't give and, distracted by his failure, giving all his attention over to rendering his victim naked, Marley did not notice Laure's hand slip into the right pocket of her skirt.

In one swift movement, her arm came up, and in her hand was her derringer. Without a moment's hesitation, she aimed it at Marley's heart and fired. A startled look crept over the raider's face and was quickly replaced by a glassy stare.

413

Laure backed away from the man, but he reached out toward her, then fell at her feet.

Laure groped for the corner of the *escritoire,* knowing that she, too, would fall if she didn't support herself. She stood there, panting, gasping for air, for three long minutes. Then she started to cry, releasing all the tension that had built up inside her. Finally regaining some composure, she walked to the door of the study and opened it, then slowly walked down the hall to the dining room, oblivious to all the shouting and shooting that was going on in her once-peaceful home.

While Laure fought off her attackers in the study, Dan Weinbold and Bud Corley took the butts of their rifles and smashed the window of the drawing room. From where she sat on the edge of her chair in the dining room, Clarabelle, her heart pounding, heard the noise of shattering glass and screamed for help. Dalbert Sattersfield heard the cries and came running, meeting Buford Phelps in the hallway outside the drawing room. They heard the thud of a rifle dropping onto the floor of the room, and Dalbert whispered to his friend, "Crouch down low. I'll push the door open, and then we'll shoot anything that moves!"

Reaching up for the knob of the door, he silently turned it, then swung the door wide. He and Buford flung themselves on their bellies, and with their guns covering the room, they caught both Weinbold and Corley in the act of retrieving their rifles. "Drop those guns, or we'll fire!" Dalbert snapped. "You're breaking and entering, and that's good enough reason in my book to shoot you dead on the spot! Drop those guns, I tell you!" He cocked his Colt revolver, and Corley and Weinbold dropped their rifles, slowly raising their hands.

Dalbert gestured to his friend to pick up the rifles and throw them out into the hallway. "All right, now, take those hoods off and let's see just which scum you are."

Dan Weinbold doffed the pillowcase that served as improvised hood.

"I know you, Weinbold, and I know your trouble-making brother," the mayor of Lowndesboro drawled. "Well, I'm sure Herb never goes anywhere without you, Dan, and vice versa—so after we catch him, both of you are going to be out of circulation for a while, and there'll be that much less mischief in my town. Buford, tie those fellows up. I don't

414

think they'll be needing those hoods again, so here"—he tossed over his penknife—"cut them into strips. That's it! All right, you two poor excuses for men, turn around and put your hands behind your backs—and incidentally, I may have just one arm, but I'm a crack shot with a Colt. I've got six bullets in it—three for each of you, if you try any tricks!"

Magnus Borden had heard the first gunfire from the house and believed it to be the signal that his band had been successful in making entry. "Let's go, men. We'll make the Bouchards pay for foisting niggers on us the way they have!" he said in a low voice. He had pistols strapped in holsters at his sides, and in the pocket of his jacket there was a hunting knife with a thick bone handle. Drawing a pistol in his right hand, he galloped forward with Sam Arlen, heading their horses toward the Wests' cottage, remembering the sensual attractiveness of young Felice.

As Borden fired a shot through the window of the cottage, two shots rang out from the neighboring cornfield. The bullets missed Borden, but one of them felled Arlen's horse, and he went down with a violent oath, screaming, "Son of a bitch, I broke my goddamned leg! Oh, Jesus, my leg, my leg!"

Herb Weinbold, who had been riding not more than ten paces behind, now turned and spurred his black mare toward the cornfield, where Lucien Edmond, young Lucien, and John Blake were hiding. He was almost upon Lucien Edmond, when the younger Bouchard spotted him. Lucien brought his rifle up and hurriedly fired, not bothering to take careful bead. But his aim was true, nevertheless, and Weinbold fell heavily to the ground, rolled over onto his back, and lay with his sightless eyes gazing up at the dark sky.

"Thanks, Lucien—that was quick thinking," Lucien Edmond praised his half brother. "You saved my life."

Now there came a fusillade of gunfire from the cottages, and four of the masked riders went down, three never to rise again and the fourth wounded with a bullet through the side. He would die an hour later from loss of blood.

"Christ, we've ridden into a trap! Who the hell spilled the beans so these goddamned Bouchards were ready for us?" Magnus Borden snarled as he wheeled his horse around and headed back toward the river and away from the deadly fire. The other men fired aimlessly at some of the cottages as they rode away with Borden, but two more were wounded and a third killed. As Borden raced toward the bank of the Alabama River, desperate to get out of sight, his horse suddenly reared, and Borden slipped from the saddle and fell heavily to the ground. His horse bolted and followed the direction of the escaping raiders.

Lucien Edmond, following on foot, sent off a shot with his rifle, which sent a cloud of dirt into the air near Borden's feet.

The flash of the Spencer gave the infuriated racist a target, and he fired his pistol twice, each time narrowly missing Lucien Edmond. Young John Blake wheeled and, drawing his pistol, fired twice. Borden stopped, suspended like a statue. The gun was still clutched in his hand, and his eyes blazed with rage and hate and pain. Then, very slowly, his knees began to buckle; he sank down upon them, then bowed his head, uttered a choking cry, and rolled over onto one side.

Borden had been badly wounded, but not fatally. He lay in the center of the fields, groaning with pain. He had taken one bullet in the thigh and the other in a shoulder.

It was completely quiet now, and Lucien Edmond suggested, "Lucien, go over to the cottages and tell the men it's all over. Then let everyone in the chateau know that it's safe for them to come out. But just in case any of the wounded attackers are playing possum, be damned careful!"

"I will be."

Lucien hurried forward toward the cottages. Cupping one hand to his mouth, he called out, "Come out! We've won!"

The doors of the cottages opened, and the defenders emerged, brandishing their weapons, raising a loud and happy cheer. They clustered around the young deputy and Lucien Edmond, obviously waiting for orders.

"All right, now, let's round up these men. Elmer, Doug, can you have your wives come out with water and bandages for the wounded? I realize this isn't the most agreeable task, but even though these men are our enemies, they're still human beings, and they need to be taken to the hospital. You'd better tie up those that aren't seriously hurt. We'll take the wounded that need to lie down to town on the buckboard; I'll send Boyd ahead to Dr. Kennery. Ben, you hitch up the buckboard, and Larry, can you take care of the big carriage?

416

We'll use that for those that can sit up; we'll take those bastards to jail in real style!''

"Right away," came a chorused answer of assent from Ben and Larry as they went toward the stables. Following them, Boyd went to saddle a horse to ride to Montgomery, while Doug Larson and Elmer Gregory went off to find their wives.

In a few minutes, the less seriously wounded men had been bound and forced to where Larry Gregory stood waiting with the carriage. Dalbert Sattersfield and Buford Phelps led out the two men that had been captured in the drawing room. Larry Gregory had harnessed two sturdy bays to the large carriage, and Lucien, exulting in the excitement and the victorious conclusion, called out, "We're ready, Lucien Edmond!''

"Get along, you!" Deputy John Blake gestured with his revolver, as those of the survivors of the raider band who could still walk hobbled painfully into the carriage, their wrists and elbows tightly bound behind their backs.

The courtyard was filled with cheering, laughing men and women patting each other on the back and sneering at the raiders. Lucien Edmond leaped into the carriage to take up the reins, while Ben Brown climbed up into the buckboard, into which were being placed the most seriously wounded. Suddenly Lucien, who was helping to lift the last man into the buckboard, caught sight of a pale wreath of smoke rising from over across the courtyard. "Look!" he shouted. "The barn is on fire!''

The workers turned and began to run toward the barn, as Ben Brown jumped down from the buckboard and directed them. "Get buckets of water from the well. Form a brigade, men—two rows, like we did before. We can lick it! If the fire starts spreading too fast, get the horses and cattle out as quickly as you can!''

"Look, Mr. Brown!" John Blake, who had been about to get into the carriage, called out and pointed. A spiral of smoke was coming from Ben's small house.

The workers instantly formed bucket brigades and within half an hour the two fires were well under control. Suddenly, smoke rose from a nearby shed.

"What the devil is all this? Who could be starting all these fires? The raiders were all driven off!" Lucien Edmond an-

417

grily exclaimed. "C'mon, Lucien. Let's see what's going on!"

They began to run toward the shed, and suddenly a figure emerged from the shadows and hurried down toward the river. The man, who wore a hood, was taking long strides, madly dashing this way and that in a frantic effort to elude his pursuers. Lucien, drawing a deep breath, gave a desperate burst of speed that caused him to pull ahead of Lucien Edmond. Closing the gap between himself and the fleeing figure, Lucien gave one last sprint, then lunged at the man. His outstretched hands caught the hooded figure around the knees and brought him down. There was a grunt as the man fell heavily on the ground and was momentarily stunned. Lucien ripped off the hood, then uttered a startled cry of astonishment: It was Enoch Washburn, the black contractor.

"You little white son of a bitch!" Washburn panted, scrambling to his feet. Launching a right hook to Lucien's jaw, he sent the youth sprawling, then started to run again in an easterly direction. As Lucien struggled to his feet, Lucien Edmond caught up with Washburn and seized him by the collar. Washburn turned and tried to fight, but Lucien Edmond sent a savage left jab to the black man's belly and a right to his head, toppling him to the ground.

Standing over him, panting, Lucien Edmond exclaimed, "You were on their side! Why? How could you be, Washburn?"

"I don't have to tell you anything. Go ahead and lock me up. Do whatever you want; you white folks always get your way anyhow." The black contractor's face was twisted in a furious scowl as he got up slowly, rubbing his jaw.

Lucien Edmond said to his half brother, "We'll tie him up and take him along with the others and let the deputy put him in jail, until there can be a trial."

The battle was over. And yet, although none of them on Windhaven Plantation could know it, the racist war was only beginning. . . .

Chapter Forty-one

After Enoch Washburn was put into a cell at the far end of the jail, away from the white prisoners, Deputy Sheriff John Blake turned to Lucien Edmond and his half brother and said, "I feel much better now that these outlaws are behind bars. I'm only sorry that we couldn't have all of them here."

"I don't think we have to worry about the other four, John," Lucien Edmond replied. "They're much too physically impaired to move anywhere of their own volition. The hospital is the best place for them."

"Nonetheless, Mr. Bouchard, I'll rest easier knowing they're being watched. I sent two men to guard them, you see, just in case," the young deputy said.

Boyd Gregory was standing by the wash basin in the corner, mopping his forehead and neck after the long ride he had made from the plantation at breakneck speed to fetch Dr. Kennery. He now spoke up, saying, "Your guards were just arriving when I delivered Dr. Kennery to the hospital, Deputy. They were there to help Ben unload the patients from the buckboard."

"That's good to know. And Boyd, we all appreciate your masterful horsemanship," Lucien Edmond said to the youth. "By the way, does Dr. Kennery know that the men here also need medical attention?"

"Yes, Mr. Bouchard. I told him. The doctor said he'll be here as soon as he can after treating those four at the hospital."

"Ah, good. Kennery's a man who's devoted to his practice." Lucien Edmond paused a moment, then continued, "I'd like to question Enoch Washburn again, if you feel it's okay, John."

"Certainly," the deputy replied. "I can't think of any reason why you shouldn't."

Lucien followed his half brother down the row of cells until they came to Washburn's.

The black contractor stood gripping the bars with both strong, fleshy hands. He glared at them, his lips curled back in a vicious sneer. "You got me, didn't you? I guess you're real proud of yourselves, you whiteys!" he growled at them.

"For God's sake, Washburn," Lucien Edmond sighed, "what the hell made you do it? Didn't we treat you fairly?"

"You wouldn't understand."

"Try me. Look, you're facing a long prison term. Maybe if I could understand the reason you did what you did, I could help you—maybe even drop the charges. But I definitely deserve an answer. Lucien reminded me that you've always had it in for him, always treated him contemptibly, and yet, to Lopasuta Bouchard and to me, you always showed courtesy and—"

"And humbleness. That is what you mean, *Mister* Bouchard, sir, isn't it?" Washburn sarcastically interrupted. "Well, yep, I hate whiteys—might as well tell you why, 'cause you can't use it against me. My daddy and my mammy were slaves, see? But they were forcibly separated when I was only five."

"Go on."

"They sent my daddy to a sugar plantation in Louisiana, and they worked him so hard he died about six months later. My mammy knew because the slave dealer who sold them both came by one day and told her about it. He said the sugarcane plantation man who'd bought my daddy said he hadn't got his money's worth and wanted the slave dealer to give him some of it back." Enoch Washburn spat on the floor of the cell.

Lucien Edmond shook his head empathetically. "I'm so sorry . . . but that still doesn't explain why you turned against us, when we hired you for a job you seemed to want and paid you what you asked for."

"You talk just like that nice, fine white gentleman who bought my mammy," Washburn sneered. "She was a good-lookin' woman, she was. He bought her so he could take her to his bed. And he liked to use a whip on her, when she didn't show enough lovin'. Two years after he bought her,

420

she died, too, bearing his pickaninny. Then he whipped me regularly, cursing me out, calling me a little black bastard, a scrawny nigger, who he got stuck with. He said my mammy was the best poke he ever had—when he made her show some life. Then he used to laugh. Well, I don't like *any* whiteys, and I won't ever. Besides, I know what whiteys think about us niggers, and it'll always be that way, Mr. Bouchard. I was just gettin' back at you and your kind for all that's been done to me. But it hasn't settled the score at all, not hardly. I wish to hell those whiteys would have burned you out tonight. I most surely do, Mr. Bouchard, *suh*! Now get the hell out of here and let me catch some sleep!''

With this, Washburn spat again on the floor and then turned his back and flung himself down on the hard cot in his cell.

Dr. Kennery had administered what first aid he could to the four injured men in the Montgomery hospital, and then had made a hurried visit to the jail to treat those attackers who had sustained less serious wounds. Both Lucien Edmond and Lucien had remained at the jail, and Lucien Edmond had accompanied the physician into the cells in the event that a prisoner should try to escape.

After Dr. Kennery left, nearly at dawn, Lucien Edmond turned to the young deputy. "My brother and I will be glad to press charges against these men and appear as witnesses," he told John Blake. "Do you think you can get this up for trial quickly?"

"I don't think so, to be honest with you, Mr. Bouchard. When Sheriff Brennaman comes back, he's gonna be mighty riled. Let's face facts. He knew all about this attack—that's why he told me not to bother if I had any message asking help for Lowndesboro. He's on the side of these rednecks who'd like to lynch blacks."

"Well, what do you think he'll do?" Lucien Edmond asked.

John Blake shook his head. "I don't like to second-guess anybody, Mr. Bouchard. But if you ask me what my *opinion* is, I'd say he's just gonna turn these white fellers loose."

"Turn them loose?" Lucien Edmond indignantly echoed. "But you saw them shoot and try to kill people. You know what they had in mind. Murder was the intention, and that knowledge belongs in a courtroom with a judge and jury."

"I hope Sheriff Brennaman won't release them, Mr. Bouchard, and as long as I've got charge of the prisoners, you have my word I won't let them off. But when the sheriff comes back from wherever he went, he's still my boss, and I'll have to do what he tells me."

"I've a good mind to stay in this jail until he comes back," Lucien Edmond angrily declared.

"If you want my opinion again, Mr. Bouchard, I don't think Brennaman will be in Montgomery until probably Friday night, maybe even Saturday. So you and your brother might just as well go home and get some sleep. I'll bet you need it. I could use some myself, come to think of it," he wryly added.

"Well, I suppose we'd better. Come along, Lucien."

Arriving back at the chateau, Lucien Edmond and his half brother immediately went to find Laure, whom they had not seen since earlier that evening, before the attack. They found her in the drawing room, resting on the chaise longue. Her face was pale, and she seemed drained of vitality.

"Mother, are you all right?" Lucien asked as he hastened to her side, his concern evident in his voice. "You weren't hurt in the fracas, were you?"

Laure had already decided that she would say no more than was necessary about the two men whom she had come upon and subsequently shot. She had no wish to repeat the details—particularly about Bevis Marley's attempted rape—and just wanted to put the terrible memories behind her. Now, she slowly sat up, carefully arranging the folds of her dress as she framed her response to Lucien's question in her mind. Finally she responded, "No, dear, I wasn't hurt. But I'm afraid I had to—" She broke off, the words catching in her throat. "I had to kill two men," she said, her voice rising in pitch and intensity. "My God! I've taken human lives! I've . . ." Despite her intentions, she started to sob.

Her son dropped to his knees and put his arms around her shaking shoulders. "Please don't cry, Mother. You wouldn't have done what you did if it wasn't absolutely necessary, I'm sure. You've nothing to feel guilty about. Here, let me help

422

you lie down again. May I get you a cup of tea? Or perhaps you'd like some brandy?''

Laure sniffed and dried her eyes with her handkerchief. She smiled wanly at her son, then declared, "Yes, brandy sounds like a good idea. But only a small amount, please. I'm afraid if I take more than two sips, I'll fall asleep while talking to you.''

"Well, that's probably the best thing you can do for yourself, Laure," Lucien Edmond told her. "Are you sure you're all right?''

"Yes, thank you, Lucien Edmond. I'm just feeling the aftereffects, the shock of it all. And of course I was terribly worried about you two. After all, you were in the thick of things a lot more so than I. I was so relieved when Dalbert came in and told me that everything had gone according to plan, and that you had rounded up the survivors and taken them off.''

Lucien walked back to the chaise longue, holding a snifter of brandy. He bent down to his mother, handing her the glass. "Do you still want to go to Atlanta tomorrow morning? Perhaps you should rest for a few days. After all, you wouldn't want Father to know what has happened—because surely he, too, would then feel guilty and responsible.''

Laure cocked her head up at her son, then smiled. "Yes, you're absolutely right, darling. Leland would naturally decide that it was all *his* fault, because if he had been here, I wouldn't have needed to fight off those two men myself. Yes, I can certainly see your point. I want to be feeling my absolute best when I go to see him, because I don't want him to have any worries whatsoever when he goes in for surgery.''

Lucien Edmond spoke up. "Incidentally, for your own peace of mind, Laure, I want you to know that I'll stay on here until you and Lucien get back from Atlanta. I don't want *you* to have any additional cause for concern, either.''

"That's most generous of you, Lucien Edmond. I'm sure you know how much your help has meant to me," Laure said. "I suppose I'll wait until Saturday; that should give me ample time to feel my old self again." She suddenly smiled. "Did I say old? That was, of course, just an expression.''

The three of them laughed, and the sound was heartening, for it reminded everyone who heard it that the Bouchard spirit was indomitable.

Saturday was yet another hot, humid day, and as the train passed through the Alabama countryside, steaming toward Georgia, Laure stood up to reach for the window shade. She pulled it halfway down, blocking the strong rays of the late afternoon sun.

"That's better," she declared, as she resettled herself in her seat and turned to face Lucien.

The youth yawned and stretched his long legs out into the aisle of the car, grimacing as the train ran over a particularly uneven length of track that shook the passengers severely. "I can't help but wonder if we wouldn't have been better off going by carriage, Mother." He had to shout to make himself heard over the noise. "Certainly it would have been quieter— and probably smoother as well—even though it would have taken considerably longer."

"You're probably right," Laure shouted back. "But I really want to reach Atlanta as soon as possible, to bolster Leland's morale as much as I can."

Lucien looked down at his lap for a moment. Then, leaning forward toward his mother, he spoke almost directly into her ear. "Are the doctors sure that surgery is absolutely necessary? I mean, it seems such a great risk to have to take—experimental brain surgery. Aren't there any potions or medicines that they can administer to Father?"

Lucien's voice broke, and Laure saw that he was close to tears. She patted her son's hand, trying to reassure him as well as herself. Filling her words with a bravado she didn't feel, she said, "Don't worry. Leland will come through the operation just fine." She then bit her lip to fight back her own tears as she declared in a firm, fierce voice, "He's *got* to!"

At virtually that same moment, Lucien Edmond reached Montgomery and rode directly for the sheriff's office. He tethered the reins of his horse to the hitching post outside and walked in, nodding a greeting to John Blake.

Sheriff Tom Brennaman was seated at his desk, thumbing through a sheaf of papers. Lazily, he looked up. "What can I do for you, mister?"

"My name is Lucien Edmond Bouchard, and I came to

make a deposition against the men you have locked up, Sheriff Brennaman,'' the tall Texan avowed. "Deputy Blake must have given you a report—"

"Oh, yes, Mr. Bouchard,'' the sheriff interrupted with a mocking smile, "he surely did that. That boy's got one hell of an imagination, indeed he does.''

"I'm sure it doesn't contain a single fictitious word,'' Lucien Edmond fiercely declared. "He was there, as was my half brother, as well as Mayor Sattersfield and the men he brought along from Lowndesboro. All of us can testify that those men who rode into Windhaven Plantation were attempting to rob and burn and even kill.''

Again Brennaman interrupted. "You can't say that because you don't know it. And anyhow, it was up to the mayor of Lowndesboro to do something if he didn't like what was going on. I told young Blake—and I'm telling you now, Mr. Bouchard—despite what the court says, Lowndesboro's out of my territory, and any intervening I did there would be illegal.''

"Don't you think what those men did on Mrs. Kenniston's land was illegal?'' Lucien Edmond was getting angrier by the moment. He clenched his fists, for he was itching to pound some sense into this grinning, mocking excuse for a sheriff.

"Well, I didn't see it. I know some of these men; they're good, upstanding citizens of Montgomery.''

"And that's your answer, Sheriff Brennaman?''

"Yup, you might say that's what it is. Anyhow, Mr. Bouchard, I don't take kindly to you trying to teach me my business, or trying to interfere with my prisoners. I'll handle matters the way I'm supposed to. Don't you worry none about that.''

"I'm not the one who should be worrying, Brennaman. You leave me no choice. I'm going to see the state's attorney general first thing Monday morning and bring charges against you for dereliction of duty. You may well find yourself a defendant in court on the same day as those buddies of yours who're locked up back there.''

"Mr. Bouchard, you're plumb annoying me now. There won't be a judge sitting in court until at least a week from next Monday. Besides, I think I'll save my peers the trouble of declaring my innocence, 'cause I've decided that I really

425

need a long vacation. Yep, I'm damn tired of this job and all the responsibilities that go along with it. As a matter of fact, I think I'll just be getting on home right now."

"Sheriff Brennaman, I resent your blatant disregard for the law!" Lucien Edmond flared.

"Oh, do you, now?" the sheriff sneered. "Isn't that too damn bad! Not much you can do about it. Fact is, I got a feeling things are gonna be taken out of your hands before much longer, Mr. Bouchard."

His last words were almost obscured because as he spoke, there was a sound of voices in the streets, angry and mean, coming closer and closer to the jail. "What the devil is that?" Lucien Edmond demanded.

Sheriff Brennaman shrugged. "The will of the people, you might say. They don't take kindly to a nigger's setting fire to a white man's property like that Washburn bastid did. I've got a hunch they're gonna give him a trial right now."

"You mean—lynch him?" Lucien Edmond gasped.

"That's right. After all, there's just Blake and me here—you being a private citizen, I couldn't ask you to defend the nigger. You wouldn't want to, anyhow—by all rights you oughta be glad they want to lynch him; after all, it *was* your property the nigger was trying to burn—so I guess we'll just have to let them come in and take him."

"But that's murder! He'd have a right to a fair trial, even if he were guilty of all the crimes in the book!" Lucien Edmond heatedly shouted.

There was a commotion at the door, and five men barged into the room. One of them bawled, "Sheriff, git that nigger out here, quick! There'll be trouble if you don't, Brennaman!"

"You see? It's the will of the people, just like I told you, Mr. Bouchard. You better stand aside. Blake, don't you go for your gun, or I'll shoot you down myself," he shouted, for the young deputy had instinctively put a hand toward his holster. The sheriff glowered at him, his own hand gripping the barrel of his Colt. "Take off your gunbelt and toss it into the corner. I *mean* it, Blake! If you use that gun, I swear to God I'll kill you. Or the mob'll kill you. So you can have your choice."

"Mr. Bouchard, I—I can't do anything—" John Blake faltered.

"I know." Lucien Edmond looked directly at the smirking

lawman. "Sheriff Brennaman, in my book, you're a murderer. And I think in God's judgment, too. We'll all stand trial one day, and you won't get away with it."

" 'S'cuse me, Mr. Bouchard; these men'll wreck my jail if I don't meet their demands—won't you, men?" He smiled at the leader of the mob. "All right, all right! Hold your horses. There won't be any trouble!"

But the man was not easily placated. "Give us the nigger! And let those white men go you've got locked up, Brennaman!" the hulking, black-bearded man in his mid-forties bellowed, clenching his fist and shaking it in the sheriff's face.

"Don't get huffy there, Ezra! I told you, you'll get what you want! Here, take the keys and do it yourself." With this Sheriff Brennaman took out his bunch of keys and handed them to the burly, bearded man. Lucien Edmond stepped forward, but two men seized him by the elbows and dragged him off to one side. John Blake stood by helplessly, his mouth agape, unable to believe the cold-blooded act of his superior.

A few minutes later, five men dragged Enoch Washburn out, kneeing him, smashing their fists into his face, taunting him. Five others hurried down to the other end of the cells, opened them, and released the white raiders, who stumbled out, jeering and yelling names at Lucien Edmond.

Bud Corley stood in the doorway when the rest of the mob had gone out. "Now you just stay here nice and peaceful-like, Sheriff. We got nothin' against you." He started to leave, then turned back. "Oh, yeah, one other thing—you'd better send for Borden's assistant. When we get through with this here nigger, you're gonna need an undertaker."

Lucien Edmond Bouchard put his hands over his ears trying to block the agonized screams of the black victim. They had taken Enoch Washburn across the street, tied him to a lamp post, and stripped him naked. One of the mob had whipped him brutally, until the black man's skin was a mass of bleeding tissue. Finally—and by then it was an act of mercy—they wound a hemp rope around his neck, and two burly men took each end and pulled in opposite directions till Washburn was strangled to death.

The noises finally subsided as the lynch mob moved away, leaving their hideous handiwork in the street to mark their show of irrational hatred against the black. "You better go home now, Mr. Bouchard," Brennaman said in a quiet voice. "Hell, nobody could do anything. If you'd tried to, or Deputy Blake, or me, we'd have got a bullet for our efforts."

Lucien Edmond didn't respond. Instead, turning to John Blake, he made a helpless gesture with his hands. Clearing his throat, he said to the deputy in an unsteady voice, "Thanks for what you did. Things'll balance out. They always do."

Chapter Forty-two

It was Wednesday, July 11, exactly one week after the aborted attack took place at Windhaven Plantation. As Laure Bouchard sat at her husband's bedside in the Atlanta, Georgia, hospital, the memories of that terrible night were far removed from her thoughts. Indeed, as she sat bolt upright in the ladder-back chair, watching Leland as he slept, there was but one conscious impression, one bit of information in her mind: Leland was going to live. He had undergone surgery to remove the growing tumor on his brain, and he had survived.

Nevertheless, the doctors were cautious in their prognosis, for the Irish-born entrepreneur had yet to regain consciousness. The ultimate success or failure of the delicate surgery was still to be determined, and Laure had been sitting patiently, silently by him, waiting for a sign.

Lucien came back into the room now. He had gone to look for his stepfather's surgeon, hoping the doctor could tell them more than they already knew. But the man had left the hospital and wouldn't be returning until early that evening.

The youth sat down in the chair that was placed alongside the bed, and he surreptitiously watched his mother, on the other side of the bed, as she in turn watched her husband. Lucien thought to himself how strong she was, how steel-willed, to have gone through so much in such a short time and yet to show such fortitude to persevere. Her pale, beautiful face was quite serene now; she had not shed any tears since Leland had been wheeled back into his room. Lucien thought that her bearing accorded to her the countenance of a marble madonna. Indeed, earlier that afternoon, overwhelmed with fatigue, he had found himself very nearly startled when the statuelike figure sitting opposite him had suddenly blinked.

Now Laure raised her head and smiled at her son, expressing wordlessly the feeling of comfort his presence gave her. She broke the silence, asking, "Aren't you hungry, Lucien? You haven't eaten anything since breakfast—and you barely ate then. Why don't you go back to our hotel and have an early dinner? I'm sure you'll feel better."

"No, Mother, I'll wait here with you until you're ready to leave. Besides, I want to be here when Father wakes up," Lucien replied matter-of-factly, refusing to entertain the possibility that Leland Kenniston would perhaps never regain consciousness.

"I understand, darling, and that's sweet of you. You know, you've certainly changed a great deal since you went off to boarding school in Ireland," Laure reflected, "more than just growing older can account for. You've learned to be considerate of others' needs in a way that's most commendable. I'm very proud of you, Lucien."

The youth stared down at his lap for a moment, slightly embarrassed by his mother's words of praise. When he lifted his face, there was a slight touch of pink to his cheeks. "Thank you, Mother," he softly replied. "I—"

His next words were never spoken, for from the bed came a sound of soft moaning. Laure jumped up from her chair and stood by the bed, listening intently. The sound was repeated, but it was quickly drowned out by Laure's own sharp cry.

"Oh, thank God!" Laure exclaimed. "He's awakening, Lucien! Leland is regaining consciousness!"

"Laure . . ." The word was feeble but distinct. "Laure . . ."

"Hush, my darling. Don't try to speak. I'm here. I'm with you. You mustn't tax yourself. Just rest." Her tender words were interspersed with sobs as Laure felt herself overcome with joy. She picked up Leland's limp hand and kissed it repeatedly, then held it tightly, stroking the fingers.

Lucien sensed that this was a time for his mother to be left alone, so he came around to her side of the bed and kissed her on the cheek, then said, "I'll leave you and Father by yourselves. I'll just go out for a short walk. . . ."

Laure was barely aware of his words. She merely nodded, saying nothing, giving all her attention to the figure lying on the bed between starched white sheets, as the youth slipped silently out of the room.

* * *

He wandered around Atlanta for what seemed like hours. He had briefly stopped at a restaurant, intending to dine but changing his mind at the last moment, suddenly feeling so exhilarated that he was no longer hungry. Leaving the restaurant, he had headed east, toward the center of the city. Now, as he rounded a corner, he suddenly was brought up short, for before him, tacked onto the side of a building, was a large multicolored poster advertising the coming appearance of the dance troupe of which Eleanor Martinson was a member.

Lucien stepped up to the sign and read all the details. The company would be giving three performances, starting the following evening. To the youth's surprise, Eleanor's name had been given featured billing; obviously she was more than just a member of the corps de ballet now. A broad smile suddenly spread over Lucien's face, and he felt his heart quicken at the realization that he could meet with Eleanor once again, if he so desired. He thought back to their parting, recalling that the beautiful dancer had had reservations about seeing him, and now he was sure he knew why: He had probably given her the distinct impression that, as an entertainer, she was not the kind of woman one would wish to bring home to meet one's family. With a pang of remorse, Lucien realized that the impression she had doubtless received was probably accurate. Deep down, he *had* felt that she wasn't quite a lady.

Lucien sighed and shoved his hands into his jacket pockets. His right hand closed upon an envelope and he drew it out. It was a letter he had received the day he and Laure had left Windhaven for Atlanta—a letter from Samantha Haynes. Lucien looked at the letter for a moment, his lips curled in disgust, then crumpled it into a ball before shoving it back into his pocket, giving a sardonic laugh at the memory of the letter's content.

Samantha had displayed in her writing the same contrariness that she had evinced in person—only this time her fickle nature was even more blatant. She had written at length about a college man she had met at her cousin's house, extolling his manly virtues in paragraph after paragraph. Then she had had the temerity to declare her fondness for Lucien, expressing her hope that when she came home for Christmas holiday, he would be waiting for her.

Lucien now snorted in derision—both at her and at himself

for having been such a blind fool and for having allowed his head to be turned easily by someone so shallow simply because she was also so beautiful. Walking along, he came upon a wastebasket, and digging into his pocket once again, he pulled out the letter and without a moment's hesitation tossed it into the trash. He then turned on his heels, and whistling merrily, he headed back toward the hospital.

Dr. James Townsend removed the stethoscope from his ears and hung it around his neck, satisfied that Leland Kenniston's heartbeat was strong and steady. The surgeon then asked his patient to tell him how many fingers he was holding up, and Leland answered correctly.

Dr. Townsend turned to Laure. She had been sitting on the edge of her chair, her apprehension keeping her from making either sound or movement. When the physician smiled at her, indicating that he believed Leland was going to be all right, Laure exhaled a long breath—seemingly the first one since the doctor had begun examining Leland. Suddenly her chin began to quiver, and the tears she had held in check for so many hours now coursed freely down her cheeks, and her sobs, which were as much a release of tension as they were expressions of her joy, echoed off the walls of the small private room.

"F-forgive me, Dr. Townsend," Laure said, when she at last composed herself.

"Don't be silly, Mrs. Kenniston. There's nothing to forgive. In fact, I would have been surprised had you not given in to your emotions at this time. You have gone through almost as much as your husband—albeit in a different manner, of course."

Laure was silent for a moment, her head slightly bowed. She then looked earnestly at the surgeon and asked, "How long will Leland have to stay in the hospital? How long will it be before full recovery has taken place?"

"As to the first question," the doctor began, running his fingers through his wavy brown hair, "I should think that your husband can leave here in about three weeks' time. The surgery was, of course, extremely delicate, and we certainly don't wish to take the chance of releasing him too soon, thereby undoing all that we have done." He paused and rubbed his chin. "As to your second question—well, that is

432

the more difficult to answer . . . if, indeed, I even *can* answer it. You see, we have done so little surgery of this nature that there is very little in the way of statistics to go by."

Dr. Townsend turned and looked down at Leland Kenniston, who once again was sleeping peacefully. Taking Laure by the elbow, the physician steered her out into the hallway and closed the door to the room. He led her down the hall to the visitors' lounge, which at the moment was empty, and directed her to a large leather armchair. Smiling at her as he himself sat down, he commented, "I'm sure that chair is much more comfortable than the one you've been occupying for hours."

"Yes, it is, Doctor. But that isn't why you've brought me here, is it?" Laure responded, worry creasing her forehead.

Dr. Townsend stared at her a moment, then answered, "No. No, it isn't, Mrs. Kenniston. I want to be frank with you, and I didn't want to speak with you in front of your husband. You see, the human mind is most amazing, and your husband may in fact be capable of absorbing and retaining all that is said in his presence without even being awake." He reached into his pocket and drew out a pipe, filled it with tobacco, lit it, then continued, "I want to reassure you, Mrs. Kenniston, that your husband's post-operative condition appears to be quite sound. As best as I can determine, all of his vital signs are normal, and his reflexes are within reasonable bounds. However—and I cannot stress this fact too strongly—when we removed the growth on his brain, we of necessity had to eliminate a small portion of the surrounding healthy tissue. And, too, there is naturally some trauma—shock—to the brain as a result of such dramatic interference.

"What I am trying to say, Mrs. Kenniston, is that we have no way of knowing what the effects of the surgery will be. I cannot say for sure that Mr. Kenniston's personality will be exactly as it was; I cannot say for sure that his interests will be the same, or that whatever drive and ambition and motivation he had will be as they were. In short, I cannot say for sure that your husband will be the same man, Mrs. Kenniston."

Laure's green eyes were very wide, and her hand was held to her mouth as she stared at the surgeon, unable to speak.

"I don't wish to alarm you, of course, but I feel that you must be fully prepared for whatever exigencies you may encounter. You see, we know that the various aspects of behavior are controlled by particular segments of the brain. What we do not know is what behavior originates where, and so I cannot tell you what facets of your husband's personality may have been tampered with by the surgery. He may, for example, be less aggressive—or more so. Only time will tell. But one thing you *can* be certain of is that physically he will make complete recovery. That I can guarantee. Do you have any questions, Mrs. Kenniston?''

Laure sat silently for a moment more, then she said in a small voice, ''No, I can't think of anything that you haven't already answered. I thank you for your consideration and your concern, Doctor. You've been most kind.'' She rose from the chair and held out her hand to Dr. Townsend. Then she excused herself, and with a brief smile, she left the room to return to her husband's bedside.

It was the beginning of August, and as Laure looked out of the train window, she thought to herself that she could not remember when she had last known a summer to have felt both so short and so long at the same time. The train had left Atlanta four hours ago, so within a few hours' time, she and her husband and son would finally be home.

Laure smiled, thinking how easily Windhaven Plantation had become home for her once more, despite the nearly three years she and her family had lived in New York City. Still, she worried that Leland would not be able to adjust so readily to the bucolic and relatively isolated life on the Alabama homestead—just as she worried that it would no longer matter to him.

As the train pulled suddenly into a long tunnel, the window beside her reflected the image of her husband, dozing in his seat. She stared at the reflection, as if transfixed. So often during these past three weeks she had found herself looking at him in just this same way, hoping to discern reassuring signs that would indicate he was making a full recovery, and that in the end, there would be no change in him at all. She had had to remind herself repeatedly, on these occasions, that Leland could not possibly have regained his strength in such a short time, and that just because he had not immediately shown his old vigor, or plunged himself back into the business world, ready to pick up where he had left off, did not mean that he would not do so as soon as he was physically able. She sighed, recalling Dr. Townsend's final cautionary words, just before releasing Leland from the hospital: The surgeon had reminded her that full physical recovery would require many months.

She turned away from the window and looked over at her son, sitting in the seat opposite. He was absorbed in a newspaper he had bought at the Atlanta train terminal, and didn't notice her watching him. Laure felt a pang of remorse to realize how different her children's lives would be from now on. No longer would they be free from financial care as they had always been; no longer would they be able to have everything they either needed or wanted. It was a far cry from the absolute luxury and freedom from want that Luke had been able to provide. For the first time in their lives, they would have to count their pennies and scrimp and save to buy those things they had always taken for granted but that now were extravagant luxuries.

Laure felt tears spring to her eyes, but she willed them back. Then Leland stirred, and Laure turned toward him, watching him as he came fully awake.

He opened his eyes and looked at her blankly for a moment, but then he smiled and picked up her hand and patted it. "Poor Laure. I'm afraid I'm not very good company this trip, am I? I guess I find the motion of the train quite soothing, and it puts me to sleep just like a baby in a cradle." Looking over at his stepson, Leland asked, "Anything of interest in the newspaper, son?"

Lucien looked up from the tabloid and smiled. "As a matter of fact, I was just reading a news item that I think is *most* interesting. There's a section of the paper given over to reports from other major Southern cities, and the one from Montgomery is very satisfying, though I admit my sentiment is not very charitable. You recall us telling you about Tom Brennaman, the sheriff of Montgomery County. Well, it seems he was shot and killed by an irate citizen when he was found leaving the man's house when no one was home. Apparently the sheriff had learned that the man would be away and decided to help himself to the fellow's collection of gold coins—which were found in Brennaman's possession. I guess after he left office, no one would hire him, because of what he had done. Folks around Montgomery may have agreed with his prejudices, but it seems they didn't want to admit it

435

outwardly by hiring him for anything, so he turned to burglary as a way of getting by.''

"Well, I can't say that I feel particularly sorry for him,'' Laure wryly admitted. "Indeed, I would say that Sheriff Brennaman received his just deserts.''

Lucien nodded his agreement, then turned the page. His eyes scanned the columns of news as well as the advertisements until he found what he had been looking for. There, on page twelve, was a notice about Eleanor Martinson's dance troupe, declaring that following the tremendous praise they had received in Atlanta, the troupe was extending its original itinerary in the Southern United States and would be visiting a number of additional cities before returning to Europe. The next stop on the tour, it was noted, would be Montgomery, Alabama.

Lucien smiled to himself, and he felt the thrill of anticipation. He thought of his brief, but warm reunion with Eleanor in Atlanta, when he had gone backstage after the show. He had declared himself to be much wiser than she had known him to be when they had met on board ship.

"I'm sure you found me to be a snobbish little twit,'' he had declared, "and if you did, you undoubtedly were correct.''

Eleanor had smiled at his confession and told him that his candor made it easier for them to be friends—and perhaps something more than friends.

Lucien recalled how he had pressed her, wanting to know if this meant they might be lovers again, but the beautiful dancer had simply replied, "The troupe will be passing through Montgomery in about a month's time. If you wish, we can meet again then and . . . talk some more.''

Lucien now sighed and folded up his newspaper. He closed his eyes and let his mind conjure up all sorts of delicious fantasies. Soon, the rocking motion of the train lulled him to sleep, a smile planted firmly on his lips.

As Laure sat in the seat opposite, watching her son, she idly wondered what he was thinking that cheered him so. She soon found herself hoping fervently that the youth would not lose his apparent tranquillity in what were sure to be times of hardship coming for them all.

Shortly after Laure, Leland, and Lucien arrived home at Windhaven—after the children had joyously welcomed their

436

stepfather, and after the convalescent had been settled in his room to rest from the tiring journey—Laure suddenly felt the need to seek the solace she always found at the top of the towering red bluff overlooking the river.

She changed into more comfortable clothes, put on her walking shoes, tied on a large straw hat to shade her face from the sun, and walked out of the chateau into the late afternoon heat. She slowly followed the well-worn path that led up to the gravesites of old Lucien, his beloved Dimarte, and his grandson, Luke.

It was just before sunset when she reached the top and, as always, Laure was awed by the beauty and the aura of spiritual love that seemed to isolate this spot from the rest of the world.

She knelt to pray, entwining her fingers and bowing her head. Many separate thoughts crowded in upon her, and she addressed them all: "Dear God, I thank You for Your tender mercy shown to my beloved husband and to me in restoring his health. I promise You that I will stand by him no matter what adversities may yet occur, for nothing could be worse than not having him by my side. I thank You also for Your protection of my loved ones, keeping them safe from harm during the terrible tribulations we have born of late—and I pray You will keep us from further wickedness on the part of wrong-thinking men who would dishonor our creed."

Laure made the sign of the cross, then rose. She stood looking down at the three graves for a moment, then turned and started toward the path. However, just before she began the descent, she glanced over at the chateau, suffused in the pink glow of the setting sun. Tears came to her eyes as she stood looking at the beautiful mansion, the home that had meant so much to generations of Bouchards. She reminded herself that all her loved ones were together; they were all healthy, and they had the comfort and peace of this beautiful home. She made a vow that no matter what else might happen, they would always have Windhaven. And as long as they had Windhaven, they would always have hope.

THE END

437